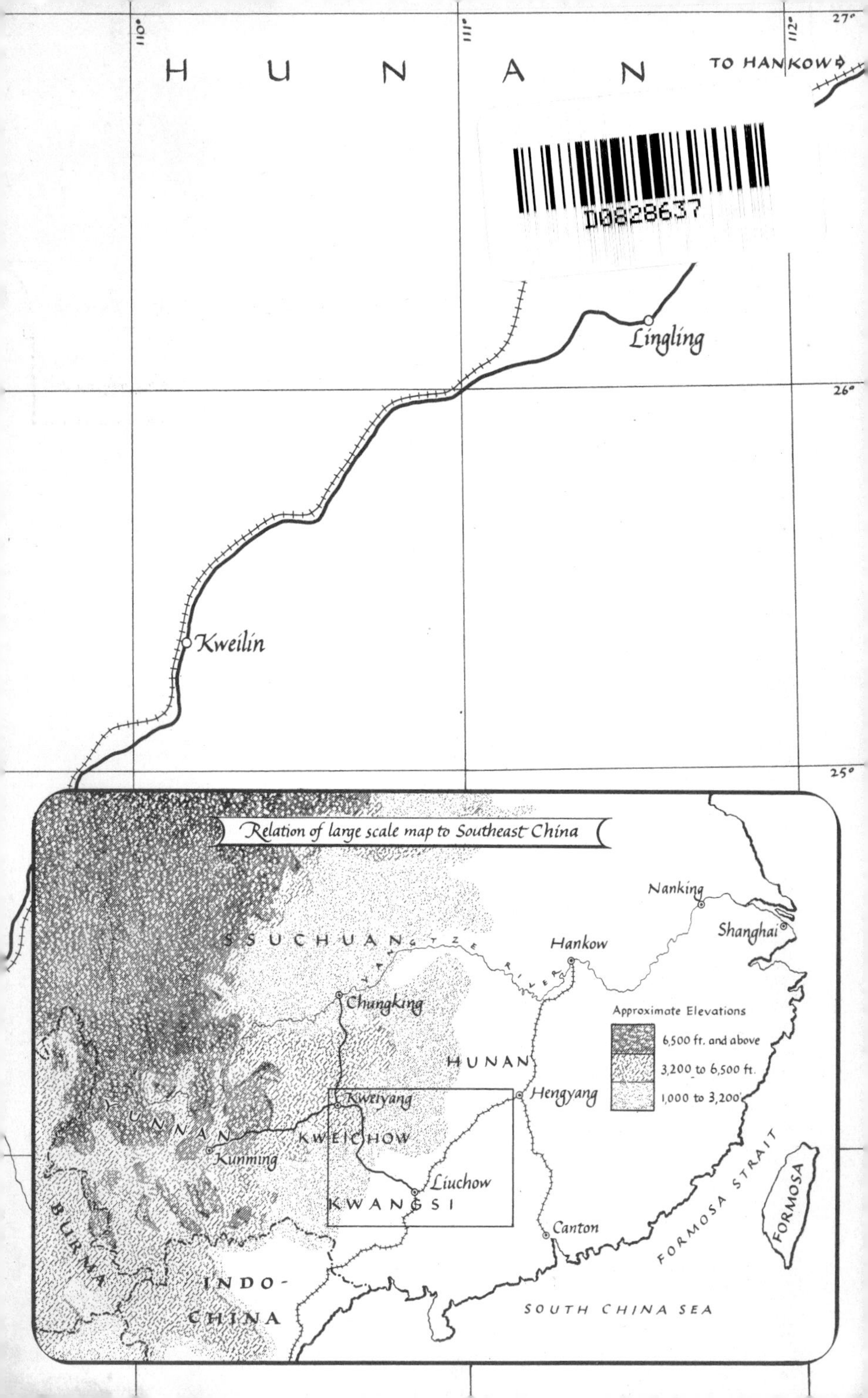
110°
111°
112°
27°
26°
25°
H U N A N
TO HANKOW
Lingling
Kweilin
Relation of large scale map to Southeast China
Nanking
Shanghai
Hankow
SSUCHUAN
YANGTZE RIVER
Chungking
Approximate Elevations
6,500 ft. and above
3,200 to 6,500 ft.
1,000 to 3,200'
HUNAN
Hengyang
Kweiyang
YUNNAN
KWEICHOW
Kunming
Liuchow
KWANGSI
Canton
FORMOSA STRAIT
FORMOSA
BURMA
INDO-CHINA
SOUTH CHINA SEA

THE MOUNTAIN ROAD

THE MOUNTAIN ROAD

By Theodore H. White

WILLIAM SLOANE ASSOCIATES

NEW YORK • 1958

Published simultaneously in the Dominion of Canada
by George J. McLeod Limited, Toronto.
Printed in the United States of America.
Library of Congress Catalog Card No. 58–6394

PRINTED IN THE UNITED STATES OF AMERICA BY
KINGSPORT PRESS, INC., KINGSPORT, TENNESSEE

TO NANCY

AUTHOR'S NOTE

THIS story is told against the background of the campaign for East China in 1944. All its characters are creatures of my imagination and any relation between them and any soldier or officer of the United States Army, living or dead, is coincidental.

I have taken certain literary liberties with the actual events of the East China disaster:

The breakthrough and pursuit of the shattered Chinese armies by the Japanese, from Liuchow to the plateau, actually began on November 9th and continued until December 2nd, 1944, when the Japanese reached Tushan in the mountains. The dispatch of the first elements of the Chinese New Sixth Army to stop the breakthrough was not, in point of fact, ordered until December 5th, 1944. I have compressed the time span of these events into approximately a week.

American demolition units blew up airfields and installations all over East China during this campaign. But no American demolition unit, to the best of my knowledge, made this imaginary trip through the entire retreat, although their adventures in many parts of China were of the same or greater order of violence than those I have described here. The blowing of the Tushan dumps was, of course, performed by Americans—not AT DISCRETION as I have made it appear here, but on direct orders from Theater Headquarters, China. Finally, the total confusion of Chinese command at the loss of Changsha that summer has never been clarified; and, though the senior Chinese officers in that battle were indeed executed, responsibility was never as clearly fixed as I have made it here.

All the rest—the flight, the death, the problems faced—are as true as memory and witness can make them. From this catastrophe, on the eve of victory, China was never after to recover.

THEODORE H. WHITE

Fire Island, September, 1957

CONTENTS

FOREWORD

NOVEMBER—1944

AGES AGO, some unseen hand had carved the face of China in a contour of endless mountains. From the green flatlands that rose gently out of the Pacific, step by step it had squeezed the land up through barriers of hills and mountains, pushing each higher and higher as it traveled west to the inner distances of Asia.

Time, the pressure of countless mouths, and the ambitions of nameless conquerers had for centuries been driving the Chinese up into these mountains, to die in flight or earn the right to settle in the fertile pockets within the protecting hills. Now the hills were bare of either grass or trees, all long since consumed by the ravaging hunger of man. Ugly and bare, speckled here and there with yellow adobe villages, the mountains rose gray along the backbone of China, from its arid north to its steaming south. And nowhere did they rise so barren as from the low ever-warm ricelands of Kwangsi province to the southwestern plateau that glowered above them.

Now, in November of 1944, from Kwangsi to the east, all

was summer. Oranges and flowers, persimmons and herbs, rice and melons mingled their perfumes hundreds of miles to the shore of the Pacific. But from Kwangsi province to the west, the cold and wintry mountains crowded up like ramparts of stone, three thousand feet high—then paused, to widen on the south to the great plateau of Yunnan, and dip in the north to the protected basin of Ssuchuan. Between the plateau, where the American army at its great Kunming base brought in the planes and supplies from the Hump to revive the feeble armies of China, and Ssuchuan, the fertile basin where the Chinese government had taken refuge from the Japanese, crouched the mountains of the desolate province of Kweichou.

Whoever could penetrate Kweichou, could tear apart the base of Chinese strength in the Ssuchuan basin from the base of American support on the Yunnan plateau. But whether the Japanese meant to do it now—no one knew. No eye could tell by sweeping the landscape, for a strange quiet hung over the fields of East China as they rolled flat under the mountain wall to the bulge of the East China Sea.

This quiet was the last triumph of the Japanese army, but no foretaste of the peace that was soon to be. The Japanese army had come because Japan was trapped. Far away in the broad Pacific, Japan's navy had been destroyed, her garrisons exterminated. Now, at last, her own great cities had been brought under bombardment. Slowly, too, the Japanese were being strangled. As American submarines explored their deadly way through the innermost of Japan's sea lanes, the Japanese islands fed from a merchant marine that dwindled and withered as each convoy faced ever more certain destruction. Soon they would have no oil, no rubber, no coal, no food. Only one sea channel could, with any hope, be cleared and defended to feed the islands of Japan until defeat would bring peace: the channel that ran through the East China Sea, between the mainland and the palm-fringed island of Formosa.

But the channel of the Formosa Straits lay naked under the bombing sights of American planes that struck again and again from the airfields of East China's flatlands. In little more than a year, the Americans had spread a net of almost twenty fields in East China, from the very lee of the mountains almost to within sight of the coast. And from these fields they had hammered and sunk the ships on which Japan's life depended, in the channel that was Japan's last hope.

By the summer of 1944, the planners of Japan's doomed ambition had had no choice but to erase these American fields. And since to do so, they had first to erase the Chinese armies that defended the fields, they had mounted in June their last great offensive, Operation ICHIGO. Due south from the Yangtze valley they had driven, down the great railway that runs in the shadow of the mountain wall from Hankow on the river, to Canton and Indo-China in the south.

Along this mainline now in November, after months of fighting, the cratered, burned-out faces of all the once-noisy, chattering cities and towns that beaded its tracks were dumb and silent. All the American airfields in the flatlands had been seized and wiped out, the air purged of their menacing drone. Now a Japanese corridor sealed off all East China from the mountain barrier to the sea, separating it from the mountains, behind which the Americans on the plateau and the Chinese government in the basin still planned their future together. And no one knew whether the Japanese armies meant to, or could, mount the barrier to divide the Allies.

All this meant little to the people flowing out of the ruined cities, up the little mule-cart roads, up the dusty footpaths into the mountains, in flight. The hundreds of thousands who walked, or dragged, or rode as they climbed from the November heat of the tropical lowlands to the piercing November cold of the winter highlands wanted food, or shelter, or warmth—but they would settle for safety and food.

Up every pass, through every ancient trail, for weeks and months, the Chinese had been trekking to the shelter of their government on the far side of the barrier. But now, of all the passes, none was more crowded than the great cleft which led two hundred and sixty miles from Liuchow, in Kwangsi, up to Kweiyang, the capital of Kweichou. Through this pass ran the only motor-road from the lowlands to the rear, the only road that made junction with the interior highway net that connected the government in Ssuchuan and the Americans on the plateau. Through this pass, sometimes close to the road, sometimes several miles away from it, ran the lone, single-tracked railway spur which the Chinese government had built to supply its East China war fronts.

Up this road, as far as the eye could see, an endless procession of people, rich and poor, people dressed in rags, in silken gowns, in uniforms, riding in rickshaws, on carts, on trucks, in buses, on horseback, on foot, continued to flow toward the safety beyond the hills.

And behind came the Japanese. Sometimes hours behind, sometimes days behind. Tormented by the knowledge of certain doom, intoxicated by this last taste of triumph, the Japanese wasted and ravaged the land as they swept on, hastening to disperse and annihilate the remnants of the Chinese army; or jubilantly seeking vengeance, when they could trap them, on the little bands of Americans who lagged behind in the retreat to destroy the airfields and installations that had provoked the campaign.

Whether the Japanese sought to do more than disperse the Chinese armies, whether they sought more than vengeance on a few Americans, whether they sought actually to penetrate the high plateau and cut the junction at Kweiyang thus dividing China and America in their own moment of disaster, no one at the moment could tell. Least of all the isolated Americans on the road, caught in a torrent of alien retreat, in a strange land.

TUESDAY

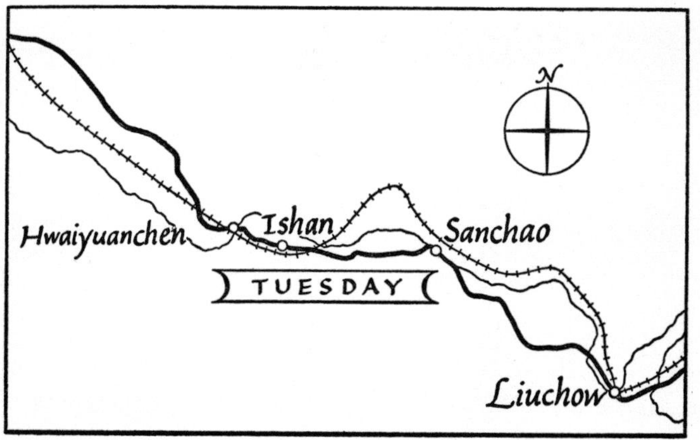

CHAPTER 1

At Your Discretion

EVEN IN THE TWILIGHT, with the color of his uniform a smudge, the figure he made against the sky was American. The dirty battle jacket hung loosely about his lean frame. Oil fouled his rumpled suntans. His cap bore a faint stain of sweat. Only the slouch, the little sag of his stomach, the half-droop of the sandy head, betrayed that the man was either tired or a civilian whose major's leaves rested on him unnaturally. In Philip Baldwin's case, both were true.

His tanned face, darker in the evening light, his deep black eyes, his wrinkled brow—all were cramped in thought as he stood at the edge of the paddy field, on the hill above the little village of Sanchao. He could see clearly below and far beyond Sanchao, the drift of smoke from the town of Liuchow he had left flaming five hours before. He wondered whether the Japanese were in Liuchow yet or not, and when they would begin the chase again. He wondered whether they really meant to come all the way up the pass to the junction at Kweiyang. He could not guess. But he knew he had to do something about it. He could not explain how—but it had become his job.

Behind him, he could hear the voices of the men about the fire. It was good to hear American voices this evening.

Miller was doing the cooking and, through his tiredness, Baldwin felt his stomach straining with hunger. The fragrance of the hot food floated in the air. Into the big enamel basin, full of GI pork-and-gravy, Miller had chopped some Chinese red peppers and onions and was stirring the stew as it simmered, with a long bamboo stave. Baldwin's mouth watered and he remembered he had not eaten hot food since General Yang's noodles early that morning at the station. Was it this morning? Yes, he recalled, only this morning, it was still Tuesday; and now, at last, they could stop for the night and rest. He turned, his eyes inspecting the convoy: The four trucks and jeep were parked operationally, ready for quick getaway, pointing out to the road from the dry paddy where they stood. He turned back and his eyes searched once more the outlines of Sanchao down below which now, at dusk, its whitewashed walls slowly graying, seemed gentle, at peace, and the war far, far away.

As if to remind him, his hand went up, touching his blouse pocket, feeling the message that rested there—folded, wrinkled, imperative.

He reached in, pulled it out, and, though he knew every word, unfolded the paper and read it once more, looking for a clue:

HDQ YOKE FORCES FOR

COMMANDING OFFICER LIUCHOW BASE PASS

TO MAJOR BALDWIN OIC

DETACHED DEMOLITION TEAM YOUR HDQ COLON

DIRECT YOU ATTEMPT WITHDRAWAL WESTWARD VIA HIGHWAY STOP AT YOUR DISCRETION RPT AT YOUR DISCRETION ACHIEVE

MAXIMUM DELAYING EFFECT ON MAIN MOTOR SUPPLY ROUTE SPECIAL ATTENTION DEMOLITION AND WRECKING VICINITY ISHAN RPT ISHAN COMMA VICINITY HOCHIH RPT HOCHIH COMMA DUMPS AT TUSHAN RPT TUSHAN STOP RECOMMEND MAXIMUM USE AVAILABLE EXPLOSIVES MATERIAL WITH DUE CONCERN SAFETY YOUR MEN AT YOUR BEST JUDGMENT STOP DIRECTIVE CLEARED CHINESE GROUND COMMAND LIAISON END

SIGNED HUTCHESON FOR CHIEF OF STAFF

It was "AT YOUR DISCRETION" that bothered him. Hutcheson must have thrown that in to protect him. But it made it worse. It loaded it all on him, one way or the other, the safety of the men, the delay of the Japanese, the possibility of being trapped—all on him. Should he or shouldn't he? Go fast, wheel the convoy right on through, and be safe? Or keep them back at the tail of the retreat, one jump ahead of the Japanese?

He folded the paper again, tucking it in his pocket. The stew should be ready soon and, listening for Miller's chow call, he could hear the men talking. They were arguing it out for him already. He sat down noiselessly, letting his legs dangle over the paddy wall, his back to them. He did not want them to think he was eavesdropping.

"Man," that was Lewis talking in his high-pitched voice, sputtering with its weakling's profanity, "we don't mean a goddam thing up there. We blow the frigging fields, they hand out medals in Kunming. They get medals when the fields get built, they get medals when the fields get blown. Then they get promoted out of China. Some general promises us we get to high-tail back when we finish blowing the Liuchow job; then he gets promoted out to Europe, and the next guy doesn't know a mother-frigging thing about it. He sees he's got eight men and all that demolition equipment on the way back by road and he says, let's blow the frigging road, we got a war on. Then he goes out with his Red Cross girl and we're stuck here sucking the hind-tit."

"General, hell, the general doesn't even know we're alive," said Prince in his teasing, wise-guy voice. Baldwin remembered that Prince was a bookie, a gambler. He did not like the voice. "It's some tight-pants lieutenant bucking for a promotion who goes in to the major and says, Major, look, G2 says the Japs are gonna push their way up that road into Kweiyang, don't you think we ought to get that road wrecked? So the major doesn't want to be bothered, but he listens and says, How can we do that? So the lieutenant says, Well, Air Force Base Engineering got this Detached Demolition team out there, and they're rolling back by truck, they can do a little blowing on the way. So the major finally says why not. So the major takes the pitch in to the general as if he thought of it all by himself, see, it's his idea, and the general says O.K. The general figures it's been checked out by staff, he doesn't think any more about it. Then we get one of those rockets and they tell us, 'Go blow up China.' The hell with it."

"The trouble with those guys up there," cut in Michaelson, the rasp of his voice and its authority grating over the others, "is they've got the big picture. They have maps. They been brought up on that book. MacArthur, he's unloading in the Philippines. The marines, they're practically unloading in Japan. Bradley, he's already dumping the stuff into Germany. So the war's won, they figure, give or take a couple of months. This East China isn't worth fighting for now we've lost the airfields, so let the Japs have it. But still they have that book. It says you can't give anything away to the enemy so they got to deny it, so they say, 'Wreck The Road.' *Sounds* right. But there's not one of them in Kunming ever even seen what goes on in these blow jobs."

"Yeah. Not one of them ever seen what goes on in a Chinese blow job." That was Miller, the echo, talking.

"Yes," said Niergaard, in his soft, slow-and-firm recital of the obvious, "that's what worries me, too, those Chinese. The time we were burning the village outside Liuliang. I never knew why we had to burn it, but old McNeil said it was too close to the field to leave and it took a whole company of Slopey soldiers to drive those people out of their houses so we could do the burn job, and I bet if we hadn't beaten it out of there that afternoon they'd've taken us apart with their pitchforks and pig-stickers. If we'd had to walk out of there, it would've been like what happened to Morgan."

"You know," said Prince, "you're right. I'll bet it was Chinese deserters killed Morgan that time they gave us that crap about Jap plain-clothes men sneaking down the road. If they'd been Japs they would've just taken his ring, or maybe his gun, but they wouldn't have taken off his uniform and cut him up that way. Those were Chinese troops, or bandits that used to be Chinese troops, or deserters that ain't made up their minds yet whether they're bandits or troops. Half this goddam Chinese army's in the hills already, and I'll bet the rest of them are getting ready to take off right now. Say, Mike, you figure this guy Baldwin knows what the score is? You figure he's gonna piddle on the way in, or he's gonna take us barreling right back?"

Baldwin listened intently. What did Michaelson think? It was important:

"It's his outfit now," snapped back Michaelson, "and he hasn't told me yet. All I know is—he's got these orders and they're discretionary."

So Michaelson had told them, thought Baldwin. Good.

"How many miles we got to go into Kweiyang, Mike?" asked Ballo. Ballo was a mechanic; a good one; no word-waster. He always wanted to know how much, how many, Baldwin had noticed.

"Two hundred and thirty miles from where we are now; if we get an early start, we can make it day after tomorrow," said Michaelson. "These roads are already lousy with refugees and if we waste even another day, with Liuchow gone, they'll be rat-racing all the way up to Kweiyang. And deserters, too. And then we'll be in real trouble because these people are hungry. And they hate us."

Michaelson's voice shifted back to the conversational. "I tell you they hate us and I hate them, and if there's one thing I want to do before this war is over, it's put a bullet into one of them. I'm sick and tired of hearing people putting out this big-picture stuff, about how poor they are, how we're supposed to be friends, how we got to understand them."

"You talking about me, Mike?" said Collins whose voice, Baldwin now realized, he had been listening for.

"Yup," said Mike, "I'm talking about you if you want it that way. I don't know what they taught you in that interpreters' school at California, or where you picked it up, but you're always trying to buddy up to them. You better watch out." It was not a threat, it was a warning.

"Listen," said Collins coolly, "I'm just as scared of this thing as anybody. I don't want my neck creased by a bullet in the dark either. But you figure out what we'd do if the Chinese came through, say, Illinois, and started to blow it up, claiming they were doing us a favor saving us from the Japs. I bet a lot of us would start cutting them up, too."

"All right, all right," growled Michaelson, "that part I get, but you act like you like them, and they don't even like each other. You tell me—what makes them so mean to each other? They're the meanest people on earth. And I hate their guts."

But Baldwin had made up his mind to break it up, before

the tempers that had been simmering for weeks in the sun and the exhaustion of the retreat stretched too tightly. They were his team now. He should have broken it up earlier, for the decision they were arguing was his alone to make.

He had wanted to join them, and break into the conversation for minutes now, but he could not and it bothered him as it had always bothered him even before the war—how to talk to people, how to be friends, whether in giving others friendship too easily they would respect him less. In those long sweeps of daydreaming that had so infuriated Helen he could always see himself as easy in conversation, finding the deft opening, the right response, the masterful phrase, the sharp or delicate rebuke. But it never worked out that way when he spoke. And thus he had become at thirty-five a quiet person, grave, somewhat solemn, with little small talk. Even at the desk, back in Boston, he could not talk unless he was talking about substance, about the things that had to be done and how to do them. Baldwin liked the army precisely because it lifted the uncertainty that hung between man and man. Everyone knew where everyone else belonged. A captain said 'sir' to a colonel, a colonel said 'sir' to a general, and so on to the very top. You did not have to fumble around for a relationship in the army. Except, of course, with the men. That was what McNeil had said again last week, when Baldwin took over, "This is a damned good outfit; they all volunteered for the detail; but don't get too chummy with them. They'll eat you out just like any other bunch of men if you give them the chance."

So there was no way to join, or steer the talk, except to get up, which he did, and walk over to the circle about the fire and ask:

"Have you got the guard worked out, Michaelson?"

"Yup, same one as usual," replied Michaelson, and then,

turning back to the others, "Any beefs, anybody sick?" When no protest came in the half-second of wait he allowed them, Michaelson turned back to Baldwin and said curtly, "We're all set."

"Fine," said Baldwin. "How about checking the radiators and filling the tanks before we eat? We'll be starting early tomorrow and I don't want any time wasted moving out. Bring the water to the top because we'll be climbing the hills tomorrow and pushing our engines all the way."

They scattered slowly, lugging the jerry cans to the truck that carried the gasoline drums, filling them, going about it all quite easily, and Baldwin reflected on how smoothly discipline worked when it was routine.

But whether he could keep it this way, calling out the same automatic responses they had given him up to now, whether he could hold them to the job this smoothly if he chose to hold them back on the road, he did not know. Indeed, under the whole pattern of the last two days was the restless stirring of uncertainty again, which was so old in him and which he thought the army had erased. He could see himself as if he stood at headquarters in Kunming far away, looking at himself through a telescope on this Kwangsi hillside, a bug in the distance uncertain whether to flee or to stay and sting. Where were the Japs? he wondered. And what could an eight-man team of Americans do now with all China in retreat about them? His thinking floated on weariness. It had been one whole day of work and one whole wild, red, thunder-popping, banging night and another day without sleep until now, at dusk, for all of them. And his thinking slipped off into the daydreaming: Philip Baldwin-At-The-Pass, The Men-Who-Held-Thermopylae, the image of Philip Baldwin-Back-At-Base in Kunming saying modestly next week, "Damned difficult job, General, but it went all right." But before then, he would have to make things happen, or break and run. It was now his to command. And he was uncertain, as he had been uncertain ever since General Loomis had casually slipped the message out from under the stone paperweight last night, and given it to him, and said, "It's a bastard."

Everything had gone like clockwork all day yesterday, Monday, until he got the message.

Loomis, who commanded Liuchow Base, had decided on Terminal Phase Demolition at 8:00 A.M. as soon as the Chinese generals had reluctantly, politely, but unequivocally agreed that they could not guarantee base security beyond nightfall. The Japanese were within forty miles, which meant that the base was already insecure, at that moment.

Only a skeleton crew of Americans remained at the base anyway, to service the last operational planes. General Loomis, a tactical man, had passed it from there to Colonel Magnusson, the base engineer, and Magnusson had it all organized. The evacuation priorities and tonnages were all long established, and up at Kunming the troop carriers and Hump cargo-carriers were already standing by to fly in and evacuate all remaining ground personnel and essential gear.

Within two hours of the morning decision, the first of the whale-bellied C-46s were lowering onto Liuchow field from Kunming, and the first of the men and gear had begun to go. By early afternoon the first sound of thudding in the clear and distant sky had sounded in Baldwin's ears, and he knew his own team, Detached Demolition, was at work. For four days, Baldwin had been planning each crater and demolition in a thirty-mile arc around Liuchow and, gradually, as the infrequent and sporadic thudding grew louder, and the muffling of distance grew thinner, he could tell that his two-man teams were falling back, on schedule, from the road net they were blowing about the great base and town.

By three in the afternoon, Loomis had cleared the last of the B-25s with their fragmentation bombs, charged to hit the advance Jap elements on the road, and fueled to fly directly back to Kunming on the plateau without ever returning to Liuchow. Watch-dogging his own timetable, immediately thereafter, Baldwin had checked with Magnusson, and Magnusson had already begun to use the Chinese labor troops to dig and pit the field with the thousand-pounders. It was a tricky job because they had to pit the field, plant the bombs, cover them—all except the de-fused nose socket—without interfering with the continuing traffic of evacuation planes. By nightfall, Magnusson had promised, Detached Demolition could start to fuse them up again, and link them with the detonating circuit that would blow the long runway to rubble.

Baldwin had eaten with the unit when he assembled them again at the signal tower at four in the afternoon, and had run over the final steps. But in November, nightfall came fast, and by five-thirty—just about this time yesterday—while there was still light, he had left Loomis and Magnusson at the signal tower, climbed into his jeep, and set out to make the circuit of the field to check.

It was then the feeling of being alone began to settle on him: The shadows sprawled across the field, and over the installations and barracks, the little hills of Kwangsi, the dormant baby volcanoes only four or five hundred feet high, brooded malevolently. For months, the little hills that had sheltered the bamboo-and-clay buildings of the Americans had seemed like smiling paper cutouts, friendly and ridiculous. Now they were hostile.

Baldwin heard the crack of a rifle bullet far away, and the tiny sound jerked his hands at the wheel. Who could it be?

Suddenly, counting to himself, he knew there were now not more than fifteen, twenty Americans at most left on the post. There had been two hundred Americans at the base in the morning; and fifteen hundred a month before. Now they were alone in China, and the Japanese were coming. This was when men got picked off.

But the Japanese could not be here yet. The Chinese had reported them forty miles off in the morning. And the roads were blown. And the Chinese base-guards were still about the field, they had not pulled out yet. But the Japanese were using cavalry, old-fashioned horsemen. And plain-clothes men. Intelligence had been reporting all summer on Jap plain-clothes men, dressed as Chinese peasants, moving ahead of the columns, mingling with Chinese in flight, picking off Americans if they could find any on the road.

The distant rifle crack made the field resoundingly silent. No lights gleamed in the empty barracks. All the noise, the yelling, the motors grinding, the activity had evaporated in the course of the day. Baldwin was conscious that no planes sounded overhead; the last of the evacuation flights had gone out. No trucks or jeeps mashed their gears or blared their horns. No voices rang or called in American tones along the road. The American personality of the huge base had been obliterated, as if Americans had never been there. He could hear, now, the far-off sound of a Chinese bugle in its melancholy off-key tones mustering some one of the Chinese companies in the area. But no flags would rise here in the morning. The base had already ceased to be a base and had become a somber, mysterious flatland lost in the mystery of China. And somewhere, far out to sea, a rusting, thumping Japanese convoy, sneaking through the Formosa Straits, would pass the narrows safely because there was nothing more to fear from the sting of American planes based on Liuchow.

Already, too, in the strange silence, Baldwin noticed that the Chinese were oozing about the field. Loomis had once said that the big problem was to keep the Chinese off base-limits: the peddlers, the girls, the houseboys, the hungry, the laborers, all who considered the American base an island of fat in their world of starvation. Now they were pillaging it; men rummaging in the abandoned barracks, hauling mattresses, chairs, tables, old uniforms out into the roadways of the base, looking for anything they might save or sell from the abandoned wealth of the Americans. A muscle in the back of Baldwin's neck twitched—which of them might be a Japanese plainclothes man, not a peasant? Which one might conceal a gun under his long blue gown and lift the gun and fire it as he went past? He stepped on the gas pedal and the jeep roared down the graveled road.

Beyond the runway, and behind one of the little hills his headlights picked up what he was looking for, two men in American uniform: Prince and Niergaard.

The two men were facing what appeared to be a long bamboo shack, covered with thatch. It might have been a barn if the Chinese had built barns that way, but actually represented the American Air Force's guess at what would appear to an enemy plane to be a peasant compound which could not hide, as in fact it did, several hundred drums of high octane gasoline.

As the jeep's headlights picked up the two men, Baldwin noticed how nervously Prince's carbine slipped off his back into a ready position, crooked in the elbow. Then he walked out so that Prince could see him clearly.

"Going well?" Baldwin asked.

"O.K., no trouble," said Prince, relaxing. "We've got a couple of hours' work on this gasoline, that's all. Everything's stacked just right."

Niergaard, who had come closer, threw his flashlight into the dark shack and, through the doorway, Baldwin could make out two GI drums standing one on top of the other set back slightly into the interior.

"You want to try it, Major?" asked Prince.

"Yes," said Baldwin, the impulse overcoming hesitation and restraint.

"There's a trick to it," said Prince. "I keep the flashlight on the drums. Then you hit the top drum with the first shot—it's full of ordinary automobile low-octane—and if it doesn't flame on the first shot, you give it a minute or two to leak, and those fumes they fill the shack. Then you cut loose with the second shot and if it's right, the fumes have taken hold and whammy, the whole thing goes. Once, at Hengyang, we blew the whole roof off with the second shot."

Baldwin sighted along the carbine, squeezed, felt the sharp crack, imagined he heard the bullet ping through the drum's iron skin. He waited. Prince, behind him, was kidding with Niergaard.

"Boy, get a box of cigars ready for the major. A bull's-eye gets him a box of cigars for himself, or a kewpie doll for his little girl. Step up one and all, step up and try your skill."

Annoyed, Baldwin squeezed again and the shack seemed visibly to bulge and shudder as, with a huge roaring gasp, the entire room burst into flame. The interior of the shack suddenly lashed back and forth in yellow and red flashes, seethed and rippled with light, and then the ridgepole caught. The flames gushed down from the ridgepole, tongues of liquid red, orange, white, yellow pouring down through the dry thatch, and then the whole roof was a sheet of brilliant orange-red, streaked with black gusts of oil-smoke burning.

The evening was vivid around them, and Baldwin's eyes blinked at the brilliance stabbing through the dark. He could feel the heat caressing his face, and growing stronger, brighter, and saw that Prince and Niergaard were also bemused and glazed by the fire, staring at it quietly with wonder and destruction on their faces, as children's faces glaze at a summer bonfire in the night on a quiet beach.

"Win, place and show," said Prince, subdued, no longer kidding. "Pay off at the end window for the twenty-dollar tickets." In the dancing flame light, even Prince's dark, saturnine face, with its thin, twisted nose had a little boy's look.

"I sure never get tired of watching them go," said Niergaard, softly, his slow simple farmer's voice even slower. "I'd rather see gasoline go than anything. Ammunition is dangerous, but this is something to see."

Baldwin was conscious of the little bubble of joy in him as he watched the flames in the wind's ballet, and remembered, oddly, that sometime in the past year the plans for these installations must have passed across his desk in Kunming when they were being built. And he felt, within the bubble of joy that the flames brought, an uneasiness that the only field job he had commanded after all the years and plans of building and construction should be this job of destruction, and his first outfit a wrecking crew in uniform. But he was glad the shot had been so clean, and that they had seen it. It made him more sure of himself.

"Stay with it," he said, "until this row is finished. Then find Michaelson on the field and see where he wants to use you. And wherever you are, I want you back at the alert shack at ten. We want to pull the big blow as soon as possible; then get a night's sleep; and then we're out."

"Right back into Kunming, Major?" asked Prince.

"A day and a half into Kweiyang, another day into Kunming," he said, feeling they were at the end of it and it had not been much of a job after all. Then, conscious of the fact that he must not get chatty with them, he said, "Back at the alert shack at ten. And stick together. The field is crawling with looters and there may be Jap plain-clothes men among them. I'm going to check the runway with Michaelson. Get me there or at the alert shack if you need me."

He ran the jeep down the road that twisted in and out among the little hills and supply shacks, turned it onto the taxiway, and, dependent on his headlights in the gathering darkness, paused before he took it out on the runway.

There were no more planes to land or take off, and the bombs with which Magnusson should have sown the field were absolutely safe without their fuses. But he waited.

Gradually, his eye noticed a pattern of dim lights on the field, neat rows, severely geometrical, and then his eye recognized them as torpedo lanterns, smoking with a little yellow light; and the little yellow lights made real to him the neat diagram for destruction he had planned on paper just two days ago. Each light flared beside a sunken thousand-pounder, to make the bombs easier to locate in the dark. There were to be twenty cross-ties, with three of the thousand-pounders to a cross-tie, according to the plan Baldwin had worked out for Magnusson's approval and execution. Each cross-tie linked its three bombs with a simple length of primacord. And each of the twenty cross-ties was hooked into the one long main cable that ran down the length of the field to the detonator behind Ramp Ten. Michaelson should, by now, have some of the men working on fusing the bombs and as Baldwin stared to the limit of his headlights he picked out the dark, lumbering form of an American truck, and beside it two Americans in uniform. Michaelson and Miller. He approached them slowly in his jeep, noticed that Michaelson's carbine, too, dropped quickly and easily from the shoulder to the ready-at-the-elbow. He strode out to be recognized.

"Any trouble?" he asked.

"Nope," said Michaelson, "they got them all marked up with these little smoke lanterns. No trouble finding them. This guy Magnusson's a pro—he's got it set up for us."

Baldwin knelt to inspect their work. A maroon-red snake of rubber-covered wire curled off the reel on the ground beside the truck and ran away into the dark. The wire had been spliced to a length of waxy-yellow cord, off which a clove-hitch led a tendril that came to a tit in a bronze, four-inch, pencil-like rod—the cap. The cap lay on the ground beside a little hole, scooped out to the depth of a fist. Baldwin gingerly probed the little hole and there it was, the snout of the de-fused bomb under the surface, metallic, cold and naked as an empty bulb socket.

"Where's the Composition-C?" asked Baldwin.

"We were just going to fill it," said Michaelson. "It's right here."

"Yeah, it's right here," said Miller, and Baldwin realized again that when Miller usually spoke, he spoke what someone else had said first.

Miller knelt and offered him a brown, heavy paper on which lay a large lump of a dull yellow claylike substance. Baldwin kneaded it, feeling its waxy give under his fingers, pinched a handful off and plugged the socket. He liked Composition-C because he liked the feel—soft and smooth as beeswax, the malleable plastic packed a punch as powerful as dynamite. He pushed his pencil down through the clay and the hole the pencil made would just take the cap, when the time came.

"Don't rub it too much," said Miller from the dark. "It gets in your fingers, Major, and gives you a jag. You know something, sir, you can eat it, too, like dynamite. You leave dynamite in the field and the cows will eat it. It's poison they say. But a little lick doesn't hurt you and gives you a hell of a lift, like taking a drink. Only you get a hell of a hang-over in the morning and a headache that makes you feel your brains are coming apart."

Baldwin handed the gobbet back gingerly and rubbed his hands dry on the paper. There was a lot that men learned in the field, he reflected, that never came across an office desk. He straightened and got up.

"Who's working the rest of the runway?" he asked of Michaelson.

"Lewis, Ballo, Collins—down at the other end. Prince and Niergaard are going to check in as soon as they finish the firing detail."

"Fine," said Baldwin. "Try and have everybody at the alert shack by ten. I really want to blow this before midnight and get some sleep before we leave tomorrow."

"Yup. We'll have it done by then," said Michaelson. "Only sixty of them to do. And then we barrel back tomorrow?"

This time the question irritated Baldwin. There was the job to do first. He ignored the question.

"Let's clean this one up first," he replied, "and let's make it good. See you at ten then, at the alert shack."

The alert shack had become the nerve center of what had once been a base of power and command. Now it existed only to supervise the base as it ate itself up. When Baldwin arrived, it had shrunk to a forlorn and frail two-story shack, made of Chinese bamboo and wicker, meaningless. On the ground floor, where the pilots had gathered to check their flight plans and spin their yarns, were eight men: six enlisted men playing poker and two junior officers idly talking. They had been drawn in together, as Baldwin had been drawn in on the shack, because it was all that was left.

"Where's General Loomis?" Baldwin asked, and one of the officers pointed up the rickety stairs to the observation floor.

"He's upstairs, sir," said one of the enlisted men, and Baldwin climbed the stairs to the tower.

"Hi," said Loomis when he came in.

"Hi," said Colonel Magnusson who was beside him.

They were standing by the windows of the tower, looking out at nothing, and a Coleman lamp hung from one of the beams, gently moving to the drafts, and the shadows swayed with it. Even in the dark, Loomis was a handsome man, over six feet tall, husky, with pride of carriage and bearing, his baggy air-force uniform hanging with grace because its wearer had grace. Magnusson, beside Loomis, was shorter—chunky—full of flesh, bespectacled, with the bearing of a doctor. They were both good men, Baldwin told himself. He spoke first:

"Fine job on those bombs, Colonel. It makes it a lot easier."

"Thanks," said Magnusson. "The Chinese did the backwork on it."

Baldwin waited, and since no one spoke, he turned to Loomis.

"Any more news, sir?"

"Call me Slick," said the general, "the hell with this Kunming garbage. Not much. We signed off the air about an hour ago. Your boys can burn this tower anytime they want. Message for you. The last one that came in."

Loomis walked over to the desk, lifted a rock off a blue topcopy message and handed it to Baldwin. Baldwin had read it then for the first time, not knowing what was being dumped on him. It seemed to make good sense at first glance, wrecking the road all the way back, although the names—Ishan, Hochih, Tushan—were unfamiliar. But what pleased him, at the moment, was "AT YOUR DISCRETION," for somehow it seemed a compliment. They had given it to him to do at his discretion and he liked it. He straightened, hoping he did not look happy and heard Loomis say:

"It's a bastard, hey?"

Baldwin stared back, puzzled.

"I hate these goddam discretionaries," continued Loomis. "They're always passing the buck. It's no way to run an army."

"But," said Baldwin, flustered, "but . . ." searching for words, winding up lamely, not wanting to sound like a boy scout, "it makes sense, I guess."

"What makes sense?" asked Magnusson.

"Well," said Baldwin, acutely embarrassed now, "you just can't leave that road open." He was in it too deep to back out now and had to go on. "If they come up that road and cut Kunming off from Ssuchuan, the game is over. The whole point's been to keep the Chinese together long enough to build something out of them, hasn't it? We have to keep them together at least until the war's over. We can't leave that road open . . . it's . . . it's the whole point of the war."

"The whole point," growled Loomis, "is to break the stupid back of the Japanese. When this base goes, there isn't any more to do out here."

Baldwin was certain that he would sound like a fool if he went on, or tried to explain it the way it looked from staff up there in Kunming, on the Yunnan plateau, where he had sat. And he admired Loomis. Loomis was a West Pointer, a general at thirty-one, younger than himself. There was something about what West Point did to a man, teaching him to divide his mind in compartments so that he could obey or command with equal ease, and though he must get tired and scared like everyone else, a West Point man never showed it. Loomis could relax up here in the dark room because he had done all that he could do, and there was no sense worrying in between the times you were actually doing things, once you had ordered them done.

"Well, hell," said Loomis, "it's up to you. I was just going to say you didn't have to do it. I can countermand your orders orally. I'm going out off the taxiway in the morning, with ten men. I can dump off some gear and take your eight men out too. It's a tricky thing with that many men in a '25 off this taxiway, but we can just do it, I think. If you want to come—well—you make up your mind."

Loomis was being a friend and Baldwin liked that. He liked Loomis more at the next question.

"This your first blow-job? You feel funny about having to blow things up?"

"Yes, some," he answered.

"Your first command, this job?"

"I guess you'd say so, sir," answered Baldwin.

"This was my first command, too," said Loomis.

Baldwin knew that already. The East China Task Force had brought Loomis his first star at thirty, and made him famous in the dispatches and given him a future in the air wars of tomorrow if there were to be air wars. But it must hurt him, seeing his first command about to go up in rubble.

"If only those Chinese had held," said Loomis bitterly, as if to himself. "They must have had half a million troops in this campaign. The Japs didn't put in more than eight divisions."

There it was: it was odd, coming from an air-force man. Only the ground-force people hated the Chinese, Baldwin had thought. The air-force people were usually all for the Chinese. At least in Kunming. The old staff arguments repeated themselves in Baldwin's mind, the ground forces arguing that if we hurt the Japanese they'd clean out East China and the Chinese couldn't stop them; the air-force people arguing that if you could punish Japan from East China it had to be done, and, of course, the Chinese would hold. But Loomis was now angry at the Chinese the way the ground-force officers were.

A shot rapped in the distance. The three men tightened together, and when the sound was lost in silence, they relaxed.

"God damn them," said Loomis softly. It took a minute for Baldwin to know that Loomis was still talking of the Chinese, not the Japanese.

"You never can tell what makes them shoot," continued Loomis. "It could be a rabbit, it could be a light, it could be a plain-clothes Jap, it could be a private fight, it could be because they're just nervous. I never did like having Chinese in such close support on a base. Look, Baldwin, you sure you can handle the Chinese on the way out?"

"I've never had any trouble," said Baldwin. "We deal with them all the time in Kunming. It's the Japs that worry me, not the Chinese; it's operating blind, not knowing where they are." That did not sound good. He stopped short. He had learned long ago to keep his mouth shut when he was worried, not to show it.

"Well, O.K.," said Loomis, in the command voice again. "You've got until tomorrow until we take off to make up your mind. Now, as I get the picture from Maggie here, you'll have the runway blown by midnight. Right?"

"Yes, sir," said Baldwin. "We have sixty bombs in. We're wiring them on a single circuit with cross-ties of primacord. We should get eight-foot craters staggered all across the field. The Jap can fill the craters, of course, but that takes manpower and time, and there'll be no air-cover for hot pursuit. If they really try, they can make the field operational again in a week. But they'd have to work on it. Hard."

"You're set to blow, when?" asked Loomis.

"At eleven," Baldwin said, confident.

"Right," said Loomis snapping off the conversation and going friendly again. "Now, how about a shot of bourbon while we sit it out."

They had sat thus talking for hours, rambling and waiting, nipping bourbon carefully, and Baldwin knew he liked the army, the easy way it braced you to do the things you had to do. He found himself talking about the army, asking Loomis about what the regular army was like in peacetime, and what he thought it would be like when this was over. They had all called each other by their first names and Baldwin was thoroughly relaxed when Michaelson had climbed the stairs, cleared his throat, and said:

"We're all aboard, Major, we're ready."

But the blow had been an absolute foul-up.

Loomis and Magnusson had come along in their jeep and joined the men behind the earthen ramp to watch them push the plunger on the blasting-machine and see the runway go.

"Everybody down under the ramp, with your back to it, facing away," Baldwin had said. "We're far enough away to be safe, but a freak could carry one of these runway cobblestones all the way out here. . . . God help any of those Chinese if they're still wandering around out there, but this is when she goes. Miller, you climb up there and give the call; Michaelson, you push it off when he's through."

Baldwin liked this moment of ceremony, the thrice repeated yelling of "Fire in the hole!" which the engineers of the army had called from time-out-of-mind, in all the wars long gone, to clear the last lingerers from whatever it was that was about to be blown to bits. From the top of the earth-ramp, he heard Miller's voice halloo in the dark, "Fire in the hole!" then wait and repeat the phrase, then wait and repeat it for a final time, and then scramble back.

"Push it off," said Baldwin to Michaelson, and saw Michaelson's back stoop as he thrust the plunger down, sending the magneto's current through the wires to rock the earth.

And then nothing had happened . . . nothing.

The men crouching with their backs to the ramp untangled with a single reflex and scrambled over.

"What happened?" said Baldwin.

"Nothing. There's a foul-up," said Michaelson.

Baldwin ordered the men back, and thrust the plunger down himself, a second time, a third time. Nothing happened. He quickly unhooked the wires from the poles of the detonator, and checked the detonator. It seemed good.

"Is this magneto working?" he asked.

"I checked it myself when we got here," said Lewis. "It's good."

Baldwin reached in his pocket for the galvanometer, scratched the two wire leads, watched the needle. Not even a flicker.

"A break," someone asked, "bad splice?"

"No," said Lewis, "those wires have been cut. Somebody's been cutting the stuff after we've been stringing it."

Baldwin knew he should have rigged the circuit both mechanically and electrically; he knew that he should at least have checked it with the galvanometer before he ordered Michaelson to push it off. It would have shown the break. The blow would not have worked anyway. But he would not be here, naked in the dark, in Loomis' presence, a fool and he wondered how to make the gaff look better. For a moment, Loomis was more important than the Japanese, and then the sense of the Japanese pressed in on him—the field still had to be blown; it was his job; how long would it take to blow by hand, how much time before the Japanese came?

"Can we find out where the break is?" asked Baldwin, aloud, knowing the answer as he asked the question, furious with himself for asking it, feeling the need to say something.

"Not if it's been cut on purpose, sir," said Collins answering the open question. Baldwin noticed the sure, conciliatory tone in Collins' voice. "If it's sabotage they just make a nick under the insulation, cut out the wire, leave the insulation jacket, and it looks so good you can't tell whether the wire's in there or not unless you go over every foot of it. We must have at least twelve or fifteen reels, more than a mile of wire down this runway. We couldn't check it quickly even by daylight."

"What makes you think it's sabotage," asked a new voice. It was Loomis. He had joined the circle about the blasting machine.

"I don't know, sir," replied Collins, "but the Chinese have been warning us of Jap agents in the refugee flow; any of the peasants out there tonight might have been a Jap with some wire cutters up his sleeve."

"Aw, shit!" said Michaelson, and Baldwin stirred uneasily, for it was clear that Michaelson had not noticed in the half-light of the jeep headlights that it was General Loomis who had joined the group and was asking the questions.

"Aw, shit," said Michaelson again. "Japs, hell. Those were Chinese. Collins, you got a frigging new excuse for the Chinese everytime something happens. I'll bet one of their officers got patriotic at the last minute and decided to screw us and save the field by cutting the wires. Or maybe somebody followed along after us in the dark and saw the wire there and cut out a couple of hundred feet just to sell. It was the Chinese, not the Japs. They messed up the whole night's work."

"Pipe down!" said Loomis in his hard West Point command voice and Michaelson choked off.

"Baldwin," said Loomis, "is this serious? Are you going to get this field blown, or is it going to be here for the Japanese when they come?"

"It's serious," said Baldwin, "but we'll get it blown."

Under Loomis' command authority, in Loomis' presence, he began to be sure of himself again and could say briskly what he had to say, without flinching because he disliked doing it.

"We can't check these wires by night," said Baldwin to his men, "but we still have to blow the runway tonight and the taxiway tomorrow morning. The main circuit is too long to check, and we'll have to blow each cross-tie individually. Or maybe each bomb individually. We'll try it by individual cross-tie first. With safety precautions and clearance for misfire that's all night's work, and into the morning before we kick off."

He caught himself. He was about to say, ". . . and then we're through." But he could not. He had almost forgotten the Discretionary. It occurred to him he had just received it all on his own shoulders and now he was in this mess. He *had* to get the field blown tonight; but he had no promises that he could make to stimulate them. He had to lead them, or drive them. And the field had to be blown.

"Can I help?" That was Loomis, friendly again, but in command.

"Not a thing you can do, sir, but thanks anyway," said Baldwin. "I'll see you in the morning at the alert shack before you take off."

When Loomis and Magnusson had left, Baldwin turned back to the men. Already, they had wilted. The long day and night of labor, of cutting, hauling, digging, lugging had worn them out. And behind this particular day and night, he knew, lay all the summer weeks since June. He could see them slumping as he felt himself slump inside; each tired nerve-strained muscle pulled on him to quit. But out beyond the ramp lay a dark, empty field which the Japanese would like to have and it had to be made useless. He must make them go.

He chose Michaelson, the strongest.

"Mike, you and Miller start at the far end."

Michaelson quivered as a tired horse does when it feels the whip.

"O.K.," he said. "Let's go, Miller."

Sometime that night, last night, only Monday night, during the nightmare and the sound, he realized that the impulse that had brought him down to Liuchow had trapped him in something bigger. It was the Discretionary that had sprung the trap, so that now he had far more than he had ever sought or bargained for. It had all somehow come into a foggy shape during the night in his mind, so that now if he drew back from it, he would feel less than a man. Once you saw what was right, you could not escape it. And if he went on with it—would he get them all killed? You could not flirt with the Japanese army in pursuit on the road. Nor with the Chinese either.

Baldwin could see the impulse clearly now; he remembered exactly how it happened up there in Kunming a week ago, when he had asked for this. He had been sitting across the desk from Hutcheson at the big headquarters on the plateau, five hundred miles away, by the big window beside the blue lake, where he could see the Red Cross girls walking through the courtyard, where they had movies every night, where newspapers and magazines arrived every day with the mail, and the hum and howl of planes roaring in from the Hump with supplies for China went on night and day.

No one was ever alone in Kunming. In the infinitely intricate, interlocked, oscillating adventures that made up the whole round of the war, Kunming was one of those headquarters where the fury and charm of battle had bound strangers together in a tight, warm partnership of a common thing to be done together. Together, in Kunming, all of them had watched the American bases thrown like a net in the past eighteen months farther and farther east toward the Straits; and, together, in the past six months, as the Japanese retaliated, they had watched the Japanese army coil, strike, pause, coil again, strike again as the fields fell one by one. Hengyang, Paoching, Lingling, Nanning, Kanchow, Lintan, Kweilin all had gone and only Liuchow had remained, doom closing on it, when, a week ago, Hutcheson sitting across the desk had read the Liuchow message and said:

"McNeil's had it."

"What's happened?" Baldwin had asked.

"Malaria. The medics want him out as soon as we can replace him."

"He's done a fine job," said Baldwin, mentally noting to himself how fine a job McNeil *had* done. He had met McNeil several times on McNeil's flight into Kunming from the field—a hard, middle-aged engineer, out of the New York building trades. McNeil had commanded the Detached Demolition unit from the time it had been organized in June to blow the fields on the pull-back from the east until just now. McNeil was an outdoors engineer, good with men at work in the field, but all awkward and out of place in the office up in Kunming. When McNeil came in on his visits, the three of them, Hutcheson, Baldwin and McNeil would talk it out whatever it was, and then Baldwin would put the data down on paper, staffing it out as he had done all his life.

Maybe it was just this staffing that had lain behind the impulse. Because he had slowly become aware that the Army was using both McNeil and him as they had been used all their lives before; McNeil, field-bossing the operation out there in the east, roughing the plans into stone. But himself investigating, consulting, giving the engineer's analysis, the engineer's opinion to the men who had to make the decision. It was just the way they had used him at Lowry & Moody: After he had clarified it, the senior partners always put the price on it. And this thought, always with him as the months at the desk in Kunming had worn away like the years in the office back in Boston, was almost certainly what had made him say, impulsively, yet casually, to Hutcheson:

"He's done a really fine job. We should have relieved him two weeks ago. Look. Why don't I fly down to Liuchow for the final blow and handle it myself and get McNeil up here to the hospital fast?"

"I suppose somebody's got to go down," Hutcheson had said. "Do you really want to do it yourself?"

"It's only four or five days until they close in on Liuchow and we ought to make a clean job of it. I'm not doing anything this week up here. Why not?" Baldwin had replied. He had really wanted to go. It would be quick. It would be useful. The war would be ending soon. And he did not want to go back to Boston without having done part of it himself.

But the impulse had had deeper roots than that, Baldwin knew. It was something about Lowry & Moody, and Helen, and home and all the years since college. He really wanted to boss it. Engineering had once been and still was a beautiful thing and in his daydreaming where he could talk without being embarrassed, he called it 'the poetry of solid things.' Engineering was taking an idea, a dream in someone's mind, and weaving it on the loom of arithmetic into stone and concrete, with men and machines, leaving something rising from the land, stark, perfect and content in itself.

But engineering had turned out to be not quite that simple. The family had gotten him into Lowry & Moody. It had been Uncle Will's idea. The money, Uncle Will had always said, lies not in the substance but the deal, and Uncle Will had made a lot of it, which was why Father disliked Uncle Will. Lowry

& Moody was an investment house, a good one. Big enough to finance moderate New England projects on its own, big enough to be called in by the really Big Houses, both on State Street and in New York when a major flotation was going. Lowry & Moody needed engineers—but not to build, for they were not builders. They needed engineers to analyze, survey, consult and finally give advice before the senior partners made a decision on the financing requested of them and set a price with which to bid.

Baldwin had loved it, too, for years, feeling very young to be inspecting great projects on which he would otherwise have served as a junior draftsman, or a working-gang boss had he been an operational engineer. But instead, representing Lowry & Moody, and the financing, and asking the questions, he had been important; and it was on his judgment and his reports that the senior partners based, in part, their final decisions.

It was Helen who had first made him discontent. There was always Helen's cold observation of the world and men; it went with her strength. It was she who noticed that though his responsibility grew, and Lowry & Moody liked him, and showed it, it was not he who sat in the big board room when the decisions were made. It was others; always others; and just before the war, even younger men were among the others. It was always Baldwin off on survey or analysis, on the trip to Michigan to look at the mines, or up to Canada to see the properties. But he did not go down to New York, where the big deals were knit. When he had given his advice, which was sound and clear, and where with the clarity of engineering he could show the shape, the size, the structure of the problem, then someone else made the decision, or set the price. Helen had noticed it. He could hear her now, as she caught him daydreaming, "Phil, where are you now? Now what are you dreaming about?" or, goading, "Phil—I don't mean for you to be pushy. But Phil, you have to handle other men or other men are going to handle you."

But he had always waited for Mr. Lowry some day to call him in and ask, "Baldwin, what do you think?" and not have Mr. Lowry mean what did Baldwin think about the engineering of the project, but whether, yes or no, Lowry & Moody should go into it. And it had been the same in the army, the same in Kunming. His hand had been over all the plans of all the new fields built in the past year; his thinking had shaped and altered half a dozen of the beautiful gray strips that had streamered the paddies of East China. But, yes or no, whether they were to be built or not, lay beyond him. When the yes or no was made, if it was yes, someone else was sent to do the building, someone like McNeil whom the army felt could handle men.

Baldwin could see all that, and how the impulse had spurted when McNeil's command was thrown open, and he had asked for it, to have this little command, for these few days, and blow Liuchow. That was how the impulse had carried him into the trap; and the trap had closed just last night, before the blow, with the message.

He could not see how he could get out of the trap, either, for the shape of the problem had an engineering truth and clarity to it. You could not come down from a staff desk in Kunming, where the whole war was spread on global maps in the map room, and think like Loomis who commanded only two medium-bomber wings and fought his war from the air over the limited waters of the Straits. *China* was important, Baldwin knew, not just the Straits; it was important that the plateau and the basin be held together, not cut. He would have insisted on it back in Kunming, in staff. There *was* more to the war than just getting the Jap, or breaking his back. The American base on the plateau, the Chinese base in the basin, they had to be held together because vaguely, he knew, China and America had to be held together. And if any man could do anything about it, he must do it. Baldwin could insist on this with the one part of his mind that was staff. But the other part was now in command of Detached Demolition here in Kwangsi. And the command-mind had to do what the staff-mind said. Because it was right. At whatever risk. That was the trap. Because it was right.

There was even more to it than that, Baldwin knew, scarcely wanting to think. It was all part of being from Boston, and spending the summers at Salem, and seeing the museum of Clipper ships at Salem, and remembering the celadon vases from China that his mother had inherited. It was part of going to school and the Open Door and being friends, and he liked the Chinese. And China was so big, there were so many of them, you could not let anybody give it away, you could not let it be offered to the Japanese whether or not the Japanese meant to follow, whether or not they meant to execute their death-dance at China's dismemberment. He had only wanted to boss this team at the last rites of Liuchow, and had done it, for himself and his pride. But now there was the Discretionary, and above that was the vague weight of China and America being held together, and it was all mixed up in his mind, for Duty was somehow involved. It ought to be done. But the Japanese were coming. And the men were tired. Linger too long on the road, and he could lose them, get them killed. He owed them something, too. He knew Helen would have laughed at him if he had talked to her about Duty. That was what made it difficult for him to tell her what he was really thinking. She would say, he could almost hear her, "Phil, you're mad—simply mad. You're daydreaming again. You and seven men—why it's idiotic."

And all through the frenzy of the night on the field, trying to coordinate the individual blasts as the bombs slammed off one by one, wincing at the occasional slap of rifle bullets that nervous Chinese were firing in the fringes, snuffing the warm breezes carrying the odor of smoke and the acid taste of explosive in the night, scanning the starlit horizon and the little hills, imagining there might be horesemen, Japs, there or there or there, charging at them, all through the night AT YOUR DISCRETION had grown worse and worse.

It was only when the sun had risen in the morning, and the sun-washed green and violet of the dawn had comforted him with its radiance, that he had decided not to go out with Loomis.

He would go out by road, with the trucks, and he would go fast or slow as it seemed best, and make up his mind whether to linger and destroy as he went.

CHAPTER 2

The Station

In the morning sun, this morning, Tuesday, as he had readied to leave the Liuchow base, the Japanese had seemed far away. The fires had burned out and the graceful plumes of smoke tasseled lazily in the haze. It was the dark that had brought fear, and the light brought security again. The Japs were close, Baldwin had known, but they came on foot or horse over broken roads, while he had wheels and could move at his own decision.

Baldwin had assembled his men at the signal tower after the sleepless night's work, the job done on the runway, and had sought Loomis to say good-bye.

"Hi," said Loomis, his voice fresh with sleep which somehow he had stolen from the night's tumult, "we've got coffee and sandwiches for you."

"Are you pushing off now, sir?" Baldwin had asked calmly.

"Yes," said Loomis. "What about you?"

"I've decided to go out by road. We've got the gasoline, the food and the gear, and I'll play it by ear whether we demolish or not as we go."

"O.K.," said Loomis. "If you're sure. We can still get you off with us."

"Thanks a lot," Baldwin had replied, "but there's the signal tower to burn and the taxiway to go after you take off. And I ought to check the town and coordinate the bridge south of town with the Chinese command. We'll finish it here, lay over in the hills outside town tonight, and figure it out tomorrow."

"O.K.," said Loomis. "It's yours for the blowing."

Loomis picked up his gloves, adjusted his cap, and had an afterthought.

"My jeep," he said, "want it?"

"No," said Baldwin. "We have a truck extra now anyway."

"Then turn it over to General Yang at Chinese command at the station for me, will you? The Chinese can use it. And get a receipt for it, too, will you?"

Baldwin drove Loomis to the taxiway where the B-25 was ready. Loomis squinted down the perilously narrow, perilously short, gravel-paved taxiway that had never been made for take-off or landing, then clambered in.

A long leg in American suntans hooked down out of the hatch, caught a rung of the belly-lid, lifted it with a toe, pulled it shut with a snap. The engines coughed. The props lazily windmilled. The cylinders puffed their black vapor, caught with a roar, and the B-25 bumped its way unsteadily down to the end of the taxiway for the tricky take-off.

Loomis gunned it very hard with the brakes firm on. He released it abruptly and the plane waddled, then ran, then streaked, then lifted into the air before it had used three thousand feet, as if Loomis wanted to suck her up into the air as soon as the rudder stirred and came alive under his feet.

The plane lifted over the field, cleared the hills, and, as Baldwin watched, he saw it turn on wing-end circling over the far end of the runway. Then, still only five hundred feet in the air, Loomis stood her on wing-end again, and came darting back straight up the length of the runway, his engines howling, the wind screaming over the wings, his prop-wash buffeting the plumes of smoke and dust from the blasted field. Straight as a surveyor's line he held the plane on course saying farewell, saluting his first command, and then was up and gone, a black dot fading rapidly away to the west. He would be in Kunming and under a shower in two hours.

Baldwin was alone now, all alone. In command. With the last chores to be done: the tower which was easy, and the taxiway which was harder, and telling the men, which was hardest. And after that, the road.

He had checked Michaelson on loading the convoy and Michaelson had reported they were already loaded to standard—six drums of gasoline, full loading of rations, three battalion demolition kits, the explosives, the portable generator, the BAR.

"Standard loading for field trip," reported Michaelson. "Whether we need it or not."

"Well, we may need it," replied Baldwin.

Michaelson had frowned at him, and Baldwin knew he had invited a question. He decided to answer the question before it was asked.

"We had another message from Kunming last night," he said. "They want us to stay out on the road for a few days and see what we can spoil on the way back into Kweiyang."

"Are we going to do it?" asked Michaelson, his voice at once surly, hostile and incredulous. "I told the team that once we get this Liuchow job blown, we barrel-ass right back into Kweiyang with no stops. McNeil said so."

"We'll play it by ear," said Baldwin. "Let's finish up here first and get in town to check the Chinese operation. It's a discretionary. . . . We'll see how it goes."

"You mean we have a choice," Michaelson said but Baldwin made believe he had not heard. He was glad he had told Michaelson; Michaelson would tell the others; thus, no speeches or explanations.

It was ten o'clock and Loomis must already be touching down at the Kunming field, when Baldwin finally assembled the seven men of Detached Demolition, the job done on strip, taxiway, and signal tower. He lined them up in road formation, his own jeep first, followed by Loomis' jeep for General Yang, the four trucks following next, and led them off to town.

Collins rode with Baldwin in the lead jeep, as he had whenever Baldwin had left base in the past few days. Collins was the unit interpreter, trained at some army school in California. McNeil had explained about Collins before he left. "A smart kid, a good one, gets along fine with the Chinese. I can't figure out what he tells them when they talk, but they like him; he's a college kid." When they got to the railway station Baldwin was very glad indeed that Collins was with him.

Liuchow station was the last unoccupied switching yard on the long railway that ran in the lee of the mountains. From Liuchow to the west, through the pass, paralleling the road along which they were now to retreat with their trucks, the single-track spur ran up into the hills to a railhead marked Tushan, one hundred eighty miles away. The spur had been in process of demolition all week, as the Chinese ripped out the rails, backed the rolling stock up on Tushan, prepared—or should be preparing—the bridges for demolition. But so long as Liuchow station and the switching-yard itself were intact, they were important. From his memory of the big map in the Kunming war-room, Baldwin knew that the switching-yard *must* be destroyed to keep the Japanese from using the north-south mainline to ease the strain on their sea-transport.

And yet, they found at the station that nothing at all had been done.

They sat with General Yang in the stationmaster's office, and in high, falsetto, South-China accents, the general explained.

"There is no way, Major," Collins translated from the general's lips.

"Ask him what he means when he says there is no way," Baldwin countered.

Collins and the general jabbered away, and Collins said:

"He says, '*Mei yu pan-fa.*' They say it for everything. It usually means that there's no way of doing anything. He says: there is no way of blowing up the yards. The people will not listen to him. They are waiting for the trains to start. They will not leave the trains. The soldiers cannot make the people go. The people will not move."

"But this is the end of the line," protested Baldwin impatiently, "the trains can't go up the spur to Tushan, it's out. And they can't go north or south because the Japanese are closing in. It's as simple as that. It's all over. Nobody can get anywhere from here by rail, it's got to be blown."

The general spoke and Collins translated in short bursts:

"My soldiers have told this to the people. But the people do not listen to the soldiers' words. They are sure the trains will carry them further. They have paid for their tickets. In America sometimes the people do not listen to their army either? True or not true? The people are too tired to walk farther. They have been walking a long time, these people.

The soldiers do not want to fight with the people. These are our own people."

The general stared disconsolately through his gold-rimmed spectacles at Baldwin, and Baldwin felt uncomfortable. The general's fingers drummed on the table. They were talking, but Baldwin felt no contact.

"If the major wishes, I will show him. Please come," said the general.

The general rose from his chair, and Baldwin and Collins followed. The general clipped an order to one of the sentries in a falsetto even higher than his conversational tones, and in a few moments a sergeant and six Chinese soldiers arrived to escort the three into the yards.

It took minutes for Baldwin to grasp what he was seeing. Into the yards had been stuffed locomotives and wagons of every vintage and model, rusting, shiny, new, old: flatcars made long ago in Manchuria, Belgian boxcars, French wagons-lits, Japanese passenger trains, tank cars marked still in German as made in Düsseldorf. South and north of the station, for hundreds of miles, bridges had been blown, rails had been lifted, culverts exploded. Now the trains had clotted here at the end of their existence, immobile, they could go no farther. One or two locomotives hissed lazily, the steam still simmering in their boilers. The rest were cold.

And over locomotives, boxcars, passenger trains, flatcars, bristled the people.

A great symphonic stink eddied and blew about the crowded railway yard, fouling the crisp, blue, midmorning air. It was the stink of a thousand human smells, of urine and excrement, of vomit and sickness, stained with the many shadings of garlic, and underlain with a sour, basic, sweaty body odor that touched everything. From the roofs of the cars, men, women, and babies peered down from beneath the crust of their possessions. Cow-catchers, decks, couplings bristled with paper parasols, bundles, chairs, packages, poles, baggage. Out of the sliding doors of the boxcars, peered peasants in blue, merchants in black, young men in Western business suits. The red silk of infant's wrappings darted from the drab coloring of the mob, and here and there the stained silken-pink of the pleated bridal robes said that a newlywed was caught in flight. Babies cried. Women moaned. Men talked in all the crackling tones of all the Chinese provinces.

"You see," said General Yang, "we have no way. The people will not leave the trains. We cannot blow them up. The people will not let us."

"But the Japanese will be here," Baldwin persisted, "today or tomorrow, don't they know?"

"We have told them that," said General Yang. "But many people do not believe us, they do not believe their government. Many people do not care now. They have walked too long. They will wait for the Japanese to come, and try to go back home after they come. Tonight we ourselves will leave, and tomorrow morning, after that, when nobody is here, those who believe us will start walking to Kweiyang and those who do not care will wait for the Japanese to come and hope for mercy. There is no way. *Mei yu pan fa.*"

A mother carrying a baby wrapped in red silk lifted herself from one of the mattresses and came crying over to the two Americans and the Chinese soldiers. A man followed her, holding out his hand, babbling hysterically. In a moment, all the wagons and cars were pouring out people who coagulated in a shrieking, crying knot about their group. General Yang barked an order to the sergeant, the sergeant shrieked another order to the soldiers and the soldiers, lifting their rifles in both hands, crosswise, like gymnasium bars, made a little circle about Yang and the two Americans and began to push the people back. The sergeant cursed and yelled until the cords of his neck stood out and his normally high Chinese voice reached a menacing soprano shriek. A boy of twelve ducked under the barrier of the soldiers' rifles and ran, pleading, to the Americans, clutching at Baldwin's field blouse. A blow from General Yang's arm sent him tumbling. The boy picked himself up from the gravel, blood running from his scraped cheek, and scuttled whimperingly back into the mob.

"He says he is hungry; but he has no discipline," said General Yang somberly. "Chinese people have no discipline, a rope of sand, these are our people, that is what our Sun Yat-sen said. The generalissimo also says we must have discipline. But we have no discipline. Let us go back to the office. You see there is no way to blow up the railway station. The people have no discipline. They will not let us."

Baldwin had not liked to agree with General Yang. It was not clean to leave the railway yard undamaged, the rolling stock intact. It was a frayed ending to the long summer's work. In the office, back in the station, General Yang had explained again.

"There is no way," said the general, "except to shoot the people to make them go. Do the Americans want us to shoot the people?"

Baldwin felt the anger rising in him. There was something unreasonable and unfair in General Yang's question. His orders, Baldwin reflected, read ISHAN, HOCHIH, TUSHAN. But did "AT DISCRETION" include the station here, too? He did not know; and he did not see how he could handle General Yang. The general was so courteous.

"Tell him," said Baldwin, "tell him we are not ordered to shoot the people, we do not like to shoot people. Tell him we are Americans who have orders to delay the Japanese, and Americans obey orders. Oh hell, Collins, tell him we've got a job of work to do and we're doing it, not because we like it, but because we've got to. Tell him," concluded Baldwin, wearily giving in, "that blowing the railway yard and the town is Chinese responsibility, not ours, and if he can't do it that's up to him."

"The major is right," said General Yang. "Besides, what good would it do to destroy the railway yard? Where will the Japanese take these trains? All the rails are destroyed. What will they do with the metals? They cannot take it anywhere. When they take Liuchow, they have taken all of East China. Then they cannot go anywhere else. Besides," went on the general, "do not the Americans say we are winning? Soon the war will be over. MacArthur is soon in the Philippines. The American airplanes now bomb Tokyo. China has eaten bitterness for a long time. Maybe it will be easier to build again if the railway yard is not destroyed."

The general smiled at them both, a wide, mirthless, nervous smile.

"Will you have tea with me? Will you have noodles? You are hungry?"

"We aren't getting anywhere are we?" said Baldwin to Collins and waited. "Ask him if he'll let us have some soldiers to blow the bridge south of town if he won't blow the yards."

"Wait—" Collins held up his hand. "I think he's afraid of us, sir. The important thing is to make friends with him first. We have to make friends. May I feel him out?"

"We haven't time to make friends," Baldwin said, hearing his own voice sound stuffy. "This is his job, too."

"The jeep, sir, if you're going to give him General Loomis' jeep, let's give him the jeep first, and have the noodles and then talk about the bridge."

"O.K.," said Baldwin, "let's get on with it." This, he knew, was the point where he always dropped out, where it was not a matter of logic or substance but of some quicksilver something extra that irrationally swayed a deal.

He watched Collins—a tall, lean, brown-haired boy, at twenty-two not yet a man, his jaw muscles still smooth, with no sag, his brown eyes bright and full of warmth, a smile now curving his lips—as he leaned forward to sip the tea, and Baldwin knew the smile was reaching out to General Yang and touching the general, too. Collins was the youngest man in the outfit, but there was an air of deftness and sureness about Collins that he, Baldwin, had never known.

The noodles came almost instantly after the tea, fragrant with the faintest touch of garlic, egg-yellow, hot, steaming, with dark leaves of cabbage twisted into the noodle soup. Collins twirled the noodles about his chopsticks, complimented the general on his noodles, and Baldwin, not understanding the language, sensed that Collins liked the noodles, liked the general—and the general liked Collins, too.

Collins brought up the matter of the jeep. The Americans were driving back to Kweiyang, he said. They had one extra jeep. General Loomis had asked them to give it to his good friend, General Yang. The jeep was outside.

General Yang became very grave. He pushed away in the air with his hands, palms outwards. America and China are good friends, he said, but this is too much courtesy.

America and China are good friends, indeed, said Collins, this is why General Yang should have the jeep, it was no courtesy at all.

It was too much, said General Yang.

It was nothing, said Collins.

Then, abruptly, the general changed the conversation and Collins translated.

"The town is burning," said General Yang.

"What?" Baldwin asked, puzzled.

"The town is already burning," said General Yang, offering the information as if he were making a gift of destruction to the Americans in return for the jeep.

"What town?" said Baldwin.

"Liuchow," said General Yang. "Already. We do not have to shoot the people in the town. There is a big wind. We burn a little of the town at the edge, and the wind will burn the rest."

It pleased Baldwin that the town was burning. Yet it irritated him that the general should offer the burning town in gratitude for the jeep. This was a job to do, not a bargain. He picked at the noodles with his chopsticks and swallowed them tastelessly and was angry.

"Now ask him about the bridge south of town," said Baldwin, "tell him we ought to take that one out, too. We need some of his soldiers to help us do it."

"Of course," said General Yang. The jeep had changed his tone. He was now a friend. He was helpful. "The bridge is not too difficult to destroy, but the people may bother you. You need soldiers to guard you while you work. I will send you the soldiers. When?"

"Now," said Baldwin, putting aside his chopsticks. "It is late. We do not know how near the Japanese are. We should do it now."

When they had wiped their mouths, put aside the chopsticks, finished the tea, they went outside, and Baldwin gathered the men in a huddle to explain the work. He would go into town himself with Collins and Michaelson to check the fire; they had to be sure that the Chinese had blasted the town's little generator. The others would go out of the city by the south gate, and wire the bridge for blowing; the team had prepared the cavities three days ago. But they were to wait for Baldwin and the other two to rejoin them before they blew.

"Wait for us," Baldwin repeated. "We should be back by noon, but wait for us at least until three in the afternoon. Don't blow the bridge until we get back across with the jeep. Don't blow it until we're back, or unless you're fired on by Japanese you can see."

The town Baldwin entered was full of silence. The poplars and willows that hung over the streets swayed gently in the breeze and the breeze twirled little puffs of dust before it in graceful glittering cones. Underneath the whitewashed columns of the arcades, the shops were boarded and shuttered, the teahouses and warehouses empty. In the bright sun, the cafes and bars, where the American airmen from Liuchow base had spent their pay and brought their goods to trade with the merchants, looked forlorn and shabby. The "Modern," the "Red Plum," the "New York," the "Three Principles," and all the other tawdry rendezvous whose signs in English implied that American soldiers might here find drink and girls, were now exposed by the brilliant light in unpainted, timbered ugliness. No rickshaw men yelled, no peddlers chanted their wares, no peanut vendors hooted at the corners. Down the bare and mud-walled side streets as far as Baldwin could look, was a loneliness. No children shrilled, jeered, hooted; no floppy-bellied pigs squealed on the way to market; no housewives laughed or squabbled. It was a Chinese city without Chinese, its whitewashed walls, its old hanging trees, its rainless gutters all without sound. He could hear only the high whine as the telephone wires quivered under tension in the wind at the poles; and, above that, loudly, the whistling roar of flames approaching.

Picking their way through the eastern half of town, judging

the fire as they went, the smoke scratching their nostrils, Baldwin agreed that General Yang's judgment had been correct; the town would fall to the flames with no more work to be done. It was only when they stopped the jeep to explore Green Alley by foot and see whether the town's little power generator had been thoroughly demolished, that they could see the flames work at close hand.

The wind was picking up clumps of burning thatch and sailing the clumps up Green Alley, to burn out fitfully if the clumps fell on a tiled roof, but to smolder and then blaze if it found wood or more thatch. It was a valiant wind, and its whistle, combined with the hoarse roaring of fire draft in the alleyways, combined with the sound of the joints of bamboo rafters popping as the flames ate them, promised that the whole town would burn in a day. It had been a dry, hot summer over East China and the city, like the countryside, was parched and ready to become cinder.

It was after they had found the generator neatly blasted and had turned back toward main street that they came across the thing. They heard it tinkling and crying through the flames before they saw it. It was the old leper, the old beggar who for months had sat outside the Red Plum cafe, panhandling the GIs in from the base, who had become familiar to the Americans because he was the only leper any of them had ever seen. His face was ridged and knotted with the bulbous tumors of leprosy, and, long ago, trachoma had blinded his pus-filled eyes. One hand tapped with a stick on the ground, and the other hand was a stump, eaten off at the wrist, braceleted with little brass bells that tinkled musically to announce his coming. The leper was stumbling, leaning on his stick, crying, tears running out of his blind eyes, calling to the dead, burning and peopleless city for help.

He must have heard the sound of voices, for he was stumbling toward the Americans, wailing the beggar's chant in the old singsong:

"*K'o-lien, k'o-lien, hsien-sheng, k'o-lien*"—have pity, master, have pity.

Then the leper would change his chant, his tongue shaping his trade call by habit.

"*Ch'ing-kei ch'ien, hsien-sheng, ch'ing-kei ch'ien*"—please-give-money, master, please-give-money ran the singsong, with its traditional half-wail, half-sob that now in the leper's throat was a real sob. And the leper, obviously, no longer needed or wanted money, only help, some hand to take his, and thread him through the fire to safety.

"What's he saying?" Baldwin asked Collins.

"He's begging," Collins said. "He wants help. He wants us to take him along," translating the meaning, not the words he understood.

"Well, we can't take anybody," said Baldwin.

"No, he doesn't want to go with us, he's blind, he can't see us," Collins said. "All he wants is for someone to get him out of here; if we leave him, he'll burn."

"God damn it, that's a leper, Collins," said Michaelson, breaking in. "You know if you touch him, you catch it."

The leper had begun to cackle furiously, crying and moaning as he came closer to the sound of their voices, and Collins was becoming, as every interpreter does, not translator, but advocate.

"No you don't," he said sharply. "It says that only prolonged and intimate contact makes leprosy contagious."

"For Christ's sake, Collins, are you giving us that bookcrap again. What are we doing here anyway? We ought to haul out of here and get back to the unit. Leave the son-of-a-bitch and let's go."

"If we leave him here he'll burn. He hasn't got a chance; he can't see a thing."

Michaelson's unsteady temper exploded.

"Oh my God," he yelled. "Collins, you're going to get all of us in a sling someday. This ain't the Y.M.C.A. We can't do a damned thing about him and even if we could, we shouldn't, we got to get out of here, they're waiting for us."

"If we don't help him out of here, nobody will," snapped Collins, his lips taut in anger.

The two stood facing each other, bristling with temper. Michaelson, short, stocky, his balding head glistening in the sun, his hard, tanned face flaring at the nostrils, was cocked like a bull—his chest thrust forward, his muscles working, his hands on his hips. Michaelson was the oldest man in the outfit, Baldwin knew, perhaps as old as himself, or older; there was fury in this man. Collins, leaner, taller, slight but tensile, was equally furious, his boy's face now hardened into a coldness, his fists clenched like a boy's.

Baldwin caught himself. They must not fight. Without thinking, he snapped:

"Shut up!"

They looked at him, their anger stilled and ebbing, the beggar still wailing, and Baldwin said quickly, "Both of you! Collins, drop it! This whole place is dangerous. The Japs can be anywhere. It's too bad for him. He'll find his way out, or he won't! Leave him! We're going back to the jeep."

Collins tightened himself again, made as if to speak, looked back at the beggar who could not see them, shrugged his shoulders, and followed the other two. They quickened their pace through the flame-lined corridor of Green Alley and, as they withdrew, they could hear the leper tottering after them for a moment, stick tapping the ground, his chant pursuing the echo of their voices.

They found their jeep undisturbed, and making their way out of the town reached the bridge span to rejoin the outfit by noon. They waited until two in the afternoon before they blew it to let a Chinese convoy pass and permit an angry Chinese colonel to file his regiment across. Refugees darted and sidled in and out of the troop column, enraging the colonel, and soldiers and refugees cursed each other. Then, as soon as the troop file was across, Baldwin pushed the plunger and the bridge went out neatly, as it should.

If the Chinese had cut the railway bridge, then any wheeled thing would have to pause on the edge of Liuchow before entering the mountains. Whoever followed would have to follow on foot, fording the stream, or come by horse, or rebuild the bridge which would be difficult. Baldwin listened for sounds after the bridge had blown, and looked at the smoke-drift from the town. Except for the smoke, the day was a perfect Indian summer day, in its full heat, with its soft white clouds in the pale sky. That might be the muttering of artillery far away, there, from the hills on the other side of the town, and he could not be sure, and even though there was a blown bridge between himself and the Japanese, Baldwin decided to move.

It had been three hours from then to this evening, three hours to make the twenty miles into the foothills, plowing through lines of stalled Chinese trucks, parting the streams of soldiers and refugees, threading in and out of the clots of the evacuation, fighting the shouting, noisy congestion all the way. But when they came up the little rise overlooking the village of Sanchao, the traffic had begun to thin, and there was a day's march between the bridge at the river and here he was, a day's pursuit for Japanese on foot to catch up with his convoy on wheels and it was safe, finally, to rest and eat and catch up with his thinking.

Now, on the side of the hill above the little village, they were relatively alone. The men had begun to eat as soon as the trucks had been gassed, and Baldwin joined them. The pork-and-gravy, with its peppers and onions, hot-and-wet-and-heavy, soothed Baldwin. A drowsiness settled on him as he shoveled the hot stew from messkit to mouth. Some of the men were already spreading their bedrolls on the ground behind the truck, and, already exhausted, they were crawling in.

Prince and Lewis had the SCR-300 on the ground, Lewis fiddling the dials. Lewis' face was puckered, his eyes squinting, all the wrinkles curving about his eyes, on his forehead, at his lips, as he listened under the earphones. Every now and then he would wince as the radio screeched with static. His fingers slowly coaxed the dials back and forth, gently feeling out the air, but he shook his head after a few minutes.

"Nothing," said Lewis, "can't raise a thing. I think I get a Jap field radio now and then, but nothing I can make out."

Baldwin knelt, took the earphones, adjusted them over his own head and listened. He expected to hear nothing; the radio was only line-of-sight in range, twenty-five or thirty miles at the most. But the surge and hum of the set teased at his ears. His fingers stroked at the dials and it seemed as if at any moment a sound might break into a voice he could understand, coming out of the dusk to say he was not alone. But there was nothing, only the whine now and then of an errant wave, or the squeal and screech of static, or the sputter of a dust particle. He listened for a moment, then gave it up.

"We're out of contact," he said to the men watching him. "We won't pick up a signal until we get nearer Kweiyang. Let's knock off now and get some sleep. All of us."

He spread his own bedroll now and was ready to crawl in, when Michaelson approached, stood tentatively as if he wanted to speak, and Baldwin motioned to him to squat. Baldwin did not know Michaelson yet. Michaelson was a six-striper and, McNeil had said, ran the outfit. McNeil had also said Michaelson was O.K.—a hard man, who knew demolition, who had worked in a Chicago foundry before the war, a foreman. What McNeil had said about Michaelson had reminded Baldwin of what the older men at Lowry & Moody used to say about the occasional survey problem that came to them in a reorganization financing: that no plant was worth anything unless it had good supervisory personnel and this was the most difficult thing to judge. A foreman, they used to say, had to be smart enough to understand what the manager or engineer was trying to do, but not be too smart. Just smart enough to know more about the job than any of the men under him, and make the men understand what management needed. Michaelson was not the man he would ever have for dinner at home. The thought was inconceivable. But for what he had to do now, Baldwin realized, he needed Michaelson.

"What about tomorrow?" asked Michaelson falling in with Baldwin's thinking. "Are we going through? Or are we going to do some more work on the road?"

"It depends," said Baldwin, "it depends on what we find."

He rose from the ground for he did not want to show Michaelson he had already decided to try because somehow it was right that they should. Nor did he want Michaelson to know that he had heard the men arguing the decision before supper. "The less talking the men do about this the better, nothing's set yet. Make sure the guard is posted," Baldwin said, and walked away.

Baldwin walked across the paddy to where the slope of the hill broke sharply in a terraced descent of many little crescent fields. The village below was now almost completely clouded with the night. Here and there a fire, or a lantern, or an oil lamp pricked the gathering dusk. It must be crowded. Beyond, far to the east, where it was full night, he could see a rosy far-off glow, making the sky luminous. Liuchow burning. The Japanese would have it tonight or tomorrow and General Yang would melt away into the hills to join the hundreds of thousands of soldiers and refugees who had already straggled into these hills in previous weeks, all of them now converging on the little highway he must try to wreck.

In the west, deceptively close, he could see the sharp black silhouette of the mountains he would enter tomorrow on his way to Kweiyang and Kunming. There they were, edged against the sunset light in the west, huge against the sky. Behind the wall of the mountains lay what was left of China that was not Japanese; somewhere deep in its shelter was the American base at Kunming and the Chinese capital at Chungking. Between them was the junction at Kweiyang for which he was heading and for which the Japanese, too, would be heading.

I asked for it, he told himself, I asked for it. Not exactly this. But somehow it had come to this, AT DISCRETION.

He stood staring at the big hills, bare and naked in the dark. He could almost feel the snow that lay within them, now, in November, when winter had surely come to the highlands. A night breeze blew, as if the mountain cold reached out to warn him. He shivered and started to get into his bedroll. Suddenly, the leper emerged on the sleep-dulled image of the day just past. The leper had been no part of the adventure he had asked for when he came down to relieve McNeil. He had wiped the leper out of his mind, like that, and had not even thought of him again, till now. Where did the leper sleep now? He shivered again in the cold wind from the high mountains and stooped to the warmth of the bedroll, the fleece comforting him as he let exhaustion flood over him.

WEDNESDAY

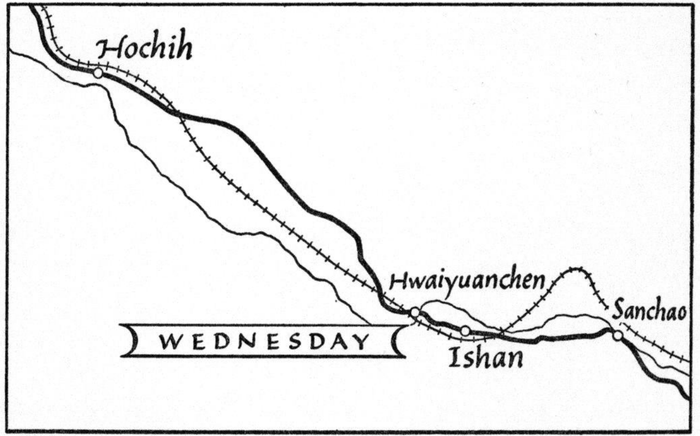

CHAPTER 3

Into the Hills

THE SKY GLOWED milk-blue over the mountains as they set out the next morning. A white mountain fog rippled in billowing pockets in the low hollows, folding them in gray when the road dipped, while a clear sun increasingly dazzled them as the graveled highway twisted steadily out of the fog into the heights.

Baldwin liked the feel of the convoy. Listening to the trucks wheezing behind him, slowing as his jeep slowed, accelerating as the jeep accelerated, he felt as if he were playing snap-the-whip back home in Boston, years ago. Collins drove the jeep and Baldwin, silent, could reflect on the train they made. Behind in the trailing six-by-six came Michaelson and Miller, an odd team, but they liked it together, and they carried the explosives. Prince and Niergaard followed third, with the gasoline drums, more than enough to carry them on to Kweiyang. Lewis followed in the fourth truck, and Baldwin worried about Lewis driving alone, carrying the three Battalion Demolition chests, the generator and the air hammer. Morgan, he knew, had once been Lewis' road-partner—he was the one who had been killed before Baldwin arrived. Oddly, he did not worry about Ballo at the tail, alone at the wheel of the truck that carried the rations; Ballo was self-sufficient. McNeil had been right. It *was* a good outfit; now it was his to use, these men had probably destroyed more in the last two days' work than the value of a good engineer's lifetime of building. If you figured back to the whole summer's operation the outfit had probably destroyed more than *any* engineer had ever built in any lifetime. And only eight of them. The feel of their power rose in Baldwin.

The weather, too, pleased him. The brisk chill of late fall had greeted them in the morning as they rose, cutting sharply across their bodies' summer adjustment to the lowlands where the heat had lingered until yesterday. They had shifted from suntans to woolens this morning and wore their field jackets zipped, but the warmth was gone. It was crisp not cold, almost picnic weather in the fall, if the procession that eddied about them on the road had let the illusion of picnic rest.

But it would not. Baldwin had thought in the morning as they pulled out that the crowd was only the early morning boil-off of the refugees who had sheltered about Sanchao for the night. But as the morning lengthened, the procession stretched on with it, endless before the American trucks as it was endless behind. On the flats, the procession crawled at foot pace, the plodding shuffle of lost soldiers, dazed wanderers, families, children only slowing and annoying the vehicles plowing through them. But at each upgrade, the horse carts and wheelbarrows, loaded with the mattresses, bedrolls, sacks, and belongings of the refugees, choked the narrow highway, forcing the trucks to grind in the torment of low gear; or to inch their way back and forth across the road to keep traction; and now and then to halt entirely before starting once more. Frequently, an empty truck or bus already rusting lay pulled over to the side, abandoned where its riders, at some earlier crest of the summer-long flight had run out of gas and simply quit to continue on foot. Occasionally, over the ledges and fall-offs of the mountain road they could see below a Chinese army truck, battered and broken where it had fallen, or had been pushed off the road once it was useless in the retreat.

At the crest of the first ridge, Baldwin signaled to the trucks behind him to stop and pull over. It was ten o'clock already, and time for the first relief stop. From the saddle of the pass through which the road crawled, he could see both the route they had come and the route they must take. As he looked back, the road they had already come wriggled toward him up the side of the mountain behind, then, as he turned, it wriggled away from him down the foreslope before them, then wriggled up the range facing them and certainly, he knew, it would go on like this, mile after mile, over a dozen more ranges higher and higher until it finally reached Kweiyang junction on the high plateau beyond. And at the bottom of the foreslope, Baldwin could see a bridge over a deep stream bed, in which water trickled and glistened.

The bridge looked very narrow and small from the high point at which Baldwin stood. But he knew it was a problem; like a tooth beginning to ache, this problem, and its decisions would come back again. There was no name to the bridge, he knew, as the highway itself had no name. Standing there on the saddle, Baldwin was perplexed by the problem. They had passed thirty, forty, perhaps fifty Chinese trucks and buses in the twenty miles they had come this morning. How many more lay behind him, chugging along as a charcoal-burner did at that instant? To blow the little bridge meant that every wheeled thing behind was trapped until the Japanese overtook them, that the riders would have to walk on foot. Horses, mules, foot-wanderers might lurch or scramble across the ravines and shallow fords of the winter streams. But with the bridge blown, no automobile could possibly pass. How much more gear behind him, or around him in the hills, did the Chinese army still plan to get out? And the jeep he had given General Yang yesterday at the station—it would be useless now, too. AT YOUR DISCRETION, he told himself, meant simply to make his own guesses and his own mistakes. But the message had said SPECIAL ATTENTION VICINITY ISHAN. Here they were.

He squinted down the long incline to where the little bridge spanned the stream several miles away. Four tiny figures, two at each end, paced it. Soldiers, he told himself. Chinese soldiers? Of course, Chinese soldiers, he reassured himself; there could be no Japs here yet, the morning was too quiet. But under whose command? Someone who had authority over the bridge? Someone he should consult to share the decision? If he could find him. How long would it take? It had taken two hours to do the twenty miles this morning. The Japanese must be in Liuchow now. Or beyond.

He turned back to his men who were smoking and gazing over the mountains. It was time to say something to them; he knew they wanted to know. But he did not know himself. He must say something now, but not a speech, and no promises. Finally, he walked back to them and began.

"We're forty miles out of Liuchow now," he said, "and I think we're far enough ahead of the Japs to be out of it. You know about these orders. Michaelson told you. I don't think it means anything more than a few days delay on the way out, at most. And the weather's great."

That was the wrong thing to say. Baldwin saw Prince pluck his cigarette from his mouth, carefully fix it between thumb and forefinger, and snap it away into the air like that. The gesture spoke. They had had enough outdoor weather of all kinds this summer and they wanted to be in. He shifted tone, harder, trying to find the key.

"We're almost two hundred miles from Kweiyang. We're supposed to tie this road up and slow down the Japanese pursuit. It means taking out a bridge here or there, perhaps a good side-hill blow if we can find the spot. Most of the bridges will be little ones, like the one down there. If we take out the one here, and another say fifty miles up the road, we've given them a week's work. We're going down now to look at the bridge there and see if it's the right one."

He cut them off before there was any questioning. He saw Michaelson viciously stubbing out another cigarette butt in the ground, grinding it with his heel.

"Keep the trucks in second all the way down. No coasting. Some of the brakes are pretty thin by now. Let's go," concluded Baldwin and turned on his heel and walked back to the jeep.

Cautiously and slowly, the convoy rode its way down the pass, blaring its way through skidding animals, scrambling children, cursing men who skittered out of their path as they clanked down.

They crossed the little bridge at the bottom and pulled up at the far side, the incurious Chinese sentries glancing at them without notice. Baldwin observed the bridge and saw it instantly as a simple thing: two stone piers in the bed of a deep stream in a sharp ravine that was almost dry, and log beams across which ran a planked roadbed—two hours' work at most. Above the bridge, the hillside rose gradually to a puckering crest and now Baldwin could see what an excellent position it was. It commanded all the valley north and south, it commanded the far slope of the hill down which the convoy had just wound its way. Into the contours, Baldwin's scouting eye noticed, the Chinese had cut machine-gun emplacements and somewhere, if it were a rich unit, there might be a mountain-howitzer or two. But he doubted it.

They were dug in well, Baldwin acknowledged, the cuts being rounded over into the hill's curve, the gun slits and pits visible only when one was almost on top of them. It was a good place to fight. But the half-remembered conversations in Liuchow came back to him, of Americans wondering why or when or what made Chinese fight. Divisions had melted away this summer when a battalion might have held, abandoning positions that might have been defended by boys. And then there were contrary stories, of Chinese companies wiped out to the last man, holding in desperate tenacity against all the weight of Japanese divisional or corps artillery, down to the last Japanese banzai charge. No one really knew what made Chinese hold and fight, or break and run. Anyway, this was a position, still manned, not yet abandoned, and he must find the command.

He beckoned Collins to accompany him and both strolled over to the two sentries on the near side of the bridge.

"*Ni-men shih na-i pu?*" asked Collins, which Baldwin understood from having heard it so often. "What outfit are you with?"

The older sentry stared at them respectfully, then gave his regimental designation. Evidently, the American uniform gave them the authority to have their question answered.

"*T'uan pu na-li?*" asked Collins. "Where's Headquarters?"

The sentry motioned up the hill.

"*Pu-chang tsai-pu-tsai?*" he asked. "Is the C.O. there?"

The sentry shrugged his shoulders. This was more information than he cared to give. Or he did not know. Collins and the Chinese jabbered further as Collins asked directions to regimental headquarters and then reported that they were there, up the hill, off the little road to the left, just before they reached the top of the hill, in the temple.

The jeep frisked its way up the hill, leaving the trucks on the road by the bridge, and found the little trail off the highway without difficulty. It was just wide enough for a jeep and Baldwin reflected on how nicely a jeep fitted into the China war and the mule-cart widths of ancient Chinese roads. Twisting and bumping, the jeep found its way in a few minutes into a clearing behind one of the hill folds. Chinese soldiers, in short yellow-green knee pants, sat on one of the slopes, cleaning their rifles. Others, naked to the waist, lay in the grass, dozing in the sun. Two sentries stood alert beside the black temple doors and through the open doors, between the red and yellow columns, Baldwin could see people walking across the courtyard; in uniform.

This was the command. But almost too beautiful to be a command, Baldwin thought. Two old trees, the ridges of their ancient bark swollen with age, pushed up through the stone-cobbled paving of the courtyard, the breeze tossing their leaves and boughs. Through the gate he could see moon-gates, one framed by the other, and the always-slanted Chinese roofs that so amused his engineer's eye, their tips curling up to the sky. It was quite warm now in the late morning sun, and peaceful here where the sound of birds and the occasional purling of water running somewhere rose softly above the far-away sounds of traffic on the highway behind the hill, the distance hushing the urgency of the traffic to a blurred chorus.

A lieutenant greeted them in an off-chamber, after the sentries had passed them, and invited them to wait. An orderly brought two bowls of hot tea, and Baldwin and Collins sat.

The minutes ticked silently by. It was almost eleven. Down below, Baldwin knew, the men were itching. The sun was warm, it was a good time for rolling up the road and getting ahead of the refugees. But they sat.

Collins broke in on Baldwin.

"Do you have that pass, Major?"

"What pass?" Baldwin asked.

"The Chinese pass that McNeil used for these field jobs. It's signed by Chang Fa-Kuei, and gives us authority to operate anywhere in his war area. We'll need it on this deal."

"You mean this?" asked Baldwin, pulling out the packet of papers that McNeil had handed over to him last week, and extracting the wrinkled, folded document in Chinese characters which had puzzled him.

"That's it," said Collins as Baldwin opened it and spread it over his knees.

Collins' finger pointed to a large rectangular tracery of vermilion lace-lines at the bottom of the parchment; above were column after column of black, bold Chinese characters.

"That's his seal, Chang Fa-Kuei's," said Collins. "His command runs all the way through South China, from Kwangsi down to Canton. It's supposed to give our unit authority to operate anywhere in his command, calling on all Chinese to cooperate with us in pursuit of our high mission, and the execution of our common duty."

Baldwin smiled. Suddenly, he liked the way Collins spoke.

"And?" he asked.

"And it works out something like a hunting license back home. Sometimes these little units honor it, sometimes they don't. It depends on what they think of Chang Fa-Kuei. It means that if we can persuade them to do what we want, it's O.K. with Chang Fa-Kuei; and if we can't talk them into it . . ." Collins shrugged his shoulders, ". . . *Mei Yu Pan Fa.*"

"What does it actually say?" Baldwin asked.

"I don't know," said Collins, "they didn't teach us to read Chinese in Counter-Intelligence. It was a six months course in Monterey—but only spoken Chinese; they crammed as much into us as you get in two years at college, everything except the reading of it. That takes years."

It made Baldwin feel better that Collins could not read Chinese either. He looked at the boy, as if seeing him for the first time, and Collins smiled back, mischievously, the way he had smiled at General Yang yesterday.

"How did you happen to go to a C-I-C school, Collins?"

"It seems crazy now," said Collins slowly, reflectively. "My father's in politics back home. In Brooklyn. He's a city magistrate; he's been aching to be a justice for the past ten years. In politics, he's well-connected because he's been friendly with the Flynn people in the Bronx and now that the Brooklyn machine's broken down, all the Washington patronage goes through Flynn. You know how it is, Major."

Baldwin did not. He disliked politicians. His face, he hoped, was showing nothing, but Collins said:

"I like my father, you know. Anyway he wanted to arrange a commission somewhere in Washington. Well, you know how we all were back in 1942—patriotic as hell, and I was just a kid. I put in for Counter-Intelligence before he could fix the commission or even OCS, and told him I wanted to do it my own way. He's still angry. They sent me to Monterey, to one of the language schools and I chose Chinese. And there I was a year later at one of these Chinese training schools in Yunnan where we teach them to use Lend-Lease material. This spring they sent me up to the Hengyang front with McNeil because he needed an interpreter and wanted an American, not a Chinese. I can't say I'm sorry either. This summer has been wild, but all the things you see at a time like this—no book carries it. As a matter of fact, when I go back to school, I think I'll take a course or two about China."

"What school?" Baldwin asked.

"Columbia. I've got two more years to go. In government. Then law school."

"Law's good," said Baldwin judiciously and he knew that Columbia Law School was fine.

"If you do it right, yes," said Collins, "but I think somehow I'd like to work over to politics. It's been in our house since I was a child, politics every day of the year. This is all politics, here."

"What? China?"

"China, this war, the whole summer. They run this country the way the Hall used to run New York. Not that that's so bad, mind you. I'm not making a moral judgment. That's the way the country is and the way they have to do it, but it makes a difference when you run a country in a war the way Tammany ran Manhattan. It's interesting."

"You like China, don't you?"

"Why yes, I do. So do you, I noticed."

Somehow the conversation had led them to this and he felt himself no longer a major and Collins no longer a sergeant. In the silence, as the waiting stretched out, they were together.

It was fifteen minutes before the lieutenant told them that the commander, Colonel Li, was ready to see them, and the two Americans followed him through the courtyard. Baldwin, vaguely aware of the quiver of excitement and eagerness in Collins' stride, knew that it would be like yesterday at the station with General Yang. The bridge had to be cut; but this colonel had to be made to agree first; and if the colonel did not agree there would be a bargaining, a quid-pro-quo involved. Baldwin wished that Colonel Li were an American colonel, in the American army, to whom he could explain the deal in his own way, get a fast yes or no, and get out. The bridge and the blowing of it was technical and no problem; but dealing with this colonel would be. And it came back to him that that was the way it was at Lowry & Moody. Baldwin was at his best either in the substance or the technique, before or after the deal was made, when he could make concrete the heart of what had been talked about, put the engineering figures on it, plan it, organize it. And now here he was tongue-tied among Chinese, with Collins to do his talking, conscious that Collins was more than an interpreter, that the boy had learned to be, or was by instinct, at home in the deal. And yet was good. Baldwin did not like being dependent on the boy.

As soon as Baldwin saw Colonel Li, he understood the delay. Colonel Li stood before him immaculate, ramrod-stiff, his pants pressed to knife edge, his tunic faultlessly draping his form, his hair oiled and clinging without a stray to the skull. An odor of perfume, strong and fresh, reached Baldwin's nostrils. Colonel Li must have bathed in perfume; the colonel must have spent the fifteen minutes dressing himself for this conference with the Americans. Now he was flawless. Beside him was a young Chinese lieutenant, his aide. Behind him another Chinese officer, thin, small, expressionless, stared darkly at them.

"Please sit down," said the colonel, after the introductions.

"Tell him we're in a hurry," said Baldwin to Collins, and he listened to Collins spinning gracefully through Chinese phrases that seemed anything but urgent.

"He says please have some tea with him," said Collins,

then added, "We'll have to anyway, or he'll be insulted."

The colonel, Baldwin, Collins, the two Chinese officers all sat down at a black-lacquered table and while Baldwin fidgeted, the colonel clapped his hand and a servant appeared to pour the tea.

"America is China's best friend," said the colonel, abruptly and solemnly, through Collins, as he raised the tea in invitation to his lips. "We are glad to have a visit from our American friends. Today is sad. Today we eat bitterness. But the final victory will be ours because China and America are friends. Has Major Baldwin been long in China?"

Baldwin squirmed. He had been through this courtesy routine at every conference with the Chinese in Kunming for a year and a half, and had sometimes enjoyed it. But in Kunming there was always time; now there was no time.

"Get through this business as fast as possible," he said to Collins, fixing a thin smile over his exasperation, "and tell him we want to talk to him about an important thing."

Collins cheerfully snaked his way through the Chinese courtesies, smiling, meandering, then wound up on business.

"What is the important thing?" asked Colonel Li.

"We are the American Detached Demolition Team of the East China Task Force," said Baldwin, and continued, while Collins translated, to sketch the situation, his orders, and why the little bridge should be blown. As he spoke, he realized how odd the idea must sound to the Chinese.

"Is this a good idea?" asked Colonel Li.

"I do not know," said Baldwin, "but my orders say the vicinity of Ishan. Headquarters think the Japanese may come up this road onto the plateau and if they do, they will cut the roads at Kweiyang junction. Then all our communications between Kunming and Chungking will be cut, too. So they want us to destroy it. Your headquarters also agree."

Somehow, talking to Chinese, Baldwin always got down to kindergarten level, one-and-one makes two—Colonel Li had a map, he knew the situation, there should be no need of this.

"How will you do it?" asked Colonel Li, and Baldwin explained how simple it was.

But since the colonel was in command of the bridge, said Baldwin, pressing on, the Americans could not blow it up unless the colonel agreed. Besides, said Baldwin, pulling out his blue-copy of the message from Kunming, then pulling out the Chinese pass, his immediate orders were in English, and he needed some Chinese authority, did he not, for certainly the colonel's soldiers would not let just anybody blow up the bridge?

The three Chinese ignored the message, studying the Chinese pass, and Colonel Li's knee began to jiggle in nervous oscillations of toe and ankle. He rose, went to his desk, rummaged about, and returned with a large map of China which he spread on the tea table. It was not a detail map, Baldwin saw at once, but a large old-fashioned German relief map of China, the low coastal plains in green and yellow, the foothills marked in tan shades, the mountains in maroon and brown, the snowpeaks in white.

"I do not think the Japanese will come," said Colonel Li, running his finger up the road on the map, "They *will* come, yet they will *not* come. It is very cold in the mountains now. Their soldiers are summer soldiers. They cannot do any good unless they go all the way to Kweiyang. They will send some horses up the highways to see how far we have gone. But they will not follow us into the hills. They *will* follow yet they will *not* follow. They will not stay. They stay only in the low country. Now they have all the low country of China. Soon they will be defeated. They will not come."

"What does he mean, Collins?" asked Baldwin, baffled by

the translation that came in fits and jerks, to the colonel's rhythm of Chinese.

But the dark, expressionless officer spoke, for the first time, as if he understood Baldwin's puzzlement. Collins translated:

"He says they will go as far as Tushan. He speaks a different dialect, not Kwangsi like the others. His name is Colonel Kwan."

Colonel Kwan's fingers ran up the map, past the green and yellow band, through the maroon and brown, and stopped, and he repeated, "Tushan."

"That's where the rail spur ends, isn't it?" Baldwin asked Collins. "That's a hundred and twenty miles from here—why?"

"It is not the railway," said Colonel Kwan. "It is the ammunition at the dumps. The Japanese know it is there. They will go to Tushan. Then they will stop."

"The little bridge," said Colonel Li, "it is all right. Tushan . . . it is all right. But not too much."

Baldwin's head was beginning to swim. He was not following. He was completely confused. Each sentence was reasonable enough in itself, but nothing was being said.

"Look, Collins, just what is going on here? I'm not catching this. Tushan's way up the line. We'll think about it when we come to it. How about the bridge?"

"I think they're afraid of us," said Collins. "Li is afraid of us. Kwan maybe isn't."

"Afraid of what?" asked Baldwin.

"Afraid that we're going to blow everything. They keep saying 'not too much.' I think they're trading with us, at least Li is—blow up this bridge if we want to, then go to Tushan and blow that, but not too much, nothing local, that's what I think he's saying."

"What does he think I am? Attila the Hun?"

Colonel Li was speaking again:

"Too much," he said. "The war will soon be over. The people are angry at the government. They do not want more destroyed. Too much is destroyed. In the beginning it was all right. They helped us. Now they are angry with us. They do not understand the government. They do not understand the Generalissimo."

Baldwin did not want to talk about the people and the government. That was politics. It had nothing to do with the conversation. He did not know what Colonel Li meant. What kind of Chinese was he? The thing was to pin the talk down to the bridge, the one bridge here, and blow it.

"Tell him," he said to Collins, "tell him the war is sad, we Americans are sad, tell him China and America are friends. Tell him anything. But tell him we're trying to get back to Kweiyang and we have orders to delay the Japanese somewhere in this vicinity. Let's get something settled. Just this bridge."

Collins translated and the cadence, even in the American-accented Chinese that Collins spoke had a different, fluent, diplomatic ring. Colonel Li visibly relaxed.

"This is good," he said. "Our people are divided, our people must be one. The people are divided from the government and the Generalissimo tries to make them one. That is why the Japan-dwarfs came to attack us, because they were afraid what will happen when the Chinese are one. Now we need the people to help make China one. After China is one, then it will be great. That is what the Generalissimo wants to do. That is why it is not good to destroy everything. The people do not like it."

"But," interposed Baldwin, struggling to get the conversation back on its tracks, "it is the idea of the Chinese army that we blow up everything from here to Kweiyang. It is not our idea only. They have agreed. It is not the Americans who decide to burn the cities."

"Sometimes," said Colonel Li, picking his words slowly, hesitantly, "the Generalissimo does not have the right advisers. He is in Chungking. He does not see the people any more. He does not know the people are angry. My regiment is from Kwangsi. I am from Kwangsi. My soldiers do not like to see Kwangsi destroyed. Nothing should be destroyed any more. Only the bridge here. The bridge is all right to destroy, it is too close to Liuchow."

"Fine, then," said Baldwin, seizing the agreement, not wanting it to slip away. "I get it. Now how about the bridge, can he help us out?"

"You are right," said Colonel Li. "I must write you an order."

The dark officer raised a question as Colonel Li finished, the Chinese chatted, then Colonel Li said again:

"Are you driving all the way to Kweiyang now?"

"Yes," said Baldwin, "but slowly. There may be other bridges."

Colonel Li nodded, then:

"Colonel Kwan will go down to this bridge with you and talk to my soldiers. Then he will go on with you to Kweiyang and he will carry the orders and if you have more trouble on the way, he will explain for you."

"Now?" asked Baldwin.

"Now," said Kwan rising, "as soon as I can pack my bedroll."

It was worth a ten-minute wait, thought Baldwin, to have a Chinese officer with them on the way out. He settled back and looked about.

"Perhaps you would like to see the courtyard and the

pool while you wait," said Colonel Li. "It is very pretty, this temple."

He led the Americans out of the room, into the courtyard, excused himself to say that he must talk to Colonel Kwan for a moment, and left them.

"What do you make of it?" asked Baldwin when he and Collins were alone.

"Interesting," said Collins. "Everything in this country is interesting. This is a Kwangsi unit, they're on home soil. But I wonder about Kwan."

"What about Kwan?"

"Kwan is a Central government man, one of the Generalissimo's men, I think, and Li is trying to get rid of him to us, and Kwan wants to get out and come with us. Kwan's probably Central government liaison with this local command and wants to get back to a Central government outfit because Li's probably going to melt these Kwangsi troops off into the hills. They're in home country."

Vaguely, for the year and a half in Kunming, Baldwin had heard talk like this. But usually from the ground-force Americans who talked a strange jargon of which Chinese belonged to whom, of what divisions belonged to the Generalissimo's Central government, and what divisions belong to the provincial governor, of what warfront was held by which armies which had come from what strange province and how great was whose control over them. Back at Kunming there had been the gunfight between the Yunnan governor's Third Son and the Central garrison, when Third Son and his provincial troops had tried to use some of the American artillery against the Central troops in the fight over how the American gasoline was to be shared, and U. S. Ground Forces had had to step in. There was something strange going on here at this headquarters now, but Baldwin did not want to appear innocent before Collins. He would play it by ear. He could not tell how all this affected the bridge he had to blow down below; and he was glad that it was Collins with him and not someone who would bleat about the 'gawddamn slope-headed bastards' as the ground forces always did, or lose his temper. He replied to Collins reflectively:

"It would be logical though to have Kwangsi troops here defending Kwangsi, wouldn't it?"

"Well, yes and no," said Collins. "Logical if they fought the war our way, but not logical for the Central government. What they've done is to use the war to bring all the local troops out from their home provinces and station them somewhere else. That makes them dependent on Central at Chungking—southern troops up north, northern troops down south. Most of the Kwangsi troops, or the best of them, are north of the Yangtze now, about eight hundred miles from here. You see, if you take these provincials away from their home province and their home supplies, then they've got to look to Chungking for supplies and the Generalissimo can command them. If he distrusts them, he chokes off their supplies. There aren't enough supplies to go round anyway, for any of them, so naturally the Generalissimo's own Central troops get the best of everything, what there is. And some of those Central troops are damned good units. So are these Kwangsi troops in battle. But I didn't know they'd left any of them down in this area. I thought they'd all gone on north."

"You've seen a lot of this, haven't you, Collins?"

Baldwin realized that, after all, he did not mind appearing ignorant before Collins.

"All summer. The Generalissimo put some real good Central troops in around Changsha and Hengyang, but they got chewed up completely in July. Most of the fighting since's been done by provincial armies, only I haven't seen a Kwangsi outfit under its own command for weeks."

"How can you tell what they are? Do you ask them?"

"It's feel mostly. This country's really like New York. The Central people come from all over—from the north, from the south, from the coast, from Kwangsi, too. Only they feel Central, they belong to the Generalissimo, they went to his schools. The rest of them come from the same places, only they went into the provincial armies and their connections are at home. Like New York. You know how New York is; you used to get these aldermen back home who ran strictly as Irish, or Italian, or Jewish. But then some of their kids get to go away to college, or learn somehow, and come back and run as—well—American. My old man, for example, he'll never make the Appellate Court; he's too Irish, or perhaps he just isn't important enough as Irish, and his base isn't broad enough to run as a New Yorker. Look: Let me put it this way—take West Point, for example. They take these country kids from California, or Texas, or Nebraska and when they come out they're American, they all talk the same and act the same; and since California hasn't got a private army, nor Texas a private army, nor New York a private army, they know that if they want to earn stars, they have to wear them in the United States Army. Here there's the Central Army —what's left of it. But then there are all the local armies, what's left of them, and this regiment is something left over from the old Kwangsi armies. Their loyalty is here. This outfit can probably melt off into the hills and live off its own peasants after the Japanese pass through, and maybe form again in a couple of months. I'll bet this Colonel Li is thinking about that right now. But Kwan is probably a Central government liaison man, and he wants to get back where he belongs, to the Central Army, if he can find it up ahead."

Baldwin pondered what Collins had said, reflected on his bridge below, was about to speak again when Collins whispered:

"Oh look, look . . ." very softly.

Collins pointed.

Across the pool by which they were standing, there had silently appeared a woman's figure. Her dress was a deep blue, pleated in sea-green, and in her black, glistening hair gleamed an amber comb. She had not noticed them and was following the passage through the water of two ducks who had glided out from behind the miniature arch of the little stone bridge. Now she looked up, as Collins whispered, stared at them, unfrightened but surprised, and turned soundlessly and disappeared again behind the bridge.

"I wonder who she is?" asked Baldwin.

"I wonder, too," said Collins. "They all have their wives at headquarters if headquarters settles in long enough in one place. Could be the colonel's wife; or his daughter, but I suppose he's too young for her to be his daughter. Or just his woman."

The mood had been broken and Baldwin could not resume the conversation. Exasperation was growing in him again as the minutes stretched out and the woman, in her serenity and silence, had irked him. This was no way to fight a war. He watched the brown-and-orange ducks swimming in the pool and decided they were mallards. They swam closer and as their bodies breasted the surface, forming a silvery, shimmering V of trailing ripples, he noticed a glint of gold and red flashing in their wake. He bent, against his will, to see what it was, and they were goldfish, flashing beneath the surface of the pool as their large, transparent fan-tails curled and waved them on. He knew they pleased his eye and his exasperation and pleasure struggled with each other and he said, "Handsome, aren't they?"

"I'll never understand this country," said Collins. "You walk on foot through this retreat, week after week, month after month, and it's all just one color—brown, yellow, mud-color, the walls, the houses, the fields, the people, the soldiers, the soldiers' uniforms, the faces. And then you come to a village and hole up for the night in someone's courtyard, or in a temple, and you find it drenched with color—blue enamels, and red silks, and whitewash, and these vermilions they use, or you come to this, with a pool and a bridge, and these ducks. Some day after the war, I want to come back and find out how China really works."

This was all different from Kunming, thought Baldwin, as Collins finished. This is how China really is. Then, once again, he sensed the exasperation growing in him, the baffled anger of delay rising to indignation. Time was escaping. The sun was directly overhead and it was noon, or past noon now. They had been through all the courtesies. Down below with the trucks the men must be grousing, and there was work to do. And still they lingered. It was as if there was no war, no haste, as if the noon sun, now as hot as it had been below in Liuchow in the summer weeks, shone on a land of peace. The minutes slipped soundlessly away and the ducks, curving through the water, appearing and disappearing through the arches of the pool's miniature bridge, made silver patterns which glowed in the light and vanished and rippled again and vanished.

It was more than an hour before Colonel Li returned. "We are ready now," he said, and led them back into his office.

Where the tea table had stood there was now a huge rosewood table. Eight pieces of fragile porcelain chinaware, and eight pairs of black chopsticks had been set. Bowls of white rice fumed with steam. In the center sat a platter of black and red meats; glistening albuminous eggs sliced to show their black sulfurous centers; flaked gizzards; red peppers; flaked bamboo roots; green, translucent, glistening pickled vegetables. About the table, stood six Chinese: Colonel Li, his aide, three others, all smiling and beaming, Colonel Kwan erect, impassive, still expressionless.

"You must eat before you go," said Colonel Li. "Please sit."

With difficulty, Baldwin capped the temper explosion that flared inside him at the sight of the lavish table. So they had held him an hour for this courtesy, an hour for the meal which the headquarters cook must have begun to prepare as soon as they had been announced, two hours earlier.

"I thank the general," said Baldwin stiffly, "but we are in a great hurry, we must go; I know we must not stay. If Colonel Kwan is ready then we must leave at once. For God's sake, Collins, tell him we have a job to do."

Colonel Li's face fell. On the faces of the staff officers the smiles thinned out. They watched him.

"You have not eaten today. Colonel Kwan has not eaten today. China and America are friends. You are hungry, please just taste a little—there is nothing to eat, only a little," said Colonel Li.

Suddenly, all of China seemed twining around Baldwin as Li spoke—with its delicate tentacles, its courtesies, its hidden impulses, its pockets of delay. He was strangled in it. He could not refuse to eat unless he were to cause Colonel Li a complete, irreparable loss of face. And he knew he could not. It would be easier to slap Colonel Li as he stood there than to walk away from the table of steaming foods.

"Just a bite then," said Baldwin and moved to the table as

the smiles instantly flowered again on the Chinese faces; Baldwin sat at the center of the table, Collins on one side, the colonel on the other, and the colonel lifted his chopsticks over the food as an orchestra conductor lifts his baton.

"*Ch'ing*," he said, pointing, "Please . . ."

First came the cold cuts, the sliced livers and gizzards and eggs and vegetables, with the pickles and mustards and sauces. Then came ham, roasted, spiced and toasted in a puff-white bread. Then came chicken chopped fine with peppers and pricked with the raw ginger; then an egg soup creamy with beaten whites. Baldwin felt himself relaxing against his will as the foods slipped down his throat.

They paused and a fat officer rose from the table with a cup in his hand. The officer's forehead was beaded with sweat which ran down his hairless, plump cheeks into his neckband. Where medals or ribbons might have been on someone else's chest, were fountain pens; fountain pens in his upper tunic pocket at the right, in his upper tunic pocket at the left, fountain pens clipped to his side pocket, new, shiny arrow-pointed American fountain pens. The officer opened his mouth and a squeaking, high-pitched voice came out speaking what was unmistakably English.

"You are glorious, Major Baldwin. You are glorious, Captain Collins. America is glorious. The 212th Regiment is sorry there is nothing to eat for its glorious guests. China and America are friends. China and America will win the final victory. Down with the Japanese dwarf-bandits." Then squeaking, he concluded, "Hip, hip, hooray!"

Baldwin blinked in total surprise and his face burst into a smile he could not control. Everyone but the dark officer, Kwan, smiled too. Colonel Li beamed at his triumph in producing an English-speaking officer in his own headquarters. He stood up holding his cup of yellow wine.

"*Kan-pei*," he shouted, "Bottoms up!" and tilted his cup to his lips. Everyone followed suit, and the fat officer stood on his feet waving his hand and began suddenly to sing, in Chinese this time, a tune which gradually and awfully became more and more familiar through its nasal intonation. The fat officer was singing "Onward Christian Soldiers," in Chinese. So were several of the others, all happily staring at the Americans to mark their response. Only Kwan was silent, stiff, unsinging.

Collins leaned over to Baldwin and said,

"I was talking to this fellow at my side. He says the fat one used to be an officer in the Northwest army of Feng Yuhsiang. That was the Christian general, remember, the one who used to baptize all his troops with a fire hose. He taught them all to sing "Onward Christian Soldiers" as their marching song. I'll bet that's where he learned it."

"Thank you, Captain," said Baldwin. "Now tell me, how the hell can we get this thing speeded up?"

"I thought you'd notice that 'Captain Collins' bit. I can correct their impression right now if you want me to and tell them that your principal aide in this high diplomatic encounter is only a sergeant. But that won't help any either. This is the colonel's big day; he's having a negotiation with the Americans, just the way the big brass does in Chungking, and it gives him 'face.' All his officers are happy, he's happy, he likes us and there are going to be speeches."

Baldwin groaned but he knew he was trapped.

"Who's the fat one," he asked.

"God knows," said Collins, "but I figure by the fountain pens and the wrist watches he's wearing that he's been moving some goods on the trade flow through the Jap line; whenever a unit stabilizes long enough in one area, its officers get into business. Or maybe he's just traveling through like everyone else and has friends here at this headquarters—in that case, the fountain pens and the wrist watches could be his life's savings, all he's got."

The party was now in full rowdy swing; the yellow wine was poured again and again; and Colonel Li was calling across the table to the fat officer once more. The fat officer lurched to his feet again and began to talk:

"America and China is friends," he began once more. "Why is America and China friends? America and China is friends because they are democracy. America is rich. China is poor. But China loves America not because she is rich. America loves China not because she is poor. China and America love each other because they are friends, because they is democracy. The Japanese bandits hates China. The Japanese bandits hates America. Together, China and America will destroy the Japanese bandit."

The fat officer stopped and went into Chinese, obviously translating what he had just said, in a full, firm bellow with much more conviction. Baldwin listened and watched the fat one. The smooth, round, unwrinkled sweat-glistening face of the Chinese beamed with goodwill; he meant what he was saying, and deep inside Baldwin there stirred the irrepressible answering of friendship with friendship. Colonel Li spoke quickly to the fat officer who resumed in English:

"What does China needs? China need airplanes to bomb Japan. . . ."

Here the fat one puffed out his cheeks and blew with a loud humming sound, his hands waving in the air like an airplane swooping, and went: "Boom! Boom! Boom!"

"China needs artillery."

More Boom! Boom! Boom!

"China needs guns." His mouth narrowed and his throat tightened as he coughed in the half-bark that children everywhere use to make the sound of a machine gun.

"Why does China wants airplanes? Why does China wants guns? Why does China wants artillery? To help American friends fight Japanese. If American friends give guns and airplanes, we will fight the Japanese for them. Chinese soldiers not fear dying. Chinese soldiers not fearing hungry. Generalissimo Chiang says, 'People have money, give money, people have strength, give strength.' America have guns, give guns. We are friends. We are friends."

The fat one suddenly switched to Chinese, an impassioned Chinese now, and Baldwin noticed that with the wine that was flowing the fat one's face was growing flushed and blood-swollen. Abruptly the fat one sat down, and the company at the table turned to gaze at Baldwin. A reply was expected.

"What do I say now?" asked Baldwin of Collins.

"This is standard," said Collins. "You say the same thing, tell 'em China and America are friends, what a fine regiment they have, what a fine staff this is, how America will quickly send what they want. You know, the same line any politician gives any meeting he visits."

Uncomfortably, Baldwin got to his feet. Even here on a hill in Kwangsi, with the world ending, he could not say that sort of thing.

"We are going to Kweiyang," he began matter-of-factly, breaking his phrases so the fat one could translate. "In Kweiyang we will see the Americans again. We will tell them that the 212th regiment is here in Kwangsi and that they are friends of Americans. We will tell them that the 212th regiment is very brave and does not run away. We will tell them that the 212th regiment wants guns and airplanes and tanks. In Burma the brave Chinese army with the Americans is advancing. Soon, the Burma Road will be open again and American guns and tanks will come for all the Chinese army to fight the Japanese. We will tell the American generals about the brave 212th regiment."

Baldwin sat down as quickly as he could.

"*Kan pei!*" shouted Colonel Li, and drained his glass. "*Kan pei,*" shouted all the others and followed suit. Again the waiters bustled about the table. A clear, cold almond soup began the second half of the dinner and the chill sweetness erased all the spices and sauces of the first half of the banquet. A dish of red peppers laced with sliced beef came next; a platter of hot wet steaming buns stuffed with brown sugar and nuts succeeded this; then came green peas inches wide; then bean sprouts. And long after Baldwin and Collins had ceased to eat, because they could no more, there came a platter of chicken livers in pepper crusts, a fish in sweet-and-sour sauce, and then a bowl of glistening cold tangerines.

"*Mei yu shen-mo tsai,*" the fat officer kept saying loudly, and Collins groaningly translated, "He says forgive them for the poor food, there's nothing to eat."

A final round of toasts, a burst of "Onward Christian Soldiers," a speech by Colonel Li, and Baldwin got to his feet.

"Tell them," said Baldwin, "that it's now two o'clock, that the rest of the team has been waiting for us down the hill for four hours and that now we must go no matter what. This time I mean it."

Baldwin's sharp rising from the table needed no interpretation. Two orderlies ran to him with a bowl of steaming towels and he bathed his face in the scalding, hot perfume of the towels.

Soldiers began to shout, Colonel Li began to snap orders, the officers at the table rose chattering, some noisily swishing bowls of mouth-water through their gums and spitting it on the floor, and in a babble of instantaneous commotion everyone moved to the gate.

At the gate, in the jeep, sat Kwan, already installed on his bedroll in the back seat. Beside him on another bedroll, sat a second figure swaddled in a shapeless blue cotton gown. As she turned, Baldwin saw it was the woman by the pool. But now he could see her closely. She was in her twenties perhaps, with a broad, round and handsome face, clear and fine of skin, her glossy black hair drawn back thickly to a bun above the nape of her olive neck. It was a good face, strong and calm; but now Baldwin was annoyed by her presence. She was in his jeep uninvited.

"Who is she?" asked Baldwin.

"This is Madame Hung," said Colonel Li. "Since you are going to Kweiyang, maybe you can take her too. Madame Hung is the wife of General Hung. General Hung was my friend. General Hung was killed this summer at Changsha. If you take Madame Hung to Kweiyang in your trucks, she has friends there who will take care of her."

Baldwin was speechless. McNeil had insisted that the one thing to watch out for was women; that Detached Demolition trucks had to be kept stripped of all Chinese, but especially women. The air-force trucks that had been coursing the highways of East China during the summer retreat had crawled with women—hitchhikers, mothers, students, wives of refugees, earning their soft way south and west to safety. McNeil had explained that Detached Demolition carried no one "not because of the V.D., and there's plenty of that, but because a lot of these air-force boys get fond of these Chinese women and it fouls up the job." McNeil would never have let anybody load a woman on his trucks on the way out like this. But Baldwin knew he was stuck. Colonel Li had given him an escort officer; they had eaten well together; they had sung "Onward Christian Soldiers" together; they had somehow been woven by the strands of Chinese courtesy into a brief friendship which now he could not repudiate.

"What do you want me to say?" asked Collins, offering no advice.

"There's nothing to say, we're stuck. Tell him how dangerous the journey may be for her."

The colonel replied that Madame Hung understood how dangerous the trip was, and that it was more dangerous for her to stay.

"Thank him for his kindness and let's get out of here," said Baldwin.

He climbed in behind the wheel, wanting to drive himself, Collins beside him. He turned around and shook hands with Colonel Kwan, nodded to the woman who nodded back. He pressed on the starter and the motor responded; he felt better. It was an American motor, an American jeep, he could control it, it would move when he thrust in the clutch, it would turn when he turned the wheel. After the agonizing delay and the insubstantial, still incomprehensible net of courtesies and resistances that had wasted the morning, he felt good just pressing on the gas treadle, and feeling the engine answer as it should.

"Good-bye," he shouted to Colonel Li, "and thanks."

"Good-bye," said the fat colonel in English. "Good-bye, glorious Americans, China and America is friends."

"*I lu ping an!*" said Colonel Li in Chinese and Baldwin recognized that one. He had heard it often. It meant "To the End of the Road, Peace and Safety." He hoped so.

They spun quickly out of the courtyard, down the cart path, onto the main highway, and headed down the slope.

"Tell her," said Baldwin to Collins as they drove, "that

this is going to be a pretty rugged trip and that we're all soldiers. Tell her we sleep out in the open. We have to get rid of her. Ask her if she'd like it if we put her on a Chinese bus. If we can find one moving up the line, we can trade some of our gasoline for a passenger ticket."

Collins turned to the back seat to repeat it all in Chinese. But Madame Hung leaned forward.

"Thank you," she said in perfect English, "thank you. Please don't worry about me. I know you don't want me with you but I'll try not to be a bother."

He was glad he was driving. She could not see the astonishment or embarrassment in his face. He was carrying a woman who spoke English, perfect English.

"I didn't mean to be rude," said Baldwin talking over his shoulder, trying to apologize, "but this is a difficult trip we're making and we aren't supposed to be carrying women."

She was quiet.

Unable to think of anything else, he said:

"I'm sorry about your husband, it's been a bad summer."

"Yes," she said, and offered nothing more.

So he had hurt her feelings. But it was just as well. He would not try to make friends. They ought to get rid of her. As quickly as possible. There was so much to do. And a woman would be in the way. And the men would not understand. He would not bother to explain her to the men before he put her on the bus. Let Collins explain to the men, he could do it better than anyone else.

He saw the team now, as the jeep came down out of the twist at the foot of the hill and approached the bridge through the incessant throng.

He pulled the jeep up before the trucks and Michaelson walked over to them, staring curiously at the Chinese colonel and the woman, but addressing himself to Baldwin.

"We thought they picked you off," said Michaelson. "We were arguing about whether to go up after you or just take off. Getting late."

"We had trouble at headquarters, clearing the bridge for the blow. But it's untangled now. Let's move on this bridge right away and then get out. You've fed, haven't you?"

"Yup. K-rations."

"Fine. Have you figured out what the bridge will take?"

"I figured we want to take out the main span and the piers. Three pressure charges across the center roadbed, maybe twenty pounds apiece, and we drop her in a V-cut. Then I suppose we ought to do the piers, too. Do a wrap-around on them—twenty pounds on each face, ten on the sides."

"Good," said Baldwin. This team could almost operate itself. But it was he who had had to arrange the deal. Aloud, he said, "That's the way I see it. And put it on time fuse, not primacord. I want to save the primacord."

Colonel Kwan had not spoken to Baldwin since he had placed his finger on Tushan and the ammo dumps on the map in the morning. But he needed no instructions. As the Americans divided in pairs to crawl under the bridge and prepare its soft sandstone pillars for the charge, Colonel Kwan spoke to the sentries on the near end of the bridge and they crossed to join the two sentries on the far side.

When they were halfway through the work, Baldwin took Collins with him to speak to the Colonel, who was silent and stiff as he watched the Americans at their work.

"We'll be ready to blow in half an hour," said Baldwin to Kwan. "Will you have the sentries stop the passengers and hold up the flow a couple of hundred yards from the other side before we set it off?"

Kwan nodded and went off to post himself on the other side. Now and then a Chinese truck would roll along; people continuously walked by, trudging unhappily on their way, but the Americans had been numbed by the procession now and no longer noticed. Baldwin took off his shirt in the warm afternoon sun and went out to join the men; his stomach was heavy with the meal and he wanted to work his body. The orange-colored fuse cord, unwinding through his fingers, felt greasy but substantial; it was a good feel after the subtleties of the morning.

They were through with the wiring by three-thirty and ready to blow. Baldwin checked the connections himself, walked back to the trucks, looked around, consulted with Colonel Kwan. Kwan pointed with his finger to the far side of the bridge and there, very high, on the road that wound its way down the valley, was a bus. It was coming down slowly on brakes, coasting. They waited as this last bus out of the lowlands slowly grew larger, slowly came nearer. We can blow the bridge now, thought Baldwin to himself, with Kwan's authority and mine, and the bus will be stuck there on the other side for years, or until the war is over, or until the Japanese take it. But we'll give the bus ten minutes more to come down, and cross over, and they'll barrel on and maybe be in Kweiyang tomorrow or the next day and never know we let them through.

The bus chuffed down to the bridge, the driver pounding the outside of the tin door to warn of his coming. With a swish of the stinking vegetable oil its diesel engine was burning, the driver snapped the engine on as it passed them, and then began the crawl up the ridge that lay ahead of them.

"O.K. now," said Baldwin to Kwan, and Kwan shouted to the sentries on the far side. The four sentries spread themselves across the road and began to walk slowly away from the bridge, herding the uneven procession of stragglers backward before them. Up the hill on the other side of the bridge, as far as Baldwin's eye could see, they stretched in ones, in twos, in groups, in clots, all winding down toward the valley and the bridge he was about to cut. They would see the bridge go up from where they walked, an eruption of smoke and dust. Would they understand? Did they know why he was doing it? Did they know that Americans were doing it? If they knew Americans were doing it, would it make any difference after the burnings, and bombings, and flights of the months and years past? Baldwin looked down at the river bed in the ravine. It was ankle-deep, the water clear-green with its fall purity. No wheeled vehicle would cross this unless the Japs could bring up something like a Bailey bridge. But none of the stragglers would have any trouble wading it on foot—unless they were sick or old. But he could not think about that.

He found Michaelson beside him.

"Ready?" he asked.

"All set," said Michaelson.

"O.K., let it go," said Baldwin.

Michaelson knelt to the pale-orange length of safety fuse, snipped it and frayed the end, then rose to give the call. Then he knelt again and touched his cigarette lighter to the fuse. The end of the fuse sputtered and spat sparks, began to writhe and smoke; then it wriggled with great deliberation down its length to the bridge in a convulsion of twisting and spitting and the charges, with an echoing, banging slam, went off. The log beams of the bridge cracked from their supports, plunging down into the water, the planking falling after them with a clatter. At the same moment, the stone piers heaved and shuddered, then crumbled like a child's building blocks being swept away by a casual flick of the hand.

If Li holds the position this will stop the advance Jap element for a day, two days, Baldwin told himself. If Li abandons the position, then how long will it take for the Jap to bridge it again? Longer than it took us to blow? he asked himself. But how did one count time—it had taken little more than an hour to destroy the bridge. But it had taken most of the day to arrange for the blowing. It was not the substance of things, he realized again, that ate up time and nerves; it was the arranging of them, the deal.

Imperceptibly, the day had slipped from his control. They had come only twenty miles. They had ripped out one little bridge. It was already late afternoon and growing sharply chilly. The hours had been lost up there on the hill with Colonel Li, in China. He had eaten too much, drunk too much, and he was stuck with a woman whom now he had to get rid of.

"Let's load and get out," he shouted at the men in a large voice. They were loaded already, he noticed, as he shouted. They, too, knew the day was lost. Sullenly, in a knot, neither talking nor chattering, they waited for him by the jeep. They climbed into their cabs as Baldwin dismissed them and when the jeep started, the convoy rolled.

As they ground up the hill again, they were catching the night wind from the highlands; the sun was sinking, the sky had lost its glow, the dust whipped the road and it was cold. The traffic on the road, the endless chain of people, was thinning now, for the cold was thinning it, and Collins, at the wheel, held the gears back, trying not to separate the jeep from the four trucks behind as the gaps opened before him.

Halfway up the hill, Collins cursed:

"Damn it," he said, "there's a block."

Baldwin had noticed it, too. The big bus, the last to cross the bridge, was just ahead of them, planted squarely in the middle of the road, leaving barely enough room for the single jeep to sidle by. There would be no room for the big trucks behind. Collins' foot came down squarely on the brake pedal, the jeep stopped, Collins turned off the ignition. Behind them, the other four trucks ground to a halt, too.

Baldwin and Collins got out without saying anything to each other. Kwan unbent and stepped out with them. Kwan had had no conversation with anyone except for the interchange at the bridge, but Baldwin noticed that he did not have to be asked. He came on his own, the same speechless disgust that moved Baldwin showing on Kwan's face, too.

The three strolled forward to see what was happening. In front of the bus, to the side of the road, lay a mule, its load of long timbers still lashed to its back, bleeding and hoarsely roaring and screeching. Baldwin had never heard a mule make a sound before, and the agonizing, whistling braying from the beast was almost human in its pitch. One of the bus's headlights was shattered, and Baldwin could almost guess what had happened. The bus with its horn blaring had startled the mule carrying the timbers; the mule had probably swung wildly in surprise or fright, and, as it swung, the protruding end of the timbers must have hit the headlight, breaking the glass, and knocking the mule over to the side of the road where it lay bleeding. Chinese animals down from the hill farms still panicked and pranced at the sound of engines or horns.

What Baldwin could not understand was what was now happening. A man in dirty, peasant blue was kneeling on the ground, sobbing and wailing. His body rose and fell as he swayed back and forth, knocking his head to the road in the jackknifing, bobbing motion of the *k'o-t'ou*. And every time he bent his head to the ground, he was kicked. The uniformed bus driver and another uniformed man were yelling at him; and each time the man brought his head to earth, they kicked it with their boots in the nose, the mouth, the eyes, and it was beginning to bleed, and under the blood it was probably pulp. A boy of fourteen or fifteen was kneeling on the ground beside the blue-gowned peasant, crying, howling, pleading in total terror.

"What's happening?" Baldwin asked Collins.

"I don't know," said Collins, but Kwan had taken over.

He had marched over to the two uniformed men and begun to yell at them. They turned to Kwan, and, their faces still hardened in rage, stopped kicking and began to expostulate. The peasant and his son turned to Kwan also, their fingers cupped beneath their chins for mercy and began to cry to him. The uniformed man pointed to the broken headlights and the shattered glass, pointed to the mule by the side of the road, pointed to the crying couple. Kwan's voice modulated from the bellow to an icy cold, a clipped, harsh interrogatory.

"Kwan's stopping it," said Collins. "They say this mule broke the headlight. They say they're sorry. I can't catch all that Kwan is saying. He's telling the peasants they're wrong. He's telling them they're interfering with the national defense, now he's telling the driver that the army shouldn't beat up on the people."

Gradually, the talk began to simmer down. The driver and his helper climbed back into their bus which, Baldwin could now see, by its numbered markings, was an army bus, loaded with women and children. They must be headquarters' families from somewhere, being sent ahead to safety. The peasant and his son went over to the mule, trying to tug it to its feet, now coaxing, now scolding it.

Collins walked over to see the animal. He came back quickly.

"Scratch one mule. They'll never get that one on its feet again."

"What did they say?" asked Baldwin.

"I can't follow any of these local dialects. I suppose that wipes them out. The family's capital was probably in that mule."

The bus had ground under way again, and Kwan, Baldwin and Collins walked back to their jeep.

When the convoy rolled forward again it was dark. Again and again, Baldwin had noticed this happen when he traveled. As the day deepened on the road, as the sun slanted, as the hours wore long and the light faded, there came a moment of pause, a break. On one side of the break was daylight and you could reach back to morning. Then, sharply, after the break, it was dark, it was evening, it was time to stop, to rest, to eat. He wondered how a drink would taste.

They had come to the crest of the hill and the black night lay before them. Their headlights picked up few wanderers now, but they traveled slowly. It was cold, too cold to sleep in the open unless they had to, and Baldwin asked Collins to ask Kwan if he knew the country.

"The road is level now for about twenty *li*," reported Collins. "That's about six miles. We pass through Ishan and then come the mountains. But before we come to the mountains there's a place called Hwaiyuanchen, a big village. He says we should stay there tonight and not cross the next range in the darkness."

They pushed through Ishan in the early evening and another half hour brought them to the village. The crowded streets, clogged with trucks, buses, an old sedan, animals, people, bustled and surged as forms detached themselves, crossing and recrossing, momentarily visible and vanishing, in the twinkling bonfires that the refugees had built on the cobbled main street for warmth. In the hard light of the jeep's headlights, people's faces turned up to stare, pale, blank, curious. Some darted out of the way as if jabbed by the surprise and pain of the light; others dragged themselves heavily to the side as if nothing could make them move faster. It was as if the jeep's lights had pried up a huge boulder of dark under which a squirming tangle of flesh writhed; or as if, in a dark hall, a light had been flashed to reveal it full and pulsing with a thousand intimacies. The convoy slowed, and behind the jeep, Baldwin could hear the trucks blasting with their horns; the men were tired, too.

Kwan finally spoke. "In a few minutes, at the other side of the village. Colonel Li's regiment has a transport post. We can stay there."

And in a few more minutes he said, "Here we are."

It was easy now. With Kwan to smooth the way for him, Baldwin could handle things. His spirits began to rise again. A large room, on one side of what appeared in the dark to be the courtyard of an inn, was cleared away for the Americans. Chinese soldiers brought two large iron charcoal braziers, and as the charcoal began to glow, the room warmed. Two oil lamps were brought, and as the yellow flames fluttered they began to see each other again. Miller had brought in a gallon can of the pork-and-gravy and a carton of the five-in-one ration. Kwan spread his Chinese quilt-roll in a corner, excused himself from the Americans and said he would go to speak to the commander of the transport post. No, he was not hungry, he said, and left.

Slowly, as the food began to cook, Baldwin realized he would have to talk to the woman. If he were going to get rid of her, it was best to be firm about it, and now. She had already spread her quilt in one of the corners of the room away from the men and was sitting, watching them, self-contained. Baldwin was aware of her dignity as he went over to join her.

"You'll eat with us, I hope," he said. "We have plenty,"

as if he were asking an uninvited guest to stay for dinner.

"Thank you," she said. Her voice was proud, yet resigned, and again he was impressed by the perfect American-tonality of the voice coming out of the shapeless swaddle of the padded gown. It might almost be from New England, he told himself.

"You can use my mess kit," he said, and then, "You do eat American food, don't you?" Some Chinese, he knew, did not.

"Yes," she said simply. "At home in Shanghai, we used to eat American all the time. But I have my own bowl, thank you, I don't want to bother you."

She rummaged in her bedroll and came up with an enameled Chinese rice bowl and some chopsticks. Baldwin was still trying to place her voice. There was something of Helen in it, not just the home sound, but the way she made him feel uncomfortable. He unslung his mess kit and together they walked over to the cooking. Miller ladled out two big helpings into Baldwin's mess kit and Baldwin reached down, took some of the hard crackers and added them to the stew to sop up the gravy. He stooped again, took another handful of crackers, offered them to her, and when she nodded, he put them on her rice bowl, brimming with Miller's helping of stew. He was conscious it was slum, and aware that she made him feel that way.

"Want to join us here?" Baldwin asked.

"I'm all right," she said and walked back to her corner. Baldwin hesitated, then followed her. It was best to get it over with right away and he squatted beside her, munching away. He waited for her to say something, to give him an opening, and when she did not, he said, hoping he sounded polite:

"Wouldn't you be more comfortable if we put you on a Chinese bus?"

"If you want to put me on a bus, do it," she replied, with no give in her voice at all.

He began again:

"Well, I didn't mean to sound harsh. But we have three or four days of work, perhaps, to do on this road before we get to Kweiyang. There's no telling what will happen. If we could get you on a passenger bus, you'd go right on through."

"Have you ever been on a Chinese bus?" she countered.

"No," he said.

"Have you been in this campaign long?"

"No," he said. "They flew me in last week. Special job."

"You need protection at one end or the other," she said. "After Changsha fell, my husband's officers put me on a bus down to Hengyang. We went only ten miles before the driver stopped the bus and asked everyone for more money, for himself. I paid him. But he threw a woman and child who had no money off and made them walk."

"I thought there were trains for officers' families," said Baldwin, puzzled.

"I didn't know anybody in Hengyang, so I bought a ticket on a refugee train down to Liuchow."

She made no further reference to her husband and Baldwin did not want to press it.

"Have you ever seen a refugee train?" she asked.

"No," he said.

"They built platforms in the refugee trains so that people could lie down in three tiers. There were three tiers of people in every wagon, and people dying, and a woman had a baby in the tier just above me. It was better than being on the roof though. There were people on all the roofs, holding on with their fingers, and our train went through a tunnel just before it came into Kweilin and you could hear the people on the roof being scraped off in the tunnel because it was so low, and they were screaming and shouting, and I never knew it was like that. I'd always been with my husband on a retreat. When we came out of the tunnel, the engineer stopped the train, and we all went out to get some air. There was an old man still lying on the top of one of the cars, bleeding. I saw a student, a handsome-looking boy, lift the man's head up by the hair and look at his face. Then he pushed the old man off the roof and lay down in his place."

"What happened to the old man?" asked Baldwin.

"I suppose he was dead," she said, and went on, "I sold my watch in Liuchow to get food and then I located Colonel Li. Li was a student of my husband's at the military academy when the Central government was trying to train Kwangsi officers. I've been with his regiment ever since, at his headquarters. If Li's regiment had a bus, he might have put me on it. But it didn't. He told me I'd be safer with you."

Baldwin, never adept at the game of parlor psychology, knew that fundamentally she was begging. He wondered if she realized it, too. Her voice did not show it. She was not pleading. It would be difficult to put her out on the road after hearing her story. But he did not want to yield at once, either.

"It's a rough country, isn't it?" he said.

"You don't like it, do you?" she countered.

"Why no," said Baldwin. "Why no, as a matter of fact I like China," he added, wondering whether he was denying what might well be true. In spite of himself, her story had shaken him, and he thought of the bloody peasant they had just rescued from the army bus.

"Except . . . I'll never really understand the brutality—that peasant with his mule being beaten up like that."

"The bus driver was furious," she said. "Kwan told me about it. The driver will have to pay for a new headlight out of his wages; it may cost him a year of his pay. You see, nobody trusts drivers. They steal all the time—gasoline, tires, anything. If they're short when they report, they have to pay up or be flogged. That's why he was beating the peasant. Was he badly hurt?"

She might have been explaining a lesson to a child, her voice cool and distant. Without thinking, Baldwin replied:

"You can't tell with a Chinese," he said.

Her voice had made him forget that she too was Chinese, but now abruptly, she turned.

"Oh, what makes you say that?" she said, her voice rising for the first time. "Because he's Chinese? Because he was knocking his head on the ground? Because he's a native?"

"I didn't mean it that way," said Baldwin trying to draw back from this woman who was suddenly all thorn and prickle.

"I know what you mean," she said.

"I'm sorry," he said, trying to cut it off, remembering her husband had been killed for China and women were emotional. "I only meant that I couldn't speak Chinese."

He wanted to get away from her now, but he did not mean to leave her thinking of him like that. Doggedly, he groped his way back to the original purpose of the conversation.

"Somehow," he said awkwardly, trying to show sympathy, "it seems you shouldn't have to hitch-hike like this. I suppose it's just that the retreat disorganized everything. But a general's wife . . . I mean. . . ." he knew it sounded pompous, but went on, "I mean provision should be made to take care of a general's wife . . ."

"T'ung-ling was shot," she said.

"I know, I'm sorry," said Baldwin softly.

"He was executed," she added, tonelessly, explaining.

"What?" he said, not believing he had heard.

"We lost Changsha. And the senior officers were executed," she said, dropping her voice, closing the subject.

He could say nothing now that made sense as his mind tried to put the fragments together. Her husband had been executed by the government. Li had foisted her on him. He wanted to be rid of her, and who was she? He looked around the room, and saw that Kwan had returned and wondered if he could trust Kwan or anyone. But even Kwan would serve as an excuse for leaving her. He rose from the bedroll, abruptly, knowing his shock must show to her, and said, "I have to speak to Kwan, he may have some news."

Still dazed, he beckoned Collins, and approached Kwan. The officer's face was cold, stiff, ungiving.

"There is no more telephone to the 212th regiment," said Kwan, when Collins asked for information.

"What happened to it?" asked Baldwin.

"Colonel Li has gone to the hills," replied Kwan.

"But . . ." stammered Baldwin, "I thought he was going to hold. He was dug in."

Kwan stared at him.

"Colonel Li is very brave. He was wounded twice by the Japanese when the Kwangsi brigades fought in Shanghai. They fought well. But they are not Central troops. Central troops stay to the end. For Colonel Li it is better to live with his troops in the hills for this winter. He is from Kwangsi."

From Kwan's calm voice, Baldwin gathered that he must have known of Li's plan even before they had left the regimental command this afternoon. It had all been an act—the banquet, the speeches, the mock heroics.

Kwan continued, "And the Japanese are in Liuchow. They entered this afternoon. They are following. That is why Colonel Li left."

So the Japs were on their heels again. And he had all but wasted the day, taking out a bridge which Japanese cavalry could probably ford now that Li had left, and eating a banquet that he did not want, and acquiring a woman who might get them in trouble. There should be something to show after a day like this. And there was nothing. Somehow he had failed.

"How far is it to Tushan?" he asked of Kwan, and Collins relayed from Kwan not an answer but a question.

"How fast will you go to Tushan?"

"We have to cut this road tomorrow, either near here or near Hochih," he replied.

"It is one hundred twenty-five miles from Tushan," said Collins, translating the Chinese figures. "It is one day if we drive all day he says, but several days if we must stop and work. He says it is better to stop near Hochih to destroy the road, than to stop in the morning near here. Japanese patrols may be coming. And they will want to go to Tushan, fast, too, for the ammunition."

Baldwin reflected that he would have to decide it all by himself. He could not trust anybody now. His command, his decision, and he had made no gain today.

Without replying to Kwan he closed the conversation.

"We'd better all turn in," he said. "We've got a full day's work tomorrow."

He would make tomorrow count, no matter what.

The men were already sleeping, curled in their bedrolls about the charcoal warming pans on the floor. Dangerous, that charcoal, Baldwin thought, throws off carbon monoxide. He scanned the ill-fitting doors, sensed the draft of cold air leaking through the cracks in the badly jointed walls. There would be enough fresh air, no danger. He looked around the room once more and saw she was still sitting on her bedroll, looking at him. In the charcoal's glow, he saw her hair glistening, and the light reflecting off her high, smooth cheekbones, making pale her throat and her eyes dark. When she saw him return the gaze, her head drooped; she had shut him out. He knew he resented her; she made him feel awkward; she was an unknown quantity. But he could not see how he could put her out now to walk on the road.

THURSDAY

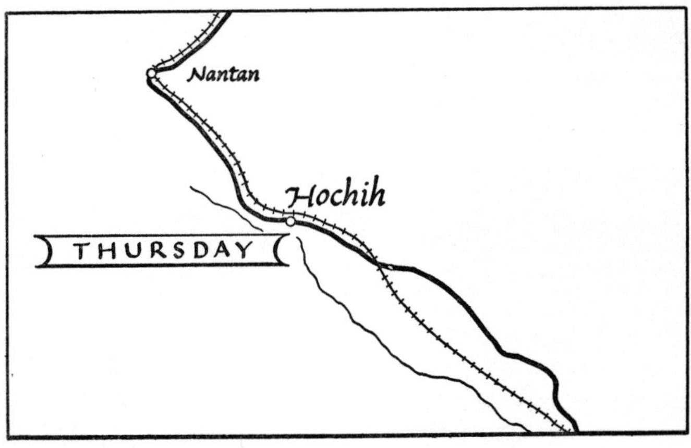

CHAPTER 4

The Cotton Truck

IT WAS WINTER when they woke next morning in the heights.

The sun had vanished as if it had never shone. The clouds weighed thick and gray above, while underneath, a dull cold wrapped and hugged them tight, seeping in under the woolens, slowing their bodies, stiffening but not quite numbing their fingers.

From the moment Michaelson climbed into his truck, he knew it was going to be a bad day. Prince had told him Lewis was sick, and Michaelson had said, Let me warm up my job first and I'll look at him. But he could not warm up the sullen six-by-six. The truck's engine turned slowly through its piston chambers, sucking helplessly on the tired battery; yet the motor would not catch. Cold, thought Michaelson, and it's going to get colder and they're sticky with summer oil. He climbed down in anger from the cab and yelled Miller over.

Then he lifted the hood and jiggled the fuel pump delicately; when he judged the chambers were filled with just enough vapor, he told Miller to crank it up and got back into the cab. Miller turned the engine stiffly through a few turns and, on the second try, the engine took and barked alive. Michaelson babied it for a few minutes with the gas treadle, then gradually fed it more gasoline until it was roaring in full-hearted vigor. Then he cut it back, letting it idle, and turned to see how the other trucks were doing.

They were all having trouble, but two would not start at all.

Then Baldwin was approaching him.

"Trouble?" asked Baldwin.

"Yup, trouble," said Michaelson. "Lewis is sick and two of the six-by-sixes won't start."

"What's the matter with Lewis?"

"I don't know. He's got a fever. They're all tired out. Maybe he's just worn down."

"Serious?"

"I haven't looked at him yet. Maybe it's that malaria of his come back. But you can't tell with Lewis."

They both stood there, two men pondering a problem. Lewis was strictly sad sack. If they had to hike, it was Lewis' sock that rubbed, and Lewis' heel that blistered. If the mosquitoes bit at night, they bit through Lewis' net which was torn. Lewis had had malaria all the way down the retreat from Hengyang in July to Kweilin in October, and had stuffed so much atabrine into himself that his face had stained to saffron yellow. He had also, naturally, poisoned himself with atabrine overdose. Something in Chinese food made Lewis' face and lips puff, so Lewis ate only from GI cans. A full-blown hypochondriac, Lewis would long since have been shipped back to base at Kunming, except for the fact that he did not want to go. Lewis liked being with Detached Demolition which was home to him in the confusing army; and, Detached Demolition needed him because he was a licensed electrician who had learned his trade in Cleveland and the cunning of his fingers with wires and circuits made him indispensable to the team. They did not need him now for what remained to be done, and it would have been smarter to have sent him out by plane from Liuchow. But it was too late now; they would have Lewis sick on their hands for the rest of the trip.

"Well, I'll go look at him," said Baldwin. "What about those two trucks?"

"Just the frigging cold. You know something—we should have figured on it. The batteries are all fried out from summer, we bring them up here in the cold and they have no juice. Prince's job turns a little bit, if we push her she'll start. Lewis' job is cold as stone, all frozen up; we'd have to thaw her out first and then push her, and then maybe she'll crap out on us for good when we get to the first upgrade."

"How long to get them turning?"

Michaelson reflected. Fifteen minutes anywhere back home to get a truck started. But here? In China?

"An hour, maybe more. Depends on the luck."

"An hour," said Baldwin frowning. He did not like it. There was no telling how quickly the Japanese were following up out of Liuchow. And yesterday had been fouled up. Today he *had* to get enough distance between them to turn and *do* something to the road. But he could not abandon a truck just because it was cold. "All right," he finally said. "We'll give it the hour. You work on Lewis' truck, and I'll have Prince's truck pushed on the road so we can start it. I'll get some Chinese soldiers to help you. I'll look after Lewis myself."

There was no trouble with Prince's truck. Kwan assembled enough soldiers of the transport post to hand-push it into the street, and a shove from another six-by-six spun its engine handily into action. But Lewis' truck was stone-cold, cumbersome and helpless on the flagstoned paving of the Chinese courtyard. Irritably, Michaelson settled into the job of starting it. Over the hood of the cold engine, the men draped a tarpaulin; under the tarpaulin the Chinese soldiers of the transport post thrust charcoal braziers so that the heat, rising, could thaw the cold-congealed cylinders. Michaelson noticed, with a grunt of satisfaction, that Ballo had brought a handful of used spark plugs from his own cab and was now filing the points. It would take fifteen or twenty minutes to warm the engine enough to give it a chance; and with fresh plugs, perhaps it would go. But meanwhile . . .

Meanwhile, the soldiers of the transport post had gathered in a knot about the Americans working on the truck, gawking and staring at the new entertainment. Through the gates of the open courtyard, Michaelson could see little boys, young men, curious strangers all crowded about for a look at the strange tinkering of the Americans. The children laughed and jeered at them and Michaelson's temper began to simmer as they laughed. He had once asked Collins what Chinese kids yelled at the Americans, and Collins had said Chinese kids thought Americans were funny and called them "Big Nose," or "Hairy Legs," or simply "Foreign Devil." He hated the way anywhere they had stopped on the road this summer, a crowd had instantly bubbled up about them to pry, to comment, to laugh, to watch. He did not want them close to him, nor anywhere around. This morning their faces rubbed his nerves raw. This truck had to start, to show them it was American. He did not like the woman at the courtyard door holding the cackling chicken by its bound legs, head-down; nor the Chinese soldiers good-naturedly commenting on their work; nor the edging and shoving about the gate.

Nor did Michaelson like the way Ballo was clowning it. Ballo had begun to file the plug points, and was brandishing the plugs high in the sky to examine them, stroking them with his file in an arm-sweeping flourish, gagging it for the mystified Chinese audience. Ballo fingered one of the plugs, muttered, "No damn good," then flung it aside. Three Chinese soldiers, laughing, scrambled after it on the ground. "Fat lot of good'll that do them," said Ballo, but Michaelson lost his temper.

"Ballo, goddam it, I keep telling you guys, don't fool around with them!"

"What's the matter?" asked Ballo, astonished.

"I just don't want them close to us, I keep telling you. These people are dangerous."

Ballo shrugged and went back to work on the plugs.

Prince spoke.

"What's the matter, Mike, you nervous?"

"I'm nervous—so what? Those Japs are on the road already, and we're stuck here in this Chinese crowd, and we've got to get this job rolling, or we're going to be trapped."

"That frigging Lewis," replied Prince languidly, "wouldn't you know it'd be his truck that conks out. Give you three to two odds that Lewis is goofing off on us, soon as we get back to Kunming he's all right again?"

Michaelson was silent.

"No bet?" said Prince. "Make you another—this joker Baldwin's gonna get us all in trouble. Bet you two-to-one before we see Kweiyang, we'll have a real run-in with these slopey bastards. We ought to ditch this truck, and barrel on right out, now."

"This truck'll go," growled Michaelson. "Quit yakking."

He judged now that the weak charcoal warming pans might have begun to take effect and ordered the tarpaulin off. He backed his own truck around into the courtyard gate again, opened its hood and began to connect some wires from his own battery to the dead battery on Lewis' truck. A Chinese soldier reached to touch one of the clamp-on terminals. Michaelson yelled at him, "Get the hell out of there," and the Chinese jumped back. The other Chinese laughed uproariously, and the soldier he had yelled at scowled. "Goddam bunch of monkeys," growled Michaelson, "they'll eat anything, touch anything, screw anything, steal anything you let them get their hands on."

Quickly and efficiently, Michaelson now clamped the wires from his own engine to the dead battery of the Lewis truck and snapped on the ignition. Lewis' truck roared alive and Michaelson felt good; he had shown them. The Chinese cheered, clapping their hands as at the climax of a play, and Michaelson found himself smiling at them, then closed it off. The Chinese kept laughing, and the soldiers who now pulled the charcoal fires back from under Lewis' truck, looked very proud, almost strutting. They lifted their thumbs in the *Ting Hao* gesture, and Michaelson realized that they must feel they had helped. Partners. He looked at his watch. It had taken only twenty-five minutes; he felt better. Awkwardly, the big six-by-six nosed its way out of the compound and fell into line. Michaelson hopped out of the car and went forward to see Baldwin.

"All set," he said.

"Fine," said Baldwin, "nice work. I was just wondering whether to leave it."

"Lewis okay?" asked Michaelson.

"No, he's sick," said Baldwin. "I've fixed him up on some bedrolls, and he's lying down in back of Ballo's truck. We'll let him ride that way today and keep him warm back there under the blankets. We'll take another reading on him tonight; I doctored him with aspirin and atabrine. Look, Mike, I'm changing convoy order today. Niergaard takes the wheel on Lewis' truck. You and Miller bring up the rear in your truck." Michaelson did not like riding tail on the convoy. But he walked back to his truck, joined Miller and waited for the signal. Baldwin stood up in the jeep, lifted his arm for the signal, sat down and the jeep rolled. They were off finally, late as usual.

"Is Lewis really sick?" asked Miller of Michaelson as they jounced along in the cab.

"I guess so," said Michaelson. "If I thought he was goofing, I'd kick his pants off myself."

"Yeah, kick his pants off," said Miller, the echo.

"But he isn't, he's just a sad sack."

"Yeah, sad sack."

"There's one in every outfit," continued Michaelson beginning to unwind, now they were off. "You take the foundry I used to work in on the South Side. We had this hillbilly come to work there once—you know we're getting a lot of these hillbillies in Chicago, now; they come up from the South for the heavy jobs, the way the Negroes do. Well, this fellow cuts his arm the first day, a big gash all the way up the elbow. I was shop steward then so I had to take it up through the grievance machinery. Then one day he spoiled a plate-mold, next time he spilled a pot of hot iron; finally one day he spilled a pot of the melt and it damn near killed a man—caught him in the heel, just burned the whole shoe and the inside of it right off—hell of a thing to look at. Stank like a piece of burned meat. When they fired him, we didn't say a thing. A foundry's too dangerous a place to have a sad sack. Accident-prone is what they call those guys. Union never defends an accident-prone man."

"Yeah, a guy ought to be able to take care of himself."

"Only you can't fire a guy in the army. You're stuck with him. They should have screened Lewis out before they sent him overseas, kept him at some base back home. He's a hell of a good electrician but he's not worth a damn outdoors. And I think this time he's really got it."

"What do you think he's got, Mike?"

"It's either that malaria of his come back again, or something he ate. Or maybe he's just had it. When it gets cold overnight this way, with us coming up into the hills, you're ready to catch anything, and if anybody in this outfit catches anything, it always has to be Lewis."

"You're right about that weather, back home in Bridgeport we got this funny weather. Bridgeport's real nice, but in the fall sometimes it'll be hot as a furnace one week and the next . . ."

Michaelson rode directly over Miller's talk as if Miller had been mumbling to himself. He always did. Miller wasn't important.

"What we ought to do is get Lewis back fast and turn him over to the hospital in Kunming. We all ought to get back fast."

"You tell that to Baldwin this morning, Mike?"

"He knows."

"What did he say?"

"He didn't say anything. Went around to look at Lewis, said he was sick, said we'd wait until tonight and see how Lewis is and how far we get. Maybe he just got a chill. Hell, Baldwin's no doctor either. I figure Baldwin'll have to do something if he ain't better tomorrow."

"You going to talk to him about it again, tonight?"

"Listen, for Christ's sake, Miller, turn it off. Baldwin's running this outfit, not me. I'm just a god-damned sergeant, not a wet-nurse."

"Yeah, sure, you're not a wet-nurse, I just asked."

"O.K.," said Michaelson, turning off the conversation as if he were snapping a switch.

Michaelson was irritated again. He realized he was losing his temper too easily. But he couldn't help it, he thought. I've got a right to be tired, too. And they're all slobs. Big fat Miller's a slob, Prince is a slob, Niergaard's a slob. Only Baldwin's not a slob, and Collins isn't either. I suppose they think *I'm* a slob, he said to himself. You're either a man or a slob.

All the bitterness came welling up in him, choking. I'm not a goddam wet-nurse, he told himself, let Baldwin handle it. Let him handle the whole thing. I'll make it out safe to Kweiyang. But there'll be trouble. And that Lewis, what am I supposed to do about him? Miller thinks I should talk to Baldwin tonight, but this is the Army, and I'm not a shop steward in the union. I've had that union crap, I've had that up to here.

Michaelson shifted on the seat, reached in his pants pocket, felt for the pack, thumbnailed a cigarette out, put it to his lips, waited for Miller to give him the light, puffed, blew out again.

Why should I? he reasoned. I'm through sticking my neck out; that's the only thing I learned from the union, and the anger took him again.

For he had believed in unions once, when they shoved the union down the throat of Big Steel. He remembered the fights, the time he let the cop have it with a baseball bat, and the guys getting shot down at the Carnegie Works, and ten hours a day for twenty-five bucks a week, and then they had the union. Stick together, "Solidarity Forever." "Nobody's going to take care of us unless we all take care of each other." "One man alone doesn't count." Stick together. And they made it.

And then, after it's all over, after the picket lines, after the fights, after being hungry, after sticking your neck out, then you're a shop steward. But somebody else who's never seen a melt, or smelled the sulfur, or never tapped a furnace, sometimes somebody who's never been in a mill at all, those guys all of them sitting behind the union desks. Lawyers writing contracts. Guys with white collars running the show, big shots from Washington staying at the Palmer House, the Blackstone, the Congress when they come to Chicago. Economists and college boys interviewing you as if they were doctors, taking twice your pay out of the union payroll, looking at you as if you're a slob. And you're a shop steward with all the other slobs nagging you, whether they got an ingrown toenail or tuberculosis you're supposed to do something about it: "Can you fix vacation for me in October because the ducks start coming over my old man's farm about then and I want to get in a little shooting?" "Can you fix it to switch me to the nightshift for just a couple of weeks, I think my wife's cheating and I want to give her a little rope and come home some night and catch her?" "The foreman yelled at me, can you do something about it?" "Say, Mike, I figure I got a right to work on the new four-stand roll they're putting in, I been here ten years and I got seniority." . . . All the slobs wanting you to take care of them. Because they bought protection with their two bucks a month union dues, and you're the guy who has to pay off. You got to have unions all right, but it's they who've got to have them, only the slobs.

So you go to night school at the plant and they train you for a foreman. You learn about high-carbon, low-carbon, about job-ratings and work loads, and then you're a foreman, you're no longer a union man. But where does it get you—fifteen bucks a week more. The union's got it fixed now so there's no percentage being a foreman. You're still a slob. You come in once a week to the plant superintendent's office in the yard, you listen to the engineer explain the new process, the super spells it out to you as if you were too dumb to understand English, and then you spell it out to the men. Where does it get you?

Then the Army, and for a while the Army was a damned good thing. Time to save some money and think things over. It doesn't matter where you come from: You're either one of them or you're a slob. Or you're in between and you've got to make it on your own, take care of yourself. Even in the Army. Now take Baldwin. Baldwin was going to be an officer from the day his old man brought him home from the hospital, he was one of them. And Collins, with his father a politician he was one of them even though he wasn't an officer. He could have gone to officers' training and come out with a bar, but he was having himself a good time when he went to ASTP. But Collins was moving, even though he was a kid. Some day he'd be a lawyer or a newspaperman, or get on civil service. And all the rest of them were slobs, with himself still in between. Come to think of it, a hell of a lot of six-stripers he'd met in the Army had been foremen just like him.

And what was a foreman, or a six-striper anyway but a goddamned in-between. They make up their mind upstairs what they want, then they tell Baldwin, then Baldwin tells me. Then it's up to me to keep the men together, to tell Baldwin how to get the job done. All through the summer, even with McNeil, that's the way it had been, stuck in between, getting hammered from on top, hammering at the men. Get off your butt, get your back into it, stick together, don't get separated, nobody's goofing off today. Or: Major, we'd better lay over, the guys need some sleep; or, we'll need six men for that job, Major, two guys can't do it alone; let's turn them loose in Kweilin for the weekend, Major, they've got a load in their pants, let them work it off. Still, even in the Army, in-between all the time.

And now, Lewis gets sick. . . . Somebody was going to have to take care of Lewis. Baldwin was a good guy, as those kind of guys go, maybe soft. But he had orders in his pocket. These quiet guys take the job seriously. The road-blowing was more important to Baldwin than anyone being sick. But if Lewis is really sick we ought to high-tail it back to Kunming and the hospital. . . .

. . . Hell! We ought to be high-tailing it back to Kweiyang and Kunming anyway; this trip is crazy, the whole goddam idea is crazy. If Lewis is worse tonight, the slob . . . then Baldwin ought to do something about it. If Baldwin couldn't see it, he ought to be told. There'll be trouble.

So Michaelson around and around to himself. But out loud, in exasperation, as he saw the convoy slowing down, he burst out:

"Those goddam Chinese!"

They were in traffic now, the traffic they had been breasting and cleaving for two days, and the traffic was at its mid-morning peak. Up ahead, the lead jeep was slowing down, edging to the side of the road to get by two Chinese trucks. Both Chinese trucks had stopped, one of them with its engine still running, the other resting on two tireless front rims as several Chinese worked on the jacked-up rear, stripping the tires.

"We give them this stuff and they ruin it. That's a new weapons-carrier," Michaelson said.

"Yeah," said Miller, "a new weapons-carrier."

"We just started bringing that stuff in over the Hump this spring, and they're ruining it."

"Yeah, they ruin everything."

"Look," said Michaelson, "did you ever see anything like this, how in hell do they expect to fight a war?"

Through their windshield they stared out at the winding, unending traffic jam that had bewildered their eyes for so long they now but rarely thought of it. The flight was now worse than at any time since they had left Liuchow. All the floating population of East China that had been pushed onto the roads and thrust back to the mountains for days and weeks and months was trekking along with them, slowing the buses and trucks in the procession to a creeping foot-pace.

Younger men walked briskly along, some with foot-staffs, in determination; others in unencumbered nonchalance. Family groups shuffled ahead, mother tugging children, father carrying baby pick-a-back on his shoulders. Other families pushed wheelbarrows, and the squeal of the unoiled barrow wheels screeched above all the other noises, of yelling, of braying, of chatter, of motors, of congestion. Others, peasants, carried all they had on bamboo staves, from both ends of which their bundles jiggled up and down in yo-yo fashion. Still others, thongs over their shoulders and bodies bent almost parallel to the ground, pulled two-wheel carts loaded with blankets, or suitcases, or wicker baskets. On one cart sat a little boy, his head wrapped in a shawl against the cold, his nose dripping, his bright black eyes serenely surveying the road from the mound of baggage on which he perched. Above the shoulder height of the procession, an old crone in a high, open sedan chair bobbed up and down on the shoulders of her two half-naked carriers, whose flesh, despite the cold, glistened with the sweat of their burden. Her lips were chattering in silent dialogue with herself, and in her lap she clutched an enamel chamber pot. On another cart, the face of a grandfather clock poked its head above the clutter of goods it surmounted.

"Man, I've seen everything now," said Miller as they watched and wormed their way along. "Hey, look, hey look, Mike, there's a camel."

It was a camel, too, red-tasseled, gaunt, sway-necked, a child perched on top, a woman leading it.

"Where in hell does that come from, Mike?" asked Miller.

"How do I know?" said Michaelson. "Camels are supposed to be in a desert. Maybe come down from the north in the retreat, maybe come out of a zoo, but every goddam thing in China is being pushed along this road like a sewer pump pushes garbage. One thing I know, that camel's never gonna make Kweiyang; he'll make camel-meat before he gets there if you can eat camel-meat."

"Them cows, too," said Miller.

"Those aren't cows, dope, those are oxes," said Michaelson as they passed a pair of plodding oxen, feet wrapped in old rags, laboring up the incline.

Now, at the next incline, they began to run into wheeled traffic again, for the trucks and buses that pounded through the foot traffic on the downgrades and levels, slowed to a single, winding clot on the upslopes.

"It's these hills that bother me," said Michaelson. "I don't mind the levels or downgrades, because if worst comes to worst you can just step on the gas and barrel through them. But on these upgrades, when you can't make any time, these Chinese can jump you, and once we lose our wheels we don't stand a chance. I wish Baldwin would move faster."

It was at this moment that Michaelson felt the convoy slowing again and lifting his foot from the gas, grunted, "Now what?"

They waited impatiently in the cab, smoking for a minute, two minutes, three minutes. An urchin tried to scramble up on their fender—a mother's hand reached up, whacked him, hauled him down, began to beat, and the child to wail.

Michaelson leaned out and yelled:

"Ah, for Christ's sake, let him alone."

The mother looked back at the American, her face slowly veiling to a cold expressionlessness, and spat. Michaelson laughed. They waited a few more minutes and Michaelson said:

"You take the wheel, Miller. I'm going forward and see what's happening. Pick me up if we start moving."

Forward, the lead jeep stood at the head of the American convoy, drawn up double-file beside another lane of Chinese trucks and carts. Square in their path, stood an old, rust-flecked, sagging truck with Chinese army markings, loaded with cotton bales, and planted solidly, directly, in the middle of the road.

"What's happening, Collins?" asked Michaelson as he picked out the slim, alert figure leaning against the hood of the jeep, surrounded by a knot of children.

"This, sergeant," said Collins, "is China, the land of ancient culture and the fast buck."

"Oh don't give me that crap again," said Michaelson, not in any anger at Collins but because it was the role they played with each other.

Collins went on in the same tone:

"Here we have half a million people walking out over two hundred miles of road and maybe a hundred thousand of them will die before they get to shelter. But the truck up there belongs to some clever gentleman, or officer, who cleaned out the last bales of cotton in Kweilin or Liuchow before he evacuated, and is now expediting them north to Kweiyang and Kunming where he will make a small fortune if the cotton gets there safely, which it will not. Anyway,"—here Collins broke tone and style of his talk and went on, "the joker with the truck is set right in the middle of the road and he won't back off or let anyone else pass unless he gets a push, because his truck won't work. And the bus behind him has pushed him up this hill halfway and the bus people say they won't push any longer because their own engine is overheating and beginning to conk out. So we're all stuck."

"Well, let's shove him off the road, and get going, what are we waiting for?"

"Because it's a Chinese army truck and the three guys with it are in uniform and have guns, and probably a cut of the profits if they ever sell that cotton in Kunming. And Baldwin and our Chinese colonel are up there arguing with them now, and the colonel has got the woman with him up there to translate. I don't see how we can move them without a gun-fight and that's not a very bright idea."

At this moment, one of the children gabbled in Chinese at Collins and he reached in his pocket, took out a cellophane-wrapped sourball, peeled it and popped it in the child's mouth. The child's face was radiant, and all the children clamored.

"So what the hell are you doing here with these kids?" Michaelson asked.

Collins, leaning against the jeep, stared coolly back at Michaelson, deliberately reached in his pocket, pulled out a D-bar, broke it in bits, and began to pop chocolate crumbs at the children. Then he answered.

"I'm giving some candy to the kids."

"Jesus Christ, Collins, we're in a jam! What the hell do you think you're doing?"

Collins' voice was very deliberate as he looked at Michaelson.

"I know we're in a jam. And we're going to have to do something about that truck, because nobody else here dares to. In a couple of minutes our major up there is going to realize it, because he's a pretty smart guy, I think. And when we do, this crowd can go either way—for us or against us, and I'd like to have the crowd with us if we have trouble. See? See those people watching us?"

Michaelson looked away from the children, to where several older Chinese were regarding them and smiling.

"They like kids. I like kids. Kids like candy. Same all over the world; make friends with the kids, you make friends with their parents. That's how you make votes."

At that moment, one of the children broke away from Collins, ran to his mother, whispered to her, and came back with his hand dangling some red paper cut-outs. He gave them to Collins and Collins spread them out—they were cut of stiff red paper, paper moons, paper stars, paper designs.

Collins smiled, thanked the child, turned to Michaelson.

"See—he's saying thank you for his candy. The Chinese cut this paper stuff up all the time to make toys for their kids. Cheaper than our toys. Some people think it's an art-form, but I suppose you wouldn't be interested in that."

Michaelson's temper blasted off as if the pressure within had blown the safety-cock.

"Oh my God, Collins, you're a jerk. We got to get this convoy rolling. This ain't the time to make friends, we got to do something with that major. Collins, if it were up to me, I'd break your back."

Collins smiled, then was very grave, and spoke slowly.

"Listen, Mike, we may or may not have trouble here in a minute. But if there's going to be trouble we're going to need some support. You can't ever have too many friends, that's the first rule of politics. Besides, I like the kids."

"Go ahead, make friends," yelped Michaelson, "some day they'll beat your goddam brains in," and he turned, pushing his way through the crowd to where Baldwin, Kwan and the woman stood facing a swart, dark man in an officer's uniform. From the uniform dangled a belt in which a pistol hung and the officer's hand lay on the pistol. Kwan was bellowing, Baldwin's face was frozen with anger, but the stubbornness of the uniformed Chinese in command of the truck needed no translation. He stood, legs spread apart, unmoved, interrupting the flow of Kwan's invective with flat, negative ejaculations. His truck would be pushed up the hill, or no one would move.

"What's up, Major?" asked Michaelson.

"We're going to have to move that truck off the road, Michaelson. I'm glad you came up. Stand by."

Michaelson's mood quickened—he realized he was happy that the major was glad to see him, but happier because the major suddenly sounded like McNeil. McNeil had taken no crap from the Chinese on the road.

Baldwin beckoned to Madame Hung, who beckoned to Kwan; a hasty consultation took place, and Kwan went back to the uniformed truck man again. Baldwin turned to Michaelson and speaking quickly, as several Chinese faces pressed in on them to catch their incomprehensible English words, said:

"Now listen, Michaelson. This is a fast one. We have to shove that truck off the road. But it's going to have to look like an accident. And we don't want any shooting, remember that. Kwan is asking him now to let you look his engine over. You're supposed to be my mechanic. You're going to look that engine over—and look it over, too. Maybe you can pass a miracle, or find a wire that's come unstuck and fix it—and then we're going to offer to push it. Got that?"

"Yup."

"Prince is going to bring his truck up behind the cotton truck. Kwan'll get the other Chinese trucks to inch back a bit. Then you're going to get at the wheel of the cotton truck as if you were trying to get it started. When Prince starts to push you, you will simply guide that wheel slowly over the side of the hill and let the truck tumble. You've got to get out of the cab just as soon as she starts to tip. But it's an outside curve so I think you can do it. Can you?"

"Major, it'll be a pleasure." This was going to be good.

Baldwin checked him.

"And listen, we're not doing this for fun. This is because we have to, see?"

There was, as Michaelson could tell immediately, when he lifted the cotton truck's hood, nothing he could do about it. And his disgust rose, as it always did, when he saw a piece of machinery abused. Crusted rust, layers of dirt, grease rags, fouled the inside of the engine. The fanbelt had been hammered together with nails and was about to slip its raceway. There was no spark. A trickle of water from the radiator showed that it leaked. Michaelson tapped the distributor head, tried to work the horn, tried to work the starter, acted briefly as if he were working, then pulled his head out.

"No miracle, Major, let's go into the act."

Again a babble of voices, Baldwin to Madame Hung in English, Madame Hung to Kwan in Chinese, Kwan to the truck driver in formal-deceptive Chinese. Behind the cotton truck a backing and filling of the other Chinese trucks took place and a space was cleared. Collins deftly maneuvered the jeep, with Madame Hung now in it again, beyond the cotton truck and to the front of it. Prince maneuvered his six-by-six into position behind the cotton truck.

Michaelson got in behind the wheel of the cotton truck,

and noticed the alternate Chinese driver still sitting there, on the outside, the side that would fall off down the slope.

"Hey, what about him?" he said, leaning out of the cab, yelling to Baldwin.

"Get him out," yelled Baldwin, "get him out."

"Let him stay," yelled Michaelson above the engine sound of Prince's truck which was now gently nudging him, "what the hell difference does it make?"

"No," yelled Baldwin, "no, hold it."

Another conference took place. At the end of it, suspiciously, the uniformed man with the pistol came over to the far-side of the truck and asked his driver to get out.

Michaelson let his arm drop out of the cab in signal that he was ready, and behind him Prince came nosing with the bumper of the six-by-six. With a lurch, the cotton truck jolted ahead, settled back against Prince's bumper, lurched again, rolled. The wheel quivered unsteadily in Michaelson's hand, he twisted it, the truck let itself be guided, he could feel a drive wheel, a front wheel, slipping over the edge. By reflex he pulled it back, his hand reached for the cab door, he tugged the wheel again, the off-end of the cab tilted, he could feel the far-end slipping, it was going. . . . With a quick motion, Michaelson had the cab door open, was on the running board and as the truck, awkward, like a sinking vessel slowly careening into the deep, began to fall away from his foot, he leaped for the road, made it, danced on tiptoe and, instinctively, let the carbine slip from the shoulder sling into the ready position at his elbow.

Between him and the uniformed truck man there was now nothing but space, the people drawing back in a circle of audience, and across the space the twisted raging face of the uniformed Chinese truck man thrust forwards toward Michaelson and the hand of the Chinese had the pistol out of the belt and the two of them, guns in hand, stood there, staring at each other as the truck bounced, and bounded, and crashed and rattled down the hillside. Above the noise of the truck, and in the silence, Michaelson heard Baldwin yelling:

"Don't make a move, Mike, don't shoot, hold it."

But he knew that if the Chinese hand with the pistol lifted even an inch, he would fire first and get him.

The truck driver and Michaelson faced each other for seconds and then around them, like the clap of cymbals, came a peal of Chinese laughter; the crowd was with the Americans, the crowd was laughing at the way the driver had been tricked, and it was over. The truck man had lost face, thus lost all—the right to fire, the right to ride, the right to the fortune that was now tumbling down irretrievably to burst and waste in the winter snow. The horns behind them blared. They could hear the trucks behind coughing into action. There was the sweet stink of an alcohol-burning motor, the sour smell of a diesel motor clearing cylinders to move again.

Baldwin signaled with his arm, and Prince rolled by, followed by Niergaard in Lewis' truck, followed by Ballo, followed by Miller.

Miller halted.

"What happened?" he called.

"Get in," said Baldwin to Kwan who was still with them, and taking him by the elbow, thrust him aboard. "Get in," snapped Baldwin to Michaelson. But Michaelson said, "You get in, I'll ride the running board." Baldwin scrambled in, the door slammed. Michaelson caught the handle and was on the running board as the truck started. He shrank against the truck door, wincing. The shot came as he knew it would, a pap from the pistol, a whiz through the air, and a clean miss.

He could not swing the carbine with the one arm free, with the truck bumping, but some day he would shoot one of these slopeys, before the war was over he'd get one.

Baldwin rolled down the window and leaned out.

"We'll put a couple of miles between us and that swine, and then I'll shift back to the jeep," he said. And then before rolling the window back up, "Nice work, Mike, nice work."

They reshuffled on the level, on the down-side of the slope, and Baldwin, taking the wheel of the lead jeep himself, with Collins beside him, the woman and Kwan behind him, jabbed the jeep off with a jack-rabbit start. An elation, a strange exhilaration had entered him. He had not meant to destroy the truck when he first saw it; he had simply known what he had to do and had done it. Best of all was the swing with which everyone—Michaelson, Kwan, Prince, all of them—had fallen into the act, had caught his command when he had made it, gears meshing with no clash. And now three Chinese racketeers were walking out in the cold. Philip Baldwin, Scourge-of-the-Highway, Baldwin-Takes-Over, Baldwin-Clears-the-Way, his daydreaming whispered, and he chuckled, for he felt good all over. Not even Helen could have faulted him on that one, and he remembered how every now and then, but more rarely in the later years, he could shake her out of criticism and wring the soft praise, "Oh, good, Phil, oh, good." He would write to her about this; he knew he had done a clean job. Vaguely, for a moment, he wondered whether he could have done it had they not been racketeers, not been so clearly wrong. Or whether he could have done it had they been Americans, in an American truck, not Chinese. And he knew he could have.

A hand tapped his shoulder—it was Kwan.

"*Hao,*" blurted Kwan, "*hao!*" Baldwin knew it meant good.

It was the first time Kwan had opened a conversation since he had joined them. Baldwin turned from the wheel momentarily to cast a glance back at Kwan—leaning forward, talking—and then Baldwin flicked his eye back to the road. But the momentary glance had shown a new Kwan. You could talk with Chinese for hours; and if they did not trust you, or were not there for you, it was as if they were in retreat, curtained and veiled from any understanding behind the meaningless stare of their eyes. Then, suddenly, they would change, something would wipe the expressionless gaze from their eyes, their eyes would sparkle, they would be with you, alive. All yesterday he had sensed Kwan aloof, remote, possibly hostile. But the slight, taut Chinese, leaning forward to say "Good," had now lost his rigidity and glowed with warmth and approval. Baldwin found himself liking Kwan. And as he warmed in response, the woman spoke, too, in English.

"Well done," she said. "Oh, that was good."

"There was nothing else to do," said Baldwin and Collins translated.

"There is never anything else to do," said Kwan, "but sometimes people cannot do it."

It was the woman who translated Kwan's Chinese this time, and Baldwin realized they were becoming a group in the jeep, almost friends. The day had started well, and he did not want to lose the feeling. Today was the day to get something really good done. The road ought to be ripped to pieces some place before Hochih—VICINITY HOCHIH, the message had read—and any place would do. The refugees were an annoyance, he was making slow time, but he felt he was doing it for them, too. Cut the road and keep the Jap out. Simple.

"Where do they all come from?" he asked out of his thinking, throwing the question to Collins to throw to the two Chinese in back.

"From the cities now," said Kwan, "from the cities and the villages. Wherever the army can reach them. This is the rule. When the army goes, the people must go. If the army goes and the people stay, the Japanese will use them. This is the rule: 'Scorch the earth, fill the wells.' "

Collins hesitated for a moment in the translation, trying to interpret the Chinese phrase. The woman's voice broke in pleasantly to correct Collins' translation. When Kwan resumed, it was she who was translating:

"If the Japanese find houses, they can sleep in them. If they find food, they can eat. If they find people, they can use them. They tie our people with ropes and make them pull the guns. They make them carry ammunition. If they find Chinese people, they do not need trucks. Whatever they need, they make our people do. They do not care if they kill our people. Because they cannot make friends with our people, they make animals of them. The men, the women, the children all must carry for the Japanese or work for them. So we must make the people retreat."

Baldwin could not tell whether it was Kwan's voice or the woman's translation that suddenly fell from a rising tone of bitterness and wrath, to a note of sadness on the last sentence.

"But what if they don't want to go?" asked Baldwin.

"Then they must go, then the army must make them go. We must burn their houses, burn their bridges, make them take their food away or we must burn it to keep it from the Japanese. There is no way. The people must go when the army goes."

"It's rough on the people."

"They eat bitterness. Especially these people."

"Is this any different from other retreats?" asked Baldwin.

"Yes," said Kwan, "these people are different. In the beginning, everyone retreated, the peasants, the workers, the merchants, the students, from Shanghai, from Canton, from Nanking, from Hankow. Now most peasants no longer go. They stay. Only the city people we can make go now. And these people. They have come once already from the coast, at the beginning of the war they came here to Kwangsi and Hunan. They were very good people, who hated Japanese. They would not stay behind under the Japanese. Now they must go again. The second time. But it is better than at the beginning."

"Why is it better?" asked Baldwin.

"Because in the beginning, only the Japanese had airplanes. In the beginning they would kill everyone on the road. Everyone walked at night. Now only the Americans have airplanes, so it is better. They walk by day."

Baldwin considered the thought for a moment and then, the woman, speaking for herself, added:

"I don't know whether he's right or not. It's safer, I know, if this is safe. But in the beginning we only hated the Japanese who used to strafe us on the road. Now, I guess we hate each other."

She had now thoroughly joined the group. He found her thought interesting and began to study the road again. Ahead, several miles away on a level, Baldwin could see a footpath cutting across the fields, marked by moving clumps of plodding people, the path curving into the main road as a tributary pours its stream into the parent river.

"And those people, there, where are they coming from?" he asked.

"More people," said Kwan. "There are many foot-roads in China. The people who walk from the East take the little roads across the mountains. But there is nothing to eat in the mountains, they cannot buy food. So they come back to the main road. This is Kwangsi, there is still food. In Kweichou, there will not be food even on this road."

"Why?" asked Baldwin, and Madame Hung answered without waiting for Kwan to reply.

"Kwangsi is a rich province. Rice," she said. "But these hills are the border of Kwangsi. Kweichou is a mountain province, the poorest in China; it hasn't even any history, and the other edge of Kweichou is Tibet, it isn't even Chinese. By the time we get to Kweichou, everybody walking out will have to come down to the main road to look for food. It's the only real road in this part of China."

Her words brought him back to the problem again: the road. The exhilaration of the fray with the cotton truck was still with him. He had to, he would, today, soon, do something about this road. The meandering gray-yellow strip that stretched before him teased and tantalized him. The ground never came to rest, it pushed and swelled, rose and fell, the folds and gray ridge-lines stretching colorless ahead as far as he could see. It is a bad road, thought Baldwin. It has no majesty. It should be blown. And then, some day, built all over again. Just one good blow before we get to Hochih, just one and that will fix it. His jeep wheel caught in a frozen rut; he jerked the steering wheel, got out of the rut, annoyed by the road. Tear it apart, then rebuild the whole thing after the war was over.

"How long has this road been in?" he asked Kwan.

"The road is very old. And very new," said Kwan. "It is very old because it was built in the days of the Emperors. For the couriers. For horsecarts. For mules. For hundreds of years, this road goes through this valley down to Kwangsi. Also for opium. In the beginning the opium went up this road from Canton to Yunnan, to Ssuchwan. Then, the people in Yunnan began to grow poppy, and the road was used to send opium down to the cities. Then the war, and the Generalissimo built the road over again for trucks, and the little railway for the ammunition. You do not think this is a good road?"

"Well," said Baldwin, not wanting to put a strain on the sense of comradeship that had just developed in the past hour, "we build them differently back home."

"With machines," said Kwan, "I know. China needs machines. Much machinery. Even more than guns. Machinery to build roads, factories. Like America. But this road, the peasants built. With their hands."

Baldwin peered. Winding and kinking and coiling about itself, the road was flung over the hills. Every now and then the road's builders had had to lift it from one watershed to the next, switching from the bed of one little stream to the next, following the water back up to the parent plateau. Whenever this happened, the road's engineers working with coolie labor, mattocks, hand-baskets for dirt-hauling, hand-picks for chipping, had been forced to scratch inches off the mountain side, twisting the highway back and forth above itself in a series of hairpin curves, one above the other. Baldwin could imagine he saw fingernail marks on the sidewall of the mountains where men had scratched away with bare hands. How did they do it? Where did they teach Chinese engineers to use people like this? All the calculations of his education faded to shadow. No slide rule multiplying cubic yardage by tonnage, total fill by haulage distance, multiplying bulldozer days by truck capacity by cement requirements by union wages so as to get a cost estimate or an engineering judgment—none of these constants of his training fitted into China. I couldn't build a thing their way, Baldwin told himself, I couldn't build a thing my way in this country either. But I can destroy.

This isn't a good road, it's a bad road, and it's dangerous, just dangerous enough to let the Japanese in.

Now where shall we do it, he asked himself, clutching back at his problem, and, aloud:

"Tell Kwan," he said to Collins, "I'm looking for a hairpin bend, a real good horseshoe, something that'll make a side-hill blow for today's work and cut this thing permanently."

Collins struggled to explain and Madame Hung took over again.

"Let me," she said, and went into Chinese.

"Yes," said Kwan, "that is right. On the side of a mountain. Where the road goes back and forth on top of itself. Five, six, seven times before it crosses the top. We call it a noodle road. Like that . . ."

And he pointed.

Baldwin looked off into the distance as Collins' finger pointed where Kwan had first indicated. As his eyes focused, the road trace against the immense hills became clearer and clearer. And it was a beauty, he told himself. He counted. There were seven bends, one directly above the other as the road mounted the high range beyond them. With one or two craters at the bends, possibly a ditch on one of them—that would hold the Japanese for a long time. Or maybe, with luck, find a snout at one of the bends where they could shave the nose of the mountain right off.

His spirits soared. The job ahead was so clean it might have come out of the Field Manual. He could even remember the language, almost see the page in the book:

"EXECUTION OF A DEMOLITION REQUIRES,

I. THE OBJECTIVE SOUGHT (MISSION)

II. TIME AVAILABLE

III. EXTENT OF DEMOLITION NECESSARY TO FULFILL THE OBJECTIVE SOUGHT, ETC. . . ."

There were twelve points, said the book, in planning a demolition, but already Baldwin's mind surged ahead to the hairpin climb, with its clean complications, the formulas of charge, the substance of the equation with its variables of roadbed consistency, the resources in his trucks, the skill of his men, the mathematics that put these together. This was why he had become an engineer. And now he was bossing his own field operation, his own command, there was no pricing on this, it was destruction, and up to him.

He turned around in his seat to Kwan, almost happily, then squelched the eagerness in his voice as he realized he *was* happy and, to a Chinese, the destruction of a Chinese road might not seem quite so gay.

"That's it all right," he said, "that's where we take her out."

"It is a good place," said Kwan.

"Halfway up," said Baldwin, "the third or fourth turn from the bottom, try to slide as much down on the lower turns as possible."

"Excellent," said Kwan, "then, if they want to fix the road, then their trucks must come up three bends, and the road is too narrow for them to turn around."

"Right," said Baldwin, proud that his reasoning was so clear and that Kwan understood and approved.

CHAPTER 5

Sidehill Blow

QUITE CONFIDENT NOW, determined to keep the rhythm of the day from slowing, aware that the thinking was his alone and there was no point in talking, Baldwin curtly halted the convoy at the bottom of the escarpment, and, freed of his cumbersome tail of trucks, gunned the jeep, with its company of three, up the hill.

The grade here, he sensed from the jeep's angle, was steeper than at any of the foothills they had climbed in the past two days and he knew this must be the first shelf of the plateau they were defending. There was good geography in the cable stipulating: VICINITY HOCHIH.

It was at the second horseshoe from the top that Baldwin found what he was looking for—an outside curve. To the right, the mountain fell off from the shoulder almost sheer, tumbling down through slopes of stunted scrub and naked rock to a little river far below. On the left, the mountain face had been chipped away with an arching half-tunnel effect that left a rock overhang over the roadbed ten feet thick. He could see still the drill marks of the Chinese laborers who had bored the solid stone with hand-irons to place their black powder and chip it to bits. His eye, following the drill marks, could see that the rock face of the mountain was only partly naked here, creviced in spots, a pudding of boulder and stone at the bottom of the arch—an entirely dirty, unstable formation which any American engineer would have cleaned out when the road was built. But the instability of it all delighted him now. With luck, with good calculation, if the rock formations were right, they would not only ditch the road here, and trigger a rock-fall; they would shave a nose clean off the mountain face, cascading boulders and rock down the slopes to all the levels below, to block the Japanese on the twisting bends beneath until it could be cleared.

He got back into the jeep, wheeled it briskly about, headed down the slope again to the trucks, his horn and brakes alternating as he threaded the one-way traffic against him. The rise at the horseshoe, he figured, was something over twenty feet in a radius of one hundred fifty, a gradient of fourteen per cent, and his mind, automatically, told him that the Chinese engineer who had done this was mad, a genius, and had probably never gone to an engineering school in his life. If they slipped it, with any luck at all they should leave an elevation of some twenty feet for the Japanese to face when they brought their vehicles up the road. To slip it meant work, though, all the rest of the day, back-breaking work; and everything would have to work, the auxiliary motor for the air hammer, the hand-augurs, the men most of all. Hours of work, under strain. But if five hours' work of eight men could slip it, it would take the Japanese fifty men, with heavy equipment, three days or a week to repair it. There was a margin there. Of how much? Of perhaps one hundred to one.

Some day, he thought, I'm going to rewrite the Field Manual. There should be a mathematical formula not only for physical earth-moving, but for the supreme calculation of demolition. If one man's work required the repair of effort of two men, did you have a profit? Should the minimum margin be one man's effort at destruction to ten men's effort at repair? And how did you figure instrumentation? When you smashed the traversing or elevating mechanism of an artillery piece, how many man hours had gone into making it, how many into assembling it—how many into getting it there? Getting it there was a factor in the equation. The gasoline they had blown in Liuchow was high-octane aviation fuel—probably a dollar a gallon back home. But what was it worth when it had been tankered to Karachi, road-hauled from Karachi to the Hump, flown over the Hump, each gallon delivered having burned up another gallon of similarly valuable fuel to get it across, then flown across China from Kunming to Kwangsi and stored? And the planes and lives lost getting it there? The gasoline wasn't valuable in itself, it was valuable because it was where it was. But how valuable? Two bullets and five seconds burned a gasoline shed, the margin of destruction must be a million to one there. A road, this road now, must rank pretty low in a trade of destruction, compared to the gasoline. Except that there was a time factor, how did one weigh the time of eight Americans today against the time a Japanese column might be delayed the day after tomorrow?

He was approaching the trucks now, and he could see the men smoking, and the usual Chinese wayfarers lingering in a circle to watch them. The thing to do was not to explain to the men but to excite them. Everything was going well, except for Lewis being sick. Lead them back up the hill, show them the job, break it down, move them fast, keep going. Ride them up to the overhang, then stop, then get to work.

Half an hour later, in the shadow of the overhang, with the trucks parked by the side of the road, tilting into the gutters out of the traffic, beyond the overhang, Baldwin gathered them together.

They had acquired, already, a part-Chinese look. Prince had, from somewhere, annexed a Chinese soldier's winter-padded, cotton-quilt vest. Miller was wearing an ankle-length khaki overcoat, over an air-force fleece jacket, and the overcoat draped his tubby body like a tent. Niergaard wore a Chinese soldier's peanut-vendor hat. Several had fleece-lined pilot's jackets, all wore paratroop boots. It was not the way an American outfit was supposed to look. Baldwin stared at them for a moment; bleary-eyed, sallow, unshaven, all dirty. They looked back at him suspiciously and Baldwin edged into it carefully.

"Mike," he asked, "have you any idea of what we're still carrying?"

"Well," began Michaelson, whose truck carried the explosives, "we've got maybe fifty sticks of the dynamite that's making me nervous. It's so cold today, it could freeze on us; and if she freezes we just can't carry it in the trucks. The way this road bounces, it could flash any time once it freezes. The dynamite ought to go right away if we use anything here. Then we've got three full cases of the TNT in the half-pound blocks, three hundred pounds all told. Figure another twenty, thirty pounds in loose blocks. We got a couple of cases of the nitro-starch half-pound blocks, that's another two hundred pounds. We got one cratering charge left, lots of time fuse, maybe a hundred of those small reels of primacord, anyway plenty. Plenty of caps, all kinds of caps. I guess that's it. We're loaded with gasoline, plenty of rations. That's it."

"Fine," said Baldwin. His mind had been working on the calculations all the way down the slope and back up again to the overhang. There was no deal involved in this, no negotiation for permission, nothing but the clean work itself. The equations hung easily in his grasp, and he had only to fit the charges to formula; and fit the men to the work.

"Listen, now, all of you," said Baldwin clearing his throat. "I want to try for the jackpot on this one." He thought that sounded right, and could tell it did by the slow shuffle forward of Niergaard in interest.

"We could spend all day hand-boring some chambers in the road on the flat, and have perhaps three or four ditches on the road of about ten or twelve feet deep at the end of a day that the Japanese could fill with refugee labor in another day."

He could see Michaelson looking at him intently, and he remembered Michaelson was a foreman who had to understand the plan; you could get Michaelson if he was interested in the job. Now he was speaking to Michaelson:

"Or we can really try to take this road out, which is what I propose to do. This is a tough job, but the tougher it is for us, the tougher it's going to be for the Japanese to fix."

He was telling them, he felt fine, he placed his hands on his hips, his voice fully confident.

"This is the first big step up to the plateau. Up to now, we've been coming out of Kwangsi through the low hills. From here on, the mountains climb and keep climbing into Kweiyang and Kunming. This is the first big elevation. And this overhang strikes me as thoroughly unstable. If we can slide it down, and slide the roadbed out at the same time, here on the curve, the Japanese won't be able to use this road again until they move heavy equipment up to work on it.

"Now here's the layout," he continued. "It goes in two parts. The first part is the road itself. I want to shave this whole curve off, the whole lip of the curve as it winds around here. We'll dig two strings of bore-holes parallel with each other in the road. The strings will be about ten feet apart, and they'll run with the curve of the road right around the bend. Seven bore-holes to each string, on the standard pattern, alternating five-foot and seven-foot depths. That's work with the big hand-augurs, and we'll chamber out the bore-holes with the half-pound blocks until they're big enough to take a major charge."

He had turned and was pointing out the pattern on the road when he heard one of them groan. He realized at the groan, the work and labor he was demanding. But he did not know who it was, and did not want to find out now. His mind was working on the calculations as he spoke. He had five hundred pounds of TNT and nitro-starch and fourteen holes. Twenty-five pounds to a chamber would be enough, more than enough, but there was no point in saving explosives. And then there would still be some left over for the overhang.

"Now the second part is the overhang."

He pointed up to the dark rock, the shale, the limestone, the brute face of it. It would be dirty work.

"We'll have to use the air hammer, hooked up to the auxiliary ninety-six pounder to get in there. Either just under or just above the arch. Five holes, sixty inches deep for the dynamite."

"Do you see?" he went on, hoping to excite them. "We'll hook them all up on one circuit, and we blow simultaneously. The road does a double ditch, the overhang hammers down at the same time, and the whole lip falls all the way down.

With enough concussion, we may loosen up a major fissure in this rock and take the whole nose of the mountain off."

They were alert, listening to him now; they were pros, Baldwin knew; they had volunteered for this outfit, and destruction excited them. Deep within himself, Baldwin could feel faintly stirring the same excitement, the almost sexual stirring that came before the explosion, the rending, the tearing apart.

Then he spoiled it, knowing too late he was saying too much.

"That's the rest of the day's work, right here, and it's hard work, I know. But if we can stop the Japanese here, even for a few days, it gives the people back on the plateau time to form some sort of line to stop them. If we rip this road out, here, now . . . why, why," . . . he paused—"we may be the ones who hold the whole thing together."

His preoration had fallen flat, he could see on their faces. They did not care about holding the whole thing together. He had sounded like a Sunday-school teacher.

"All right, let's get into it," he snapped, harshly.

"Oh my aching back," he heard Ballo say as he turned away from them, and then Prince, mimicking him, softly, almost out of hearing, "We're gonna hold China together by blowing up their frigging road, everybody's gonna be happy. Two to one we're here until night-time. And then it'll be screwed up like Liuchow. Wanna bet?" and Michaelson growling at both of them, "Shut up, for Christ's sake, let's get this thing over with," and Prince snapping back, "Ah, blow it out your barracks bag," and he realized their nerves were all on edge too, and they were snarling at one another because they could not snarl at him. But he must hold them to it. That was why they were here. It was a simple, uncomplicated job and he could see it clearly. But he ought to check Lewis while they were setting up for the job.

In the back of the truck, Lewis was obviously worse, and a train of annoyance began to build in Baldwin. The job had to be done, but he was the only one who wanted to do it, and all of them were dragging at him, not helping, and though he could scarcely blame Lewis, it was Lewis who kindled his anger first.

No, said Lewis, he didn't want anything to eat. No he didn't want any coffee or water. Only a glass of milk. The permanent whine in Lewis' voice had become a whimper and Baldwin could see how deep Lewis' brown eyes had sunk into his scrawny face and how the hair was thinning, and how useless this man was. Lewis could not take pressure. The request for milk bothered Baldwin more than Lewis' appearance. This was China; there was no milk; there was only milk in America, far, far away. And Lewis' petulant insistence on milk, warm milk, meant that Lewis had no grasp on what was happening to him now, and was beginning to wander, like a child in fever. Baldwin's determination to carry through today, with today's work, could not erase the fact that by tomorrow, if Lewis were not better, Lewis would be the big problem. He would have to get him back in. Which was all the more reason for making today good, as good as it had promised to be when he pushed the cotton truck off the road, as good as it still might be if they could only blast the nose off the mountain.

Covering Lewis with another blanket, promising him to open a can of condensed milk when they broke to eat, he walked back down the line of trucks, and saw that four of the men were already working on the road with the hand-augurs, two to an augur, straining away at its long twist-handles. But Prince and Ballo were sitting on a chest of TNT, the air hammer on the ground beside them, doing nothing.

He stared at them coldly for a minute and said, "Well?"

"We were waiting for you to come back," said Prince, dead-pan. "Michaelson put us on the first trick with the air hammer, but he couldn't figure how to get in there either. He said you'd know."

He could not order Prince, or Ballo either, to stand to attention. He could not order them to do anything until he told them how to do it, and he repressed the anger in him.

"What's the matter?" he said.

"Well," said Prince, pointing to the underside of the arching rock, "I don't see how we get in there, even if we brought a truck up to stand on the cab. And if we loosen anything, it's liable to fall right down on us." He said it patly, not pressing his point, acting stupid; and Baldwin knew that Prince was not stupid.

It was up to him then. He could not leave two men sitting around while the others worked; nor could he give up the hope of the overhang falling, as it could fall and must fall if it were done right. The way to do it was to get on top and look for a fissure or crevice if there was one, topside. And if there were none, to drill the holes anyway.

"Let's try it from on top," he said. "Get your truck around the bend, over to the side, so I can climb up."

Prince got in the truck, and deftly maneuvered it around the bend, as the road rose around the curve, close to the wall. Baldwin and Ballo followed on foot and Baldwin realized that Ballo was not gold-bricking, he was simply tired.

Unsteadily, Baldwin clambered up to the top of the cab. Leaning from the cab to the shoulder of the overhang, he could swing onto the rock shoulder and then was on top of it.

And he saw he was right. It was unstable. Rain, or frost, or natural erosion had cut several fissures in the slope that was the roof of the overhang. Studying them, Baldwin decided that at least one of them was wide enough for a man to get into. But it would be dirty. The man would have to lie down on his side within the crevice; then, cradling the heavy air hammer with one elbow and hand, direct it horizontally into the crack where it narrowed. Could anyone, he wondered, hold the twenty-pound hammer long enough on the horizontal, from that position, to dig into the necessary sixty inches? Was the rock hard or soft? he wondered. Would each hole take half an hour or an hour? He wanted five holes and time moved on.

He clambered out of the crevice, knowing he could not escape it, and yelled down to the two beside the truck.

"Get the hammer up here to me. And hook it up to the auxiliary. I want to try it."

In a few moments, he could hear the auxiliary chugging, and Ballo had clambered up with the hammer, and since there was room for only one man in the crevice, Ballo had climbed down again, and Baldwin, supporting the hammer with his left hand and guiding it with the right, had the star-bit against the rock and it was biting. The rock was soft, he could tell, and in good position he knew he could take out the sixty inches in less than half an hour. But the hammer was heavy, and as it bit and beat and shuddered and jolted his body through the arm, through the elbow, through the wrist, through the gripping fingers, he wondered if he could last it, and he knew he must. Every now and then, he turned, flexing and releasing the cramp in his numb left hand, triggering the air hammer to blow it clean, panting as his body began to ache, hating it, hating Prince, Ballo, Lewis, the road, China and the trap into which he had taken himself. If Hutcheson could see him here; or Helen, he thought. Helen would know he was a fool.

He pulled out the hammer after a while and with a huge effort, sat up erect on the edge of the crevice to let his back muscles ease from their torment for a moment, and looked at the long drill bit. He bent and unbent his stiff fingers, mechanically; but the hammer had drilled forty inches he saw, measuring with his eye, and through the trembling of his body he realized it could then be done, after all. A rock rattled and he looked around to see Ballo climbing up to him. Baldwin tried to control the panting so that Ballo would not see it, but he panted none the less, as Ballo said:

"Are you into it, Major? Will it work?"

"Yes," said Baldwin, still panting, still angry.

"It's my trick now. Want me to take over?"

"This bit's getting dull," said Baldwin. "Have we got any more in the kit?"

"Yes, sir," said Ballo, and Baldwin realized the man was saying "sir." "I'll get them right away, sir," he heard Ballo say as he scrambled down to the truck, and the "sir" rang in Baldwin's ears; it sounded good.

Baldwin was back in the crevice, forcing the bit deeper, hoping to take out a few more inches before handing over to Ballo, when he was aware that Ballo was back. Turning, he could see that Prince had come up with Ballo and they were both ready. He crawled out, stood up stiffly and said, "Twenty minutes is all anyone can take on this. The hammer is heavy. I want five holes, five feet apart. Sixty inches deep. Ballo on the first trick, Prince, you next. And I'll have Michaelson rotate the rest up here for their trick, too."

He climbed down from the truck before they could reply, and still holding his breath from panting, but conscious he looked as filthy as any of them now, he explained the rotation and the job to Michaelson, and walked away. He wanted to be quiet for a moment, while the irritation and the cramp passed. Without thinking, he found himself wandering up to the lead jeep to look for the woman. It would be good to hear her quiet voice.

She was not in the jeep and, for a moment, concerned, he looked for her and then saw her, sitting on the edge of the road, looking out over the hills.

"Hello," she said, looking at his dirt-smeared woolens. "Is everything all right?"

"Fine," he said. "Except for Lewis. How are you?"

"It was cold sitting in the jeep. And I felt so useless. I thought I'd walk around a bit."

He sat down beside her, found a comfortable niche for his feet, and looked out on the gray-and-lavender heights descending before them over the road they had come.

"It must be different for you," she said softly. "I'd forgotten how all this must look to an American."

"Why?" he said.

"People change so gradually that they never see themselves change," she answered. "And then something or somebody holds up a mirror of how you've changed and everything has a new shape."

"Do you see a mirror here?" he asked.

She pointed down the road, with the people winding on it.

"I'd become so used to it," she said. "I've been with my husband's headquarters for four years. I've become used to seeing people on the road like this. But then, watching you, I could suddenly see it the way it looks to an American."

"How?" he asked, puzzled.

"In America, when the roads are crowded, it's always for fun. Everyone is coming or going to a good time. That's what roads are for in America. And I've grown so used to this in the last few years—" she waved her hand out into the distance —"here, whenever the roads are crowded, there's been a disaster. There's been a flood, or a famine, or a retreat. The roads are always sad here. We use them only for flight. I never thought about it before until just now."

"This isn't really much of a road," he said. "Just good enough to be dangerous."

"I know," she said. "In America it used to seem that the roads went where you made them go, like driving from New York to Boston, they go right over the hills, right across the rivers. Here—doesn't the road seem to crawl? It seems to go only where the mountains let it through."

"You've been in Boston, then?" he was bemused by the thought.

"Yes," she said. "You're from Boston, aren't you?"

"I didn't know it showed," he said, smiling. He was always hoping he did not sound like Boston, though he knew it was home, but now, being so far away, he was glad it showed. So she had been there. What had she seen of the brown-and-russet city, with its parks, and its river, and the golden dome?

"When were you there?" he asked.

"I was there for four years. At school," she said. "At Radcliffe."

He wanted to know more.

"Oh," he said. "How did you happen to go there?"

She was silent, somehow withdrawing from him as he pressed too far.

"It's a very long story," she replied. "I know you have to work. You're really going to cut this road today, aren't you?"

She had turned off any questioning, gently but firmly, and

he was back in contemplation of the road again, the irritation stirring underneath.

"I hope," he said. "We have a few more hours of work."

"It's dangerous, isn't it?"

"Not very," he said, "if you know what you're doing. We do."

"And the people . . . the people on the road. How do you get them out of the way?"

He had not thought of the people. The team had been working like divers up to now, as if under water; the flow of people, carts, animals, vehicles coursing continuously about them. And however much Kwan had cursed and yelled to keep them moving, not to cluster, at least once every fifteen minutes the knots would build up until they had to be dispersed with shouts and threats. And now the people were going to complicate the job. He had not thought of the people in calculating the poundages, the chambers, the depths. He had thought briefly, earlier, of the danger of debris, without mats to cover the tamping. But he had decided to get his men far enough around the bend on the upper level before blowing, and to rely on distance alone to protect them against the fling of the explosion. But he was hoping for a spill down the slope, to all the hairpin bends below, where the refugee procession moved. How could he halt the procession long enough to blow? He was conscious of a new source of irritation.

"Why," he said, embarrassed to admit he had not yet thought of this, "why . . . isn't that why Kwan is along . . . to handle the Chinese. . . . He'll think of something."

"Not you?" she asked.

"We'll think of something," he said, trying to sweep the problem away until later.

"Like what?" she pressed.

It was now suddenly enormously complicated, and he resented her pressing. Hastily, he tried to improvise for her.

"Maybe we can talk some of these stragglers into cordoning off the road just below the cut, holding them down there. There's no more truck traffic, we've cleared the last trucks that passed the bridge we blew yesterday. It's only foot traffic now. I guess most of them will be able to scramble across the cut after we blow it."

If it worked the way he hoped it would, he knew that most of them would not. Not the animals. Not the carts. Not the old people. Or the sick. But some would. It was beginning to come to Baldwin that there was a difference between the cotton truck this morning and this job. The cotton truck had been a racket. But the refugees below were innocent. How would he stop the procession long enough to blow without blowing the road from under the feet of people who could not understand? How?

"Maybe we can stop them just below the cut," he went on, reaching for an answer, "by giving some of the stragglers some cigarettes, or some of the sugar, and they can make a cordon just below the blow. If there were enough food, I'd open a couple of cartons at the cordon and that might hold them long enough to let us make the blow, or . . ."

She broke in on him, her voice sharp as it had been last night when he had spoken of the peasant and his mule in the same way.

"You mean leave some food as decoy . . . as if they were animals you want to bait. . . . And what about everyone down below when it tumbles down on them?"

Suddenly, he felt his irritation vent. The temper had been there for years and years simmering away at people who could not see when he saw clearly, who would not listen when he explained. He should not have to explain, now. She knew, somehow he expected her to know, that the road *must* be blown, someone must know he was right.

"Do you think I like it?" he flared. "What do you think I'm trying to do? This isn't my job. I'd rather build a road than tear it down. Right now there's only eighty miles between us and the Japanese back at Liuchow, and if they get as far as Kweiyang, they'll cut every road between Kunming and Chungking. They've always wanted to separate us, and if they separate Chungking from us you can wrap up this government and this country and this war and the whole damned thing is finished until the Navy lands in Shanghai. Nobody knows what the Japanese are going to do. But I'm not leaving this road as an open invitation for them to come along. It's up to me, and, damn it, I'm trying to save what's left. We'll make some kind of barrier. As good as we can. How would you do it? Just blow the road right out from under their feet? Like a Chinese general would?"

He had jabbed her with the last question, as he had meant, too, because he was angry inside. She winced as if he had slapped her. He got to his feet, brushed his pants, trembling with anger, but aware that he had never spoken that way to a woman before, not even to Helen, even when she had goaded him further.

Furious with himself, the road, the men, with her, with the problem she had now focused so sharply that he could not ignore it, he got to his feet and walked back to where the men were working on the two-string ditch. As he approached them, he saw Prince flipping one of the yellow-paper half-pound blocks of TNT to Niergaard who stood by the shoulder of the road, packing a bore-hole for chambering. Niergaard fielded it deftly, placed it on the ground, raised his hand for another, and Baldwin lost his temper a second time. He knew the blocks were inert, that the TNT was stable and safe, but this was sheer carelessness.

"Just keep on horsing around, you fools," he yelled. "Just keep on horsing around and you'll never even see Kweiyang, let alone home."

They looked at him blankly for he had never yelled at them before. He must get a grip on himself, he realized, and turned away angrily to inspect the strings of bore-holes the team was digging on the road. He paced around the bend, checked their work, found himself elbowing one of the men off the twist-handles of the augur to work it himself and realized that it was easier to work the augur, sweating and straining, losing himself in it, than to figure out what to do about the people coming up the road.

At two, Baldwin called a lunch break. By half past three, with five hours of work gone by, Michaelson had begun to stack the explosives by the side of the road and Baldwin had come to check them and run over once more his final calculations. The dynamite and TNT for the overhang were stacked neatly in one pile. More TNT and nitro-starch blocks were stacked separately for the chambers in the ditching holes. The detonating wire was ready in its reel, and the leads, he noted, were clean. The primers were ready. The caps in their compartments, eight to a box, were there. He calculated once again—fourteen primed blocks for the ditching chambers, five sticks of dynamite to wire up for the overhang. That made nineteen which fitted easily into the capacity of the thirty-cap blasting machine. He had far more explosive here than he needed; but everything was going to work this time, he knew, exactly as he had calculated. Except for the people; he had left them out of his calculation. And now he must do something about them.

Telling Michaelson to spoon out the chambers and wire them up as soon as he could, ordering him to load all but fifty pounds of the excess TNT into the crevice of the overhang, Baldwin dismissed the technical job to Michaelson's care and called for Collins to interpret. He was going to talk to Kwan. He had decided to turn the problem of the refugees below over to Kwan. Kwan was Chinese.

"There is no way, from the beginning, there is no way," said Kwan when Baldwin had explained the problem. Kwan must have seen it from the moment in mid-morning when they had stopped to dig. There was no way.

"Ask him if he can stop them for just ten minutes," said Baldwin.

"How?" said Kwan, and it was back in Baldwin's lap.

"If we set up a couple of empty gasoline drums across the road and string a rope across it, will that work?" asked Baldwin.

"They will go under the rope," said Kwan.

"Can't you explain to some of them, some of the soldiers, the stragglers, that they should form a cordon and hold the refugees?"

"How?" said Kwan. "If I explain to the soldiers that we are cutting the road—then they will want to hurry ahead and get through."

"If we give them something?" said Baldwin.

"What?" said Kwan. "They cannot spend money here. Maybe a great deal of money, but we have no money. What else can we give them? There is no way."

Baldwin thought again.

"Food? We have K-rations. Cigarettes? We have lots of cigarettes. What would they want?"

Kwan was withdrawing from him now, as the woman had

up on the hill. Baldwin knew why this time. In Kwan's eyes he was trying to bribe or buy Chinese like animals, with toys, or bait, or gifts.

"What would you do?" Baldwin asked Kwan unhappily.

Kwan shrugged his shoulders and repeated, "There is no way."

Yet it was important. It was important that there be a warning on the road below, a warning that the refugees might ignore, a warning however meaningless and perfunctory, a warning for his conscience's sake.

It was almost dusk; Michaelson had reported ready; and a full quarter of an hour had passed since the charges had been laid before Baldwin had completed his decoy at the bend below the blow.

It was a squalid thing when they had finished, put together of the leavings of the convoy. Two empty gasoline drums had been stretched across the road, a rope between them. They had poured the remaining gasoline of one of the drums into a hollow in the road and lit a fire, hoping curiosity and the warmth would hold a few wayfarers there. Two Chinese—a soldier and a student—had been mobilized by Kwan with cigarettes, a pack of hard candy, a pair of spare paratroop boots, and wordy exhortations to warn all comers to wait for ten minutes until the dangerous road above was fixed. The refugee stream was thinner, for the dark was now fading the sky, and those Chinese who had watched them with curiosity making their ramshackle barrier had lingered to warm their fingers about the gasoline burning in the puddle. When they had halted the flow, Baldwin, Kwan, and Collins hastily climbed back aboard the jeep, raced it back up to the overhang, gingerly picked their way through the bore-holes, followed the wire up, and found the others waiting for them at the detonator.

Baldwin worked fast now. He checked the leads of the detonating wire with the galvanometer and the needle flicked across the dial, flicked back, flicked up again—it was clean. The splices seemed good. He examined the bare leads, twisted the wires around the poles of the blasting machine and screwed them down tight. They were around the upper bend from the cut and they were far enough away.

"Nobody down below?" he asked of Michaelson.

"All present," said Michaelson.

"Give it the call," said Baldwin, and watched Michaelson cupping his hands.

Then the yell, "Fire in the hole!"

It was senseless, he knew. All the Americans who understood the call were here gathered about him, and any Chinese who might overhear it would never know or understand. Yet the call of warning comforted him.

"Fire in the hole!" yelled Michaelson again, and the echo of the first call came rolling back to join the sound of the second. Baldwin saw that all the men had, by habit, pressed themselves against the mountain wall for shelter, some crouching, some balling themselves up as small as they could get. But he was sure they were far enough away. The little wait passed and Michaelson called for the third and last time:

"Fire in the hole!" and stepped back and said, "That's it, Major."

In a caprice, Baldwin turned to Kwan and, gesturing to the machine with its long handle sticking up, invited him to plunge it off. Kwan shook his head, firmly. He did not want it. Baldwin stared at the Chinese for a moment and Kwan dropped his eyes, retreating into a blank veiling of expression. Grimly, Baldwin seized the hickory handles of the plungers and with a hard, smooth downthrust pressed, and paused, and heard the earth racket around him. The sound boomed dully, rumbling, echoing, cracking; and in a moment the earthwave brought a quivering and pounding under his feet.

He straightened slowly after the sound and waited, as if he expected to hear something more. It had gone. There was quiet. He found his hands still on the hickory handles and relaxed them, then ordered the wires detached. Then, slowly, he walked back around the bend to see what he had done. A cloud of dust still hung over the cut, but by its size and as it began to settle, Baldwin could see that the blow had come off perfectly. He walked straighter now, erect. No one had been with him on this and the road had been cut none the less—beautifully. The simultaneous charges in the road had all of them together clawed off the entire curve as the road bent one hundred fifty feet about the mountain, while the rock overhang had been hammered down from above at the moment when the two ditches had been erupting from below. From the outer edge of the torn road where he stood he could just barely see the outer edge of the road where it resumed the curve, and the elevation from where he stood down to where the road resumed was twenty or twenty-five feet and there was nothing but the gullied, raw face of the mountain in between where the overhang had been ripped off. Down below he could hear boulders and rocks still bumping and bouncing as they rumbled into the twilight depths. It would take a very agile young man to clutch the face of the mountain and scramble across the gap to where the road began again. It would take work, hard work, and seasoned engineering to put a vehicle trace across the gouge. It was a good job.

The others had followed after Baldwin to see, too. It had been their handiwork and he wanted them to see.

They stared out, down the valleys and gorges, over the hideous, dusk-shrouded contours of the bleak and desolate range.

"Fine job," said Baldwin to Michaelson. "Good work. This will hold them"—but quite loudly so that everyone could hear.

"Wish I had a picture," said Miller. "We haven't got a single picture of the whole summer's work, and when I talk about it, nobody's gonna believe me."

"Damn right they ain't gonna believe you," said Ballo. "I don't believe it myself."

"Sure makes a lot of work for the Slopeys, or the Japs, whichever tries to put it together again," said Niergaard.

"Hey, look at him, look at him," said Prince suddenly.

They looked. At the opposite lip of the gulch they had cut in the road a Chinese had appeared, lonesome and frail, an old man in a black, silk merchant's robe, staff in hand and leaning.

The old Chinese stared across the gap at the Americans, the Americans stared back.

"I'll betcha the old bastard's real mad," said Prince, and the rest laughed as if it were a joke.

It was the laughter that set off the old man. His face twisted with rage, and his thin voice dribbled across the gap full of hate and cursing. He was too old to be afraid. Someone laughed again, and the old man stooped, picked up a rock, and swinging his arm wildly, flung it at the Americans. The rock traced a pathetically feeble arc through the air, then rattled down into the gap not halfway across. The old man screeched at them again, and the Americans were silent.

"All right," said Baldwin, "that's enough. Let's get back to the trucks, and get out."

Abruptly, he turned away and started to walk back, leading them. A gust of an updraft followed him as he walked and, on the wind, faintly from below, he could hear the sound of —was it screaming or crying? Or just the whistle of the wind? He knew, still, that he had had to do it and that it had been even harder than the blow at Liuchow or pushing the truck off the road. But it had been the logical thing to do. Now it was cut. He had seen Loomis come back from mission, and talked to other bombers in Kunming when they had come back from a sweep over Hong Kong, or Hanoi, where the bombs had dropped on the wharves, or close to the wharves, or in the houses near the wharves. They did not talk about who or what might be dying because they had dropped their bombs below, never. But that was because when a bomb fell from the plane you could not hear people crying. He could hear. It was no imagination. There was something crying again, there, far below, it was a voice wailing on the updraft of the wind from the level below. But it had been absolutely necessary.

It was almost eight before they were all installed in the inn at Hochih.

Baldwin had forced the convoy ahead through the night after the blow, sensing the mountains still rising beneath his wheels, heading for the town that announced the border of Kweichou. The town, as it opened up, pale and ghostly, in the light of their headlights, was carpeted with people, as if the endless procession on reaching this high point had flung itself on the ground, exhausted from the climb.

At Hochih, Baldwin had turned matters over to Kwan, as he had the night before at the little village; and Kwan had sensed that there was something there in the shifting dark, as a swimmer does who reaches with his toe and finds a hummock of unstable sand off the shore on which to balance. The town was in dissolution as all the road was in dissolution, but Kwan had found troops and their division headquarters, an uneasy island in the rout. And the headquarters had a general whose soldiers still sluggishly took his command.

Baldwin had left negotiations to Kwan, and when Kwan emerged from the headquarters to report, Baldwin had confirmed the deal although he felt vaguely it must be a dirty deal. The general was a Ssuchuanese, said Kwan, who had offered to clear out half the inn in town in return for some gasoline for his own car, and Baldwin had paid with three jerry-cans full. It was Lewis' condition that urged him to do it, the thought of Lewis sick and needing shelter, and all of the men tired after the job they had done today; it was up to him to find them bed space. After the jerry-cans had been paid, the convoy had pushed its way through the frigid, dark streets, where people froze and moaned, and had come to a courtyard. After much shouting and violent noises inside, the Ssuchuanese general's platoon had cleared the cobbled courtyard for the trucks to enter, and emptied two rooms off the courtyard for the Americans to sleep in, and they had settled down.

Baldwin was now, in recapping the day, sorry for Lewis and aware that Lewis was some part, a growing part of his obligation, and stuffing down his distaste and annoyance with the man who should not, must not, be weak at a moment like this when there were things to do, Baldwin went to tend him.

Thin and gaunt, Lewis lay stretched in a bedroll by the charcoal fire, his brow hot to the touch.

Lewis stirred to the touch of Baldwin's hands, the dark eyes opening in recognition, and he murmured, "I'm sorry, Major—I guess I'm sick." Baldwin tried to cheer him up. He forced some broth, made from the powdered beef bouillon, down Lewis' throat, and followed that with three of the multipurpose bull pills they carried in their medicine kit, and spread another blanket over the sick man's bedroll. But there was no connection between Baldwin and Lewis, and Baldwin withdrew when Miller had come to sit down beside them. Miller, with his big, bulging body should have been a nurse, thought Baldwin, as he heard Miller's voice meaninglessly droning on to Lewis as he walked away . . .

". . . so there I am, laying there, sick as a dog, and my Aunt Mary she comes in and she says, I don't hold with these new doctors, what he's got is catarrh of the chest. You know she's old-fashioned, she thinks it's what you eat makes you sick, or gets you well. You know something . . . I go along with her. These new health foods . . ."

Baldwin looked around the room. He did not want to be with any of them; he did not want to be alone; and the smell of the pork-and-gravy that was cooking again nauseated him. He reeked of pork-and-gravy, and the thought came that even Spam would taste good when they got back to Kunming. The men were dog-tired, he could see by the droop in their bodies as they squatted, and as he continued to study the half-lit room he realized that there were only three people alert. In the corner, Collins and the woman were sitting on a bedroll and Kwan, taut and slim, was talking to them. Kwan's face had come out of the withdrawal again and was alive. Kwan was speaking slowly but with animation, very slowly, so that Collins, whose attention spoke in every line of his young face, could follow. The woman's face was warm, her eyes now slowly turning up to the Chinese officer, now slowly returning with fondness to the young American.

Baldwin watched them for a moment and his ear began to pick up the rhythm of the incomprehensible flow of Chinese as the Chinese officer spoke. It was a familiar rhythm, and then Baldwin placed it. Over and over again, in conferences with the Chinese at Kunming, Baldwin had noticed that the better Chinese officers all spoke as if they were talking to a classroom, with the didactic, sequenced logic of a teacher. More often than not the logic was madly unreasonable. But, in translation, it always seemed so spuriously good as they counted off their reasons—First, Second, Third, Fourth, and so on. That was it. Kwan was teaching; and Collins was a student, with the open, excited enthusiasm of a student on his glowing face, learning new things, wanting to learn. It was a wonderful face, Baldwin thought, and for a moment a wave of affection for the boy swelled up in him. Collins was the only possible person in the convoy who might know what it was about; Collins liked the Chinese, too, and could understand why it was important that they help hold the plateau. The others were cogs.

Something tugged at him from inside, and he quietly walked over to join the warmth of the group.

"Say," said Collins when Kwan's discourse broke for a minute, "he's telling me about these troops that cleared the inn here for us."

"What about them?" Baldwin asked.

"It's one of these Ssuchuan divisions. They've been on the road to the front down from Ssuchuan, since July . . . walking. It's a real, old-fashioned division, belonged to some joker whom the Generalissimo knocked off several years ago. Kwan's been explaining this campaign. It's fascinating. He has a theory that the war is a matter of four things: first, transportation; second, bastions; third, equipment; what's the fourth? —oh, yes, loyalty."

"First, second, third, fourth," said Baldwin dryly.

Collins looked at him uncomprehendingly and Baldwin said, "Go on, I want to hear how he works it out."

Collins resumed:

"Geographically, he says, the Generalissimo has to hold the

four bastions—the north pass at Sian, the Yangtze river front, the Salween front, and the big plateau here. Then, secondly, he has to be able to move stuff by foot to each of those fronts faster than the Japanese can go by rail or truck. And then the equipment has to come from America. But the most difficult, he says, is loyalty. He has to keep the discipline in order to hold their loyalty. He has to hold down the Communists in the north, the local people in Ssuchuan, and a few other warlords, too. Every time he can move a Ssuchuan division out of Ssuchuan, that also releases a Central division which doesn't have to balance it any more. So even if this Ssuchuan division doesn't fight the Japanese, it's released some Central troops somewhere to fight the Japanese, too."

Kwan had been listening as Collins spoke to Baldwin, following the two Americans' conversation by the woman's murmured translation. But the courtliness of his attitude had been wiped out. What could be said to a student, could not be said to an equal. And Baldwin was an equal.

Baldwin wanted to hear more, too. It was easing the tiredness in him to listen to this. He squatted on his heels and said:

"I hope I'm not interrupting. I'd like to hear this."

But he had interrupted. For when Kwan resumed, it was in a different vein, in more complicated Chinese, and the woman, breaking in, took up the translation.

"What the Americans should understand," she translated from Kwan, "is that Chinese believe that every man has an exact relationship to every other person. The son to his father. The wife to her husband. The teacher to his student. The soldier to his officer. The prince to his people. This is the harmony of the good society. When each person knows his duties above and below."

Kwan folded his hands behind his back and his little figure

was very tense and school-masterly again as he concluded:

"The trouble now is—no man has discipline any more. The relations have broken down. If no man knows his duties, there is no discipline. If there is no discipline, there is no loyalty. If there is no loyalty, there is no government. There will not be government until China is one again and each man knows his duty and relationship."

Baldwin pondered it. Like so much he had heard from the Chinese it all sounded so plausible, yet he knew it did not make sense. But the woman, unable to stay out of the conversation, was adding something of her own, to Collins, as if explaining a difficult passage to a child. Baldwin remembered that he had been furious with her only a few hours before on the road. Now the warmth of her voice made him wonder why he had been so angry.

"He's talking from Confucius, of course. It's what we call the Old Learning. But he's right," the woman said.

"What's right?" asked Baldwin, breaking in.

She turned to him and he could see that she had dismissed her anger with him, too, and he was pleased as she answered, conversationally, "The five relationships Kwan was talking about. What Confucius says is that there is something like a contract between all men. The prince has a contract with the people: they must serve him and he must protect and take care of them. The father must care for the family, and they must obey him. Each man must serve the one above him, and the one above must protect. If it dissolves, then you have anarchy. If the prince cannot protect the people, he is no longer the prince."

"Did Confucius say that? I thought he was one of the gods here," said Baldwin.

"No," she said gravely. "No, he isn't a god. He was a teacher, he taught government long before Europe had any government. There are temples to him, of course, and a lot of people worship him. But he's what we call a '*kuei.*' I don't know how to translate that. Sometimes it means a ghost, or a demon. But really it means a spirit, an idea. He's an idea, not a god."

"And there isn't any God, then?" Baldwin asked.

"Oh yes," she said. "Of course. I'm a Christian, but China has gods, real gods. I think Kuan-Yin is the closest we come to the Christian God though."

"What's Kuan-Yin," said Baldwin.

She paused, thinking, and Baldwin noticed the pensive melancholy of her dark eyes looking at him.

"Kuan-Yin is mercy, I guess," she finally replied. "She's the goddess who hears. She hears people crying or praying wherever they are, and she is the one who gives mercy. She is never angry, she forgives. When a sailor is going down at sea, he prays to Kuan-Yin; she is the only one who can hear him. When a child is dying, the mother prays to Kuan-Yin, she is the only one who can hear. She gives mercy. Like Mary, perhaps. When I was a child I used to get Mary and Kuan-Yin mixed up."

"Aren't those her temples," broke in Collins who had been listening intently, "the little temples you see by the roadside, with willows around them and the incense sticks burning, those lovely temples with the yellow and gold? But I thought she was only a goddess for Buddhists. Didn't she come from Buddhism?"

"Yes," said the woman, smiling now as at a bright child. "It's part of Buddhism, and what you're really saying is that Buddhism came to China from India. Religion is all mixed up in China. But Kuan-Yin is easy to understand, for she's mercy and mercy is something everyone understands. It's not really an idea that belongs to India, or to America, or to Christianity, or to anyone particularly."

"Why look," said Collins, snapping his fingers, almost exploding with excitement, "you're right! I never thought of it that way. It's wonderful, the more you talk things out, the more you find everything fits. You take mercy. That's what my father says and I never got it. My father is a politician. He used to run a district in Brooklyn. All kinds of people lived in the district, Italians, and Jews, and Irishmen, and Norwegians, and maybe we even had Chinese somewhere there too. He used to say that none of them could understand the courts, because the courts were justice and there were too many kinds of justice. Everybody comes with his own idea of justice, and too many lawyers have messed around with it. But mercy, he said, mercy belongs to everyone, even if they can't speak English, they have the same idea of mercy, they understand it. That's what makes politics go round, he used to say, mercy not justice. It's the same wherever they come from, fixing it with the judge if the boy gets in trouble, fixing it with the commissioner if a guy needs a license, fixing a visa for someone whose mother has tuberculosis and wants to come over here from Sicily. That's the Kuan-Yin stuff. My father would love Kuan-Yin, he'd be right at home here."

Kwan had silently withdrawn from the conversation as it glided into English and now she was alone with the two Americans. But somber again.

"No," she said very slowly. "No. China's too big. There are too many of us, too many Chinese for mercy. No one loves China except a few Chinese. Confucius is more important than Kuan-Yin here, that's what Colonel Kwan was trying to say. There has to be a government. First you have to have a government, then you have mercy afterwards."

She turned to Baldwin and was speaking to him, in the mood of easy friendship they had shared momentarily on the hilltop above the blow.

"There's no time for mercy any more, is there?"

But she was not accusing him now, she was offering to forget. He winced as he remembered the afternoon. There had truly been no time for mercy then, but he had not thought of it that way at the time.

He looked at her silently, the warm feeling swelling up in him ungovernably. She understood. He could say it easily.

"I'm sorry I lost my temper up there," he said. "I just had to do it, you understand don't you, there was nothing I could do about those people."

He noticed that she waited to answer and in the pause Collins gracefully unfolded himself from the bedroll where he had been sitting, rose and walked away, leaving them.

"I was angry, too," she said, offering apology in return, "but you knew they were there and what you were doing. I see it now. I was angry, I think, about you being an American. When you had to blow it up, you seemed just like everybody else dealing with Chinese. Everything's happened to us because of other people—the Japanese, or the Russians, or the English, or the French. We don't control ourselves any more. It should have been we who blew the road. I wouldn't have minded so much if Kwan had blown the road. I know you had to do it. But it was your being American. I'd thought I'd forgotten about being American. It's terrible to love America and be Chinese. I love America."

The last phrase had been spoken so softly, with such intimacy, that Baldwin did not know how to answer. He loved America, too. But he had never said so aloud in all his life. It was the most private part of his being—along with his hopes, and Helen, and daydreaming. It was why he felt so embarrassed when, at banquets, the Chinese toasted "China and America is friends."

Awkwardly, he tried to respond and, as he knew he would, he spoiled the mood.

"You said you were in America four years, Madame Hung?"

"Please don't call me Madame Hung," she replied.

"I thought that was the way you should say it," he said, even more awkwardly.

"It is. In Shanghai. All Chinese women call themselves in English Madame Wang, or Madame Chiang, or Madame Hung. But it sounds so French. And Mrs. Wang, or Mrs. Chiang, or Mrs. Hung, sounds worse—doesn't it? I was Nyi Su-Piao before I was married. I like Miss Nyi better than Madame Hung if you have to call me anything. Or Su-Piao, just Su-Piao, that's better."

She was smiling and he saw that beneath the tan of her face, the throat rose in a warm stalk of flawless skin, and that the eyes with the skin-fold over their corners were beautiful. The hair was glistening in the dim glow of the charcoal fire, and he wondered how she would look without the cotton-quilt robe.

"I had to do it," he heard himself saying. "I don't see what else I could have done."

The smile slowly left her face, and she said, "I know."

He got up to go, to get some of the pork-and-gravy which he knew he could now eat with returning appetite. It was only when he turned away, that he realized she had lightly touched his arm, gently, but firmly, forgiving him—and that she really did know.

FRIDAY

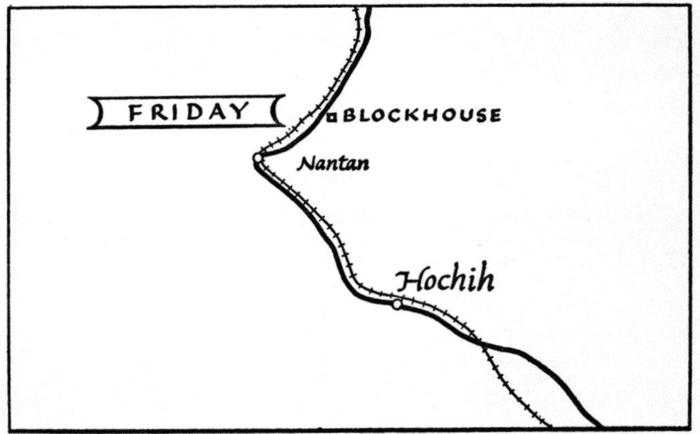

CHAPTER 6

Death in the Snow

THE NEXT MORNING, it was snowing.

Baldwin opened his eyes in the murk of the huge room and lay there, for how many minutes he could not tell, his muscles aching as he turned to comfort them, unable to pry himself out of the snug warmth of the bedroll. Gradually, as he stretched, and brought one arm out of the roll, then the other, and opened his eyes, he came awake, and was aware, first, that several of them were up and moving. Then, beyond that, gradually, his ears picked up a strange, muffled hush.

"How is it outside?" he asked Niergaard whom he now saw drinking coffee.

"Snowing," answered Niergaard. "I never knew it snowed in China, real snow. Like home."

Baldwin turned again, his muscles still sore with cramp, jackknifed his body out of the bedroll, and rose to his feet. It was snowing, and he had to add that to the rest of today and the decisions crowding to the surface of his mind. He did not want to talk until his mouth was clean, and he reached down for the canteen, swished the water through his lips, swallowed. He reached for his toothbrush, scrubbed vigorously, then tucked it back in his bedroll and looked around.

Miller and Niergaard had a charcoal fire going and, over the fire, water bubbled in a pot. They offered him coffee, looked at him inquiringly, to which he said only, "Let them sleep awhile," and went to the door still holding the coffee in his hand. The door opened directly on the dirt main street of the town, and as his mind oriented in the light, he grasped the design of the inn. It was a U-shaped building, and his men occupied one wing of the U. One door of the room in which he stood opened directly on the street, which he faced now; the side door of the room opened on the courtyard within the U where his trucks were parked. He stepped out, closed the door behind him, and noticed that the gates of the courtyard were timbered and barred and this pleased him, and he turned to look down the street.

Over the town, the snow was quietly falling in a somber white morning silence, muffling the faint noises of the crowded street, padding the sound of every movement. It was a dry snow and must have been falling half the night. But as it sifted down the street in the wind, it left the hard-frozen yellow ruts in the street bare; it caught on the curl of the tiles in little white ridgelines, designing ripples of white against the clay-red of the roofs. The town was choked as far through the snow-swirl as he could see—wheelbarrows, old rickshaws, a bicycle, pushwagons, Chinese army trucks, all tangled and snarled in the snow, here on the first ledge of the plateau. Some Chinese soldiers, he saw, were awake, working on a truck. As they stalked about the vehicle, he saw their legs naked in the cold, still ulcered with summer infections, their bare feet in straw sandals sinking into the powdery snow, and he shivered. He sipped the coffee he had brought with him, and heard the door open, then close behind him. Michaelson had come out to join him.

Michaelson wanted to speak to him, but was waiting for him to speak first. He was there, Baldwin knew, to get the day's plot but Baldwin did not have one yet. Yesterday had been solid, and he knew he had a grip on the unit, on the situation, on everything now; yesterday had been good. It had taken care of VICINITY HOCHIH, he thought. Or had it? And there remained the DUMPS AT TUSHAN, which were now a growingly-important thing. Should he go right on to Tushan, or check the local command and find what more could be done here? He knew the men must now be rising and were waiting for him to decide again—to prod them out of their frozen weariness on the way, or to hold them here. Or to galvanize them with release by telling them the job was done and they were going to cut and run for it. But where were the Japanese? Would they be following on a snow-day like this? Was it snowing all over the highland? Or was this a trick snow flurry in a mountain pocket? There was something else that bothered him. Lewis. He would have to see Lewis quickly and decide about that. Riding in the back of an open truck in the snow would be bad for Lewis. Lewis could use a day in the sack, beside a fire—it might be better than rushing him on to the hospital. If Baldwin could find out where the Japanese were, if they were far enough behind, they must certainly be on the other side of the sidehill-blow, then there was time to wait—time to investigate what to do here, time to let Lewis linger by the fire. Until it cleared? For the whole day? What?

"Good morning," he said finally to Michaelson as if he had just met him on an early morning commuter's trip into town.

"Morning," said Michaelson. "This snow sure messes up the job. I never knew it snowed in China."

"We're two thousand feet up now," said Baldwin, "and it's November. How are the men? Any problems?"

"They're getting up. What's the score for today?"

"I don't know yet," said Baldwin. "We've been traveling without information since the night before last. It depends on the Jap—and the snow. It must snow on the Jap just the way it does on us. We could use a day of rest. So could he. I'd like to let the men rest up today, if we can, because there may be a major job to do at the dumps at Tushan. And they must be tired from yesterday."

"Major, are you planning for us to do that job at Tushan?"

"We'll see when we get there." Baldwin resented Michaelson's questioning. But Michaelson pressed on.

"That's a Chinese job, isn't it, that's their work, isn't it?"

Baldwin was quiet, not knowing how to slap Michaelson down. He could have done it if the unit had been together. But alone, in front of the door, just the two of them—it was more difficult. Underneath, he knew he had been mistaken when he had said he didn't know what he was going to do today. In command, you had to know. Or give the impression that you did.

"Look, Major," said Michaelson, "that Lewis is real sick, we can't take care of him much longer. We've got to get him to a hospital soon."

"I know," said Baldwin. "But it isn't going to do him any good hauling him along these roads in the back of an open truck, with the snow coming down this way, either."

"What if the whole road snows up and we get stuck here?"

Michaelson was making a debate of it. Baldwin slowly angered. He would not let Michaelson push him.

"Listen, Mike," said Baldwin, "I'm running this outfit. And

I'm not deciding until I've found out where we stand. There's a division headquarters here and they ought to have some information. If the Japs are right on our heels, we'll move. Snow or no snow. If the Japs are stuck down in the valley, we may be able to sit here today and let Lewis and this unit warm up and get rested, and decide Tushan tomorrow. I'm just as worried about Lewis as you are, and a day in bed may give him just what he wants to lick it. Go in and make sure he's fixed up with what he needs now. As soon as I get some information, I'll let you know what the orders are."

He knew he had sounded waspish, wanted to regain the mood of yesterday, half-waited for Michaelson to challenge him again, but Michaelson went back inside.

Now he had to find the division headquarters, which meant he needed Kwan, and Collins for the translation.

He found Kwan, warming his fingers at the charcoal fire, standing, as usual, ramrod-stiff among the slouched and shuffling Americans. Kwan nodded at Baldwin's questions and suggested, through Collins, that they go looking for headquarters as soon as they had eaten.

When they emerged from the inn, the town had long since begun to rustle with the sluggish movements of morning. From wherever they had been sleeping, the refugees had begun to crawl out into the open street—out from the eaves, out from the hovels, out from under trucks, out from under the arcades and quivering mat-sheds that leaned against the adobe walls of the houses. And now they were trying to warm themselves. From somewhere in the city, from a warehouse, or an army store, they had taken straw and the white snow of the street was speckled with yellow plats of straw where people sat, or yellow-brown tufts of straw which they were burning to warm themselves. It was bitterly cold; he could see the plumes of vapor from their breath. Yet the jostle of the people gave the illusion of warmth about them as they walked.

At first, Baldwin was not aware of what he was seeing. It was the man lying across the wheelbarrow that the young fellow was pushing who first struck him as curious. The man was dressed in rags and his knees were bare halfway up the thighs, and he lay across the squealing, screeching wheelbarrow face down, his head, with its matted hair, jiggling and bobbing to the wheelbarrow's bumping. As the wheelbarrow drew nearer, the jiggling seemed stranger until it became obvious that it was not a man, but a body, unstrung and dead. After that, as they walked, Baldwin looked more closely and saw there were many dead. A woman lay stiff and grotesquely flat in the gutter of the street, her lips blue. The snow falling on her face was melting so that her cheeks dripped, but the snow remained white and dry on her eyes so that it seemed her eyes were wadded with cotton. Another woman, making the first loud sound of the morning, sat on a straw mat with a bundle swaddled in red silk that might have been a doll, but was a baby. The baby was dead, too, and the woman was keening, her voice reaching for the high shrill of the soprano-hysterical and then tumbling down through the octaves and rising again in a trill. The sound of madness in her voice hurried them past her and they had walked beyond her before Baldwin realized he should have done something or, at least, felt sorry.

They were all going to die, Baldwin slowly realized, all of them, or most of them, and he was outside it, he could not feel it because he had trucks, food, men, gasoline back there at the inn compound. Some of the bodies were naked, he could see, and he reasoned, of course, why leave clothes on a dead body when people are freezing, of course. He noticed a man with a child's sweater buttoned around his head like a shawl, to keep his ears from freezing, and others had towels, or undergarments, or fur wrapped around their heads, and they moved, when they did move, with a gentle stagger through the street, as creatures in a herd moved. Some sat on their straw, and he saw a woman nursing a baby from a flat brown breast that hung like a flap of skin bared against the cold; the woman cried as she nursed, putting the nipple back in the mouth when the child turned away to howl. Another woman sat in the snow, a man's head in her lap, her hands slowly stroking his cheeks, back and forth, caressing them, soothing them, pressing them as if she were in the privacy of her bedroom; and two little boys sat beside her, their eyes glistening, their necks, Baldwin noticed, shrunken beneath the skull.

Baldwin, Kwan, and Collins walked almost on tiptoe, not speaking to each other, not wanting to draw attention by talking, knowing they were here, in the presence of death, intruding on last intimacies which they should not be seeing.

The three walked slowly, for they did not want to appear to be hurrying, or people might follow them; we are too fat, thought Baldwin, seeing himself through the eyes of the people of Hochih as obscene. He asked Kwan how far it was to the divisional headquarters and Kwan said it was just beyond those people there, where the three trucks were. The people there, where Kwan pointed, were huddled and growling animal-like in lust about something big that lay on the ground. As the three drew abreast they saw it was the carcass of a horse and the knot of refugees were chipping away at it with knives. The skin had already been taken off and now the layers of white gristle and cherry-red flesh were being stripped away, layer by layer, as if it were a huge misshapen onion that the busy, dirty fingers were peeling. The skeleton of a mule, likewise stripped, lay further down the road, its entrails discarded, its eyes gouged out, its skeleton protruding.

Over all and everything fell the snow, muffling the sounds through which, constantly, Baldwin could hear or thought he could hear the soft sounds of crying and moaning.

Two sentries at the divisional headquarters passed Kwan and the two Americans through to an inner room, where they met the general.

It was like no headquarters Baldwin had ever seen before, even in China. It was dirty, which was rare, he knew, in a Chinese headquarters, and the cadaverous, melancholy man who was introduced to them scarcely rose from his chair in the courtesy greeting. Scrawny, his face yellower than any man Baldwin had ever seen, the general offered them tea with hands that shook and quivered. The room stank—of garlic and body odor and something sticky-sweet that seemed to be either burned chocolate or coffee. Baldwin sniffed as they sat down and saw Collins sniffing, too. Collins leaned toward him and said, "Opium." It was the first time Baldwin had smelled opium. His gorge rose, then he bound himself to the business at hand.

The inevitable, slow questioning followed the tea—from Baldwin through Collins through Kwan to the general. Then the long pause before the general started his answer on the long return. This was the general who had traded them rooms at the inn last night in return for the gasoline for his car. He was neither hostile nor friendly in any way that Baldwin could make out. He simply did not care, and Baldwin remembered last night's conversation, and Kwan's contempt for this Ssuchuan division.

He was waiting, said the general, as the conversation wound back and forth, for information. He had no information. No one told him anything. His information came by jeep courier, or by horse, from Tushan where the Central Army had a headquarters and no one had come since yesterday. No radio. No telephone. Wires cut.

Yesterday the general had been told that Ishan was fallen to the Japanese; or was on the point of falling. The general pulled out an old-fashioned Chinese map with its ink lines of elevation and pointed. A dirty fingernail pointed out several Chinese characters on the map and said, "Liuchow." Then, again pointed and said, "Ishan."

Baldwin tried to assemble the scraps of meager information into a pattern. They did not help. If the Japanese were at Ishan, then they had come fifty miles from Liuchow. The Japs had, therefore, already crossed the bridge Baldwin had futilely blown on Wednesday. But they could not have passed the road-cut he had made yesterday. Not in any force. The Jap was coming—but to seize and occupy, or to raid and reconnoiter?

The general went on. So, last night, he had sent his own jeep to Tushan to ask for instructions and find out what was happening. And he hoped his courier would be back early this morning. By noontime, the general corrected himself. Certainly by two o'clock. Or before dark. Maybe soon.

The general went back to the map, sweeping both hands back and forth over it, sullenly, as if he were personally aggravated. There were two Japanese divisions, the Third and the Thirteenth, said the general. The Third was the division coming up the road. The general knew about it. But where was the Thirteenth that was circling in a sweep through the hills? The Third could not get to Hochih up the road for another two days, thought the general. Or maybe they could. But what about the Japanese Thirteenth? Where was it? What was he supposed to do? Should he wait? The Japanese would certainly take Hochih. But when?

Baldwin had lost control of the conversation now, and Collins, too, was being left behind by the flow of Chinese between Kwan and the Ssuchuanese. For the Ssuchuanese was now openly complaining to Kwan. Kwan was Central Army. And it was the Central Army, Baldwin remembered from the night before, which had tricked this division out of the warm, fertile basin of Ssuchuan. It was Central which had liquidated the warlord to whom this division belonged and sent the division tramping over the hills for all these months to arrive here, nowhere, in the merciless cold of the Kweichou border, in the torrent of retreat, to become the last organized unit between the barrier and the enemy.

Not understanding, Baldwin could look closely at the Ssuchuanese. The sallow, drawn face of the man had the furtive, hunted look of a rabbit. The man was lost. Something had been drained from him which command should have, which Colonel Li had had yesterday, which Kwan had, which an officer has. His vitality was gone. He had lost or never had the essential purpose of the warrior which was to impose his will on other people, making them submit to what his command and mind dictated. The whine, the querulousness, was now rising in the Ssuchuanese voice.

Somewhere behind, far behind, said the general, he knew between Kweiyang and Tushan, the Central Army was making a new line. They were bringing new Central troops from the Chinese army in Burma by air up into Kweichou to make a new line—the American planes were bringing them. The Central troops would have a line and they would have American guns. But they would leave him here until it was too late. Or they would tell him to go into guerrilla action. Out of the stumbling heaviness of the opium-blown sloth, an anger began to come alive in the Ssuchuanese. How could he go to guerrilla action? There was no food in the mountains. The people in the mountains hated men from Ssuchuan. His Ssuchuan men did not even speak the same tongue as the mountain people. How could they get food? Where would they get ammunition? What could they do here? Yet he could not go back until he got orders or until the Japanese came.

As Baldwin followed the rambling, diffusive sing-song of the Ssuchuanese, he could see the man was useless, to be discarded from any calculation. There was no point in spinning out this conversation. This general could offer neither advice, nor strength, nor help; nothing but whatever scrap of information might be sent on to him from Tushan this afternoon. Baldwin decided to break it up, and, using Collins, breaking in on one of the Ssuchuanese's sentences, he said:

"Tell him we'll check back with him about two to see if he has any fresh information on the Japs from Tushan headquarters," and then realizing he wanted at least the appearance of friendship and the hope of cooperation for the rest of the day, he added, "Ask him if there's anything we can do to help him?"

"This afternoon," said the Ssuchuanese, "this afternoon perhaps I will know. I will know if they do not forget me. But they will forget. Come back."

Then, in an afterthought:

"If the Americans want some soldiers to help them, I can give some soldiers. Have the Americans any more gasoline they do not want?"

It was another trade, and Baldwin did not want it.

"No," he said, "we have just enough gasoline for ourselves."

"Or wrist watches?" said the general, "or fountain pens? Or tires?"

Kwan snarled in exasperation and anger; and the general's face relaxed into its melancholy, half-childish expression of hurt as he accompanied them back to the door.

"He is no use. He is finished," said Kwan as they walked back.

"Yes," said Baldwin, "he is finished."

"Not all Chinese soldiers are like that," said Kwan, "only now at the end of the war, we must use men like these. They are warlord soldiers for fighting warlord wars, or for fighting peasants. They are not soldiers for fighting big wars. But we had soldiers for fighting big wars once, at Shanghai. And our soldiers fight a big war for you Americans in Burma. We will have good soldiers again, but first we must have a government, without a government soldiers cannot fight. This is what the Generalissimo is trying to do, to make a government so the soldiers can fight. Maybe he is too late, maybe he does not know. But these soldiers here do not belong to him. They do not belong to anybody. That is why they cannot fight."

Michaelson met them at the inn.

"Lewis is real sick," he said, "he's boiling."

"Oh," said Baldwin. For a full day the condition of Lewis had been nagging at him under all the decisions he had had to make, and now the death outside reminded him that life was frail, and Lewis was sick and he was responsible.

"I'll take a look at him," he said, and then, "Tell the men to knock off this morning. We have to lay over until this afternoon to find out where the Jap is. Let them sack out if they want to, they can all use some rest. But tell them to stay in the inn, or in the courtyard. I don't want them out in that street until we leave. If they get restless, let's make sure the trucks are ready for this afternoon. Put them to work on the engines."

He walked over to Lewis. In the dark room, cold yet stuffy with the smell of the bodies that had slept in it, stale with the air breathed over and over through the night, Lewis lay quietly in a bedroll, and Su-Piao sat beside him on the *k'ang*, the high, brick, Chinese bed-rest. She was dipping a face rag in a bowl of steaming water in her lap and mopping Lewis' face. Baldwin's own flesh tingled as he watched; he sensed his eye muscles strain and the jaw muscles of his face tighten, aching for fingers to stroke and soothe them. The touch of hand to flesh was a language in itself, he thought. The woman stroking her dying husband's face in the street—she could do no more, but she had been speaking. The children holding hands in the cold outside, they were speaking. He wished her hands could touch him. Then he spoke to Lewis.

"Lewis?" he said, "Lewis, how are you?"

Lewis barely stirred. From his bedroll came the high-pitched voice, weak and soft.

"I don't know, Major, I don't feel good."

"What's the matter, Lewis—your stomach? Or your head? Is it like malaria?"

"I don't know, Major, but I feel weak all over, just . . . just, I feel as if I can't lift my head. I feel shivery like malaria—but it's different this time. My bones ache. And this fever, it doesn't come and go the way malaria does. It just stays and stays and I feel lousy. I want a drink of milk, cold milk . . . but I'm shivery, too."

Su-Piao shifted on the *k'ang* beside Lewis and said, "I'll get some water."

"When are we going to get some place, Major," asked Lewis.

"In a day or so, Lewis, maybe tomorrow we'll be in Kweiyang. We're laying over here this morning until we find out where the Japs are. We may stay all day and give you a chance to get some rest under a roof."

"If you're laying over just because of me, Major, I'd rather get out of here. I'm not going to get better until we get out."

With difficulty Baldwin suppressed his indignation.

"We'll get you to Kweiyang, Lewis, don't worry," he said. "We have to find out where the Jap is before we can make the next move. It's snowing today and we can't make any time. We might get stuck on the road. Spending a night on the road in the snow would be bad for you. You take it easy, now, try to sleep. . . ." It was like talking to a child. But the man was sick.

"I never knew it snowed in China," mumbled Lewis.

Su-Piao was back with a canteen cup of water.

"Yes, it does," said Baldwin, "real snow. I'll get some aspirins for you to take with the water. It'll be good for the fever."

Su-Piao lifted Lewis' head, and let him sip the water. She fed him several aspirins, gave him another sip, and let him rest once more.

Baldwin waited for her to get up, then followed her to the bench on which she sat down, and sat beside her.

"I think he has typhus," she said.

"Typhus? That's bad, isn't it? What makes you think so?"

"His fever. The way it stays steady. His bones burning, the fact he was worn out. That's when typhus comes. We've lost more soldiers to typhus than to the Japanese. It usually comes when a man is completely exhausted. A louse bites him some night as he sleeps, and he's infected; then, three or four days later his fever starts to burn. I don't know whether anything helps. Maybe penicillin would. We've never tried that. Have you any penicillin with you?"

"We've got some capsules in the kit, somewhere."

"But no syringe, nothing to inject it with, no ampoule?"

"No."

"Oral penicillin doesn't do any good, I read somewhere; I think it should be given intravenously."

"You know a lot about this, don't you?"

"I should. I've worked in hospitals quite a bit."

"Hospitals?"

"Officers' wives look after hospitals in our army, at the war fronts, away from Chungking. It's fashionable. Even the Generalissimo's wife is supposed to look after hospitals in Chungking. And T'ung-ling—my husband—tried hard to make our hospital a good one."

"Where did you learn about them?"

"Only what I learned at the Red Cross, in the beginning, at Shanghai. We lived in the French concession there and when the Japanese began shelling the Chinese city, we were furious. All my friends joined the Red Cross and we made bandages and took first-aid courses. You could stand on the roof of our apartment house and look out at the fighting in the Chinese city, and see the Japanese shelling the trenches and the houses. But the French concession was so safe, the Japs respected foreign flags then, that some of us couldn't stand it. We used to sneak out of the concession and go to the hospitals in the Chinese city, and try to help the wounded. We were all so patriotic then."

"I remember that Shanghai fight," said Baldwin. "That was seven years ago, wasn't it? The papers were full of it back home."

"We used to get the American papers and magazines in Shanghai, too, and they said we were wonderful. It all seemed so romantic in pictures. But they used to bring the soldiers into the hospitals with their feet rotting from the trench water in Chapei. They'd stay in the hospital for two days and their feet would heal—or they'd die. There were men with arms torn off, men with scalps ripped off, and dysentery and typhus.

In those days, we still had medicines, not penicillin of course, that was back in 1937, but we had the sulfa drugs, they were new then, do you remember?"

"Yes," said Baldwin, remembering how long ago sulfa drugs seemed, and how old this war must be for her which started in 1937. But she was remembering, too.

"Then, when T'ung-ling and I got married, I went off with his unit in the retreat, and his war front settled in Hunan, and we officers' wives tried to help at the hospitals. The headquarters' hospital was mostly for the rear troops; the soldiers who got back from the front were starvation cases, the wounded died on the way. And the little hospitals near the front. Some of them had herb doctors, with their thousand-year-old ideas. You know—fever comes from hot winds in the belly, so eat cold food. Stomach ache or cramps are bad winds, so eat belch medicine; and opium syrup for everything. And for sore throats, eat rotting bean curd, moldy bean curd. The funny thing was that a lot of their medicines worked. The moldy bean curd, for example. I've heard some of our doctors say we discovered penicillin first because penicillin is only a mold, too. We didn't argue with them, because we didn't have any penicillin anyway, only enough for the staff officers and their families. Look, if you have some of these oral penicillin capsules, why don't we try them on Lewis anyway. It might help."

Baldwin got up, went out to the trucks, rummaged around in the medical kit until he found the flask of capsules. Then he hoisted a case of mountain rations on his shoulder for investigation and came back in. When he had given Lewis two of the capsules, he set the case of rations down before Su-Piao and sat down beside her. There was nothing to do but wait, and it was better to be asking questions of her, than be with the men who would be asking questions of him.

He slit the case of rations open with a long knife and began to pull out the packages.

"There may be something in here we can prepare for him that'll make him feel better," said Baldwin, "this is the army's top field ration."

They began to unpack the carton, pulling the containers out one by one—the meat cans, the butter cans, the cereals, the pudding cans, the sourballs, cheese, sugar packets, cigarettes. He sensed that she was smiling and he looked at her. It was an American smile on her face, almost girlish. He had never heard her giggle the Chinese giggle, he realized. That's what makes them different from us, he told himself—the giggle, or the knee jiggling, or hysterics when they get angry, or the frozen face when they withdraw from you. She was American.

"Something funny?" he asked.

"No," she said, and then, "Well, yes. It is fun to look at these again. It's been so long. I grew up on American food even before I went to America. Our family comes from up north, in Anhui, where we have land, but father owned these apartment houses in the French concession, in Shanghai, where I was born. Father was so proud of his American friends and his American house. We had Americans at home visiting all the time—insurance people, banking people, shipping people. We had bacon and eggs in the morning, and took our milk from the American dairy in Shanghai. We had Christmas with the turkey, and Thanksgiving with the cranberry sauce. My father was so Americanized that he was hurt when the American consul wouldn't invite him to the Fourth of July party for Americans. He thought the consul was being anti-Chinese. Oh, see!" she ended abruptly.

In the carton at her knees she had found a brown waxed box.

"Mashed potatoes," she said.

"Dehydrated mashed potatoes," Baldwin pointed out. "Almost all this stuff is dehydrated. If you open it you'll find it looks like white soap chips, and when you put water in it, it tastes like dust."

But she was already playing house. She had piled several little tinfoil envelopes by her side.

"Here's chicken broth, and here's beef broth," she said. "They're both good for him. And then there's this can of dehydrated cheese, and the butter and the potato flakes. We can mash the potatoes with the cheese and butter—it should taste fine. But first we'll give him some broth."

"Fine," said Baldwin, "you take over. You can be Florence Nightingale. But let's wait until about noon when everyone eats. If we have to leave after eating, that way they'll all have had at least one hot meal today."

He looked across the room. Several of the men were playing red-dog on the floor, two were dozing. Miller was doing nothing.

"Miller," he called, and Miller looked at him in response.

"Miller, we'll eat about noontime. Get another carton of rations off the trucks and fix up something hot and good for everybody while there's time. And then give a hand to Madame Hung, here; she's going to make something special for Lewis."

"O.K.," said Miller, and then shifted his beefy body about uneasily. "Say, Major, that Lewis, are we gonna get a doctor for him? Do you think there's a doctor here in this joint?"

"No," said Baldwin, "no doctor closer than Kweiyang, but we'll take care of him." They were more than a hundred miles from a doctor, from clean beds, medicine, from someone who knew. Baldwin had never been so far from a doctor in his life. Being so far from a doctor made him feel naked. But they had to wait.

Then, because it was Miller, the agreeable, he was talking to, he offered a part explanation.

"That's why we're laying over here today, to keep him out of the cold and the snow. If we put Lewis on the back of one of these trucks in the snow, he'd have a bad time of it."

"Yeah," said Miller, "that's right, the snow would give him a bad time. Then, when it stops, we can go right on through, can't we?"

Even Miller was pushing him on. They were all pushing him on, to get in to Kweiyang and safety. But he knew he must not be pushed now, he must make the decision when he knew where he was. And tomorrow was Tushan, where the big one was. For some reason, he did not want to do Tushan today.

"We'll see how Lewis is when the snow stops," he said firmly, knowing that Miller would carry the thought back to the other men. It was best to pin the delay on Lewis.

They had eaten lunch and it was now almost one o'clock. The smell of food mixed with the smell of bodies, but no one noticed. Though their bellies were full and heavy, a nervous indolence twitched them all, some pacing, some talking, Michaelson and Collins needling each other, the inaction scratching at all of them. Baldwin felt he should do something, and ordered the room policed. Idly, they fell to, piling the leftover food, the packages of hard-biscuit, the little envelopes of sugar, the open tins of butter, the unopened cereals and jam back into the big cartons which were now overspilling in disorder.

Outside, finally, the snow was ending. Every now and then someone would open the door to peer out, leaving the door open for the welcome burst of fresh air which cut the heavy stuffiness of the room, then slamming it shut when the cold began to flood in, overwhelming the little heat from the charcoal fires. The last time the door had been opened, there was no doubt but that the snow was ending—it fluttered down in occasional gusts, but it was thin, and in the gusts it was difficult to tell whether the snow was falling from the sky or being lifted from the powder drifts in the street. The snow was no longer much reason for lingering, and Baldwin felt it was time to check the Ssuchuanese headquarters again. They were only seventy miles from Tushan and they ought to push on—at least part way.

He saw Kwan talking to Su-Piao and approached them.

"Will you ask him," he said to Su-Piao, "if he can go back to that divisional headquarters and see if their courier has arrived yet? Or any other word from Tushan. We'll be pushing on soon anyway, but I want to know what the word is."

Kwan was back within the hour, long before Baldwin expected him. He was out of breath, holding on to his dignity with an effort.

"Go back," said Kwan, "now everyone goes back. The courier says the army at Tushan wants everyone to go back because the Japanese are coming."

"When?" said Baldwin.

"They do not know. But the army has decided the Japanese will take Hochih. The Japanese Third Division moved up the road last night, with cavalry. The Japanese Thirteenth Division is north of the road and will start for Hochih soon."

"Both divisions? Two whole Japanese divisions?" Baldwin could not conceive of two divisions moving so quickly up these passes, moving from the summer of the lowlands to the winter here with no transition. Unless they had planned, really, to seize the highlands. Did they?

"This general does not know how many. He does not know much. The army has told him only they will not fight for Hochih, that he should go back quickly to Tushan. This general will go quickly, before the army changes its meaning and makes him stay and fight guerrilla battles. This general does not want to fight. He will go first himself, today, in his few trucks, and his soldiers will walk after him, slowly."

"And Tushan?" said Baldwin.

"Tushan is only seventy miles away, there are Central troops in Tushan. But they will go back, too. They will meet the new divisions from Burma near Tuyun, in the hills between Kweiyang and Tushan. They will make a new front there."

"Will the headquarters still be there when we get to Tushan?"

"I do not know, the general here does not know. The army at Tushan would not tell such a thing to this general. They do not trust him."

Baldwin let the information roll around in his mind. It was not clear. Nothing had been clear since they left Liuchow. He was tired of making up his mind in a fog. He did not know how fresh the general's information was. In an army without radio or telephone, dependent on couriers, the information might be a day old. Or it might be false, the Central Government might be trapping the Ssuchuan general.

It was a madness, thought Baldwin, there were several wars going on at once here. There were the Ssuchuan troops in this town fighting in some past century, on foot, with rifles thirty years old, and old French pack howitzers, their commander an opium sot, dependent on messenger-couriers, almost as antique as General Grant's army, except that it was worse because the Ssuchuanese distrusted their command, their government, and one another.

Then there were the Japanese. Who had begun the war with an air force, a navy, a mechanized army, electronics. And outward on the Pacific they still faced the Americans with air force, navy, radar, radio, guns, and were being punished and crushed. So that here they were turning inward on Asia in an older kind of war, moving on foot, on horse, like Jeb Stuart's calvalry, punishing China because America was strangling Japan. And there would be more people dying on this one road, of hunger, of cold, and sickness, than would die in all the battles of the Pacific. This was the old-fashioned killing, the dirty bloodless killing of women and children and refugees, the old-fashioned war in which he was trapped.

And then, ahead of him somewhere, if the general's rumor were true, reaching around the awkward distances of India, of Burma, of the Hump and the Himalayas, the U.S. Air Force was ferrying fresh Chinese troops into battle, Chinese troops of a different kind. Chinese troops that the Americans had trained and brought from the last century into this, new units who had learned to fight with American planes, radios, artillery, medicine. Somewhere up ahead, the new armies that Americans were building up for China would meet the dwindling ferocity of the old Japanese horse cavalry. And as Japanese energy ran down, as the Jap capacity to supply ran out, they would come to a deadlock with the new troops and the plateau would be safe.

But in-between was where he was right now, seeing everything come apart. And he could sway it a little bit. The Ssuchuanese general would be out by night and, of course, the Ssuchuanese general would not burn Hochih as he left. Hochih *should* be burned so that the Jap cavalry could not shelter in it. It could be flamed, not easily now that the snow had wet it, but flamed nonetheless. But to flame it was a Chinese job. To flame it, meant leaving the dying in the snow to die more quickly, leaving the other refugees still trekking up to the highlands to find no shelter. Casually Baldwin wondered whether he was responsible for burning it, and the thought ended: The hell with it. He would get out fast, the way the Ssuchuanese general was going to get out. He would get on to Tushan, close on the rear, leave the idiot war to the Chinese, letting them wreck their own country in their own way; he was responsible only for the road; and possibly for Tushan if the headquarters there wanted him to be.

"Michaelson!" he yelled.

Michaelson came.

"We're moving now," he said. "Snow's over. The Japanese are coming. We're getting out. Are the trucks ready?"

"That Lewis job, she won't start. We've worked on her all morning, but she's worse than she was yesterday. She's dead."

"The hell with it. Leave it," said Baldwin. "Off-load what gear you can into the other trucks. The demolition chests and the auxiliary motor. Dump what you have to, to make room. Fix Lewis up comfortably in the back of your truck. Get him as many blankets as you can dig up."

They moved fast. Soon he could hear the big six-by-sixes churning their motors. The men came in one by one to get their bedrolls, moving with force and vigor, for the morning's rest had helped them. Even Baldwin felt better, now that he had decided. It was almost over. Then Collins was approaching him, and Baldwin smiled because he knew that Collins was with him.

"We're going on to Tushan," said Baldwin, "and the dumps. There's no point in wrecking this town; if the Chinese want to burn it, they'll have to do it themselves."

"I always hate this part of it," said Collins, unhurriedly, "pulling out and leaving them behind. I know we can't take any of them with us. I know. But this morning, those kids, it was worse than anything I've seen all summer. It's like giving these people over to death. I wonder what they think of when they see us go."

"I know," said Baldwin, realizing that it was because of the people in the street, not because he was tired, that he did not want to burn it.

"Say," said Collins, nudging the overflowing food cartons on the floor with his boot, "are we going to load these, too?"

"Why?" asked Baldwin.

"I was just thinking," said Collins, "we have enough rations in the trucks for a week or more. And the jokers in the street are starving. We'll probably dump this stuff on the way, anyway. How about distributing it to them out there?"

Baldwin suddenly knew that Collins was suggesting expiation. The boy shifted from the slick to the soft, from the shrewd to the emotional, so easily; but there was a quality in him that came out like this. He was suggesting expiation for the people killed at the blow, for the old man left at the gap, for the leper at Liuchow, for being well fed and on wheels while the people they had seen in the cold, crowded streets this morning would remain to die. The food would save few, there was so little. But it might save one or two. The biscuits, and butter and cereals and condensed milk might nourish a few bellies for the night, so they could die farther up the road. But not on his conscience.

"O.K.," he said, "but don't waste any time."

Awkwardly, Collins hoisted one carton on his shoulder and moved out, through the door that opened on the street. Miller came in to rouse Lewis on the *k'ang*. Lewis rose, motioned to his bedroll, which Miller shouldered, then staggered after Miller to the trucks, through the side door that opened on the courtyard. Collins returned for the second carton, and left, and the room was empty except for Baldwin and Su-Piao.

"Where is he going with that?" she asked sharply.

"We're leaving it for the refugees," said Baldwin, knowing she would approve, and glad that Collins had suggested it.

Instead, her face frowned, and she said sharply:

"Oh, no! Call him back."

The alarm in her voice startled him.

"Why?" he asked.

"It's dangerous," she said. "Oh don't!"

He realized as soon as she spoke that there *was* danger. But everything was dangerous. It was a kindness that Collins was trying to do; he wished Collins were here to explain it, he could not say the words of kindness the way Collins might.

"What's dangerous?" he said in a cold voice, his face hardening. "Giving food away? We can't eat it." He groped and came up with a thought. "You were talking about Kwan-Yin last night. Mercy. We can burn the town, or leave them food. It's all the same. But I want to leave them food."

She angered him. She was Chinese, these were her people. She should approve; but she said, "Refugees are dangerous. You don't understand China. They're starving. If we leave the food in here, they can loot the place as soon as we've gone. Oh, please, stop him!"

Outside, muffled by the door, he heard a sudden noise rise, a murmur and growling, punctuated by yells, then shrieking and a howling. Baldwin rushed to the side door and looked at the courtyard. The Americans were there, he noticed, standing alertly, listening to the tumult beyond the barred gates of the inn.

"Where's Collins?" yelled Baldwin.

"Ain't he in there with you?" asked Ballo.

"Where is he?"

Outside, the din and shouting grew.

Baldwin unslung the carbine from his shoulder, snapped the safety.

"Get your carbines," he shouted. "Open those gates."

As the timbered gates swung slowly inwards, parting to show

what lay outdoors, it was as if a curtain rose on a stage. In the foreground, a mass of bodies squirmed and twisted in a tangle of forms out of which legs kicked away in the air, arms rose and fell, shoulders thrust up and crumpled again under more bodies that flung themselves on top of the growing mound. From out of the pile, a little boy was running away, dancing, holding a can of butter in his hand. A man shot out a claw, snatched the butter from him and ran off down the street faster than the boy could chase. On top of the pile now, a woman in a smeared pink dressing gown stamped with her heels in the small of someone else's back, trying to dig down through the mass of bodies to the cartons that lay underneath. From down the street came others, the fast-of-foot running, the slow and tired hobbling. Food!

Baldwin leveled the carbine over their heads and fired into the air. Michaelson and Prince were beside him and he was ordering, "Over their heads, over their heads, into the air, Collins is underneath, over their heads." And they were volleying. A shriek sliced through the growling of voices and Baldwin heard Michaelson grunting, "Winged one!" Then, dissolving, the tangle began to unsnarl itself, the edges unraveling, the animals becoming people, standing up, running away, leaving a space of snow and mud, littered with torn cardboard, packages, tins and strewn food.

And in the blank and littered filth of gray and white, lay Collins. Collins did not move. In one outstretched hand a can slowly dropped from his fingers and Baldwin saw it was a can of sardines. Baldwin stared at the body, his stunned mind slowly grasping that the neck of the boy twisted awkwardly from his shoulders and the round of his head seemed oddly shaped.

"Cover me," he said hoarsely to Michaelson, and walked across the snow, and stooped. There was a rock beside the head, and the light-brown hair was matted with blood, and the rock with which the head had been bashed in was covered with blood, too. Baldwin wanted to touch the head, to smooth the wound; he noticed that Collins' cheeks were shaved, the only man who shaved, he wanted to touch them, too. But he could not, it was over. Like that.

Through the quivering of rage in his body, through the fear, through the numbness as he tried to absorb what was happening, as his mind spun, Baldwin found himself trying to reason with the hate that rose in him. It was because they were hungry. It was because Collins was at the bottom. It wasn't because Collins was American. Whoever held the rock and was hammering his way through other Chinese to the food had not meant to kill an American because he was American. He had only meant to eat, even if it meant killing. But trying to be fair made no difference. They had killed Collins because they were beasts. He hated them because he had not been able to keep the vital, fragile distance between his men and the refugees, because you could not be kind to them.

He walked back to the courtyard gates, very slowly, not wanting to scuttle back in the sight of the mob or of his men. Michaelson and Prince were still there, facing out with their guns, covering him; behind on the jeep's hood, stood Ballo with his gun.

"I want to bring him in," said Baldwin. "Niergaard and Miller, get out there and carry him in. We're covering."

Baldwin walked out with Niergaard and Miller as they lifted the body and brought it back to the courtyard. And as he walked back, he became aware that they were still there, behind him, hungry, growling and rumbling to get back at the food which now, as the cartons had ruptured, lay strewn in the snow.

Su-Piao knelt, touching Collins' lips with her fingers, lifted the wrist, felt for the pulse, stood crouched for a moment, then shook her head.

"Oh the frigging Chinese," said Miller almost to himself. "Oh the bastards."

Kwan spoke softly in Chinese and Su-Piao frowned.

"What did he say?" asked Baldwin, hoping that some magic phrase in Chinese had passed between them that could erase what had just happened.

"He says, let us go now quickly. The shots will bring some of the soldiers here. He says the soldiers have guns and they are as hungry as the refugees. If they know we have food here, we cannot stop them. If we shoot, they will shoot back. He says go now, quickly."

But Baldwin was already moving the convoy into formation, his orders snapping flatly, efficiently, coming off the top of his mind while somewhere the same mind groped to accept what had happened, and what had gone wrong, and the ache was momentarily pushed down underneath, the ache he knew would return.

The jeep first, he ordered, impersonal and brisk, Michaelson riding the hood to fire cover. Miller on the second truck, with Lewis in the blankets behind. Ballo next. Niergaard driving the last truck, carrying Collins' body, with Prince to fall back from the gate and ride the back firing rear-cover.

They were ready to roll now. Baldwin lowered the flat windshield of the jeep flush with the hood. It gave a clearer field of sight if he had to shoot, and no glass to splinter if the crowd threw rocks.

Baldwin moved behind the wheel of the jeep, noticed and was angry that Kwan and Su-Piao were already in place without being asked, called to Prince still standing at the gate, with Michaelson, holding the crowd at its distance with their carbines.

"Prince!" Baldwin called from the jeep as his motor raced and the other trucks sounded behind him. "Fall back now. Tell every man to keep the trucks inched in close. No separations. If one of these Chinese edges in between, keep going. Don't stop. You get on Niergaard's truck, in the back. You fire rear-cover. When you're ready to go back there, fire two shots, and we take off. Mike," he continued, yelling to the burly back that stood guard at the courtyard gates, "when you hear Prince fire twice, hop back to the hood of the jeep and be ready to shoot when we roll."

He waited for the seconds it took Prince to get back to Niergaard's truck, gazing at the mob which held its distance, roaring with desire and discontent.

There were no faces he could see, only the large encircling arc of people, half-mooned about the entrance, dressed in grays and blues, rags and woolens, heads covered with old towels, shawls, handkerchiefs, fedoras. They were not people at all, he told himself, but a giant beast, swaying and pulsing like an unfed animal, panting in a subhuman passion of hunger and fear. They had killed Collins and none of them was responsible. They could not care that Collins was dead any more than they could care for one of their own Chinese dead that he and Collins had seen this morning. It was a pack. It was not human. The pack had a personality. And he hated it, hated it.

Behind him, he heard Prince's carbine fire twice and he fed gas to the jeep as Michaelson, never lowering his carbine, backed aboard, and then fired over the heads of the mob several times for warning. Baldwin twisted the wheel as he emerged from the gates. He could feel it crunch over the cartons, mashing the food into the ground, knowing the trucks behind would mash what was left and not caring. The crowd thinned and parted, and he moved out, the trucks following.

The convoy was in the clear now, slowly gathering speed

when a figure darted out at them from the side, a figure in a Chinese soldier's uniform. It ran alongside them, calling, whether to curse or beg for a ride, Baldwin could not tell. But he saw Michaelson's carbine go up again and shoot point-blank into the running figure and it tumbled awkwardly, like a football dummy carried to the ground. Baldwin noticed as it fell that the soldier had been running barefoot in the snow. Behind he could hear Prince's gun on the last truck blasting off in a volley, and then they were out of it. The last he saw of Hochih was a little girl gaily waving at them, and the mother's hand reaching out to snatch her back.

They drove a minute or two in silence and Baldwin turned to speak to Collins, but Collins was not there, only the two Chinese and Michaelson up front on the hood. He wanted to talk about it with Collins, only with Collins. He was conscious now of many things as the fright of the flight ebbed from him, that anger was hardening in him, that the boy had been precious. And that he, himself, had been a fool. Because I was a fool, Collins is dead. I was responsible. It was all right for him to have the idea, thought Baldwin. But it was not right for me to let him go. I was responsible. The flattened windshield was still down, and Baldwin was beginning to be cold, his fingers were numbing at the wheel, and Michaelson must be freezing up there. But he could not stop now because if he stopped he would be sick, he would not be able to stand up, he wanted to throw up. He must keep driving just a few more minutes until his hands stopped shaking. And what were they going to do next? He could not think about it. He would stop in just a minute and when they stopped he would figure it out. If he had gone out with Loomis it would not have happened; he had wanted to go out by road, to do this job.

CHAPTER 7

Evening in a Blockhouse

WHEN HE JUDGED they were far enough away, he halted the convoy to let Michaelson and Prince out of the cold and back into the cabs of their trucks. But he was still not sure enough of himself to try his voice. For now, with only three trucks behind him, he realized one carried a man close to death, and the other a lad just dead, and he could not think of the one just dead, still warm, even through the numbness, without the choke rising in his throat and a wanting to cry. He knew that no man in command cries, and that even a junior lieutenant on patrol in the night must bring back bodies without crying. But beyond the death was somehow a deeper personal sorrow, and, aching with it, knowing he had asked for this command, he tried to think of what he must do next, and could not, and was aware that he was alone in a jeep with two Chinese, and he did not want Chinese close to him.

If I wish, he thought, I can drop them both, right now, by

the side of the road, and force them out to join the gray-blue living ghosts streaming, mile by mile, up the road toward death in the snow, and they would probably die too. But, as bitterness toyed with the thought, came the realization that he needed her, now. With Collins gone, the team was tongueless in China. He had no words of Chinese and she would be the only link, for as long as they stayed on the road, between what he wanted and the strange Chinese army and the lost millions of Chinese he must deal with.

He drove silently and slowly for even though the snow had thinned the flow of refugees, he had no taste for hurry. The dark was falling, he observed soon, and he reminded himself that it was November, that they were high, and dark came quickly when it was cold. But he could not trust himself to speak yet, not knowing whether his voice would break in a sob or snarl in fury at them.

A gray lithe form appeared on the road, running beside them, its tongue out, and automatically, flatly, his voice said:

"A dog."

Su-Piao answered, softly.

"No, I think it's a wolf, it's following us."

"I thought wolves were thin," he said, testing his voice further, "that's a husky one."

"Yes," said Su-Piao. "It's been eating well. I've never seen a wolf before, I thought they were only in stories."

Baldwin let the jeep speed a bit, and the wolf fell behind down the file of the convoy. Behind, he could hear a shot ring out. Then another. That must be Michaelson, or Prince, with their guns still ready, firing at the wolf and Baldwin knew their carbines were still on the trigger and they were trigger-happy. Once you fired a gun, you unlocked something inside a man, and then it took enormous pressure to lock it up again. Like crying, Baldwin thought. Once the tears came, you could not stop a woman from crying unless you brought the entire episode to an end and began a new one. It would not do to barrel on into Tushan this way, with the men still nervous on the trigger, to arrive in a crowded town full of fretting, turbulent people after dark. If they had arrived in Hochih yesterday, by day, and seen what they had seen on the morning's walk to headquarters, he would have handled it better. He had handled it badly and his daydreaming embroidered what he had done: Philip-Baldwin-foul-up; no, more simply, Philip-Baldwin-fool. He did not know whether he had to do Tushan tomorrow, or could do Tushan tomorrow, but he did not want to face that decision today. He could not.

Through Su-Piao, he turned and consulted Kwan. Kwan's voice was clipped, unmoved, expressionless. He agreed. It would be better to come into Tushan by daylight and find the headquarters, if the headquarters were still there, in the morning. Then they could make plans.

Better to sleep alone on the open road, Baldwin said, if they could find a roof and walls to shelter them in the fields, than to lock themselves into a village inn, or any town swarming with refugees. But where to find a roof and walls that had not been torn down for wood to warm the wanderers, and his eyes scanned the fields as they drove.

It was Kwan who first saw it, his eyes sweeping the landscape with the skill of an old campaigner. On a crest, on a gentle rise, still miles away in the gray, it stood square and squat, like the rectangular locked-masonry of a Norman keep.

"Maybe there," said Kwan, "maybe it is empty."

"What is it?" said Baldwin as they drew nearer.

"A blockhouse," Su-Piao translated and then added, dully, on her own, "I've seen dozens of them."

"Blockhouse?" asked Baldwin.

"Yes. Everywhere, all through the hills, all over China. We

built them when we were fighting the Communists. The Generalissimo drove the Communists out of South China that way. He used to build circles of blockhouses about their areas and then squeeze them out. Sometimes, the warlords built them, too. But this is probably an old blockhouse of ours— The Communists had to march across these hills when they were escaping from the Generalissimo. That was before they turned north, on their Long March. That was ten years ago. The Generalissimo left these blockhouses all across their trail wherever they moved in China. If only this one's empty."

It was empty. On the aching surface of the day's events, luck had placed an empty blockhouse in which they could sleep. Its gates were splintered and open, its interior cold and moist, but it was empty; and in the square courtyard of its thick walls, the jeep and three trucks could stop and be guarded. On the stone flooring they spread their bedrolls and blankets; the men brought in pebbles and gravel, heaped them in a basin, poured gasoline on it and a blue fire burned. They brought Lewis and stretched him on the ground beside the fire and after a while, Miller opened another can of pork-and-gravy and they ate. But Collins lay in the truck in the cold outside and no one wanted to talk.

Someone had brought the field-radio in and snapped it on, but nothing within its radius made any sound except the occasional *da-dit, da-dit* of some unknown Chinese sender and the surging roar of the static. Baldwin knew there was probably no American call-signal closer than a hundred miles, yet he leaned forward like the other men about the radio and watched Prince stroking the dials. Once a squawking, distorted Chinese voice balanced momentarily on the edge of a wave-length, above the hum of static, and Prince handed the earphones to Baldwin, who handed them to Kwan. But by the time Kwan had adjusted the phones, the voice had fallen off again into the wild emptiness of space and though Prince twirled and coaxed the dials back, over and over again to the same point, the voice would not return. They were alone.

Baldwin did not want to eat with the men; they would have to talk and there was nothing to talk about except what had just happened. He did not want to join Su-Piao and Kwan, because the coldness that had settled on him when Collins died had made them Chinese again, and he wanted no Chinese courtesies. But he did not want to sit alone, apart, either, while everyone watched him, wondering what was on his mind.

There was nothing on his mind, actually—no plans, no program, no will. He would go into Tushan in the morning. If the Chinese wanted him to blow Tushan, he would blow Tushan. If they did not, he would leave it. Let them decide. If they got up early, at six or seven, they would be in Tushan—when? How many miles? Kwan would know and he walked over to join Kwan and Su-Piao, both eating their pork-and-gravy without conversation and without appetite.

They had just passed a town called Nantan, Su-Piao translated for Kwan, and Nantan was about one hundred fifty *li* from Tushan, "mountain *li*."

"One hundred fifty *li*," said Baldwin calculating three to a mile. "That's about fifty miles, isn't it? What does mountain *li* mean?"

"A *li* doesn't really measure distances," said Su-Piao, "it's flexible. The *li* of an easy, flat road is longer than the *li* of a difficult mountain road. A short road over the hills has more *li* sometimes than a longer road over the paddies. It's a way of thinking, really; you ask a peasant how far it is to the next town and he tells you how many *li* but that's not really the distance, that's how long it takes to get there."

Baldwin was irritated. That was China, always uncertain.

Everything sounded sensible, but the sense was always so illogical. They had not answered his question.

He said nothing, and Su-Piao continued trying to open a little the bridge of friendship which he had closed.

"If you have to cross a river by ferry on your trip, the ferry crossing is ten *li* all by itself."

"How?" he asked in spite of his restraint.

"If a road is only forty *li* between two towns and crosses a ferry on the way, that makes fifty *li* for the journey because it takes more time."

For a moment, Baldwin found himself toying with the odd logic of her statement, and felt a faint ripple of amusement inside himself. Then, he was angry with himself for being amused and at the feeling of friendship rising in him again. Collins had been killed. Chinese had killed him. These two had not yet acknowledged it.

"And today," he said, "how many *li* did we come today, how many *li* do you add when the road costs a man?" He was trying somehow to transfer part of the blame, part of the responsibility to her because she was Chinese.

She did not answer, retreating from him in her silence, then turned and translated what he had said to Kwan.

"He was good," said Kwan, "he was beginning to understand China."

"It didn't do any good," said Baldwin bitterly.

"You will take him back to Kweiyang and send him home?" asked Kwan.

"Yes," said Baldwin.

"It is good. He will sleep in the grave of his ancestors. Chinese soldiers are not sent home when they die. So their families eat great bitterness."

"Yes," said Baldwin curtly. He did not want Kwan to

equate the death of an American with the ragged soldiers dying here in the hills.

"The soldiers who die here," said Kwan, "will die without any coffin. They will die without even the straw a poor peasant has at home to wrap him. They will die like dogs, and the refugees who still live will take their clothes and then the dogs will eat them."

Baldwin stood hard and unyielding before them, still trying to make them, the Chinese, share the blame.

"I'll have to write his father that he died," he said.

Neither Kwan nor Su-Piao answered. Baldwin continued.

"Usually you never tell them how their sons died. The Army doesn't think parents should be told, it makes them imagine things. You say he was killed in action, that his loss came as a great shock, that he will be mourned and missed by all the men in his outfit. But this will be more difficult. His mother is dead, he told me. And it's always more difficult to write the father. And his father is a judge. And he'll write and ask exactly what happened."

They were still silent. Kwan had retreated now into the Chinese neutrality, his eyes bleak as if he were seeing nothing. Su-Piao sat with her head bent, looking at the ground. Baldwin had to press on.

"I'll have to tell him how he was killed. Not in action. If Collins had been killed in action, fighting Japanese, his father would think he was a hero, and being the father of a hero helps. But now, somehow, his death will seem meaningless, and this will be a private sadness for his father. His father will hate the Chinese, and hate and hate them, until he's dead. He won't understand."

Still looking at the ground, as if she were speaking to herself, Su-Piao said:

"No one will understand. No one except Chinese. You can't explain it to Americans."

Baldwin did not know whether she included him, too.

"Explain what?"

"It takes too long to say."

He could not invite her to talk, the coldness was still in him, he did not want to recognize that somewhere in the past two days the distance between them had powerfully but imperceptibly lessened. But he stood there, listening, saying nothing, hoping the pause in the conversation and his silence would force her on. Her day, too, had been full of terrors and she, too, had to unwind.

"It's all falling apart," she said after a while, slowly, speaking almost as much to herself as to Baldwin. "Nobody sees it, not the Chinese, not the Americans. But I can see it. I'm both. I'm Chinese. And I'm American, too; I feel that way. I can see it now from the very beginning. From when I was a little girl."

Unwillingly, he had been caught to attention. Baldwin had never thought of Chinese as children, except for the urchins on the road, with their scabrous heads, their bright black eyes, their restless playing and chattering, like puppies. All Chinese were grownups when he thought of them. But Su-Piao must have been a little girl once. He listened.

"There was one spring when I was a little girl," she began falteringly, as Baldwin wondered what this had to do with Collins and it all falling apart, "I was ten years old and father always took me back in the springtime to the family land in Anhui, in a town called Hofei, where the family had come from. He took me back for the spring festival every year because it was so beautiful. In Shanghai, at the apartment, he used to laugh at the old ways and say they were primitive superstitions—but he loved them. I did, too, they were so beautiful. The torches of pine for the festival that could only be kindled by the light of the sun reflecting on those centuries-old bronze mirrors. We used to polish the mirrors in Hofei with cornsilk, until they were like glass. Then, when it began, the drums would beat, and the procession would start from our house with paper buffaloes, and the dancing, and the flutes—and the sky in Anhui is so pure and blue. We had special feasts at the spring festival before the plowing, with foods of honey that people never ate except only then.

"My mother would never go. She was real Shanghai, she'd been born there and she never left except to go to Hong Kong, or the beach, or to visit America—her family taught her to play piano when she was a girl, and she spoke English, and she wanted me to play tennis and ride horseback. But she'd let me go to Anhui, because she knew papa really loved going back once a year, even though he was a modern, and made believe he laughed at all of it.

"I think it was 1925, this time. The warlords were always fighting in Anhui when I was a little girl, they'd been fighting there even before I was born. I must have been ten years old at the time."

Baldwin did the arithmetic quickly in his mind. She could not yet be thirty if she had been ten in 1925, and Helen was thirty-two and this woman was younger. She was a general's wife, but she was talking about a little girl; her voice had lost the quality of talking-to-herself and had acquired a quality of intimacy, talking to him urgently, not rapidly but with the excitement of explanation and unburdening.

"We stayed in Hofei for four days that year. Papa always did all the year's business at the spring festival too, looking over the land accounts, trying to tell his brothers and the rest of the family about the new seeds the Americans had developed and that our land should be planting, talking with them about the peasants' rents.

"Then one day he took me into town with him, he had business to do at the Guildhall. When he was in Anhui he used to wear the long silk robe, a black one like everyone else who was a gentleman, not the Western business suit he wore in Shanghai. He loved it really. Well, that day . . ."

She broke off suddenly and looked at Baldwin to see if he were following her, as if to ask if she were saying too much of herself, but his attention reassured her and she began again in the same tone.

"That day . . . oh yes, I should have said the family had told him not to go into town because there had just been one of those spring wars between the warlords. I think it was Chang Tso-lin whose troops had come down from the north and had fought some battles with the southern warlords, and now his troops were going back north, retreating so it was best to stay indoors at home because retreating soldiers always did their plundering on the way back.

"But papa had just come up from Shanghai. He thought that warlords were comic, just the way the Americans did."

She smiled as a memory crossed.

"I suppose they were, the soldiers carrying their umbrellas and their suitcases along with their rifles and some had birdcages with them for their canaries, and the warlords took their concubines with them. Papa thought they were funny too, and so he had taken me in town, and we were eating in the restaurant outside the northern gate, the *Pei-Men Ta-Tien,* after he had finished his business. Just papa and me. He was so happy to have me with him and his family in Hofei again, and the *lao-pan,* the restaurant-owner, who knew our family, made such a fuss over me—he gave me a whole plate of pastries of honey and nuts to nibble on myself. I was the little '*Shang-hai hsiao-chieh.*'

"Then the soldiers came in. The restaurant owner and all the waiters left papa and me right away and began to serve the soldiers. The soldiers were already drunk. Papa began to hurry me to finish. Everybody else in the restaurant began to call for their bill, too. Then, suddenly, a big husky soldier, so tall he must have been from Shantung, took out his rifle and slammed the butt down on his table so hard that the dishes broke. And he got up, drunk, and yelled that no one could leave the restaurant.

"Everybody was quiet. They were all afraid. Papa, too. And the big soldier yelled that the rich people did not like the soldiers who fought for them, that he knew they thought soldiers stank, that it was true soldiers did not smell good, but that was because soldiers had to sleep on the ground, or in the stables with the animals. Then he said that nobody should leave the restaurant until the soldiers had finished eating, that they should give honor to the soldiers.

"Then he saw me. I had on a yellow dress, all the little girls got new dresses at the spring festival because it was the beginning of the new year. Nobody in Hofei would have taken a ten-year-old girl in her new dress to a public restaurant, but papa was from Shanghai and so full of American ideas. We must have looked so strange and conspicuous there, me in my yellow dress, he in his black silk robe.

"The big soldier came over to us and put his hand on my head. I remember looking directly at papa when the soldier did that, and papa was frozen with fear. The big soldier smelled of onions, and his breath had alcohol on it. His face was so red. He stroked my head and his hands were rough, but he wasn't trying to hurt me. He was telling papa that little children should be taught to respect soldiers because the soldiers were China's only hope. Then he noticed papa's wrist watch and he belched over me and asked papa if he could look at the wrist watch. Papa took if off and said to the soldier that he should keep it, because the soldiers were fighting for China.

"It made the soldier furious. He yelled that soldiers weren't bandits. He was going to *buy* the watch from papa. Papa said he didn't want any money. And the soldier yelled some more and gave papa a handful of dirty paper bills, and went off with the watch. Then they upset their own table, and broke all the dishes, and went away. The money was paper money, of course. Either from some bank they had looted, or paper their warlord had printed up. It was just paper, worthless. Papa left it there. The restaurant owner came over and apologized for what had happened. But papa went home. The next day we got on the train back to Shanghai, and I think papa never went back to Hofei.

"But I'll never forget sitting there, with the soldier's hand on my head and papa being afraid, saying nothing. Papa being *afraid!* He couldn't take care of me. He couldn't take care of himself. Nobody could take care of us. He was only safe in Shanghai because the foreigners governed Shanghai, with *their* police. Mama scolded him when he came back. Of course, Mama hated being Chinese."

Baldwin found that he was sitting on the floor beside her, on her bedroll, listening to a story about a ten-year-old. He wondered how many times she had told the story before, or whether she had ever told it. He knew he could not stop her now from telling more, and he did not want to stop her. He had forgotten about Collins, without realizing it, and knew the woman was making a point, as women always do, in the long roundabout way the emotions take to illuminate and justify what they want to say.

He was listening to her now with only half-attention, aware

of what she was saying, interested, yet paralleling the story with memories of his own, from his own childhood.

She told him how she had dreamed she was American, and went to the American School in Shanghai, and had gone to Boston to Radcliffe as her mother had gone to Radcliffe and come home and found China had begun to change. There was a government now, she said, a real government, and its soldiers were not bandits, and the officers were educated, and there were universities, doctors, factories, engineers.

Except that she had gone north to visit some friends in Tientsin and in the north it was the way it was when she was a little girl. She had been walking in the street and had seen two Koreans carrying away a screaming little girl, and a father and mother crying after the Koreans. But they were Korean *ronin*, gunmen protected by the Japanese army, which already controlled the north. They were moneylenders, who had lent money to the parents, and since the parents could not pay they were seizing the little girl to take away for payment. And Su-Piao had run to the Chinese policemen to ask them to come quickly to help; but the policemen had shrugged their shoulders because the *ronin* were under the protection of the Japanese army. There was the hospital she had seen in Tientsin too, the hospital for people dying of opium which the Koreans were peddling for the Japanese army. The students in the schools were organizing a boycott of the Japanese in Tientsin but nobody could stop the Koreans from selling the drugs because the Japanese army was everywhere in North China, and it controlled the trade. So there was nobody in North China to take care of the people either, there was no protection and she had come back to Shanghai, hating the Japanese.

It occurred to him, with the other half of his mind, as she was talking, that all these things must have been happening when he was a boy, too, but he had not felt them, not even the depression although he could remember his father, so sure of himself, talking about that-fool-Hoover, that-scoundrel-Roosevelt. Father disapproved of everything that happened in Washington; father had never been a success; but he had been proud and never been afraid of anything. Nor was Helen, he suddenly realized. Helen was strong, he realized, as he listened to this Chinese woman talk. She carried herself with strength; Helen would have *made* the policemen help the child. Helen would risk far more than himself, and it was he who always saw what would happen if things went wrong. Until today, when he had risked it without thinking, and he was back to Collins again, not listening to Su-Piao talk, thinking about Collins *and* about Helen and was Helen stronger than he, and why had she wanted to marry him.

But Su-Piao had been talking, and there had been a pause, and Su-Piao had begun again exactly as if their thoughts were meshing.

"I suppose I married him," she was saying with great earnestness—and Baldwin scrambled to pull back out of his mind what she had been saying when he had begun to wander, and remembered it was about the Japanese attacking at Shanghai seven years ago, in 1937, and how wonderful it was when China, finally, turned and fought. It was there she had met her husband, T'ung-ling, who was a young colonel, an officer of the artillery, fighting, and had married him.

He was fully alert now, listening.

"I suppose I married him," she said, "because he wasn't afraid of anything. He wanted to be proud. Oh, it was easy to think that it would be all right in those first few months, that we could take care of ourselves, we had the new army, and the new officers, and the new arsenals, and everyone helped.

"But then we were pushed back inland, and as we went

back and back and the war went on, I realized what we were. We were a crust, a brittle thin crust beginning to form over the wounds. It had taken all those years since I was a little girl to build up this crust of new people over the warlords, and I thought the Generalissimo had made this crust, that it was his, that he was taking care of us. But it wasn't. He was part of the crust, he didn't make it. It belonged to him because he wanted to make China strong, but the Japanese saw it better. If they could break the crust, if they could take Shanghai and Nanking and Canton, the cities on the coast where there was just beginning to be a China—if they could wipe it out, nothing could ever be built again. I hate the Japanese, they did it, they did everything. Once the crust is gone, everything's gone."

Baldwin could see what she meant. He had never thought of himself as part of a crust in America, but of course he was. Only it was such a thick crust, it went all the way down to the bottom. He was sure that Lowry & Moody could get half a dozen engineers to do his job as well, that the army could fill his spot with twenty men just as good just by shuffling punchcards through a machine. But he could see that an engineer, or a good officer, or a good doctor, or a good anything in China would be much more important, in a much thinner crust. Yet you could not wipe out what people knew, they were still there.

Musing, he interjected:

"But they're still there, aren't they? They haven't all been wiped out."

"You don't understand," she said sharply, and Baldwin could see by the tone in her voice that she had been making a point. "That's what I'm trying to say. You don't understand that this is the end of it, here, now, on this road. Some Chinese stayed behind in Canton and Shanghai, and they're working for the Japanese. Even if we go back, it'll never be the same—those people will serve the Japanese as long as they stay, and they'll serve us if we get back, or they'll serve the Communists if the Communists come down from the north first. And the people who went to Chungking, with the Generalissimo—the war's been going on too long, they don't care any more, they're just waiting for the war to be over. Even T'ung-ling hated the people in Chungking at the end, everyone at the front hates the people in Chungking, they're safe. But these, these people here on this road—do you know who they are? These were the best. These are the people who wouldn't go north with the Communists, these are the people who didn't stay with the Japanese, they didn't even want to go on to Chungking and be safe with the Generalissimo. These are the good people from Shanghai, or Hankow, or Nanking, or Canton—not peasants. These are the people from the cities where we had the little crust, who came to East China or South China four or five years ago to settle down and start over again to help the war. They were the best, and this is the end of them, the end of everything.

"It's the end because there's nobody to take care of these people. There has to be something to take care of people. People have to be protected. There has to be an order somewhere. And there isn't any order left anywhere in China. The Americans take care of the Generalissimo and he's safe in Chungking, but he isn't the Generalissimo any more, he's just a warlord the Americans happen to be taking care of. He can't take care of us, he isn't taking care of us. Do you think if any of these people get to Kweiyang or Kunming safely, that they'll be the same? Do you think they'd be the same if this happened in Boston and Americans had to walk out in the snow?"

"No," said Baldwin, "no, they couldn't be the same."

"They're going to die," she said, staring, her tone suddenly a resonant, carrying whisper as if she were talking of ghosts that only she could see. "Everybody back there in Hochih is going to die. Not everybody, maybe, but most of them. If any of them are going to live, it will be by accident. And life shouldn't be by accident. Death shouldn't be an accident. Dying shouldn't be something you can avoid only by trickery, or by being cruel. It should be something that means something, or because someone has come to the end of his days. There has to be something that takes care of people, a law, or a government—even here on this road, there should be a government. Any kind of government, even a government with a bad meaning, is better than no government at all. Because then people are animals.

"Do you know how many millions of people in China have walked for their lives in the past seven years? And only the cruel ones or the sly ones got out. All the good ones are used up—or their goodness has been used up. The peasants, oh, the peasants will always be the same, they're hard and they're bitter and they hate us and the Japanese both. But they stay. They'll accept any government so long as it's a government, and it can make some order in the land, or stop the war and let them work in the fields. But people like us—this is the end, we aren't people any more, we're like what you saw this morning, now. We're worse than the peasants, because we were educated; we need to have a government to protect us, and there's nothing left for us any more. We need a government so we can do something with it, or be kind, or have mercy. When there's no government, there's no mercy, it's only savage."

The team, which had finished its food, had stopped talking to listen to her voice. Baldwin could see that she was crying, without stopping the out-rush of her words, and the words were hurting her, while the tears slowly washed down her cheeks. He wanted to hush her but he could not.

"It's all coming apart," she said. "It's like an avalanche, only the very strong or the very cruel will live, along with the dirty people who stayed on the coast with the Japanese. And when it comes apart like this, it isn't even human any more, everyone dies by accident, without it meaning anything. Don't you understand? That's what happened to Collins, he was caught when the avalanche fell on him, he was trying to be kind, but it fell on him just the same; there's no time to be kind any more, it's too late, it's too late. It's all ending. You Americans can still get out—so get out, get out. You can't take care of us, so you've got no business here. Don't you see, don't you see?"

She stopped again. She was no longer crying. The entire dark room was silent, the Americans waiting for her to go on: Kwan, not understanding her English, only her tone, frowning; Baldwin tormented, feeling he understood, yet did not, not knowing what to say.

She had almost finished. Softly this time, she said almost to herself:

"I don't even know what I am. At Radcliffe, I used to dream I was an American. In America, it's so easy to dream. But I'm Chinese, I'm a real Chinese. When T'ung-ling died, I understood. But when Collins died, I didn't know what to think. When an American dies, it should mean something."

There was a long silence now and they were all uncomfortable.

Miller broke it.

"There's more coffee, lady, do you want it?"

She shook her head, voice steady, tears gone.

"How is Lewis?" she asked.

"He's sleeping," someone said.

She rose from the ground and went over to where Lewis half-snored, half-whistled in his sleep. She knelt beside him and felt his forehead.

"He's burning," she said as the sleeping man turned his head at her touch. All of them around the fire watched her, the gasoline flame lighting her face from underneath, the smooth planes of her face glistening up to the ridge of her dark cheek bones, the broad, yet delicate, Chinese nostrils curling flat like an infant's, the smooth-oiled hair coiled tight around the nape of her sun-browned neck, to where, Baldwin knew, it disappeared in the pale skin of the body. My God she's beautiful, thought Baldwin, and they've beaten her, and she's only twenty-nine. He wanted to sit closer to her, to comfort her, perhaps to take care of her. He would get her to Kweiyang safely, he would get all of them to Kweiyang safely.

But he had not taken care of Collins, and the thought brought back all the weight and force of what she said. He had lost Collins to save what? He had thought he could save China and she had said it could not be saved. What was he trying to do?

He shook his head again trying to be clear in mind for he knew that somewhere in the course of the day he had lost not only Collins but a clear idea of what it was that had made him take the team up the road. And if he did not know, what could he do tomorrow? He was confused as she was, he told himself. Except that I have to decide again tomorrow, and I have to decide for all of us, and for Kunming, and for her.

He heard her say, by his side:

"I think I'll try to sleep now."

"Yes, you'd better," he said. And then, "Good night, Su-Piao." His tongue had formed the words of her name haltingly, stumbling, but he felt better for having said it. He tried to take his eyes from her as she walked away to where her

Chinese quilt lay rolled, as her woman's figure stooped to untie it, as her legs tucked under her knees when she sat, then unfolded as she lay down beneath the quilt, and turned her back to the room.

Somehow, she had relieved him of the guilt of Collins and he would be able to sleep tonight and think of the boy again with warmth and affection. But look at it how he would, it had been a bad day. And he could not see what he would do tomorrow. Except that he would put the team on the road early.

SATURDAY

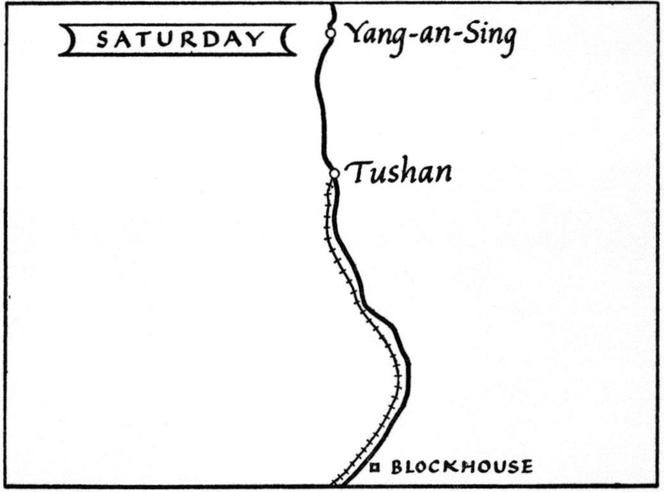

CHAPTER 8

Decision by Default

MICHAELSON was up first the next morning and grunted with satisfaction when he saw that in the night the skies had cleared. Today they could roll right through if they wanted to. If Baldwin wanted to.

He wished Baldwin would get up. He needed five minutes with Baldwin before the men were at him, nagging, to find out what was going to happen today. McNeil had always given him those five minutes at morning coffee and he had been able to lay it out to the men after that. But now just what the hell was he going to say. That he didn't know what the score was? Were they going to take the team into Tushan, and take another chance of getting jumped like yesterday? Or break their backs the way they had done the day before at the sidehill blow? Or just barrel on through? Damn it, it was a Chinese job, why in hell didn't the Chinese take care of it themselves? Did *Baldwin* know what the score was?

Angrily, Michaelson stamped on the ground to jar his freezing toes and began to flail his arms about his chest, warming up; and then when Prince's voice spoke up he was annoyed because he knew he looked stupid. There were two of them, Prince and Niergaard, up early too, and Prince was asking:

"You know what the score is for today, Mike?"

"Not yet," growled Michaelson.

"Do you think *he* knows what the score is?" continued Prince, sarcastically, but seriously.

"What do you want, a blueprint?" answered Michaelson dodging.

"Yeah," said Prince. "As a matter of fact, a blueprint would help. Even money, this joker doesn't know what he's going to do today. I don't mind a guy betting on a stacked wheel when he's betting his own chips. But I'm one of the chips. We lost Collins yesterday. What's the pitch? When are we getting into Kweiyang?"

Michaelson's thinking churned. They had a right to know. But *he* had a right to know first. Then Niergaard spoke, slowly, as always.

"Look, Prince, let me say it. It's this way, Mike, we've been talking it over, we aren't pushing you, but you're the only one who can talk to him. Why are we doing it? I can't understand it—these people are dangerous and we've done our job. The longer we fiddle around with them—well, the way I see it, we have our finger in a buzz saw, we ought to go right in—I mean, if we have to blow up these dumps they're talking about, if we *have* to, well you know us—Mike, just talk to him and all we want to know is—do we go in today or don't we, yesterday we didn't do a goddam thing and we got cut up. You see, Mike?"

The Mountain Road

by THEODORE H. WHITE

A Report by CLIFTON FADIMAN

Reprinted from the Book-of-the-Month Club News

THE chamois leap from the precipice of reporting to that of fiction writing is one few journalists have made with any success. Mr. White is one of those few. Club members may recall his *Thunder Out of China* (1946), co-authored by Annalee Jacoby. They will recall, too, his brilliant analysis of today's Europe, *Fire in the Ashes* (1953). To this brace of Club selections Mr. White now adds a third, a novel as thoroughly professional as his journalism. *The Mountain Road* combines an expert's knowledge of the Chinese people, drawn from first-hand experience; a notable ability to portray the American soldier, without sensationalism or sentimentality; and a gift for tense, condensed narrative. It is this quality that, months before publication, moved a major film company to purchase the screen rights to *The Mountain Road.*

It is a novel of both action and thought, and the two factors are so skillfully blended that only the most coldly analytical reader will be able to separate them. It is a story in which suspense, conflict and vigorous, often violent, drama play leading roles.

The scene is East China, the time November, 1944; the action is compressed within a single week. This particular moment of time was of fateful importance to our history. It marked the period of China's greatest disorganization, when Japan, herself lost in the American trap, was nonetheless ravaging the Chinese mainland; when Chiang Kai-shek's Central Government was proving itself, perhaps inevitably, unequal to the task of leadership; and when a dire political vacuum was opening. From this series of catastrophes, as Mr. White puts it, "China was never after to recover."

An eight-man detached demolition unit of Americans, headed by an ex-civilian engineer, Major Philip Baldwin, is assigned the task of delaying the Japanese advance along a 260-mile stretch of strategic road leading from the coast inland, a road along which tens of thousands of Chinese are fleeing in search of food and safety. Though Mr. White has invented his charac-

ters and telescoped the action, this episode is historical. Mr. White says, "The flight, the death, the problems faced—are as true as memory and witness can make them."

Major Baldwin is faced with three kinds of problems. The first is technical: how, with the explosives stowed away in his four trucks, to accomplish the maximum of useful destruction as quickly as possible before the Japanese catch up with him. The second is psychological: how to transform himself from a civilian, unused to making critical decisions, into a handler of men and a bearer of almost intolerable responsibility. The third is philosophical: how to achieve his brutally necessary task in the face of an alien mentality—for at every step he must secure the co-operation, or at least the neutrality, of the Chinese military and the Chinese people.

The first of these problems he solves perfectly. The blowing of a bridge (necessary, but also a guarantee that every wheeled vehicle containing fleeing Chinese would be trapped); the titanic destruction of a whole hillside; and finally the Wagnerian end-of-the-world demolition of a vast ammunition dump—all these are described in vivid detail, and with a mounting effect of excitement. One can hardly wait to see how Hollywood will handle these beautiful opportunities.

Baldwin's second problem is rooted in his past life. His wife, Helen, had told her husband, "Phil, you have to handle other men or other men are going to handle you." Baldwin, in the course of a week of strain and agony, learns how to make a team out of his seven men. All of them, by the way, are characterized with quiet precision, and one of them, young Collins, who has a politician's passion to understand people, is a character the reader will not easily forget. The major is forced to learn not only how to handle men but how to handle power—more power, as he reflects when it is all over, "than I knew how to use."

Baldwin's third problem is the heart of the book. It involves coming to an essentially philosophical understanding when the alien mentality of the Chinese when it was being subjected to unique pressures. For in 1944 China was falling apart; it was liquefying into a flood of disaster and desperation. In the face of this flood Baldwin clings, as he must, to his American conceptions of justice and responsibility. These are not the Chinese conceptions, and the consequence is a moral crisis in Baldwin's soul that goes very deep indeed. In the end he does what he has to do: he punishes because it seems to him necessary; and he finds that the power he commands has made him do a terrible thing.

Essentially this is a rapid, tight narrative involving problems of conscience and ethical responsibility. It should be so read. *The Mountain Road* is short but packed—and swift-moving. Once having begun it, most readers will not easily lay it down.

BOOK-OF-THE-MONTH CLUB, INC.
345 Hudson Street, New York 14, N. Y.

Printed in U.S.A.

Michaelson saw perfectly and, because he saw, he was furious, and because it was Niergaard, the farmer, whom he liked, he could explode without slugging him as he might have slugged Prince.

"Jesus Christ!" he yelled. "What the hell do you want? You know how to read and write—write a letter to your Congressman! Save it up until you get to Kunming and tell it to the chaplain! This is the frigging army and you volunteered for this detail! I'll let you know as soon as I know anything myself." He throttled down the burst of temper and knew he would have to speak to Baldwin, and snapped, "Let's get the trucks turning. Warm them up. We're going to roll early today." And went to find Baldwin, in the blockhouse.

He waited until Baldwin had brushed his teeth, and watched Baldwin shave, and knew by the slow deliberate movement of the man he watched that it was difficult to interrupt his thinking. But he caught Baldwin finally when Baldwin began slowly to drink his coffee from the canteen cup. Michaelson squatted, cleared his throat and said casually:

"What's for today, Major?"

Baldwin did not say anything, and Michaelson said again:

"I mean what shall I tell them, Major, are we going to do Tushan, or are we going on through?"

Baldwin turned slowly to look at him, blankly, his eyes still sleep-fuzzed and said:

"How soon will we be ready?"

"Any time, Major; about ten minutes, I guess. But they're bushed, Major, they've had it. And this thing yesterday shook them."

Michaelson could see Baldwin coming awake now and Baldwin said:

"It's about a hundred miles, isn't it?"

"To Kweiyang," said Michaelson, "yes—a hundred, hundred-twenty, something like that."

"We could make it by noon," said Baldwin, distantly, "if the roads were clear."

"By two o'clock anyway," said Michaelson, his spirits rising. "We barrel right on through then? Don't stop for anything? That's it then?" and he edged away, half-rising. It had been easy; he had thought Baldwin was going to chew him out the way he had yesterday at Hochih.

But Michaelson had moved too quickly.

"No," said Baldwin quietly. "No, you don't get me. We have to stop in at Tushan, just for a look at the dumps, whether we do anything or not."

"Why?" snarled Michaelson. "It's dangerous."

"We've paid for the look," said Baldwin, as if to himself, "so we have to look. Whether we do anything or not."

Michaelson was baffled, then angry. This was always the way. Somewhere behind Baldwin's flat, puzzling statement, Michaelson could sense a reasoning. But he could not see it, and he felt like a fool, having to go out and hammer it into the men, when he did not see it.

"I don't get you, Major," he said stubbornly.

"If we don't go in and look around today then we should have gone on through yesterday," said Baldwin, more firmly, as if it were all quite clear.

"I'm not following you," said Michaelson, not yielding at all.

"Look," said Baldwin, straightening, his voice suddenly clear and firm. "We paid the price to find out what's happening yesterday, with Collins. It's up to the Chinese headquarters here whether they want these dumps blown. But it's up to us to check in on them and let them decide whether it's their job or ours."

Michaelson was about to open his mouth, to ask Baldwin to say it yes or no when Baldwin's words hammered at him, fast, snapping:

"Get the trucks loaded. Fast. Let's get on the road. Let's move."

In a few minutes they were on the way in traffic again, and Michaelson had dodged answering any questions from the men. The road, he saw, was good today. The fog, the clouds, the snow of the past two days had evaporated and the sky was polished. The frost on the stubble in the fields below sparkled like a carpet of crystals in the brilliance of the morning sun, and along the road they traveled they could see the telephone wires bowed and snapped by the weight of the rime that sheathed the wires in an inch-thick sleeve of ice. The little bed of narrow-gauge rail that had meandered on their route parallel to the highway, now in sight, now out of sight, was finally converging with them on a city, which must be Tushan, and Michaelson still did not know what Baldwin planned to do. Nor did he find out when they had plowed through town, stopped the convoy and Baldwin got out of the jeep to speak to them.

"All you've got to do," said Baldwin as he assembled them, "for the next hour, all of you, is just sit. I'm going back to town to find Chinese headquarters and find out what they propose to do about the big dumps here. I'll be back in an hour or two at most. Don't break out any food. Don't make friends with anybody. If you're hungry, use K-rations. Eat inside the cabs. When you're not eating, I want you outside sitting on the trucks. I want them to see you've got guns. But if anybody fires a shot except to save his neck, so help me God, I'll break him and throw the book at him when we get into Kunming. Got that?"

They nodded. Prince began, "Say, Major . . ."

But Michaelson snorted at Prince, "Shut up!"

Baldwin was already in his jeep, with the two Chinese, on his way to town when Prince turned to Michaelson again.

"Listen, Mike, what the hell's going on here?" he asked.

"He says he's already put in his ante; he's paid for the next card. He wants to stay one more round because he's already paid to look."

"So now he's playing poker," snapped Prince.

"You heard it," said Michaelson. "What the hell do you want *me* to do?"

As Baldwin maneuvered the jeep back through the crowded town, he knew he could not explain to Kwan and Su-Piao, whom he needed for this conference, why he wanted the conference any better than he could explain to Michaelson. It made no difference, he told himself, what the final Chinese decision was about the dumps. One way or another, it was up to them. But the dumps should not lie undecided before the Japanese, an accident of chance. The only reason he had to make this call was to establish responsibility for the decision somewhere, anywhere. This was why he had wasted a day; and lost Collins; and unless he carried on through now, to this last rendezvous with the Chinese, however perfunctory, then all of yesterday's events made no sense. He had risen this morning, determined to go right on through to Kweiyang with Lewis, until Michaelson had spoken to him. But when he had answered Michaelson this morning, there had been this conviction waiting there on his tongue, the residue of the night's sleep and the night's unconscious thinking, already shaped. He had paid the price to force this decision, he must follow through.

He wondered what kind of headquarters this would be. The town, he noted, was even more crowded than Hochih, and he was glad he had posted the convoy on the far edge of town outside the crowd. But the drab grays, browns, blacks, blues of the refugee mass were flecked more persistently here with the slate-gray and mustard-yellow of soldiers' uniforms. The little town rang with the clanging and cursing of military congestion—a soldier pulling at the bridle of two mules that drew a pack-howitzer, soldiers sleeping on trucks piled with ammo cases, soldiers in knots, waiting, leaning against walls, soldiers about a bonfire as the breath of their nostrils steamed in the cold. And he saw an officer beating a soldier with a stick, and though the soldier yelled, he was not being hurt. Baldwin recognized that there was a thin mantle of discipline in this town and he must locate the center, which was Kwan's job. And after some questioning, Kwan guided him to a stop, before an arcade of boarded-up shop windows, which was the headquarters.

A conference was going on at headquarters, an orderly told them, once the sentries had passed them. But, as if they had been expected, Baldwin, accompanied by Su-Piao and Kwan, were admitted in a matter of minutes.

In the large, conspicuously clean room, a real fire, not a charcoal pan, burned in an open grate with an old stovepipe carrying off its smoke and making the draft. It was cozy. The wall was covered with a large American detail map, its arrows in blue and red, its circles, boxes, and designations instantly illuminating the darkness of ignorance in which Baldwin had lived for four days. The red arrow north of the road was sweeping far wider than Baldwin had imagined, and the fat red box marked with the double cross indicated a full Japanese division, the Thirteenth. Along the road they had traveled for the past four days swept another arrow, and its designation marked it as the Japanese Third Division—still somewhere short of Hochih. Did the break in the arrow indicate the Japanese had stopped, there, where he thought his side-hill blow might have been? Or did it mean that no one really knew where they were?

All this Baldwin noticed at a glance, as he heard Kwan talking to the men about the big table. It was a staccato conversation. Baldwin could catch Chinese courtesies now and his ear, tuned to the music of the language, could tell that these courtesies were flat and perfunctory. That was all right. It was just the way he felt, too.

Su-Piao spoke to him first.

"They're asking about me; I think they don't like having a woman here. Kwan says I'm the interpreter but they still don't like it. Please say something to me in English so I can translate quickly, before they ask more about me. Kwan's told them my name but not about my husband, or who he was, and they may learn, and that could be bad."

He had forgotten that her husband had been Central and that he had been executed. She had not mentioned the execution again since the first day. And all China seethed with spies, Japanese against Chinese, Chinese against Chinese, provincials against Central. This was a Central headquarters and it might, indeed, be bad if he appeared with the woman of a man the Generalissimo had ordered executed.

Baldwin cleared his throat and said loudly, "I am Major Baldwin of the American engineers."

His loud voice cut across the Chinese courtesies and abruptly he was in the conversation. They turned to him as Su-Piao translated, and, quickly, she continued to Baldwin.

"Say something else, they're waiting."

Baldwin reached into his pocket, pulled out the old faded Chinese pass McNeil had given him, laid it on the table with the red seal face up.

"We are on our way from Liuchow to Kweiyang. My team is a demolition team and we've been ordered to destroy as much as possible in the path of the Japanese advance. Find out what command this is, and whether they want us to stay today and work on these dumps. Make it sound courteous."

Su-Piao translated, Kwan breaking in now and then, obviously telling them by what route, and how they had come to Tushan.

While Kwan talked, Baldwin studied them, and found himself impressed. There were five. The one in command, the man with the presence, wore three bronze triangular pips on his throat collar which made him a lieutenant-general, and Baldwin remembered the rule of thumb that all Chinese officers were graded two ranks above equivalent American rank, so this was probably a brigadier in authority. His head was shaven absolutely skin-smooth and it shone. The young one with the thick, full glossy head of hair and the sharp, intelligent face was probably his aide. A stocky, hard-faced man beside them wore two triangular pips. Then there was an old bespectacled one-pip, wearing ancient gold-rimmed spectacles all askew on his nose; and, finally, the nervous one, chain-smoking his cigarettes. But they looked as if they could run an army, Baldwin admitted to himself. This was like a Chinese headquarters back in Kunming where he dealt with Central officers on engineering problems; it clicked. They could handle it themselves; it was all right. This will be over in ten minutes, he told himself, and we'll be on our way. He would put it to them cold; he would urge nothing; and he would get out.

The tall one in command had reached across the table to take the Chinese pass and was examining it. Then he handed it to the bespectacled officer and no one said anything. The tall one spoke to the old one and all of them conferred. Then the tall one in command spoke again, not unfriendly, but with no trace of courtesy in his voice.

"He says this pass carries the seal of Chang Fa-Kuei. Chang Fa-Kuei commands only the war zone in Kwangsi. Now we are in another war zone," translated Su-Piao.

The tall one turned to the wall map, ran his finger down a heavy line that wove its way between Tushan and Hochih on the map.

"Chang Fa-Kuei's command runs only to the border of Kwangsi. Hochih is on the border of the two provinces—Kwangsi and Kweichou. Tushan, where we are now, is in Kweichou. It is not part of Chang Fa-Kuei's command," translated Su-Piao.

"What's that mean?" asked Baldwin.

"It means, I suppose, that you have no authority to operate in this area."

Cheerfulness and regret suddenly mingled in Baldwin. I've done it, he thought. I've pushed it all the way, all I was supposed to do, and now they've taken my responsibility away. Now I've only my own men to think about. The thought crossed his mind that if he could exit now, courteously, while it was still only nine in the morning, why, the whole convoy would be in Kweiyang tonight; they could have hot baths and sleep under a roof. Tomorrow, if there was a plane, he could be in Kunming and pick up the mail from home. The thought of mail brought Collins back to his mind. It would have been easier to explain Collins to himself and to everyone else if only they could blow the dumps here. It would be worth doing. He had paid for that, too. He wished he could do it. But it was their command problem, not his.

"Fine," Baldwin said, showing he understood by standing up, ready to go.

"*Ch'ing tso*," said the tall one.

"Please sit down, he says," translated Su-Piao.

This was a switch. Now what, thought Baldwin, as the aide drew three big, straight-backed chairs about the table to replace the bench on which they had sat. Everyone sat down. These were ceremonial chairs, so high that Baldwin, tall as he was, could scarcely touch the ground. He was sitting on a throne. Su-Piao's and Kwan's legs dangled.

"*Ch'ing ho-ch'a*," said the tall one, and Su-Piao translated, "Will you have some tea?"

"Thank the general," said Baldwin, "but tell him the men are waiting. If I can't help him, I should go back to them and we'll go on to Kweiyang today."

The general turned to Kwan and said something and there, indisputably, the courtesy sound was warm in the general's voice. Baldwin turned to Su-Piao for the translation but she held up her hand to silence him, waiting for Kwan to repeat the same phrases.

"He was talking to Kwan, not me," she said to Baldwin. "I'm the interpreter and I know he still doesn't like the idea of my being here. They haven't given me any tea. I think you should be careful now, I can't tell what is going on but he says, 'The honorable American officer must be tired, he must have some tea, then will you please sit with them in this meeting and give them of your honorable instruction.' It's very flowery, not the way he was speaking before."

"Instruction?"

"That's a courtesy phrase," said Su-Piao, "it means that they invite you to offer them ideas. They want you to wait and listen to them. He must have changed his mind about you since he rejected your pass. I think he wants something from you."

"What do I say?" asked Baldwin, thinking to himself that

if this was another gasoline trade he was having none of it. If the Central Army was that way, too, the hell with it.

"Oh you say something courteous, too, like 'This is too much honor.' "

"Say it."

"*Chun-chang t'ai K'o-ch'i*," said Su-Piao to the general.

"No, no, the American general is doing us too much honor, he is too courteous," returned the tall commander.

"Tell him I'm a major, not a general."

"He knows it."

The general muttered something to his staff, and they nodded agreement.

"He says he wants your meaning on the situation, I mean, your views on the situation, I'm getting my languages mixed up," said Su-Piao.

It was difficult to associate her present composure with the last evening's outburst, thought Baldwin as he realized how smoothly this conference was going, if mysteriously. She made him feel poised. But, of course, he thought, she's almost American; and these people are the crust, her crust, that she was speaking of last night.

"Tell him the situation looks bad to me. I came here to get his ideas," replied Baldwin.

They all leaned forward around the table, the commander spoke to his aide, and the young aide began in a high, rapid, barking voice to speak as if he were reciting a monologue. He would pause, Kwan would ask a question. It dawned on Baldwin that this Chinese command had a real briefing officer, just like an American command, and they were being briefed. As Kwan questioned, the Chinese at the table began to focus on Kwan rather than on Baldwin and the talk moved too fast for Su-Piao to keep up.

Something was obviously under debate—not in argument,

or dispute, but there was a pro-and-con involved and Kwan, who had just come in from the lower road, was part of it. Baldwin began to whisper to Su-Piao, seeking to catch up.

"Whose vote is Kwan casting here?" he asked.

"Yours," she said.

"What am I supposed to be in favor of?" he asked.

"I don't know yet. Neither does Kwan. He's trying to find out what's in back of their minds."

"Well, what are they saying?"

"They're explaining yesterday's field orders, from Kunming. The Chinese-American ground-command in Kunming, the YOKE forces I think you call them, has been given authority over this sector. They want to form a new line of resistance. There's an American airlift going on and the Americans are flying in two Chinese divisions of the New Sixth Army from the Burma front. The Americans are landing the divisions in Kweiyang, and moving them by truck from Kweiyang down the road towards here. The line will be about thirty miles north of here, where the next big mountain rise is."

"Good," said Baldwin. "But what's this headquarters supposed to do? Why did they order the withdrawal from Hochih yesterday?"

Su-Piao held up her hand, restraining him. She was trying to listen to the conversation and translate at the same time and her sentences came in snatches of undertone.

"The general here says it will take about a week to assemble those Burma divisions on the mountain line. It's almost a mile high. Transport is short. The Americans control the Burma divisions—they equipped them with American arms. The Americans refuse to let those troops be fed down the road into the Japanese in pieces. So YOKE and Chinese field headquarters have jointly ordered a withdrawal of all Chinese troops up the road, to prepare the new line for the new divisions, and hold it until they're dug in. Everything now on the road is supposed to start moving back as soon as possible without waiting for the Japanese to cut them off."

"I see," said Baldwin, with a fine sense of detachment.

He had it all in his head now, clearly, because somewhere far up the line someone else was thinking clearly, too; there was American staff-work in this. They would yield the foothills to the Japanese all the way up to the main barrier before Kweiyang. That would leave a no man's land between the Chinese and the Japanese until the new barrier was ready, in force and well supplied.

"That's clear," said Baldwin, "very good, a pull-back."

"No," said Su-Piao, "it's not clear at all. There's more coming. Be careful."

The officers around the table had paused. The chain-smoker lit a new cigarette. The old one drummed his fingers on the table. The stocky one had begun a knee jiggle. Obviously, they had come to a point of climax. The tall commander was clearing his throat.

Now it was the commander himself doing the briefing, in a burst of exposition. He was explaining the Japanese situation: the advancing enemy had only two divisions, no trucks, but much cavalry, much infantry, and pack-borne mountain artillery. On the other hand, the Japs were still dressed in summer clothes and it was very, very cold. It would take at least four or five days of hard marching for the infantry, at least two days of hard riding by the cavalry for the Japanese even to approach Tushan.

Therefore, there was no immediate danger, not today. Certainly, in a week, if the Japanese wanted to strike, there would be no way of stopping them. But there was no danger to Tushan from the Japanese at the moment. The only question was a question of time: if they did not start marching these troops here, now, to the new line, could they reach it in time when the Japanese came closer? The general's troops were tired. Many were sick. They must march in the snow.

"There's something in what he says," said Baldwin to Su-Piao in an undertone as she tried to translate the long Chinese periphrases into English while the general spoke. Baldwin felt a sympathy for the Chinese general—he had a real problem. But it was his decision here; Baldwin was just an observer and beginning to be interested in the way the Chinese fought a war. Still and all, though, they had orders to withdraw. Why did they wait?

"Yes, I can't quite see how the Japanese can get here quickly," he said aloud, politely. Su-Piao translated the remark, and the Chinese officers all nodded gravely and the general said:

"Yes. That is clear, too. That is the opinion of *Chun-ling-pu. Chun-ling-pu* does not think the Japanese will be here for several days. *Chun-ling-pu* says we should wait," said the general, somberly.

"Who's *Chun-ling-pu?*" asked Baldwin.

"It's not 'who,' it's what. *Chun-ling-pu* is Operations Division of the General Staff in Chungking. *Chun-ling-pu's* orders usually come from the Generalissimo personally."

"I don't get it," said Baldwin, perplexed, "YOKE in Kunming, the joint Chinese-American command, is supposed to be running the front now. That's what he just said. They told him to pull out. But this order from Chungking says they ought to sit around and see what happens. There's a direct conflict there. What's happening? Who's boss?"

"Yes," said Su-Piao, "oh yes, it's happening all over again."

"What?" said Baldwin.

"Just a minute," said Su-Piao. "I want to listen."

A cold silence had fallen over the Chinese staff at the table.

The general rose and went to the wall map and pondered it as if somewhere in the ridge lines, the elevations, the grease-crayon overlays, there might be an answer. It looked exactly like a Western war-room, like an American war-room. But it wasn't, Baldwin suddenly knew, it was different. Kwan joined the general at the map, the other officers followed. They were talking excitedly. Momentarily, Baldwin and Su-Piao were left alone.

"They really are in trouble," said Su-Piao. "If they fall back, they will disobey the Generalissimo. If they stay and get trapped, or don't get to the new line fast enough and the Japanese come fast, the line up forward may go. Then they'll be in trouble with the field command."

"This is a hell of a way to run an army," offered Baldwin.

"Don't say that," said Su-Piao sharply. "These are brave men. These are Central troops. They aren't afraid to die, they're just afraid of the Generalissimo."

These were her people, he realized, her vanishing home. Her husband had been a Central officer. She was still loyal.

"It's just that they don't know what to do. The Generalissimo doesn't trust them any more, he doesn't trust anybody. And they don't trust the *Chun-ling-pu*. There has to be a glue to make it stick together, to make orders really orders, to make the army really an army again. The glue is gone. That's how T'ung-ling got killed. Just like this."

"Your husband? Like this?"

"At Changsha. When the Japanese attacked, our area command wanted to pull back and fight from the hills. But *Chun-ling-pu* thought we ought to fight to hold the city. The Generalissimo is always stubborn, he wants to hold everything. Then our staff divided. T'ung-ling commanded the corps artillery; he thought the area command was right and took the artillery up into the hills overlooking the city. But the infantry commanders thought that *Chun-ling-pu* was right; either that, or they were afraid of the Generalissimo. So they kept the infantry in the town. T'ung-ling wanted the infantry to dig in, in the hills, to protect the artillery, where we could support each other. The infantry command wanted the guns brought down to the city to support the infantry there. Our general couldn't make up his mind. While we were arguing, the Japanese came. They took the artillery first because it had no infantry protection; then they wiped out the infantry because it had no artillery support. Chungking was furious. The Generalissimo had the key officers executed. So T'ung-ling was shot."

"God!" ejaculated Baldwin and thought, what a way to lose a good man.

"These people are in trouble," repeated Su-Piao again, and now they were coming back to their seats around the table and regarding Baldwin.

He spoke:

"Let's stay out of this," he said to Su-Piao. "Ask them what *they* plan to do about Tushan. Our orders are to coordinate demolition with the Chinese on the way. What about these ammunition dumps here? Do they want them blown or not?"

Su-Piao translated. The Chinese general stared straight back at them unblinking, and said softly:

"And what is the honorable opinion of the Americans? What is your instruction?"

Over to me, said Baldwin to himself, jolted. This is why the conversation, this is why the switch. Let the American say. Let the American make the decision. They were handing it over to him.

He had thought he did not care any longer. But, toying with his answer, he could not escape the fact that he did care.

He had lost one man killed and another man sick. It would be all right to go on if only these people took responsibility for the dumps. Someone had to do it, and it was *their* job. But somehow it was his too, and he could not walk away from it. Grand strategy belonged to men back in Kunming, or Chungking, or Washington. But if here at the end of the war America was too busy to think about this front, or what might come after, or what it meant—he must. He was Philip Baldwin. He was line command now. This was what line command was. After all the palaver and discussion, and briefing—line command was to say "yes" or "no," or "do this" or "do that." Big or little, command was different from staff, or counsel, or consultation. This was a bigger thing, he knew, than he had ever done before, or would do again. He could not have done it last week. The reason why he was here lay buried somewhere in yesterday's snow, and the snows of Boston, and doing things right because they were right. And he must.

He lifted his cup of tea, sipped it, reflecting with half his mind that he was beginning to like tea and that he was beginning to understand China. As he sipped it, and they waited for his answer, he thought how easy it would be, if he wanted to, to say Thank you for the tea, and then Good-bye, and be off. But they wanted *him* to make *them* agree to blow the dumps, he could sense it. And so he would.

"Tell them," he said to Su-Piao, "that it is my opinion we should blow the dumps."

He was speaking slowly, thinking Chinese as he spoke, letting her translate his phrases slowly, using the pauses to think, but knowing that none of the phrases that formed almost of themselves on his lips need be logical now that he had made the basic decision.

"Tell them that no one can guess the Japanese intention.

If the Japanese are only coming here on a raid patrol and then go back because it is too cold, they will certainly destroy the dumps while they are here. We cannot save the dumps. But if the Japanese have planned a major drive, they will base here at Tushan and use the ammunition. Or maybe if they find the ammunition, they will change their minds and stay here."

He knew the logic was false, but he was amused to hear how plausible it sounded. Victory would come with the next year, he felt in his bones, and the Japanese command would not spend its last troops so far from the homeland to invade the deep heart of China at the very end. But he went on talking about the Japanese, as if it were he, alone, judging the enemy, shirking all mention of the conflict of orders in which this staff was trapped.

"So it is wise, and best, to destroy the ammunition before the Japanese get here, because if it stays here it may make the Japanese come. Or if they come, it may make them stay." Then, oddly enjoying himself, he finished, ". . . but I am only an American major who has come to help the Chinese. The general is older, he understands better, what does he want me to do?"

"You're learning to speak Chinese," said Su-Piao after she concluded the translation.

But the general spoke better Chinese and was back at him, as all listened.

"So the American general wants to explode the dumps. He has decided."

There was the responsibility back in his lap.

"Tell him it's a suggestion," said Baldwin, feeling that in a moment more he could force the general's hand.

"The American is very wise," said the general. "He is right."

Baldwin had won on the blowing of the dumps. Therefore he knew the general would also withdraw now. So he had it made. But he wanted to see how far he could force it. He reached back into his pocket for the faded Chinese document with the faded seal of Chang Fa-Kuei. He felt like one of the partners at Lowry & Moody, describing the clinching of a deal, when the papers are put on the table to sign.

"If the general will put his seal on my pass, too, I will go to assemble my men."

The Chinese faces froze. Had he gone too far? He knew that somehow for days he had meant to blow these dumps. But they were Chinese and this was so big, and it was their country. They should share the decision, once he had made it.

It was Kwan who broke the silence. His voice was no longer clipped, short and military. It was young, conversational—conspiratorial.

"Kwan's good," said Su-Piao. "Listen."

"I am," said Baldwin, "but my Chinese isn't that good. What's he saying?"

"They're talking it over now, seriously. It always comes down to this. Kwan says the general needn't issue any orders. He says you will assume full responsibility. The general's seal will be under Chang Fa-Kuei's seal, it puts him second in line of responsibility *after* Chang Fa-Kuei. It only gives you permission to do your duty as you pass through this command, that's what Kwan is saying."

There was no change in the sad features of the general. With melancholy, he explained something to Kwan.

"He says he can't. Chang Fa-Kuei is not his commander. Chang Fa-Kuei has no authority. Chang Fa-Kuei is not loyal to the Generalissimo. He could not explain this to *Chun ling-pu*," said Su-Piao. "It's because he's a Central man, he's loyal."

"I can get him off that hook," said Baldwin. He reached into his pocket, shuffled through the papers, drew out the blue top copy of the message that he had been carrying since the night at Liuchow. It was wrinkled and messy now, but the English print of the typewriter was clear and the red stamp of Signal Center reception, with date and time, that the Liuchow field reception had placed on it, looked official.

"Tell him these are joint Chinese and American orders," said Baldwin.

Kwan had it clearly now, and his Chinese was rapid, almost jocular, easy, friendly. The general relaxed and examined the blue American message.

"I think he'll put his seal on it," said Su-Piao. And as she spoke the general made a remark to his aide. The aide left to return in a moment with a pad of vermilion ink. The general reached into his pocket, pulled out a fat, crystal cube, pressed it in the ink, then pressed it on the message. The seal, a delicate intertwining of lines, stood out on it. He looked up, a smile lit his face, and he handed the document back.

"There is time," said the general. "Will you stay and eat with us? We have poor food, but we will be honored."

"No," said Baldwin, smiling now, too. "We must go, we have work to do, and we want to be on the road again this afternoon." He thought a moment, then added, "Ask him if he can give us a few of his own men to help on the job. We'll need them if we have any trouble on the spot."

The general agreed—his soldiers would meet the Americans at the dump.

Baldwin rose. Kwan and Su-Piao rose. Kwan bowed from the hips. Su-Piao bowed from the hips. The general spoke inquiringly to Kwan and Kwan expressionlessly turned to Su-Piao.

"The general has asked Kwan if he would like to come back to this headquarters and remain when today's work is done and you have gone," she said.

"What does Kwan say?"

"He didn't say. I'm sure he doesn't want to stay here."

Baldwin was happy. He wanted Kwan with him. He was taking care of Kwan as well as Su-Piao now.

"Tell the general I should very much like to please him. But I have orders to keep Kwan with me until I get to Kunming," lied Baldwin.

Baldwin thrust out his hand and the general took it in a firm clasp. He murmured something and Baldwin asked:

"What did he say?"

"He says he understands. He says also, 'China and America are friends,'" translated Su-Piao, and the conference was over.

It was not until they had left the conference that Kwan spoke to Baldwin. He said, "*Hao*," and then puckering his lips, "Gude."

"Gude?" repeated Baldwin. "What does that mean?"

Su-Piao smiled. "He's trying to speak English. He's saying 'good,' he's happy you kept him with us."

It was remarkable how boyish and young Kwan's voice had sounded in English. In English, thought Baldwin, all Chinese sound young.

As Baldwin pushed the jeep back through the streets to the convoy, he realized that even carrying the ache of Collins and the exhaustion of the week, things were now flowing in him again, as if he had been re-wired. Now there was only the blow to organize, and that meant the men, and he realized how irritated he had been with Michaelson in the morning, when they woke.

To do it well, though, he needed Michaelson with him; command was not simply a thing of ordering people but of bringing them along to act with the same purpose.

He noticed with satisfaction that the convoy was waiting by the side of the road exactly as he had left it, the men sitting on top of the trucks, their guns easily handy, as he had ordered, and there had been no trouble.

First Michaelson, Baldwin told himself; and called him over, apart from the men.

"We've been handed the job, Mike," he said. "They're going to leave it to the Japs if we don't do it. How about our men?"

"What about our men?" asked Michaelson with an undertone of surliness.

"You said they're beat," said Baldwin. "This morning. We've pushed them hard. Have they got it in them for just one more?"

They were going to do it anyway, Baldwin knew, and he knew that Michaelson knew it, too, but he was appealing to Michaelson and wanted him to know it.

"If they've got to, they've got to," said Michaelson, feeling he was being mouse-trapped, yet wanting to gain something out of it. "Say, if we could send Lewis on ahead, that would make everybody feel better. If we send Lewis on ahead, and I can lay it on the line to them that this is really the last one—well, you know, they've never blown a whole ammunition dump before, and it's still a damned good outfit, maybe we can wind them up."

Michaelson had ended in a tone of partnership, and Baldwin wanted to keep it that way. But he hesitated.

Then he said:

"If we send Lewis, that means sending another man to drive."

"Yes. Miller," said Michaelson. "He's a nice guy but a slob. He'll be like a mother to Lewis on the road. And we put Collins on the same truck. They barrel right through, maybe they can get Lewis to a hospital tonight."

"Fine," said Baldwin. "Let's move. Maybe we can all be in tonight. Get them together."

"Front and forward, you guys," yelled Michaelson, turning from Baldwin. And Baldwin knew Michaelson was with it, finally.

"Listen," said Baldwin when they were all assembled about the jeep, "we're going to split up now. We have a day's work here for some of us, but there's no need of keeping Lewis on the road any longer."

They rustled, edging forward, because now at last they could see it ending, and somebody would, right now, be given clearance to speed a truck down the road, to Kweiyang, and get out of it all.

"Miller," said Baldwin, "you're driving Lewis out. Take Ballo's truck, with the rations. We'll put Lewis in back and cover him up warm. We'll put Collins on in back with you, too. I want Lewis in a hospital as fast as possible. There's a YOKE force liaison somewhere in Kweiyang. They can get him to Kunming tomorrow morning, maybe even tonight if you make Kweiyang by afternoon. Or you may hit an American liaison group with these new Chinese divisions coming in. If you do, turn Lewis over. We'll be in Kweiyang ourselves tomorrow morning. Afternoon at the latest. We'll locate you through YOKE headquarters. Got it?"

"Got it," said Miller. "When do I start?"

Baldwin looked at Miller's round face trying not to show

its happiness, acting tough and unconcerned like everyone else, and Miller was not making a good job of it.

"Right now," said Baldwin, "just as soon as we can move Collins and Lewis over to Ballo's truck. Make sure you have enough gasoline and fill up some extra jerry-cans. The rest of of you, start turning the trucks around because we're going back to the dumps. I'll explain it when we get there."

Baldwin waited until Lewis had been transferred and then climbed up to look at him. Behind two cartons of food, on a green plywood demolition chest that carried an engineer field kit, the men had fitted Lewis a cubbyhole of blankets and bedrolls where he lay, his face yellow and drawn, his eyes deep with purple edgings.

"Lewis?" asked Baldwin bending low. "All right?"

Lewis looked up at him, nodding, saying nothing.

"You're pulling out now, Lewis," continued Baldwin. "Miller's driving up front. You'll be in Kweiyang tonight, in the Kunming hospital tomorrow morning."

From the cubbyhole in which he lay, Lewis murmured something. Baldwin bent to hear.

"Is Collins going on this truck, too?" he asked.

"Yes," said Baldwin, annoyed. "He's in back."

"I don't want to ride with a dead man," said Lewis weakly. "Can I ride up front?"

"You ride back here, damn it," snapped Baldwin, not knowing why his annoyance with this weakling was so great, why he should raise a problem when other problems were so huge and pressing. Then, realizing that the man was sick, he bent and stroked Lewis' head.

"I'm sorry," he said to the man's face. "I'm edgy. Lewis, you're better off back here, out of the wind, lying down. Collins won't bother you. And Miller is up front. You like him you know."

Lewis' head nodded in feeble assent and he closed his eyes. At the end of the truck, Baldwin saw as he straightened, the men were hoisting a flopping bedroll, bound with rope, into place. It was very heavy. Baldwin had not seen Collins' face since they had lifted him from the snow at Hochih. He could not open the bedroll now and say good-bye. But he clambered over, after the men had rested it on the floor boards, and his hand went out, resting gently on the coarse, field-green twill that covered the bedroll. Underneath, he knew there would always be sorrow, but the sun was shining and the cold air was charging him and there was the dump to be blown, and Baldwin knew he could do it.

It occurred to Baldwin now, as he knelt by the body in the bedroll, that Su-Piao had said yesterday that only the strong and the cruel survived. And here he was, sending Miller and Lewis and Collins on ahead. Miller and Lewis were weak. But was Collins? What was it that made him know he would always remember Collins? Because he was good? Or because of all the people being killed in this war hurling masses upon masses of men against each other, Collins alone had known, when the rock was hammering, that he had died on a personal purpose. Everyone else died out of strategy, or by accident. Collins had died, doing something he wanted to do. Doing something good. Was it weak to be good? How quick and live the boy's face had been, how it could glow. Baldwin touched the bedroll, whispered good-bye so softly he could scarcely hear himself, and climbed down.

"O.K., Miller, take off!" he yelled, and the truck lurched away, the men jovially cursing Miller's luck in envy. Baldwin watched it go, disturbed by the thought that only the strong and cruel got through.

CHAPTER 9

Tushan!

THEY HAD NO TROUBLE finding the dumps, which lay exactly where Kwan's directions said they should be—back through town, four miles west of the railway station, through a wooden gate in a long bamboo fence that ran along the spine of a ridge. And by the gate, a dozen Chinese soldiers were waiting to help them, as headquarters had promised.

It was when they had passed the gates, and Baldwin had stopped the truck to look from the ridge down on the hollow that he saw what he had taken on. It was immense. The gray, low wooden buildings must be the warehouses, squat one-story cubes of weathered, unpainted lumber, connected by graveled paths that ran off in three rows toward the distant ridge that formed the sheltering far rim of the hollow.

How many were there? Twenty or thirty, he thought, though his eye had not counted yet. What was in them?

Where did you begin? How did you take apart something like this?

Yet the vast field of sheds challenged him. Listening to the men talk behind him as they scrambled out to look too, he knew he could do it because this team was a tool, an instrument, committed to his hand; a precise, and elaborate tool that the United States Army had somehow thrown together from American skill. And he knew how to use it, finally. The blow itself only took figuring out.

Behind him, as he gazed, he could hear someone yelp:

"Jackpot! Man, do you suppose these sheds are really loaded?"

"Frigging Chinese," he could hear Michaelson exploding, "so that's where they been hiding it. We give them all this stuff, they hide it in these frigging hills."

"You mean we're gonna blow this *now*," he heard Prince saying. "My back is still aching from the last job—we got a whole day's work here."

"Mike," he heard Ballo asking, "you absolutely sure that this is the last one we got to do on the road?" and Michaelson replying, gruffly but not in anger, "What's the matter, soldier, you want me to tattoo it on your butt?" and he could tell that Michaelson was excited, too.

They waited for Baldwin to say something, but Baldwin was in no hurry. He could tell by the tone of their growling, by the bubble of excitement in their voices, that the itch of destruction was working in them again. The thing to do was to keep the excitement high as they worked, but his own mind clear so that he could fit the facts together and work out exactly how it should be done. When his mind had told him what to do, then he would tell them. There was plenty of time and the chill air braced him. The thing to do was to break the job down into parts, but get the facts first.

He turned back to them.

"We have plenty of time," he said, "and we'll be out of Tushan this afternoon if we get our backs into it. This could be the best blow of the summer. If we handle it right. Any of you ever blow an ammunition dump before?"

There was no answer.

"All right," he said, "neither have I. But it shouldn't be far different from the Liuchow blow. First we split up to find out what there is. There are three rows. Mike, you and Ballo take your truck and scout the off-left row. Prince, you and Niergaard, do the off-right row. I'll take the center row." He was counting now and he saw there were twelve sheds in each long row, and he continued:

"Let's see. Try to get back here to the gate all of you in about forty-five minutes, and we'll count up what there is and what we have to do."

And at last he could say what he had been wanting to say since the night of Liuchow. He could make them a promise.

"And this is the last one. The YOKE troops are making a new line with new Chinese troops from Burma about thirty or forty miles north of here. That's where they're going to stop the Japanese. I wouldn't be surprised if that's the end of the show in China. This may be the last big blow any of you will ever see. We'll be into Kweiyang and Kunming as soon as we finish and you can all sit around in Kunming and get fat until they blow the whistle. So let's make it good."

They were back within the time set, simmering, all of them. It was big, bigger even than Baldwin had thought. There was everything. There was artillery of all sizes and makes, including, Ballo reported, an entire shed of American pack-75s, all new, all with original cosmolene still greasing their parts, never used. There was a shed full of rifles and another of machine guns, with English and American, French and German, Russian and Chinese markings of origin. "Some of the stuff's real old," said Niergaard, "there's rust on these old cases and one of them says 1918." There were mortars and mines, pistols and flares, and in Baldwin's row he had come across three full sheds of small arms ammunition, of every marking, of Skoda, Winchester, Armstrong, Brandt and Krupp. There was one entire shed of TNT—German, French, Japanese and American TNT. There were at least two sheds of mortar shells, another shed of shells for 75s, another shed of 105 ammunition, all of them distributed about the dump without apparent reason or system. And then, in one shed, in a fanciful aberration of good order, they had found a collection of antique hardware assembled in one place, apparently only because everything in the shed was British—old British twenty-five pounders, Lee-Enfield rifles, mines, old imperial twenty millimeter ammunition that fitted no gun Baldwin had heard of. Some roving English arms-merchant had, perhaps, long ago, made a killing in selling the trash of the first war to some forgotten warlord who had been snuffed out by the Central Government; and his hoard had now ended here in the shadow of the Asian plateau. Michaelson reported he had found drums full of fuel in one shed. "I guess some of it's gasoline," he said, "but some of it, I guess, is alcohol. It smells like orange juice, do you suppose they made the stuff out of oranges?" Prince summed it up: "Now I know why they call them dumps—they must have bought everything they could lay their hands on and dumped it all right here. They got everything to fight a war, except Confederate money."

It was a museum, not an ammunition dump, that Baldwin was dealing with. Thirty-six sheds. And, calculating in his mind, at one thousand to fifteen hundred tons to a shed, it would be forty to fifty thousand tons of ammunition and gear that lay before him! Too much, too much to handle in one afternoon.

And yet too little. It was so clear to him now, all the arguments they had had at staff back at Kunming, as to what the Chinese were doing with what the army was giving them, whether the Generalissimo was hiding it, or saving it, or stealing it. Here, in these gray sheds, was the strategic reserve of a nation. Down there, at the far end of the rickety little rail spur which led from these dumps to the mainline in Kwangsi, then up the steaming hot paddies of Kwangsi to Hunan and the front, down there half a million—perhaps a million—Chinese troops had waited, facing the Jap for six years, nursing on this. Out of this one little gland of reserve—built of what he had beseeched or cajoled from the outer world, built of the bargains he had made with wandering hucksters of obsolete weapons through the years—out of this, the Generalissimo had had to face the power of the Japanese with their industry and their science.

Baldwin found himself saddened by the pathetic dilemma, thinking as he knew the Chinese command in Chungking must have been thinking: How does one spoon-feed a starved and diminishing mob of soldiers at the far end of the railways, shell by shell, ton by ton, weighing each shipment against each judgment, each spy's report on the loyalty, or vigor, or courage of the unit and the commander who pleaded for more to fight with. And so the Chinese command had hoarded and hoarded it, hoarded it to fight against the Japanese when the emergency might come in one last battle, hoarded it against calculations of other wars, with other Chinese, when this war might be over. Hoarded it, in fear, until it had become not a strength but a weakness, because it was alien, and now finally was useless and he, Baldwin, an American major, must erase it from the balance.

Su-Piao had been translating to Kwan as the men made their report and now Kwan spoke, his body almost trembling in anger.

"Now, now everything must be destroyed," he said.

"Why, of course," said Baldwin calmly. "As much as we can."

"Everything, everything," said Kwan.

"What's the matter?" Baldwin asked.

"Nothing for the Japanese when they come," said Kwan, "nothing for anybody. There is no way, now we must do it."

"He's right," said Su-Piao, her voice tense with emotion, too. "He's right, it has to be wiped out."

Baldwin looked at her. He could not see why she was excited; of course he was going to do the job, that was why he was here.

"Don't leave a thing for anybody," she cried. "We could have used it down front, we could have used it. Why didn't they use it? What were they keeping it for? T'ung-ling had two hundred shells for a battery at Changsha; the soldiers had fifty bullets a man. At Hengyang, they let each gun fire two shells a day, just two shells. We had nothing to fight with, and it was here all the time; it was right here, they could have sent it to us. It's nobody's, I tell you, nobody's, you have to destroy all of it."

She hated it, he could see, and so did Kwan; they hated this dump more than anything else they had been through on the road. Perhaps, somehow, because the cold dumps here in the cold sky had been more important in the calculations at the *Chun-ling-pu* than soldiers, or troops, or life itself. Here was what the Generalissimo had bought or begged, and it had been useless, worse than useless, for it had reduced him to being the client of other men and other strategies. But the Generalissimo had a point, too. Baldwin could see it clearly as if it were his own command problem. There had to be a strategic reserve; war wasn't a chess game where you committed your last piece and then there was nothing.

And the Japanese had to come after this reserve; and someone had to blow it before they got there. And he was the man. It was simple. There was no point in getting excited. The only problem was how.

He had to think it out alone, so he walked away from them to be quiet and sat on the edge of the road that ran along the ridge in the lee of the bamboo fence. There was nothing in the Field Manual about a dump; he had thumbed through its pages so often he could almost remember each section heading. The manual listed all techniques for all objectives, but nothing about a dump. Probably because a dump, a strategic reserve, was blown only in major retreats and the U. S. Army had no manual on major retreats. We're probably the only Army in the world that hasn't had to plan a major retreat, he thought. We don't retreat. Grimly, he told himself—not yet. And then—what the hell are we doing now? But it's not our retreat, it's theirs. How much is it ours, he asked himself, what's this going to cost? Then with an effort, he pulled himself together, reaching down through the vagrant groping of his mind to grasp the problem.

In a while, he had it worked out and called the men together.

"There's some stuff we're going to have to leave," he said, "and some stuff we absolutely have to blow. The rifles and the machine guns. We can't do anything about them, and so we'll forget them. If the sheds burn and the cases burn, well and good; but if not, they won't do the Jap any good either.

"Then there's the artillery. We'd have to set off a thermite charge in each barrel to fuse the metal, and we haven't got thermite. Or we'd have to set off a block of TNT in every breach and that's handwork, and could take us hours. I'll leave the artillery pieces to Kwan's Chinese soldiers—we'll have them smash out the traversing mechanisms on every piece they can find, the same mechanism on every piece so the Jap can't cannibalize parts and replace. Would you explain that to Kwan?" he finished, turning to Su-Piao, who translated to Kwan, who nodded enthusiastically.

"Then," went on Baldwin, "the gasoline and alcohol, that's standard and we can see whether it burns when the sheds burn or it's fifteen minutes of S.O.P. to put bullets through the drums.

"Now that leaves the ammunition," he said quite clearly for it was all clear in his mind, even the little complications, "and the ammunition is the heart of this job. It's all stacked for safety, with good separation, so that *could* make it tough. But I think it's almost certain that one block of TNT, to each shed, as a primer, will kick off any case of shells and the impact of concussion will kick off everything else in any one shed. But that's not absolutely certain. If each stack of shells has to be blown individually, we'd have to manhandle these stacks together to get an impact effect. Which means Kwan would have to go back in town and get more labor troops to help us shove all the ammo in any one shed into one big stack so that each shed will go with a single charge.

"What we ought to do is try one of these sheds for size right away, and if we need more troops, Kwan can go back in and get them now.

"I'm going to try the first one myself. The far shed in the middle road is stacked with mortar shells with damn good separation between the stacks, and if it goes then any other shed will go, too, when we're ready.

"All right then," he concluded, his orders brisk, "Kwan gets his Chinese troops to work right now. I take off and case the far shed of mortar shells. Mike, I want to work this dump on the same field-net we tried at Liuchow. We'll run firing wire down the field, and feed twelve cross-ties of primacord from it. Each cross-tie carries three caps to detonate a couple of blocks of TNT in each shed. Get the wire ready. Get the primacord ready for hooking in. Get out about forty or fifty half-pound blocks of TNT and prime them. If you get through that before I try that shed, you can eat. If the shed goes as easily as it should, then all we have to do is string the stuff down the field. Blow it. And get out.

"When I get ready to set off the shed of mortar shells, I'll fire a flare from where I am. That means Kwan gets his Chinese back off the field up here into this drainage ditch by the road for cover. That's when you take cover, too. When the Chinese are back off the field, give me two shots from your carbine as a signal, and I'll blow it. Have you got it?"

"Got it," said Mike.

"Does Kwan understand?" he asked Su-Piao.

"He understands," she replied in a moment.

He turned away to assemble the TNT and the primacord he needed for the shed. He wanted to test the shed alone and by himself; if anything went wrong he did not want to lose another man; he had lost one already to his conscience. But when he got into his jeep, he found Su-Piao already there.

"What are you doing?" he asked.

"I'm supposed to be with you, aren't I?" she asked.

"Not really, not this time," he said. "Do you want to?"

"Why, of course," she said, and a round full smile flourished on her face. He knew it would look ridiculous to the men to see him driving off with the woman, but he did not care. He enjoyed the thought of taking her along to see this last large thing he had to do. He thought quickly—what will I do when she's gone? And knew he did not want her to be gone. They had come a long road together; he was somehow a different person now than he had been three days ago; she was part of it. He stabbed the gas treadle hard, the jeep took off. Everything would go well, because she expected him to make it go that way.

It was the first time they had been alone together since Thursday on the crest above the sidehill blow, and so much had happened since. He had seen her angry; seen her in despair last night; she had been his partner this morning and he could not have closed the deal on the dump without her. He noticed now, watching her face out of the corner of his eye as he drove, that her head was high, her eyes bright, that she sat as erect and gracefully on the bouncing seat of the jeep as if she were in a saddle. He, too, sat straight, not hunched over the wheel as he usually did, and wanted this day to do a clean, quick, effective job that she would remember; he did not want her to forget him.

In the far-off shed, with its empty, abandoned silence, she followed him down the aisles of chest-high stacks of mortar shells. The black stencilings on most of the cases were Chinese markings; but several piles were stacked only with the yellow triple-tube cases of new American 81 mm. mortar shells. He scanned the long shed quickly, trying to organize what he must do in a precise procedure; then he went back to the jeep, brought back a hand-reel of primacord, two half-pound blocks of TNT, a toolkit, and squatted on the ground. She squatted beside him, and he was aware simultaneously of the great stillness, the bitter cold and that the curve of her leg from knee to ankle was perfect and firm.

As she watched, he tied the blocks of TNT together, deftly inserted the bronze cap in one of the prepared holes in the block, pulled out his crimping tool and crimped the primacord into the cap. Next he cut a length of twine from the ball in the kit, circled the block twice with the twine, looped it over the primacord, knotted it, and tugged the primacord to see if it would come loose. He was making a show of it, he knew, as he tied the knots firmly and squarely, but he wanted the moment to linger.

"It's like sewing," she said as she watched his fingers work.

"You don't want the cap to jerk out of the block," he explained matter-of-factly, "you have to twine the cord to the block so that the cap is secure inside. It's Standard Operating Procedure."

"It sounds complicated."

"It's not, really, it's all in the book."

"What book?"

"There's a book for everything in the army, everything's been figured out—there are books for attack and assault, for roads and cooking, for burial, ordnance, survey, supply, signals, repair. We're engineers, so ours is the book for demolition."

"Do you mean a real book?" she asked as if he were teasing.

"Here," he said, reaching back to his hip pocket where the brown-paper pamphlet had sat all week, "it's an Engineers Field Manual."

"TM 5-23. Engineers Field Manual. Explosives and Demolition. January 12, 1942," she read aloud from the cover. "Do you mean you have to study this?"

"We know pretty well what we can do and how to do it," he replied, "but it's got a lot of formulas in it that save paper work; and some odd information on situations that arise that we've had no experience with in this theatre."

He had to pull himself away. There was work to do. He rose to his feet, lifted a carton of mortar shells from its rack.

He unscrewed the cover, crammed the block of TNT in, bound it down with more twine, manhandled it back in place.

She had been reading the book and now she was reading the table of contents, almost in amusement.

"Why, it's how to blow up everything—look, here it is, tunnels, railroads and rolling stock, oil and gasoline, telegraph and telephone lines, frame buildings, wells, artillery, wire entanglements, stump blasting, ditching—why, it's a science."

"No," said Baldwin, "it's a technique. You can learn it. People who stay in the army are going to school all their lives." It was true. He had never thought of it. The Army ran on brains and learning.

"It must be more than schools," she said aloud, giving the manual back to him. "Learning isn't enough. We used to think so. In some parts of China the God of Scholars and the God of War share the same temple. In some places he's the same god and he's called 'Wen-Ti.' It doesn't help, though. Somehow we got off the track."

He saw her face fall and a soft melancholy erased her expression. There would be time later to talk to her, he wanted to see how this would work, now.

"We're ready," he said. She rose and he lifted the little plastic reel of primacord from the ground. He stooped for the toolkit but she had reached it first and had it. Letting the cord unravel through his fingers, he backed out of the shed, Su-Piao following with the toolkit like a plumber's helper. As he paced off the distance from the shed that receded in the distance, he explained, "We've got to give it good distance, I don't know how it will work." He was annoyed because the little plastic reels came only in 100-foot lengths and he wanted 300 feet between him and the blow. He was aware now that they were about to make a blast in a field of high explosives and that the bowels of the earth would rend if anything went wrong; and that she had no idea of what the primacord might do; or else she did not care. He stopped at the jeep and spliced two more reels together, strode out their length to the end, told her to get into the drainage ditch for shelter while he brought the jeep to the ditch beside them; and then finally joined her.

When he joined her in the ditch, he dropped down again beside her and she handed the greenish-yellow, rough-waxy cord to him and he cut it with a knife, carefully fraying the end for good ignition.

"Is this wire?" she asked.

"No, it's primacord, the highest-speed explosive we make. It goes twenty thousand feet a second, the book says. It's instantaneous for all practical purposes. You touch a match to this end and as soon as you touch the match to it, it's flashed at the other end. Really good stuff."

"Now?" she asked.

"No," he said, "I have to send up a flare to warn Kwan's Chinese soldiers off the field and back up to the ditch on the ridge. Then Michaelson will fire off his carbine when the field is clear, and I'll try it."

He climbed out of the ditch once more, cocked the flare pistol in the air, pulled, and the pink-shell traced a lazy, languid parabola of light in the blue sky.

It would take several minutes of waiting to get the Chinese back in and he enjoyed the thought of these minutes suspended unavoidably, in time, with this woman.

"And when it goes," she asked, "when it goes—then there'll be nothing left?"

"This takes out the shed of mortars. If that goes well, we can hook the whole field up in about two hours work, and take it out all at once. *Then* there'll be nothing left."

"That's good," she said complacently, and then, "but it's sad, too. Nothing at all?"

"Oh," he said, savoring the masculine moment, "the artillery will be here, but if Kwan does his job on smashing the traversing mechanisms, it'll be useless, and in time it will rust, and after a while there'll be nothing at all left."

"Just rust," she said, reflecting, "just rust, that's all that's left of us. But they tried, our government did try, you know they did."

"Yes," he said, "of course," wondering why her thoughts had carried her this way. It had been a bad campaign, but the war was won.

"I wish . . ." she said. "There's a poem . . ."

"A poem about this?" he asked, inviting her on.

Her voice fell across his ears, rich and warm. It was Chinese, but more beautiful than he had ever heard it.

"What's that?" he asked.

"It's a poem. It's a thousand years old. By a man called Tu Fu, about some king's abandoned palace."

"What's it like?"

"Something like this, I think:

'Of what dead prince, this palace?
Beneath these hills, who graced this ruined hall?
The beauty of his maidens now is yellow dust,
Their paints and colors faded, gone.
Of those who danced attendance on his golden chariot,
None remain—
But this, among these relics—a horse of graven stone.' "

She paused, then:

"We never had beautiful dancing girls, and no golden chariots. I don't mind that. But I mind their finding among our relics only rusty old cannon we didn't make. I'd rather they found one graven horse we left behind, some one thing of beauty we made. Because we tried, our government tried; we did try. And we're leaving nothing, no memory, no beauty."

Baldwin was embarrassed. Sometimes he read the poems at the end of the page in the *Atlantic Monthly*, but he was embarrassed if someone saw him reading them. He hoped he would not be embarrassed again, when he got back. He thought not. Aloud, he said:

"I never studied any Chinese poetry. It's quite different from ours."

"No," she said, "it's almost the same. I read all your poetry when I was in America. Do you know sometimes I would go to tea at our professor's house, and he would read poetry out loud to us. I thought America was all poetry . . . until this trip. Americans are hard too, aren't they? I think . . . I think I learned only the poetry in America, and all you've seen in China is this road, and how cruel we are."

"I wouldn't say that," answered Baldwin quickly, stirred somehow. "I've learned as much on this trip as you learned in Boston, I've learned . . ."

He stopped. He did not know what he had learned. But he was aware of her hand, on his arm, holding him softly but tight, and her deep black eyes, looking at him, and her voice, urgent.

"Tell me, tell me! What have you learned? It's important to me. Is there anything you've learned in China? I don't know what I am, I learned everything I know in American, or in America. Have *you* learned something here? Did it give you anything? . . ."

Just then came the distant rap of Michaelson's carbine. A double shot. Then another double shot. They were ready.

"It's time now," he said, reluctantly freeing his arm from

her fingers, but relieved that he did not have to answer the question.

He knelt to the cord on the ground. He took a kitchen match out of its glass vial, scraped it along the sole of his boot until the round head spat at him, and held it upside down so that the shaft of the match might catch. Then he touched it gently and carefully to the frayed cord and with the most fleeting of hisses, the cord had disappeared and was gone.

"What happened?" asked Su-Piao.

"In a sec . . ." But as he spoke a hammer sound pounded through the air, and then a racketing, bouncing series of cracks as if firecrackers were going off.

"It's going," he said, "but it's not going on simultaneous impact," and then a mortar shell landed beside them in the ditch and the bank shuddered above them, and he reached out an arm and pulled her close and they both buried their faces in the ground.

"Damn," he said, holding her close, "damn those mortar shells. They're ricocheting and kicking each other off one by one, and they're going up and coming down here."

Another shell slammed beside them and he knew they must run for it, and he grabbed her elbow and yelled, "We can't stay here, we've got to run for it." She looked at him, not hearing through the din, and he yelled as loud as he could.

"We've got to run! To the shed! The stuff is making a fountain, it's mortar shells, we'll be safer the closer we are to the shed."

He lifted himself to his knees, and, with an effort, grabbed her elbow to haul her up. She was hitching her skirt and he noticed she wore Chinese straw sandals, and he hoped she could run, and then they were both out of the ditch and running to the shed. As they ran, his hasty, frightened eye could see what was happening. The roof of the shed had fallen in, and yellow and black smoke was pouring from the fallen roof. Occasional fire gashes streaked the smoke and black objects hurtled out into the sky, arcing dark across the blue, falling again, exploding with geysers of dirt, and a rose-yellow flower of flame at the center of each instant burst. They stumbled into the drainage ditch that ran about the burning, thundering shed, and lay there. She was beside him, and he was holding her. The fountain of shells was going fine now; he could hear explosions inside the shed, explosions all about them; explosions hundreds of yards away. But they were within the arch of the spray and they could lie and hear the ground pound, and pound, and pound and shudder around them. She pressed closer, like a child. Then it was over. Two loud blasts from inside the shed ripped the volleying, a final thud and bang resounded further away, and after that they were silent, still clutching.

There was nothing to say and she looked at him, very close. Curiously she was smiling.

"Do you know what I was thinking?" she asked in the quiet.

He shook his head, being comfortable in the moment, being glad he was alive, hoping she did not notice she was in his arms, not wanting to stir.

"I was thinking you Americans may have put it all down in your book. But it was the Chinese who invented firecrackers."

He smiled and said:

"I wasn't thinking at all. We almost got killed."

But he held on to her. She lay there for a moment in his arms and he did not know whether he was holding her because it happened that way, or because of the warmth in the cold or because he wanted to. There was a yellow-clay streak on her black hair, and he freed one arm and gently brushed it off. His fingers lingered on her hair and then, of themselves, slowly drew their way down over her cheek, smooth and soft, and caressed it and stayed there, his thumb under her warm chin, his finger-tips cupping her cheek. He stared at her, not knowing what was going to happen. Then slowly her eyes veiled, the American smile left her face and it was all Chinese again, blank, dark, withdrawn—yet beautiful. He could not tell whether he had done something wrong, or whether he had pleased her. Nor did he want to spoil it. He could not take his fingers away; but she was slowly wriggling away, and sat up. He rose, too.

When they stood, Baldwin winced. He could see the shed they had blown was a mound of smoke and flickering flame; but the roof of another shed was burning, too. His stomach crawled in fear. What if it blew, too—now? His leg muscles clenched to run away. Then his mind remembered that the shed in the row at the left held only artillery pieces; it would not explode.

He turned back to her and knew the other moment had ended. There was no way back to it, and his mind doggedly reverted to business. The whole dump would go on a straight hook-up and it was best to start immediately and get out early.

"Let's go back and see if the jeep is still there," he said. "That was a damn fool thing to do. But it worked. We have it made."

The rest of the work went so smoothly it seemed to Baldwin that these sprawling dumps of Tushan, the purpose and goal of all his trip for four days had become anticlimax. By two, the long red firing wire circuit ran down the length of the field, the cross-ties of primacord ran from the circuit to the primer-blocks of TNT in each shed, and as he checked the work down the long field by jeep he knew that he was much farther away from Liuchow than two hundred miles and four days; this blow would be no foul-up.

The men of the team were waiting for him on the hillside as he drove back, sitting on the ground, their knees jackknifed up, idly talking. He saw for the first time that each had a new Luger and a holster belt and knew they had been looting the sheds. A few days ago it would have annoyed him. Now it made no difference. They would find no Luger ammunition in all China to go with the pistols they had taken, but they would have a trophy of their trip—a German Luger, scrounged in China, a memento of the wrong war, an emblem of victory snatched in defeat. It made no sense for the team to take Lugers; but he saw that some of the Chinese soldiers who had helped smash the artillery had Lugers too, and he nodded to himself in agreement—the Chinese could sell the Lugers.

Conscious of a sudden splitting headache, he got out of the jeep, aching for an aspirin. He saw that the detonator was already set up, the lead wires on the ground ready to be hooked on, waiting for his word to blow.

"Are you ready, Mike?" he asked finally.

"Yes, sir," said Michaelson and the tone of respect was a soothing touch to Baldwin's spirit and to his aching head.

"I'll push it off myself, let me take the stick," he said, and walked to the blasting machine. He lifted it by the leather handle, hefted it, fingered the wing-nuts for the wires, ran the handle up and down its travel. It was so smooth, so small, so infinitely powerful.

He turned to the men.

"We're safe here," he said, "but get down in the ditch

anyway until we see how it goes." While the men and the Chinese scrambled into the ditch, he touched the tendrils of the galvanometer to the naked leads of the wire and the needle on the dial lazily, but firmly, swung up; then back; then up. It was a good circuit. He curled the wires around the poles of the blasting machine and tightened the wing nuts.

The men were watching him and he moved deliberately. He saw their eyes peering at him from the ditch row and he made the round "O" with thumb and forefinger and yelled, "Heads down, now." The field was bare as far as he could see as he turned back to the machine, yelling, "Fire in the Hole!" It echoed in the clear day, and he waited and gave the call again, and waited and called once more, and then pushed off.

It was perfect. From where he stood, looking out over the vast dump, where everything might have gone wrong, first there were the sheds, edging other sheds which were edging other sheds, gray-yellow in their neat rows running to the far and distant rim of the hollow. Then the sheds were winking at him, in flashes and spasms of light, like a switchboard carrying the telephone traffic of madmen—amber flashes, yellow flashes, golden flashes, red flashes. Then, after that slowly the sound began to charge back, coming in waves, booming, slamming, booming, bouncing off the hills, the echoes rolling back volley after volley. And as he watched, the scene grew, unfurling in a tumult of color.

The men scrambled out of the ditch to watch it, too. On the left the sheds with the gasoline and alcohol had begun to blaze and Baldwin was watching them flower: the flames a pale red and yellow flicker in the light of the afternoon, but the black of their smoke now beginning to show too, and the flames in the fuel sheds were licking up one by one, reaching together to form what would be a fine corona of fire when the wind, which was swaying them, should marry them in an updraft.

Then he heard Ballo say, "Look at that," and he turned to the right, where out of one of the sheds, a fountain of green lights was beginning to soar slowly in the air. A whole crate, or dozens of crates, of flares had begun to go and now the cascade of their upward thrust was painting pink and yellow and green and white against the sky, with the varying chemistries of all the nations that had sold arms to China. The shed, they could see, was shuddering with flame and some of the flares were darting out flat, across the field, lancing still other sheds; while other flares were rocketing at every angle across the sky, painting their way in long slow streamers as they went, and even in daylight the pin-point of their glare was sharp and hurt their eyes.

Then there was too much to watch at once. From everywhere across the huge field came the sounds of destruction and the meaningless anger of the ammunition going—the rat-tat-tat, rat-tat-tat of the small arms ammunition, pappety-pap, pappety-pap of belts, the sky-tracing effects of the tracer bullets in their belts, the heavier but rapid chunking of fifty-caliber ammo, and the deep chug-boom, chug-boom, slam-slam, slam-slam of all kinds of shells going everywhere. It was great.

"Oh man, if we could have saved this for the Fourth of July!" said somebody, and Baldwin was aware that the men were yelling at the top of their lungs, screaming with delight, and the dump was only beginning to boil. He knew he was enjoying it, too, and could not tear himself away. He knew the sound and booming must be carrying back to Tushan four miles away, and the refugees and soldiers must be looking in the sky, their faces upturned in wonder at what was happening. He had lived with this in mind for four days, but to the thousands in the streets of the town, it must be a mystery and an unknown menace. Now, always, he would know that when something terrible or mysterious happened which he could not understand, he would know that somebody had made it happen, because one man's decision must be at the heart of it.

From within the dumps, a yellow flash larger than all the rest suddenly ripped apart, pushing smoke away with a sweep of light that overwhelmed him. Then, a column, an enormous pillar of smoke and flame went tumbling upwards, billow scrambling upwards to chase billow, and the black column reached from the ground up to the thickening layer of smoke clouds that was beginning to merge as a ceiling over the dumps, and the column, for moments, held up the entire ceiling. Then, flattening out all the other sounds, there came the roll of the explosion that had made the column, thumping on his ears, then the shock-wave, and he could feel himself slugged in the chest and staggering backward; and he knew that the shed of TNT must have gone, finally.

The trance had passed and he was alert again. He called:

"Let's get out of here, we've had it, back to the trucks."

They moved sluggishly back to their trucks by the gates, their faces still watching the rippling hollow, seething with smoke and stirred by the thunder sound of explosion. He turned himself once more, uncomfortable that he was leaving the fires burning, unable to shake the thought that they should stay and tidy up, and shook himself out of it, telling himself that that was a Chinese job for some day in the future.

"Get the lead out of your pants," he heard Michaelson yelling, supporting him. "We want to clear this town this afternoon."

He turned to Su-Piao and asked her to have Kwan dismiss

the Chinese soldiers who had helped. The Chinese soldiers clambered into their diesel truck, and as it disappeared, he noticed the two soldiers on the tail gate, with their Lugers in their laps, waving to the Americans and he waved back. It had been a good detail for them. If they could hide the Lugers from their officers, and sell them, and then desert, they would have made a good thing of it. He wondered if that was what he would do if he were a Chinese soldier and were paid thirty cents a month. But he was an American.

He got into his own jeep, pulled it around, and waited until the two trucks of the convoy had backed and twisted and were in line behind him. They had no more primacord, he realized; they were short of explosives; they were toothless and harmless. But, by God, they had done a job. One night more on the road, he told himself, and then we hand it over. Except for Collins, the trip had gone perfectly. And tomorrow he would hand over command and be out of it.

CHAPTER 10

Fire-Fight

AS THEY JOLTED out of the dumps, it was only three on his wrist watch, and Baldwin was high.

Behind him, the last detonations rumbled like a raffle of applause in his ears. The Japanese would not pause here now, for there was no point in their staying in Tushan, or what would be left of it. Now that the dumps were gone, the Central headquarters would surely burn the city before they left, and with the city burned the Japanese would find no shelter here. Nor, of course, would the wanderers. But the wanderers did not seem important to Baldwin any longer. The giddiness and the exultation could not be held back. He shook his head to shake the daydreaming from it. But with or without daydreaming, he knew he could sit again in the warroom at Kunming and see the vast chunk of China draped about the plateau and be proud of today's job.

It was still important that he had done it himself, AT

DISCRETION, yet he realized that the dumps would have been blown by someone else, sooner or later, better or worse. He understood now how the men in the front offices felt about everyone else. To decide, you had to have the energy first to see the obvious and then make the decision—and enough energy left over to make other men see the obvious, too, and force them to act. You had to *will* it. After that anyone else could work out the details. He was high now, his headache all gone because he had *willed* it this morning, and had brought it off clean.

Blowing the field at Liuchow on Monday had not counted, he told himself, as he looked back over the week—he had blown Liuchow under the shelter of Loomis' authority. The little bridge of Colonel Li on Wednesday was too small to count; he knew now he had not been outwitted there; he simply had not recognized what was obvious. Thursday had been good—the cotton truck had been good—but easy, because the racketeer had left no alternate between right and wrong; and the sidehill blow had been hard, but correct. Yesterday had been bad. He could not now recall why he had lingered in Hochih—the snow-flurry and Lewis' fever seemed scant reason. The mistake there had been to trust Collins' judgment against Su-Piao's judgment. Su-Piao had been right, he should have listened to her; and because he had not found the will to reverse Collins, Collins was dead. The thought of the dead boy ached inside him like a wound, and today's work had not evened it. Yet today's job had ended the trip solidly, not the blowing part which was technical, but the morning conference which had been hard. That part of him which was still staff told him that what he had done was clean-done, well-done, and his mind slid off as it always did to daydreaming, to his reporting of the event at Kunming, to the retelling of it, to writing of it to Helen. And he caught himself. He wanted to talk about this again, and again, to someone, and it was not Helen, but Su-Piao, who was by his side, now, quiet, wrapped in her own thoughts, but with him.

He was slowing down now, as he crossed the tracks, and came upon the town again, which he must negotiate to get back on the main road. Once more he was caught in the people on the streets, and the driving, now they were back in traffic, annoyed him more than it had on the morning visit to headquarters. In the few hours they had worked at the dump, the restless simmering of refugees in the street had quickened to an erratic bubbling and hasty movement, as if the burners of concern and worry under the town had been turned high. People were moving in currents through the crowd, files edging this way, files pushing the other way, the voices louder, and a stream of uniformed men seemed to be detaching itself from the cross-movements, leaving the refugees coagulated in clumps and clusters of dismay.

"They are moving," said Kwan as the jeep was caught in the clutch of the crowd again.

"Who?" asked Baldwin.

"The troops. The headquarters have decided to move since this morning, since we spoke to them."

It was so. And Baldwin reflected that this churning movement in the street now was somehow because he had passed through this morning and blown the dumps. It was strange; one firm decision anywhere, in a situation of uncertainty, triggered off other decisions, high and low, like an avalanche set off by a cause no one could ever after determine. The artillery he had noticed in the morning were now being disassembled and packed on mules, and the mules hauled into line. The drivers cursed the mules, their whips cracked, officers ran about screaming at soldiers in the high-pitched Chinese falsetto of command and little knots of troops stumbled and huddled together. Some officers blew whistles, others shrieked till their faces were red, and Baldwin noticed as the animals and men turned into columns that where the beasts had been, mounds of fresh manure steamed in the cold, as if they, too, were suddenly nerve-shaken.

The movement was beginning to separate the soldier mass from the refugee. For it was only the soldiers who were beginning to form. The refugees, who had heard the explosions from far away, and could see the tumult and confusion of command, knew that something was happening. About each clump of soldiers was a larger cluster of refugees, chattering, asking questions, seeking; and as Baldwin blared the convoy through them, they parted scowling, or held up their hands and waved, or smiled and called at them, asking for rides on the empty trucks. A student paced them in a lope yelling, "Americans very good, I go with you American, Americans very good, I go with you." A woman held up a baby in front of them, her face of sorrow pleading, and Baldwin knew she would never make it on foot, five days in the cold to Kweiyang. The woman was shoved out of the way as the convoy lurched forward once more and Baldwin could see that two younger women, with fat cheeks, smiling the beggar's smile, had pushed her away. The two younger women, amazingly, spoke English, and one cackled, "Hey, Joe, you take me, I make you happy Joe, for free Joe, I go with you I make you happy Joe for free no money Joe for free, I love you Joe, hey Joe . . ." and then their voices faded; they had been wiped out along with the airbases and GIs they had served in the frolic days. They were all part of the scenery. He had been sorry for all of them for three days, and yesterday at Hochih he had hated them, but now he was neither sorry nor did he hate. He was just on his way out.

Impatience began to settle on him only when they were

clearing town. He had finished the job, but he could make no speed, for the traffic still clawed at him. He noticed, irritably, how many individual soldiers seemed to be shuffling in the drift and how many of them carried guns.

"Whose troops are they?" asked Baldwin of Su-Piao, and Su-Piao, translating to Kwan, replied:

"Nobody's."

"Nobody's? Deserters?" Baldwin asked.

"No deserters, not troops," said Kwan. "Soldiers. After every retreat, this way. The soldiers must be gathered again. Some are looking for their regiments, some are looking for any general who will feed them. The soldiers are looking for a home, too. Their home should be the army. But there is no army here. In the beginning after every defeat we would gather the soldiers ourselves. And the Japanese would try to collect our soldiers, too. The Japanese take no prisoners. They kill civilians and soldiers. Only those Chinese soldiers who will fight in their garrisons, they let live. Or in the north, the Communists collect the soldiers and change their minds. Now it is much more difficult. No one wants soldiers now. The American generals say China has too many soldiers, not enough guns."

"What will happen to them?" asked Baldwin. "Where will they go?"

It was Su-Piao who answered, sadly.

"Some of them will sell their guns and sneak home; and others will find a place in some other regiment. And a lot will die because they are sick and hungry. They're all so far from home—if the army doesn't take care of them, then no one takes care of them. I suppose some will become bandits because these people in Kweichou don't know who they are and can't understand their dialect. The soldiers will want food and they'll take the food from the peasants, and the peasants will hate them and try to kill them, and the soldiers will be very dangerous because they'll become bandits."

Baldwin was glad he was almost out of it. These soldiers and refugees who were drifting in the current he breasted now, these were the strong. The weak had died on the way already, and of those behind him on the road, most would die, too. Those who had reached Tushan and could almost see the plateau ahead, concealing Kweiyang and the fugitive dream of safety, these were the ones who meant to live. The strong and cruel lived; only they. Survivors were not to be pitied, they were to be feared.

The foot-traffic was thinning now, finally. It was like a tide, this flow he had seen all week, with its crests and slacks, its congestions and openings, each crest shoved forward by some impulse of panic that might be hours or days behind down the road. The slack about the convoy now was made of those who had set out from Tushan before the blowing of the dumps, for they were now five miles out of the city, a hike of an hour or two hours in time. Thus, these people about him had started before the movement that was now beginning to boil in the town that was about to be leveled. These were the ones who had determined to reach Kweiyang before they froze to death on the road, or before they starved. Young men with strong faces, the husky and the gaunt. Few children now, fewer women. More drifting soldiers with their guns. What would you do if you were a father, thought Baldwin, or a husband? Would you leave the family? At what point would you leave the family? If you could not carry your family with you because one was weak, did you leave the one, or leave them all, or stay and all freeze to death?

His foot on the gas treadle was heavier and he was picking up speed from the crawl that had shackled him since they left Tushan. The speed soothed him, easing the foreboding that the wandering soldiers, with their guns, had caused to swell in him since Kwan had explained their meaning. Speed was strength. He no longer had to feel and fumble his way forward with the jeep as he had all week with the long tail of four six-by-sixes dragging behind him. There were only two trucks now, and he felt unburdened. Just possibly he might make some outpost of the new line by nightfall; just possibly, too, he might be able to raise an American liaison unit with them. He would try to radio again tonight, wherever they made camp; there was nothing now to concern him but himself and his men.

It was only an hour ago that they had blown the dumps, it was almost four now, and the slant of the sun, clear, bright, and austere, lay on the ochre hills. They were going north and far off, high, high away, the sun which was settling to the west was washing the snowcaps of the range on the east with its rose and yellow luminescence. In another hour, it would be deep dark. But before then would come the sunset with its burst of flagrant beauty. For the first time on the long trip he could wait for it without fear and concern for the night, thinking only of how far beyond the imagination and memory of his people these mountains reared into the Asian sky.

"I think that was an American," said Su-Piao flatly across his reverie.

He slowed down.

"An American? Walking?" he asked, unbelieving.

"No, a body."

Baldwin trod on the brake, raising his hand by reflex in signal to the trucks following.

"A lot of these people are dressed in old GI clothes, they've picked up old uniforms at the bases in the east. It's probably Chinese," he said, turning to her. He did not want to get out of the jeep and look. Yet he knew he must.

"I think it's American," she said again, softly.

"Where?"

"We just passed it. On the outside of the road. We can't have come a hundred feet."

He got out of the jeep and paced back to the trucks.

"What's up?" asked Michaelson, leaning out of the cab of his truck.

"I want you," said Baldwin. "Come on down."

Niergaard leaned out of the cab when Michaelson stepped down.

"What's up?" he repeated.

"Nothing," said Baldwin. "Stay put. I want to look at something." They had not noticed it any more than he, Baldwin saw. Dead men were dead.

He repeated the same orders to Prince and Ballo in the second truck, and walked forward. He realized he had his own carbine free, and without a word Michaelson had unslung his carbine, too.

There was no doubt it was American, Baldwin saw. No Chinese had that light-brown American hair. It lay face down on the road, its boots, its pants, its jacket stripped. In the cold, in its white underdrawers and sun-tan shirt, the body looked innocent; and the lean boyishness, the tight, unfleshy thighs, told Baldwin even before he turned the stiff, cold body over that this was Collins.

Wordlessly, they looked at the strange peaceful face, with the deep, purple-and-blue bruise where the unknown rock had killed the day before, and Baldwin felt again the frenzied, panic strength of the hand that had hammered its way with such force down on Collins' head yesterday. But out of the numbness of his mind, Baldwin slowly grasped that something more terrible had happened here today, at this point, on the road. From under the deep weight of his breeding and restraint, he could feel a rage choking its way up his throat, a yell swollen somewhere underneath that wanted to burst. With eyes surprised and stunned he looked at Michaelson and Michaelson was staring at him, muttering.

"They wouldn't have dumped him," Michaelson was saying. "They must have been jumped. They must've run into trouble. Where do you think they are?"

The others? What had happened to them?

Suddenly Michaelson screamed, almost a woman's scream, so high and sharp the pitch, so abrupt the voice speaking from the fear that had suddenly come on them.

"Get back, you son-of-a-bitch! Get back, you goddam bastard!" he yelled, with the gun, that seemed to slip automatically into his trigger-eager fingers, pointing at something in back of Baldwin.

Baldwin whirled. It was a loiterer, a wanderer on the road, a middle-aged refugee, without a gun, walking all alone, who had stopped in curiosity to see what the two men in strange uniform were kneeling over.

"Get the hell out of here," yelled Baldwin, his voice as savage as Michaelson's, knowing himself ready to kill without thinking or pretext.

The Chinese, his face suddenly fearful, held up his palms in a gesture of friendship, tried a weak smile, saw the body, his face froze, turned quickly away and hastened off.

"Get Niergaard and Ballo to carry him back to the truck," said Baldwin, and Michaelson hurried away.

Baldwin stood there over the body, his mind sorting and re-sorting the possibilities. The body could not have fallen off the truck unnoticed to be stripped later by the wanderers; Baldwin had seen them lashing the bedroll to the truck when they set off only that morning. Miller would not have dumped Collins voluntarily, there was no reason to, he was ours, not

Chinese. Then Miller had been stopped and someone else, hijackers of the road, had dumped the body. But Miller would not have let someone dump the body without a fight. Where were the others? Where was the truck? Lewis was sick, he couldn't have fought. Miller at the wheel, not watching, good-natured Miller. The hijackers had only to shoot Miller, then possess the truck. But had they gone on to kill? The road was full of soldiers with guns. Hundreds must have passed up this road today. Any of them might have jumped the truck—perhaps when it stopped for a moment. Baldwin remembered Miller was always relieving himself at every stop.

But when had it happened? They were only a few miles out of Tushan now, the truck had been no more than an hour on its way, at most, when it had reached this point. The truck had started at ten. It must have reached this point by eleven, five hours ago, before the blowing of the dumps. He should not have split his forces, he should have kept them with him.

Niergaard and Ballo were back now, lifting the body, their faces grave and frightened. Su-Piao and Kwan had wandered back too, somber, saying nothing. Baldwin followed the cortege carrying the rigid body back to the two remaining trucks of the convoy and the other men had come down to talk softly about it, too.

"What do you think happened?" asked Su-Piao. They waited for Baldwin; he did not know; but he had to say.

"They were jumped," said Baldwin. "It could have been any of these Chinese soldiers. It happened early, probably in the first hour. Miller probably stopped the truck to do something; he probably got into an argument; or they were picked off without any argument. We'll have to find the others."

Su-Piao had been translating to Kwan and Kwan spoke.

"Not here," he said. "The truck went on. We will find the truck ahead of us. But the others we have passed already."

Baldwin listened to Kwan: "First there would be the fight and they would take away the truck," said Kwan. "Then they would drive a little way ahead and stop to look at what was in the truck. That was when they found this one and dropped him here. But the other bodies they would leave where they fought—back from here. The truck will be ahead of us, the others will be behind."

Kwan knew they were dead, Baldwin knew they were dead. This had happened five or six hours ago, in a flow of men and time, and no one on the road passing now knew anything about this or had anything to do with what had happened five hours ago. The weights and pressures inside Baldwin kept shifting; he could feel himself rocking to the point of explosion. He could not go into Kweiyang and just report three men missing out of eight. These were *his* men; he had to do something.

"First we have to find them," said Baldwin. "Then we have to find the truck. And then we'll probably find the Slopeys who did it, and then we take care of them."

He did not know quite yet what he could do but his voice continued, "We'll turn around right here and back-track for a few miles looking for the others. Keep closed up and keep your eyes peeled for anything on either side of the road."

Kwan saw it first, stopping the convoy, pointing to two pair of dirty grass-sandals by the side of the road.

"They did it here," he said. "Nobody leaves sandals on this road. Everyone who has walked this far must have shoes or sandals. They do not throw sandals away for no one can walk far barefoot. The sandals here were changed for the boots the Americans wore."

They got out and Kwan was right. In the ditch by the side of the road, cold and folded over each other, like the pictures of atrocities in the magazine, sprawled in frozen awkwardness, lay two bodies—both stripped as Collins had been stripped for their boots, their clothes, their warm jackets. It was impossible to believe that the bodies were dead, but they were. Who had done it, or how they had been flung here, the bodies could not say. Lewis, almost unrecognizable, told his own story, the face blown off and the powder burns on it. It was a close shot, an executioner's shot—the killer must have found him lying in the back of the truck, and, standing over him, fired straight down into his face. Miller had it clean through the neck, one shot and that one shot enough. Miller had never been a combat man, but had he had a chance to shoot? It was important. Had they had a chance? Was it an argument over food, or over a ride, with an American gun lifted first and a Chinese shot fired quicker? Or had they been sneak-jumped, while peeing, or resting? How?

Baldwin was choking. To cry would help get it out, but he could not cry and it was the rage and fury pushing around in him that wanted out most. To shoot, to kill, that was the thing, someone must pay for this.

"Get them in the trucks," he ordered. "We're taking them home."

He watched as the men carried the two, heavily, slowly, back to the convoy. He was not out of it, there was no one on this road to whom he could report a crime and hand it over. There is no law in this whole country, he told himself. This was the way at the beginning of things, someone had to make laws at the beginning of things, and he was way back at the beginning and he was going to find the men who had done it and make them pay for it.

"What are you going to do now?" asked Su-Piao, and he realized she stood outside his rage. She and Kwan. They were no part of this. He could hate finally, anonymously, he did not have to have a reason for hating any more.

"We're going to look for the truck," he said in a dead voice that bore no tone.

"I know," began Su-Piao, "but . . ."

"I'm going to find the truck and the people who did it," he snapped, cutting her off.

She translated to Kwan and he replied:

"They cannot go anywhere in the truck, there is only this one road. They do not know it is part of a convoy and that you are behind. They will not be careful. So when we get to Kweiyang, you will tell the American army, the army will tell Central, Central will find the truck and the people who took it, and the government will shoot them."

"No," said Baldwin, stubbornly. "I'm going to find that truck and get them."

"Kwan is right," said Su-Piao firmly. "I know how you feel, but this isn't the time for it. First get to Kweiyang and they can't escape. The army will find them and hand them over to the government."

"There isn't any government," said Baldwin coldly. "You know there isn't. I lost these men, I'm going to find who killed them."

"You can't say you lost them," said Su-Piao, her voice now pleading. "*You* aren't responsible. I keep telling you this is happening everywhere. You don't even know what happened. If they were drowned in a flood, would you whip the flood? You can't punish a flood, don't you see."

"I don't care," repeated Baldwin. "Maybe we'll all get killed. You said last night when an American dies it should mean something. I've got to make it mean something, I just can't drive back to Kweiyang like this without *trying* to do something."

Her anger was beginning to rise to answer his. He could

sense it, and knew it was because they had been close, and he became even more furious as she said:

"You're trying to make yourself feel innocent, that's all. You *are* innocent and if you don't see it . . ."

But Baldwin had turned his back on her and walked away. The men had finished carrying the bodies to the truck and he did not want them to hear her; it was either fear or anger that would catch them now and he wanted anger, to be ready when he called for it.

"Get back into your trucks," he said. "You know what's happened. We're going to find the pigs who took that truck. If we have to tear what's left of China apart. Keep your guns ready. Keep your eyes on the road. If you see the truck before I do, fire into the air. I'll hear. I'll stop."

He felt mutilated as he started the jeep again. His glance back showed only the two trucks—two trucks with four men live, and three men dead, who had all been alive yesterday. He had been crippled. But he was free now, he knew, of any restraint; he could flee, he could fight, he could speed, he could blast.

She tried once more to talk to him as they started.

"You won't be doing anything," she said, "if you have a fight with these soldiers. Once they've killed someone, they're bandits, they're nothing. You can't make law here, you can't change the world when the world is ending. If you shoot somebody on this road the only reason that could be right is to save your life. You can't make law until there's government. Don't you see? All you want is revenge and it's too late for that, or it's too early."

"It's not revenge," he snapped. "Even if it isn't written down there has to be a right. I can't go back into Kweiyang if I don't do something about this."

"It *is* revenge," she repeated. "It *is* revenge and you're doing it for yourself, and it's not time for revenge, revenge is a luxury like civilization, you can't do anything with revenge at the end when nobody will know and nobody will remember." Her voice broke as she pleaded. "Oh please, oh please, I'm right, I know I'm right."

She had brought him to the verge of weakness and she might be right or wrong as she was yesterday at Hochih and he had to stop her voice, for he could not listen to it.

"For God's sake!" he shouted at her. "Stop it, stop it, STOP IT!"

She stopped.

As they drove on, Baldwin saw the sunset glowing blood-red over the mountains and the mountains were full of malice because he did not belong here. And within him, temper answered the malice. He was a stranger, with dead men in his charge, and death stretching back all the long miles to Liuchow. But he was not fleeing now, the Japanese had disappeared into yesterday. Now he was chasing, his convoy picking up speed through these mountains, black and purple, their snowcaps red and gold.

They had passed two villages, making good time, but they had seen nothing to catch their eye or give them a clue to what they sought. And then the convoy dipped over the saddle of a little ridge. At the bottom of it, the road made an "S" curve through the valley, entering a patch of huts from the left, straightening out on the single main street, twisting up to the right as it left the patch of buildings to climb up another hairpin over the range that lay beyond. The patch of buildings was too small even to be a village.

"What's that one?" asked Baldwin, as he first spied it below. He did not care about the name, for the names of the smaller villages on the Air Force map he carried were usually wrong. But he wanted to know the name, for knowing the names gave him the illusion of knowing where he was.

"Yang-an-Sing," said Kwan, leaning forward from his back seat to cast his voice up between Su-Piao and Baldwin in front.

"A *ma-fu* stop," Kwan continued as Su-Piao translated, "where the horses used to stop. This is left over from the old road of the Emperors. Where the carts would stop, every eighty *li* would be a *ma-fu* stop, where travelers could rest their horses and get food for the night. Four or five houses for the peasants who grow vegetables or food to sell the travelers, and the *ma-fu-kuan*, the hostel where the travelers and wagons stop. The compound with the white house in the middle, that is the *ma-fu-kuan*. Today, not many *ma-fu-kuans* are left in China except in the north where the camels come in from the desert. And the truck is there in front of the *ma-fu-kuan*, by the left of the road before it turns up into the mountain again," concluded Su-Piao as Kwan finished.

Had he heard the translation right? Had she understood Kwan?

"The truck? Is that what he said? Our truck?"

"Yes," she said, "that's what he said."

"*Man-man-ti*," said Kwan cautiously.

"He says go slow now," translated Su-Piao, and Baldwin's eyes squinted down the twisting incline to the village, his eyes trying to shift focus in the gathering dark from the long reach of the road to what Kwan's eyes had pinpointed in the bar of the "S" curve, in the street.

From the height where they rode, looking down on the cluster of shacks, it was like looking down from an airplane. And again, as when he had looked from planes down on the villages of China, Yang-an-Sing seemed clean, crisp, sharp-edged in its hollow. The adobe huts, with their sharp, straight lines, the whitewashed walls of the *ma-fu-kuan* seemed even cleaner against the dusk than by daylight. He strained and peered to pick out what Kwan's eye had spotted, but the haze of the evening fuzzed the distant street.

There was no wall about Yang-an-Sing, Baldwin could see, and his mind checked that off as good—it would make it easier getting in and out if there was to be trouble. For, as they kept winding down, he could begin to make out in the street darker gray shapes than the huts, and he knew these were horsecarts, or barrows, or Chinese trucks, or people and this, like every other sheltered spot they had passed in the week just past, must be crowded. Whatever had to be done, would be difficult because it was crowded, but it would be easier since there was no wall. And as they rode their brakes down the hill, Baldwin knew that whatever was going to happen, would happen here.

It was only on the last twist down the slope that his eye picked up the truck, parked to the left of the street. There it was, the olive drab of the American six-by-six unclear, but the shape unmistakable just there beyond the inn where the road twisted right and upwards against the bulk of the hill on the other side.

Baldwin decided to stop the convoy and lay out the plan before they got into town. He gathered the men again.

"O.K.," he said, "the truck's down there. Whoever jumped Miller back there on the road is with it. We're going to take that truck back. We'll go right through the town first—fast. We pull up on the far side of it, just where the road turns up the hill. There's a grade there. We'll be looking right down the main-stem. We've got a BAR in one of the trucks. I want two of you to set it up on the rear truck for cover. I'm going in with Kwan and Michaelson to get the truck. The rest of you will wait there on the slope, on the trucks, covering."

It might be wrong. He knew he was repeating the mistake of the morning, splitting his forces again. But that was always a command problem—how many to hold in reserve, how many to use for a strike. And this morning when he split them he had not been prepared for a fight. Now he was. All ready. The Chinese would still have to fire first. He could not. But once the Chinese did, if they did, he would be released to hammer back. With everything.

Tense, his hands quivering at the wheel, his nerves reaching out in anticipation, he started the convoy down the last slope to the street. It was so normal as they rumbled through the street, the scene covered with the softly crying, softly chattering, gurgling, murmuring human sediment of the retreat that it was difficult to think that he must stop here and do something. Instinct told him there was no command post here, no unit, not even a Ssuchuanese general. Only people. For an instant, as they slid through, he knew he should go right on and reach Kweiyang tomorrow. But there was Miller's truck slipping behind him on his left, high above the jeep. He could not leave an American truck to the looters simply because he was afraid, or because it was wise. The sight of the truck infuriated him.

When they pulled up about a hundred and fifty feet beyond the truck, they were out of the village, on the slope.

Baldwin got out, studied the road, saw that the sharp twist of its "S" fitted his plan perfectly; he was gazing directly down the main street, and could see the dark passage marked with the waving flicker of refugee bonfires. There could be five hundred or a thousand refugees and soldiers mingling in this village. And they all lay below him, just there. It would be so much easier to put the brand to the whole place, drive back, dump a cratering charge from the jeep, fling out a few blocks of TNT, sweep it with tracers, leave it boiling in flame to claim afterwards they had spoiled it for the Japanese. But there was no purpose to that, he caught himself remonstrating with himself; there had to be a purpose, a right and a wrong. He wanted only two or three men here, and those only if he could be sure they were the right ones. It would be so much easier to do it clean and wholesale; but there had to be a purpose.

He walked back to the second truck to find the men. They were moving fast. Ballo was on the back of the truck already fitting the BAR together and Baldwin called up:

"Ballo? You sure you know how to use that thing?"

"Had three weeks on it at Benning before I got transferred to engineers," Ballo called back.

"Don't go with it unless you hear shooting down there. Fire over the truck to give us cover, not into the white building. Don't get nervous. Are you ready?"

"Another couple of minutes," Ballo shouted back. "I'm nervous, Major, but don't worry."

He checked Michaelson next, he needed Michaelson to come with him on the walk.

"I've got Niergaard fusing up some blocks of TNT," said Michaelson, "but that stuff is pretty hard to toss far enough to be safe. Got another idea, though. We've got a cratering charge left. Those metal cylinders roll great. It'll go down the slope right into the street. If we cap it and tape a little safety fuse to it, we can blow up any rush they try. There's one of these gasoline drums, too. About half full, and we don't need it any more. If we tape a half-pound block of TNT to the drum head—we can roll her down, too. When she goes, she'll make a real fire."

"O.K.," said Baldwin, "not a bad idea. Tell them to get the stuff ready. But let's hurry. The Chinese must know we've stopped here." It might be useful, he knew. Even if it wasn't useful—he knew he no longer gave a damn, and was off to find Kwan and Su-Piao.

He found them in the jeep, their faces blank, remote. They were not with it. And he knew it was not because they were afraid. But he needed them.

"I'll need you and Kwan for the talking," he said to Su-Piao. He did not like taking her with him; but she was his tongue. He had to.

She made no reply to him but turned to Kwan to translate. Both got out of the jeep and followed him and he found Michaelson again and was ready, and started down the slope.

They reached the parked truck by the inn in what seemed a moment. Baldwin noticed that the truck had become, in the course of a few hours, half-Chinese, a driftling of the flight. It was piled high with refugees and their gear, and on the crown of the mound above the truck sat dark, waiting figures, civilians, sitting where they would sit all night in the cold to be sure to get off with the truck in the morning. The hijackers had wasted no time in selling rides out to Kweiyang. Whoever these people were, silently waiting for the truck to save them, they had probably paid all their cash or valuables for this ride out. And whoever had sold the rides was probably rich or would be rich, if he could get to Kweiyang. But now, whoever it was, he was still here in Yang-an-Sing. He had stopped too soon to enjoy his fortune.

Baldwin stopped before the inn door, and pushed in without knocking.

The room they entered was full of fug. The charcoal heating pans had fumed the air to a horrid sickliness, while within the thickness of the air hung the sweet odor of the vegetable oil burning in the lamps, and waves of human-smell washed about the room laced with the stink of rice-breath or the sour-mouth odors of hunger. In the gray light of the lamps, that swayed and smoked and reached, yellowing, far back to the corners of the room, it was not quite as Baldwin expected to find it, nor yet quite strange.

It was crowded—but not with the pack and crush he had expected. The warm room should have sucked the wanderers in from outside in the cold until they jostled shoulder-to-shoulder in this shelter. Yet it was relatively open, with only thirty or forty people sitting about the benches, or lying on the floor, near the charcoal pans, or in the corners where the bobbing light of the oil lamps would poke fitfully to show a body sleeping and then leave it to the shadow again. Someone then must be cock-of-the-run in this shelter, saying who might enter and who must endure the cold in the street outside, and as Baldwin's eyes grew accustomed to the light, he saw there was only one place to begin, only one thread to follow. He was in the dining room of the old hostelry. He could recognize the black round dining tables, and every table was cold, bare and foodless except one. It was at the table with the food that the men in control must sit.

There was a muttering as Baldwin and his party pushed their way into the room, an angry, remonstrating sound, which fell off as the people saw that here were two Americans. As the sound fell away, Baldwin pushed his way forward until he was before the one table with the food, and he regarded it. About it sat four soldiers, of the vagrant and familiar stream of wolf-like men they had been passing on the road all day. These soldiers, however, seemed relaxed and pleased with themselves. They had food—four rice bowls, with rice steaming before them, no more than that, but enough to make them rich on this night of hunger. Their rifles leaned upright against the table, muzzle-high, the muzzles snouting up between them. And one of them wore a fleece-lined American aviator's jacket.

"That's Miller's," growled Michaelson to Baldwin.

"I see it," said Baldwin, and walked forward, Kwan and Su-Piao following him.

Kwan began the conversation.

"*Ni-men shih na-i-pu,*" asked Kwan, the standard opening: What outfit are you with?

Kwan had asked it with a bark of command, the bearing of authority in his stand. And Kwan's voice bounced against nothing. He stood there before the soldiers for a moment, erect, stern, demanding—and faded, as Baldwin watched, to a frail cutout, his carriage, his trim uniform, his manner all ridiculous because there was no sounding-board in this room to give the echo that authority needed.

The room had become silent and all were listening.

The leanest of the soldiers said something; someone giggled nervously from a dark corner and then hushed, quickly, because no one else laughed.

"What did he say?" asked Baldwin of Su-Piao, wishing somehow he could speak Chinese.

"He said he doesn't belong to any outfit any more. He says he belonged to Old Hairy Lung—that's his general—until last month, now he belongs to no one. He belongs to himself. They laughed. These men are wild."

Here in this room Baldwin realized there was nothing—only guns and fear and the beasts in their lair. Kwan and the entire Chinese command no longer existed. This was hundreds of years ago. And they were laughing at him. The laughter was the worst.

The four soldiers sat satisfied, their entire bearing a sneer and contempt. Baldwin could not guess their age, or where they came from; in the dark light, all their faces bore the same wine-dark weather-worn color, the jaws of each rounded off square at the skull hinge, and seen anywhere on the road, they might have appeared either sturdy and good, or wicked and menacing. Here, in this room, they were evil and the one wearing Miller's jacket, who had replied to Kwan, was their leader—a thin fellow, with an enormously pointed nose for a Chinese, and a momentary expression of intelligence as he stared at Baldwin's group.

"Ask them who's in command of the American truck outside," said Baldwin, trying to push the firmness of his voice through the translation that Su-Piao must make, though he knew she did not want to.

The lean soldier, his voice sly and taunting, wanted to know whether it was an American truck.

"Tell him it's an American truck and it belongs to me."

A pause, then, from the lean one:

"Who are you?"

"I'm the commander of the convoy and the men who were on the truck."

"Americans are bad," said the lean soldier flatly and leaned forward, his elbows on the table, to see how Baldwin would take it.

It was like a slap in the face. In all the courtesy conversations with Chinese over the past year the phrases of friendship had been so thick a paste in the conversation that now Baldwin gasped. The room rustled as people listened. Baldwin noticed that one of the soldiers at the table had curled his fingers about the barrel of his rifle.

"Chinese who work for the Americans are walking dogs," continued the lean soldier. "Americans are rich. Chinese soldiers are hungry. Chinese soldiers fight. Americans ride in automobiles. Chinese who ride with Americans are turtle-people."

Kwan snapped an oath at the soldier at the table, the soldier snapped one back, and the sound of their voices growing more savage told Baldwin they had touched bottom.

"Shut up!" Baldwin yelled across them both, bellowing as loud as he could, and the full timbre of his voice, octaves lower than the Chinese voices in anger, stopped it.

"What did he say?" asked Baldwin when they were quiet.

The soldiers at the table looked at him as Su-Piao translated.

"This is terrible," she said softly. "I can't say it the way he did. He asked whether I was sleeping with you or with Kwan to get my ride out. He said he'd put me on his truck for the same price but he already had a fatter woman. He should be flogged," she added as her voice deepened, then broke as she caught in her breath, her lips quivering. Baldwin did not know whether she was afraid, or whether the officer's lady in her had been humiliated by the outlaws. It made no difference; they were mocking him in humiliating her; he could not even protect a woman from them, they implied.

The soldiers at the table, half-laughing as Su-Piao translated, understanding what she was translating, were peering at him to see what he would do. The knee of one of the soldiers had begun to jiggle, and Baldwin had been aware of the jiggling for seconds before he noticed that it was wearing a familiar American paratroop boot, and the quivering of the toe showed that the soldier was nervous, too. But Baldwin could not leave or back out now. To back out and show that he was afraid, or weak, would be the most dangerous thing of all. They were testing each other. The thought flicked through Baldwin that the soldiers were sitting down and he could probably shoot one or two before they could rise; Michaelson would certainly get one, too. But the crowd in the room was not neutral; he could feel it; the crowd was against them, and they could not shoot and get out safely.

"Ask him where he got the truck," said Baldwin, trying to keep his voice stiff.

"We found it on the road," said the leader of the soldiers. "Americans have too many trucks, they must have left one behind."

Baldwin pressed Su-Piao again.

"Ask him where he got the jacket."

"We found it on the truck," said the lean soldier, but this time not smiling or joking. He was being accused of murder, and he knew it. But Baldwin could prove nothing.

"I want the truck back," said Baldwin.

"How do we know it is yours?" asked the soldier. "There are many Americans in China. Too many."

This was better, thought Baldwin, feeling he had turned an important corner. The lean soldier was now no longer cursing, nor forcing the conversation. Something of the arrogance had drained out of his voice in the last reply, he was responding. But the lean soldier could not back down, could not lose face with his companions watching him around the table.

"This truck is ours, and I represent the American army," said Baldwin awkwardly, stalling, waiting for the interchange to yield him a crevice he could grip for advantage.

"We will give this truck to the Chinese army in Kweiyang. Then the Chinese army will give it back to the Americans," said the soldier, lying.

Kwan cleared his throat to speak, and Baldwin put his hand on Kwan's arm to stop him. It was better to keep this between the soldier and himself. The soldier was a murderer. In Chinese that would have to be said. If Kwan spoke, neither they nor the soldiers at the table would be able to back down. But between himself and the soldier, he could maintain the fiction for the moment; thus he could maneuver. He did not want to fight in this room.

"We will be in Kweiyang before you," said Baldwin. "We shall have to report you have our truck."

"There are too many Americans in Kweiyang already," said the soldier, his arrogance returning as he felt Baldwin backing down. There was a pause and then one of his companions said something and all four laughed uproariously. Tentatively, uncertainly, several other people in the room laughed too; then were suddenly silent, as if they burst out off-cue, their voices vanishing like the sound of glass tinkling as it breaks without an echo.

"What did he say?" asked Baldwin.

"He was speaking to me," said Su-Piao. "He said if the Americans get tired of me, he will give me a ride on their truck—he needs a woman like his friend, it is cold in the mountains."

The soldiers laughed again as Su-Piao translated the remark, but with bravado, not mirth, in their laughter. Several other voices in the room, uncertain, unhappy, frightened, quavered in laughter, then silenced.

It was best to get out of this room while they were laughing, thought Baldwin. A plan had come to him. He knew where the chip was, and how to make them knock it off. Then he could shoot. But not here in this room. Outside was the place to be.

"All right," said Baldwin to his party, "let's get out of here, I've got an idea."

"Are you going to let them get away with this?" asked Michaelson's voice over his shoulder. "We can clean these bastards up in five minutes."

"Pipe down," said Baldwin. "This is going to be rougher than you think."

As they withdrew towards the door, Kwan and Su-Piao turning, Baldwin and Michaelson backing away, one of the soldiers yelled after them.

"Tsai chien, mei-kuo jen, tsai chien tsai Kweiyang." Baldwin's courtesy Chinese was just good enough to catch it: "See you again, Americans. See you again in Kweiyang"— and this time the room burst into real laughter, a release from strain. It was safe for him to go out to the sound of laughter, even though it hurt to lose face.

He had thought it through by the time the doors had closed behind them. He could not fire the first shot. He must make them shoot first. The soldiers must knock the chip off. He wanted the truck. He was going to take the truck and let them try to stop him. It all fitted together, neatly.

It was no more than twenty strides from the inn door to the truck and the convoy was only one hundred fifty feet beyond the truck, on the slope covering the street. He was under protection now, under the protection of the BAR as he had planned it.

"Stop here," he said to Su-Piao as they drew abreast of the truck. "Now tell Kwan to tell all the people to get off the truck. Michaelson is going to drive it back and we'll go on with the convoy."

"You mean, just tell them to get off?" asked Su-Piao.

"Just that," said Baldwin. "Kwan will understand."

From above the truck, where the bedrolls, the mattresses, the sacks, the boxes, all rose in a high mound above their heads, the pale faces of the shivering passengers looked down.

Kwan looked up at them and then, using his command voice again, yelled:

"*Hsia lai!*" Come down!

"Why?" shouted someone from the top of the truck. Aloft a woman's voice shrilled and Su-Piao, below, translated to Baldwin, "She's telling her husband to tell you they've already paid for the ride." Others at the top of the truck joined the chorus—they had all paid.

Kwan yelled again, screeching, and there was an uneasy murmuring on the top of the truck, half-pleading, half-angry.

"Michaelson," Baldwin ordered, "get up there and boot someone off to start them moving."

Michaelson clambered up the side and in an instant a flow of fluent American invective mixed with the Chinese chatter on the top of the truck, and a young Chinese came down. Another followed. An enraged and puffy man in a merchant's silk gown began to derrick his bulk down the side of the truck, fell off awkwardly, picked himself up from the ground, and, full of indignation, began to expostulate. Kwan snarled at him and the man waddled off back to the inn. More were coming down from the top of the truck. One was running to the inn; Baldwin knew the bandit-soldiers would be out in a moment. And he was ready.

"Move it out, Mike, start it up," he yelled, and, grasping Su-Piao by the elbow, he thrust her forward, ordering, "Up front with Michaelson! On the front seat! We're getting out now," and with another thrust he pushed her into the cab and yelled again to Michaelson, "Fast, Mike, fast, get this truck started, they'll be coming soon," and saw Michaelson hop into the cab, and turned back to face the dark.

There were only Kwan and he at the tail of the truck now, and as they stood there, there came as he had been expecting, the shallow, flat crack of a rifle bullet.

"Duck," Baldwin yelled. "Duck, hit the deck!" forgetting

that Kwan could not speak or understand English, but Kwan was already flat on the cold road beside him and both were straining their sight toward the inn.

Another shot rang and this time Baldwin, looking toward the inn in the dark, saw the little puff of yellow-red flame where the shot had splashed, like a matchhead in the dark, only bigger, and tried to see beyond it down the street between the bonfires, where forms and shadows were darting back and forth across the street. He waited, collecting his thoughts, hoping for the roar of the truck's motor coming alive, steadying himself. Then another shot cracked from the inn, and Baldwin found that his gun, already pointing at the memory of the first flash, triggered off directly at the new fire-burst. Another gun sounded in his ear, and it was Kwan, aiming with his pistol at the target that must be too far away. And everything that had been held back in Baldwin all week, all his life, was now free on the surface and he was firing, freely. For the dark had fired first and all he needed now was a clear target. But he must not use up his clip at once. And why did the truck not start? And where was the BAR?

Someone dropped lengthwise, puffing, by his side in the dark and he heard Michaelson's wheeze and Michaelson was saying, "She won't start, she's cold, she won't start, or they've ruined her. What do we do?" But before Baldwin could answer, he saw, his eyes still on the road, a thin figure running across the street from the inn door, outlined momentarily against the bonfires, and he fired at it in the dim light and it howled, stumbled, and kept on running. And then there was yelling in the street and he heard a voice yelling, "*Mei-kuo jen, t'u-fei, t'u-fei,*" and other people screaming what seemed to be "*Sha! Sha!*" There were at least half a dozen guns going out there, flat sounds, needle points of color in the dark, and the long jabs of light streaking. There were now more than the three or four guns of the soldiers he had braced at the hostelry, and he knew they would rush him soon.

"What are they yelling?" he asked in the darkness, knowing he needed Su-Piao, but where was she.

"They're yelling about bandits," came her voice from the ground behind him. "They're calling you 'American bandits,' they think you're bandits, they're crying to kill. Why did you do it, Phil, why did you do it? We must get out now."

It angered Baldwin that they should be calling *him* bandit. But somewhere out there where everything was confused, the hijackers had fused the crowd's emotions to their support against the Americans. There had been no court to explain the crime, only the emotions of the road. All the guns of the scores of deserters in this town who had no home but bitterness, all the refugees who had longed to hate, without knowing what to hate, all in the dark had been given a target to hate. Baldwin told himself that these people were as good as dead already, soldiers and refugees alike, and they, like himself, were shooting out of reasons they could not understand, a few for loot and food to be gained by fighting, the rest out of unreason because their hate and hurt demanded it. They would be at him soon, Baldwin realized, and through the anger that was unlocking him, without fear, he began to realize they must break for the cover of the trucks soon, where his strength lay, so he could punish them and get out. He wished the BAR would fire, so he could move, for he wanted to move before they did, for in the darkness they must be readying.

Then the BAR was firing, rattling in short bursts directly over his head, stitching the street from just beyond their head almost as far as the bonfires at the far end of the village. It whisked and poked in short strokes, reaching at the individual darts of rifle-fire in the night, and Baldwin could almost imagine the delicate touch of Ballo's hands up there, back at the convoy, tracing the road, not knowing what was happening.

But if there was a time to go, it was now, with the BAR in action. Baldwin got to his knees, looked at the other three on the ground beside him and yelled, "Back to the convoy, all of you, now, NOW! Run for it!" He waited for a moment, saw Michaelson lift with a twitch and race with astonishing speed up the slope, saw Kwan following, his dignity gone, Su-Piao running, and then he was chasing after them, with a rattle of shots behind him. It was a long way, the one hundred fifty feet up the slope, and he wondered as he ran whether the few blocks of TNT they had left were really stable, or whether a stray bullet might indeed set it off, and his carbine was heavy as he ran. Then, finally, he was there, in the shelter of the convoy, under the BAR, panting, and safe.

"What's happening?" yelled Niergaard from the top of the truck and Baldwin answered, senselessly:

"We found them, they're down there."

He turned to look down the slope, wondering what next, and he could make out a glow larger than a bonfire in the street. It was the truck, something was burning in it and he chuckled, for the wild Chinese fusillade must have set the truck afire and it was no good to anybody now. But he was still angry. Then he was aware of another scattered burst of rifle fire from down in the street, wide, erratic, meaningless, but aimed at him and his convoy and so they were still trying to get him. He knew they could not reach or touch him now. His convoy sat on the upgrade, he had a BAR firing, the hill protected his rear, the road up forward could not be turned, he had explosives; they had fired first; he would get them. He would get them—for killing his men, for stealing the truck, for the whole bleeding, meaningless mess they had brought about. And the rage carried him, without thinking. . . .

"Mike," he yelled, "get that gasoline drum ready to roll, cut the fuse for a ninety-second delay. Let the cratering charge roll after the drum goes down."

But her hand was on his sleeve again, she was clutching his arm, saying:

"Phil! Don't! Don't! You don't know what you're doing! You're just like them if you do it. You can't see what you're shooting, Phil, the truck is burning, don't you see."

"We have to, we have to," he cried at her, and heard two answers at once.

Su-Piao, her hand still firm on his arm, was saying, "Who are you trying to kill? You're not shooting the right people, you can't see, oh you fool, you can't see."

But above, Prince was yelling from the top of the truck:

"Here they come, here they come again," and Baldwin fell flat on the ground again to watch them coming. About half a dozen of them were coming, loping out of the growing fire of the truck by the inn. It was the lope of good soldiery, and it wasn't strange at all, thought Baldwin, most of these deserters are combat troops and they've fought a lot of battles.

The BAR was tracing the soldiers as they came and Baldwin knew that if any of the indistinct figures of this evening's memory were the men who had ambushed Lewis and Miller, they would be among the men scrambling toward them now, hoping for more loot, and he trained his gun on one of them, absolutely sure that the silhouette coming closer was clothed in Miller's flight jacket. And in the moment the man forgot to zigzag, when he was no more than one hundred feet away, Baldwin's shot caught him in the chest and he fell like a sack, as if someone had pushed him with a timber. As he fell, Baldwin was not sure whether the man wore a Chinese cotton-padded vest or Miller's flight jacket, but he could see another falling, too, and the rush had stopped.

In the silence after they had stopped the rush, Michaelson was back beside him and he could see that Michaelson was enjoying it now as much as he did, now that they were both back on the slope. Michaelson's voice was rushed but sure of itself.

"We're ready with the drum. I got the fuse and the primer taped on one head, and some Composition-C on the other head. Now?"

"Now," said Baldwin, "and then as soon as she flashes let the cratering charge roll down after. She'll take three or four feet off the top of the road." Why it was important that the road should be cratered again here he did not know, it was no longer his responsibility.

He watched Prince and Michaelson manhandling the drum to the center of the grade, then the match went up and the lazy sputter of the fuse was visible and they were pushing it off. Idly, with a cold spasm of detachment, Baldwin wondered whether the slope of the hill was steep enough, the ruts sharp enough to keep the awkward barrel rolling on course for the one hundred fifty feet to the inn, whether it would bounce against the hillside, or fall off an edge, or catch, as it careened, in a gutter. The deserters in the street were firing at them in a scattered rattle, annoying, not worrying him now; and Baldwin could hear the barrel bounce away towards the village, and wondered whether the fuse would last the full ninety seconds, and the waiting seemed infinitely long . . . but then, finally, it came apart nicely, at the very bottom of the slope, in the village.

The primer unfolded in a white flash and a soggy "whop," and Baldwin saw the brilliant shawls tearing out of the drum as the gasoline flared out. He waited and was aware that the firing from the street had stopped and the firing from the trucks above him had stopped, and watched the dark village to see if the gasoline had spread the flame or not. He could see the first flame now, off to his right, where the inn should be. It was a small one, a little tongue of white and yellow licking its way up a wall; and there was another across the street, small, too, but with robust promise that it would not go out. If the wind was right, there would be a sweep of the little street, and he licked his finger. When he held it up, the coolness of the backskin of his finger told him the wind was exactly right, blowing away off the hill, down the street, and there was a good chance the whole thing would become cinder. He had fixed it and, as he thought that they could go now, he heard Michaelson grunting.

"That cratering charge should go any minute now, too. We had a long fuse on it." And Baldwin realized that he might have stopped the cratering charge for it was now unnecessary but it was already rolling down there into the village.

Then the cratering charge did go, far down beyond the truck, in the midst of them, with a resounding rending crack of the forty pounds of ammonium nitrate tearing apart the tin cylinder that held it, and the sound of the charge tearing open, tore the men open again, too. The BAR in Ballo's hand opened first, mercilessly, and on top of the trucks, they were yelling and cursing, and every one of them was firing, as fast as he could, pumping bullets blindly into the village, and he himself was yelling till his throat hurt, out of control, shooting with them, cursing.

It was when Baldwin's carbine triggered off in a click and did not fire that he knew he was through with his clip and could see again, slowly, painfully, as if he were coming out a drunk. For the flames were now beginning to rise to a boil, tumbling like waves upwards, upwards, with scarlet and crimson shading gaily to orange, and the light growing brighter so that he could see the stretch of road between them and the village like an illuminated stage. And across the road, coming toward them was a hobbling, swaying figure, madly twisting in its silhouette; running, but slowly, and dragging something. It was a woman, followed by a smaller black silhouette, the figure of a child she was half-dragging by the hand in total confusion to escape the fire. And there were no shots from the village any more, only his men were still firing, and he must stop them.

He could hear them screaming with abandoned passion on the truck-top, and he yelled above them, "Hold it!" and louder, "Hold it!" and wanted to yell, "We've killed enough already," but found himself yelling instead, "Don't waste that ammunition, we may be short. Hold it! God damn it, stop!" straining and heaving to cap them and press back what he had released.

Then it was quiet. He could not see the woman and child any more; he hoped they had gotten away; there was only the sound of crying.

He knew he was waiting for the strength to rise and go. In the shelter of the trucks of his convoy, facing the flames in the night as they grew, he could not rise. In the flames, he could see several bodies in the road and knew they were dead and hoped they were the hijackers he had meant to punish. He had probably gotten one himself, the man in the American jacket who had tumbled at his shot. He hoped. Now he could see another of the bodies in the road, stirring, a hand coming back from underneath the body and the hand limp, trying to feel its own hurt body, trying to caress, or touch, or comfort itself. But the hand had no strength. And dropped.

It was dying. The hand falling flat on the road as he watched made Baldwin feel sick and he clutched the ground, putting his head down flat on the dirt for he was faint. And grimly he told himself that they had killed Miller without a chance, and someone had stood grinning over poor Lewis in the back of the truck and killed him in cold blood, but it did no good. And as he lay there, suddenly ill, he heard the voices in the street again, not angry voices this time, but crying voices, questioning voices, the sound of voices in sorrow. There was a word in the Bible for this kind of crying, a word for this. He had learned it long ago—the name of a Book—it was Lamentations. The Book of Lamentations, how did it go, it was right there the sound of the book . . . "All the roads are desolate," it started, all the roads are desolate, he had made them desolate.

He knew if he watched it any longer it would do no good. It would drain him. Go, now. He had had to do it. But it was like making love, this killing. While it was happening, you had to go on with it. There was no way of stopping. Then, when it was over, you were all weak, and wondered why, and wanted to be alone.

With an impossible effort he tried to get up. And did.

"Michaelson," he called, "we're going now."

"Now, Major?" asked Michaelson.

"Yes," said Baldwin, his voice dead. "We're finished. Let's go."

"We're ready," said Michaelson.

"All right," said Baldwin. "Start them up. Then follow me."

When both trucks were humming, he got into his jeep and flipped the switch. It started easily. Motors never tired.

"We'll go as far as we can tonight," he said, "at least until we find a roof." He was talking to Su-Piao. She sat erect and distant, as far as she could sit from him on the seat of the jeep. Behind, he could feel Kwan just as cold, erect and distant. As remote as when they had first met far, far down the road on Wednesday. And it was only Saturday now. Three dead. Four men still with him. Four men and he had done this thing, and the village burned. At his command. At his command.

It was cold in the open jeep as they set out up the hill.

CHAPTER 11

Over and Out

THE ROAD was entirely theirs now, as if what they had done had swept it clean. Behind him, Baldwin felt the yellow road lights of his two trucks clinging to the back of the jeep, while before him, his own lights cut a jumping triangle of white against the black rutted road.

As they wound up the hairpins of the hill, the fire in the hollow below grew fainter, fading with distance from its slashing brilliance to a many-petaled rose of fire, then softening further to a shrinking glow that grew smaller the higher they climbed, until finally as they crossed the saddle and Baldwin looked at it for the last time, it seemed no more than a twinkling bonfire far away, gentle and without horror. When it disappeared on the far side of the black range as they crossed, Baldwin could see that the stars were out, high across the sky, flung madly in scattered brilliance and there was no sound but the uneven rhythm of the truck motors and the purring of his own jeep. It was cold—desperately, bitingly cold, so that the ridges of his cheek ached, and his nose hurt, and his fingers in their gloves throbbed. But there would be no stopping until they found shelter.

No one in the jeep had spoken yet.

Then there was a new pinpoint of light down the road ahead and after a while Baldwin forced his attention to it. It was not a star, but a fire and, for a moment, he wondered if the dark road were swinging him back to the town he had savaged, but quickly he knew it to be a fear spasm. He had left the town. This was something new.

"What's that?" he asked aloud.

No one answered, and Baldwin addressed her directly, making her answer because he must know.

"Will you ask Kwan what that is?" he said to Su-Piao.

He heard her voice then for the first time since the village —flat and defeated, expressionlessly asking the question of Kwan in Chinese, and Kwan's voice tonelessly coming back, then her voice replying as if she no longer cared.

"He says he does not know."

He marked the hollow tone of her voice. But he must first face the fire up ahead, or whatever it meant. Then, later, he could turn and face her—face what he had just done, face himself. But not now. The fire was growing bigger and he would think about that, which was easier than thinking about what lay behind.

What was it? Another village? Another bonfire? Automatically, he let the jeep slow down as they began to approach the light. There was now no chance of sneaking up to reconnoiter it. If anyone guarded the fire in the distance, they must by now have seen the beams of the convoy lights bending and sweeping around the curves. Baldwin began to draw his mind to alertness.

They slowed to a crawl, then to a creep, and then the light divided in the middle of the road as twin flares, and dissolved into two gasoline drums standing upright, with flames flickering from both of them. There was no one to be seen as they stopped their trucks, and then, sharply, from the darkness behind the fires came a shout and four figures appeared, rifles unslung, striding out from behind the fires; bold and unafraid.

By the way they stalked out, Baldwin knew it was all right. This was not a roadblock but a control point. The figures in the light were soldiers, not bandits. He could tell by the way these men bore themselves that he would not need his gun. A panic-flash pricked him momentarily and he jackknifed up from his seat, turning back to face the glare of lights from his following truck, held up his two arms, waved the old baseball all-safe signal, and yelled, "It's O.K., back there, O.K.—O.K.!" and hoped the men would not shoot.

Two Chinese soldiers were looking at him when he turned to sit down. They were smiling as he peered up at them and he smiled, too. It was the fat in their faces that made him smile. He had not seen healthy Chinese for a week, and these men were robust, muscled, their faces ruddy in the jeep's light, their uniforms the familiar brown wool of American GI issue. They must be an outpost of the new army being rushed up from Burma to the new line, the men America had trained from the discards of China's many disasters.

"*Mei kuo jen,*" said Baldwin loudly, using his sparse vocabulary of the language, "Americans!"

"*Mei kuo jen ting hao!*"—"Americans, very good!" cried one of the soldiers in response, holding up his thumb in friendship. It was spontaneous; and Baldwin knew they were in.

"O.K., Joe, O.K., American"—said the second soldier in recognizable English, his face beaming, his body squirming with happiness, and Baldwin, trying to speak to him, found it was the only English the soldier apparently knew and turned back to Su-Piao and Kwan for help.

Yes, said the soldiers as the conversation moved quickly in translation, they were part of the New Sixth Army. No, they were part of a reconnaissance platoon, a control point; the platoon was back up the road, two miles, in the temple on the hill. The captain was there, too. Did the Americans want to warm themselves at the fire before going on?

Baldwin said no. They ought to get on to platoon headquarters at the temple and bed down there, if one of the soldiers would come to show the way in the dark.

The soldiers talked briefly and Su-Piao said:

"One of them says he knows how to drive an American jeep. Do you want him to drive us to the temple?"

"Good," said Baldwin, infinitely grateful that he could hand over the wheel to someone else. He climbed in back as the soldier flicked the jeep's motor on, turned to the glare of the waiting trucks and made the "follow" signal—and they were off.

It was a good outfit, Baldwin knew, as soon as they reached the temple, on a hill slope off the road. No light shone from the inside, and he could never have reached it looking alone. Two sentries challenged the convoy, brought their rifles smartly to rest at the driver's response, and only for a moment, as Kwan went in, when the doors opened wide and the blanket behind the doors was pulled aside did Baldwin catch the dazzle of a clear white light inside. Baldwin lingered for a moment to talk to the men, told them they would bed here for the night, he would be out as soon as he cleared it with the commander; and then followed Kwan inside. He noticed that Su-Piao had lingered with him, and was by his side as he went in, still his tongue.

It was bright, clean and warm inside—the flagstoned floor of the huge temple hall swept tidily, the peeling idols and old scrolls glittering in the glare of a gasoline lamp—and a young Chinese captain, neat in American uniform, clucked sympathetically as Baldwin rubbed his frozen fingers together.

"You will have tea, Major? You will have drink, Major? Please have some food, Major? Colonel Kwan say you have much bitterness on the road." It was unmistakably English that the young captain was speaking, and Baldwin knew it would be all downhill from here. The captain had many rooms in the temple, he would be glad to bed and feed the American team here, please bring them in, he urged.

Still dazed, unsteady on his legs, the alert top of his mind organizing and commanding, Baldwin summoned the men and followed them to a room off the hall, while the underpart of his mind looked at them, as if for the first time, judging them. He noticed how their legs dragged as they carried their bedrolls, how their bodies bent, how much they looked like refugees.

He squatted beside them as the lamps were lit and the fires kindled, and looking at their faces, thick with growth of beard, noticing their eyes, bloodshot, ugly and worn, he knew that somehow they were his, and belonged to him, because the army had given them to him, briefly, to command and care for. Their exhaustion made them stumble as they moved, and they fumbled as they undid their bedrolls; somehow, they were pathetic in the night and Baldwin was glad he need not flog them any further. Together, his mind knew, they had been an instrument of power, their skills and vigor interlocking into something which had scorched and ravaged East China, and which had been given into his hand. Tomorrow night all of them would be back in Kunming; the next day he would report to staff; the team would be broken up or belong to someone else; someone else would feed them; someone else would post their guards; someone else would use them.

For what, he wondered. He would probably pass on their next mission at staff; but they would not be his. He remembered how he had not wanted to talk with them as they started up the road. Yet now he could talk to them if he wanted to, it would be all right. They had been part of each other's lives for this week, he changing them in some way they could not know, they changing him. And he wanted to sit and be with them now for a while, shrinking still from facing the recall of the day.

He undid his own bedroll and sat down by the fire with them to wait for the food and noticed that Niergaard was already dozing on his bedroll. If Niergaard's conscience had been touched by what had happened, exhaustion had now purged it. For a moment Baldwin thought of waking Niergaard to eat, then decided the man's body needed sleep more than food.

"You want this, Major? You going to do the writing?" asked Michaelson in the silence, as he plucked something from his bedroll.

This was a wallet. Baldwin opened it and there was an identification card—Joseph Lionel Collins.

"I'm glad you've got it," said Baldwin, "the others were stripped, weren't they?"

"Yeah," said Michaelson. "Clean-stripped, the bastards."

Baldwin flipped the panels of the wallet and they both looked. There was a fleshy, aging man, with jowls; and somewhere, deep in the folds of the flesh in the picture, was an echo of the fine-lined face of the boy who was dead in the truck outside. There was another picture of the same man in a silk hat and morning coat. And a picture of the same man, much younger, with a woman and a little boy. The little boy was Collins, and he was wearing knee pants.

"Looked like his old man," said Michaelson.

"Yes," said Baldwin, and for no reason, "His father is in politics."

"Nice kid," said Michaelson, "I should've broken his back." The tone was flat and mournful, not bitter.

"Lots of guys like that," went on Michaelson. "They figure they've got to take care of the world. Used to have a lot of them back when the union was starting. They work out of it in time and get like everybody else. Collins figured he had to take care of the Chinese. But all you can do is take care of your own crowd. If you can take care of your own, you've done a hell of a lot. I should have kicked his butt off when he was giving us all this college-crap about making friends with the Chinese. He might be alive now. I liked him."

Would that have helped, Baldwin wondered. Could Collins have been cured? Of what? Of humanity? Too big a word. But could anybody have saved Collins? Were the men blaming him?

"The only way," said Prince sharply, breaking in, "is the way we did today at Yang-an-Sing. Don't take any crap from them. That was a hell of a job. A hell of a day."

"You know something, Major"—that was Ballo speaking to him directly—"we didn't have any idea what you were going to do, sir, when you went down into that joint, but it sure worked. I'll never forget it."

So they approved, thought Baldwin. Perhaps that was why he was lingering with them. Because he knew they approved. Not of the job on the road; but of what had happened at Yang-an-Sing. Yet he did not want this approval. Somehow he must clear himself of it. But he could not break from them right away, and returning to Michaelson, he answered them all:

"You've got to take care of your own, Mike. But Collins had a point, too. If you just take care of your own, it isn't enough. The trouble with the Chinese is that they've ended by each one trying to take care of himself. In the end it doesn't work—it winds up on a road like this. It doesn't take care of anything."

Two Chinese soldiers came in bearing two trays of hot rice, and Baldwin could smell the spice in the meat sauce and was hungry. From somewhere, the captain must have dug up porcelain soup spoons, not chopsticks, and they began to eat, all thinking.

It was Michaelson who began again, as if he were replying to Baldwin's last remark.

"Well. Maybe. But I'd say there's a lot worse coming. Somebody's going to come along and organize these bastards and then there'll be real trouble. They're ripe for it. Collins used to say he wanted to come back and see it after the war. Not me. I just want to get back to Chicago and let them alone."

"What're you going to do back in Chicago when they let you out, Mike?"—it was Ballo asking, and Baldwin was glad the conversation was leaving him, so he could sit and listen.

"I've been figuring," said Michaelson. "My wife's been saving my allotment and she's working in Sears Roebuck and saving her pay, too. I'm getting out of the foundry when I get back and I'm going to open a garage. The hell with taking orders for the rest of my life. I don't want to worry about the guys over me, or the guys under me. I'm going to make my own mistakes. I'm just going to have my own shop, and be my own boss, and maybe have a family. Let the slobs take care of themselves."

"I get in to Chicago lots," said Prince idly, "when the horses are running at Arlington Park. I make it every year."

"You ever come through Chicago," said Michaelson, "you come round to my station and I'll fill your tanks on the house. I'll be in the phone book. 'Iron Mike's Filling Station.' You, too, Major."

"I sure will, Mike," said Baldwin, knowing they were his friends now; but realizing that the men were drifting off into their own world. He could leave to seek Su-Piao and Kwan.

He pulled himself up off the ground and said:

"They must have a radio here. I want to see if we can raise Kweiyang. They should have planes out of there, and maybe we can hook a flight into Kunming. That would put us in by early afternoon tomorrow. See you in the morning."

"Yup," said Michaelson, "last morning."

"Say, Major," said Prince, adding quickly, "Sir? Do you suppose you could get us a good slug of leave when you turn us over in Kunming? Maybe a couple of weeks? We could get shuffled into some other outfit awful easy. And we've been out on the road all summer."

"Sure thing," said Baldwin, "I certainly will. Don't worry. See you all in the morning. Time to say good-bye then."

But as he turned away, he realized there would be no good-bye, or, if there were, this had been it. He looked back at them, Americans all, his for the last night, hunched by the fire, growling in conversation as he had first heard them days ago, their faces half-lit and molded by moving shadows. They did not look frightening. Yet they were. Even in their slack exhaustion, the memory of what they could do and how he had used them made him see them as Chinese might see them.

For they were power. And Baldwin knew it was not enough to have command, or have power all by itself, for this could come to any man by accident, as it had come to him. It was how you used it, what for. He had used it well, he had learned to use it well, all the way up the road until tonight. Then it had gone wrong; he was beginning to see it. But no one would be able to understand, except Kwan and Su-Piao; and as he walked toward the hall of the temple, he hoped they were still there.

* * *

The white glare of the gasoline lamp splashed the big hall that he entered with harsh, sharp-shadowed color—bits of red wax still lying as votary offerings before the images of the idols; burnt candle ends, yellow and gray, about the altars; the red and black scrolls of Chinese calligraphy sparkling bright from the walls. And in the huge space of the temple hall, about a table, sat the three—Kwan, Su-Piao, and the young captain. Baldwin had once thought that all Chinese looked alike. They no longer did—the young captain, so fresh, was welcoming him; the other two, so tired, looked up, aloof in recognition.

He sat down at their table before the captain's courtesy invitation had spurted from his lips. Baldwin had business with the young captain and began there, turning to Su-Piao, formally, saying:

"I wonder if you could ask him whether he has radio contact with Kweiyang?"

Yes, the captain answered, the advance echelon of New Sixth Army headquarters was already in Kweiyang. Yes, there was an American liaison team with the advance echelon. Yes, perhaps, it was possible to signal them tonight; and possible that headquarters could put an American officer in contact with them. It would take time, did the major want to do it now?

"Tell him," said Baldwin, "that I'd very much appreciate it if we could pass a message tonight"; and when the captain left to set the signal up, Baldwin was alone with them once more. But now, suddenly, they were awkward with each other.

"We'll be starting early tomorrow," said Baldwin. "We'll be in Kweiyang before noon."

Both were silent.

"About eight or nine in the morning, I guess," he continued, "just time for breakfast before we go."

Su-Piao translated to Kwan. Kwan muttered something and she said:

"The captain offered to put us on one of his trucks going to Kweiyang tomorrow." She did not look at him as she spoke.

"You'll finish it up with us, though," he said. Then added strongly, "Won't you?"

"Finish what?" she asked, her eyes still averted.

"The trip," he said, wishing somehow he could recapture the mood that had bound them all this distant morning at the conference and the vanished afternoon at the dumps; remembering that when first he spoke to her, he had wanted to get rid of her; and now alarmed and angry he wondered whether she might slip away.

She did not reply quickly, stirring as if caught between impulses of silence and speech. Staring at her as she stirred, he stirred himself not knowing why he wanted her with him tomorrow morning. Was it because she was part of the convoy and she should stay? She and Kwan could not walk away now, separating themselves from what had happened, from

Yang-an-Sing and the screaming, leaving him alone with it. He smoldered at the thought. Or was it something more between them?

Then she was speaking:

"We finished it at Yang-an-Sing," she said quietly.

Looking at him directly, her eyes lifted, "You finished it," she added.

The accusation was open now.

"You're angry," said Baldwin, "I know."

"You didn't want the truck"—she cut across him—"you wanted revenge. You didn't care who paid as long as it was Chinese."

"No," he said defensively. "It was wrong, I know it was wrong, but that's not why."

"Yes," she went on, "it was because they were Chinese. I thought Americans were different, because I thought I was American, I really thought so. I would have understood if a Chinese had done it, then it would have been senseless just like everything else. But you made it mean something. You weren't just killing. You were stepping on something. You were doing it because you wanted to."

Baldwin was conscious he must not answer her anger with his own.

"Listen to me, just listen," he said. "I don't know whether it's something I can explain or not . . . it's about this power there was in my hand, and doing it because . . ."

"Because why? . . ." she snapped back, sharply.

He waited, collecting his thinking. He could not apologize; what he had done was too big for apology. He must say it out before it slipped from him, now. For in Kunming, when he told of it later, they would judge him right because they had not been there. And his men, he knew now, approved.

And the survivors at Yang-an-Sing would remember him only as something nameless in the night. Only these two, here, could pass judgment. If they were not going with him in the morning, he must make them see it now. If he could make them see it, he would not be alone with it forever.

He began again, very slowly, picking his way:

"You asked me before we blew the dumps what I'd learned in China. Whatever it is, I should have learned it before, but I learned it here in China. I asked for this team—but what came afterward was an accident. They put the team in my hands. And then there was the road to blow up. It had to be done. But I had to learn how to use the team, how to use the men."

He paused, listening to her translate to Kwan.

"I guess I was always afraid of it, not of the men, but of using them, of using the power. All my life I'd been afraid of that. And then, on the road, I found it was easy. It was easy so long as it was just between the road, and me, and the Japanese. I had the power and I was using it. But then, tonight . . ."

His fists were clenched, the white of his knuckles showing, his body hunched over the table to her, speaking so rapidly she could barely translate.

"Then, tonight, it reached out and possessed me. I was angry. You know why—they'd killed my men. The anger opened me up, and the power walked in and used me. We had the cratering charge left, we had the BAR, we had the gasoline—it was the power acting by itself."

His hands were stretched out across the table, palms down, fingers grabbing as he spoke.

"I never knew that could happen. Everything I'd done up to then was right because the reason was big enough to make it right. But tonight, the power, the cratering charge, the BAR, the fact I could do it if I wanted to—they pushed the reason right out."

She was about to speak again, but he wanted to finish, his hand motioned her to quiet.

"It wasn't because they were Chinese, then—you see, don't you? It wasn't because I was American and they were Chinese, it was because I had more power than I knew how to use. Power hasn't any face, and it hasn't any country."

He was breathing heavily as he finished, waiting; he had been pleading, he knew. And across her face, emotions he could not follow rustled and passed and she was sad now, not accusing. Her sadness drew the anger and irritation from him; he sensed again the swift pulse of warmth for her rising. He stared at her Chinese countenance, wishing this feeling did not come and go between himself and her, that he could think of her either as close and bound to him, or else as alien. But not both at the same time. His look was an inquiry and she answered.

"Yes, I see what you're trying to say. What you're trying to say is that it makes no difference whether it's Chinese or Americans, it's bad when the power seizes you. But then . . ."

She frowned, as if a new thought had hobbled her.

". . . But then it means anyone can become a beast, all the way back at Yang-an-Sing, or at Hochih, or at Tushan, everyone is a beast just trying to live or kill, and if you live with the beasts you become a beast. It's all a matter of strong or weak, and the strong people decide sometimes right or wrong, and what happens at Yang-an-Sing happens over and over again. With Americans, just the way it does with us, you're no different really."

She broke, then resumed.

"It's bad, though, it's bad all the same."

"Of course," said Baldwin. "I'm saying just that—that it's bad. But I was trying to tell you what I've learned from it. It makes no difference where you learn it, or whether it's in China or America you learn it. In the long run what you learn has to show, you have to add what you learn to what you are, that's all you get out of it. And maybe if you can carry along with you what you've learned, that's all you have to repay the cost of learning."

She sat bolt upright; her hand flicked out, stopping him.

"But," she said, "that means I'm Chinese, if it makes no difference where you learn it, only what you do with it, then I'm Chinese."

She was talking in a rush.

"I don't know what's going to happen. But I can't go back to America now, because I wouldn't be escaping anything. Because you're the same as us. I have to stay, don't I? I think there has to be kindness, whether I learned it on this road or in America—then, I have to stay, don't I?"

He knew, as she spoke, that she would have to stay, that she could do as little by trying in America, as he could do by trying in China. She had learned in America, and he had learned in China; but only about themselves.

Kwan was drumming two fingers nervously on the table, involuntarily reminding them they had forgotten him. Su-Piao turned, rapidly, to translate, and Baldwin could tell from her voice that now she was entirely with him again, she was interpreting, not merely translating.

Kwan nodded as she spoke, his taut features softening from their aloofness; whatever quality of Baldwin's distress moved through Su-Piao's voice, was changing him for when Kwan spoke, his voice was friendly, replying to Baldwin's plea.

"Yes," said Kwan, "the Major Baldwin is right. It was bad this thing that Major Baldwin did. He wanted the truck. He punished the men who took his truck and killed his soldiers. He is sorry the people died at Yang-an-Sing, I know; this is good. But he knew what he was doing, he knew his duty. That is why it is all right what he did. It had meaning. In China today, no one knows his duty. No one knows the law. That is why the government must be strong and have a meaning . . ."

Slowly through the Chinese contradictions of speech, it seeped in on Baldwin that Kwan was forgiving him. But for the wrong reasons. They were here at the end of their road, and they had all learned, but obviously differently.

"Those who do evil, must be punished," said Kwan, almost chanting now, "even if Major Baldwin must burn Yang-an-Sing." . . . The image of the woman and the child, in silhouette, fleeing in the flames in fear of him, swiftly moved across Baldwin's mind, and Su-Piao's voice was still translating. . . .

"There *must* be discipline"; the sound of Su-Piao's voice mingled with that of Kwan's as she translated. "Until there is discipline, there is no government. Until there is government, there is no strength. Until there is strength, the government cannot guard the good and punish the evil. If there is discipline and a meaning, then mistakes do not matter. Even the cruelty does not matter. It is only sad, like Yang-an-Sing. First there must be strength, like Major Baldwin. He has learned to be strong. And China must be strong, I do not care how. . . . It does not matter how."

But Baldwin did not wait for Su-Piao to finish the translation.

"No!" he gasped. "No!" not waiting for Kwan to come to the end. He could see now opening up before him, finally, all the ultimate terrors the road had pointed to, yet hidden from him. He could see the parade of men who would do again and again the thing he himself had done at Yang-an-Sing, drunk enough with power and righteousness to spread death everywhere only because they wanted to be strong, or wanted China to be strong, and did not know how to be strong. He could see them all, the captives of their tools and instruments reaching for strength through their tools and becoming slaves to it. He, Baldwin, had learned this, at least, from the road. But how long would it take Kwan, or many generations of Kwan, to learn?

"But it does matter how," said Baldwin to Kwan. "You're responsible, yourself, for whatever part of the power that falls into you. Just being strong doesn't matter, nor having someone decide to let you use it. It would have been better to leave the men dead on the road, and abandon the truck, don't you see?"

Baldwin was holding out his hands, the tips of his fingers quivering, begging.

Kwan shrugged his shoulders; Kwan's eyes veiled. He was not there. He had withdrawn. Kwan had forgiven Baldwin because they had been companions on the road and departed. Only his body sat there.

"*Mei yu pan fa,*" said Kwan: There is no way.

There was nothing to say. Kwan was too good to leave thus at the end of the road, excusing him for Yang-an-Sing. But there was nothing to say.

And then came her touch on his arm. It was almost like last night at the blockhouse, he realized, as he turned to her, for he could see in her face that she was trying to comfort him.

"Nobody's important really," she was saying. "Something will stay, even if it goes Kwan's way. Even if what he's learned is right, and we're wrong. Other people must have learned on the road, too. It can't only change by cruelty, can it?"

It was more like the night at the blockhouse as she went

on, changing from comforter to comfort-seeker, talking almost to herself.

"But I won't be alone, I don't think I will. Will I? Something else American will stay when you're gone, won't it? It can't all disappear like that."

It was his turn to comfort now, to speak from his feeling that she should be sheltered. Because, Baldwin knew, for a shorter or longer time in China, it would be the way Kwan said. Cruel. Even though Kwan was wrong. It would be a long while before Kwan or the generations of Kwan could free themselves from the tools and instruments that made them strong, yet captive. It was important to comfort her, to nurse and keep alive what she had learned.

It was difficult to say in words for he had comforted other people only rarely; but this day he had done many things that were difficult and so he was not surprised when he found himself saying:

"When I was becoming an engineer, I took a course in metallurgy. About metals. And the molecules in them."

She looked at him puzzled, but he did not wander from the trail of the long distant past, when he was learning to be an engineer.

"You hold a block of metal in your hand. And it's solid. And yet within the metal, there are molecules. All moving by laws of their own. Press a block of pure gold against a block of steel, one against the other—then when you separate them, they seem unchanged. But not really. A good physical chemist will show you that where they've been in contact, invisible flecks of gold molecules have wandered across the barrier of structure, and buried themselves in the molecular structure of the steel. And the molecules of steel, somehow, into the structure of the gold. You can't see them, but a scientist can prove they're there, close to the surface."

She was not bothering to translate to Kwan, and he was speaking only to her.

"I think," went on Baldwin, "that when people are pressed close, they act the same way. Part of you enters them, part of them enters you. They call it learning. I think you see it mostly when you dream, when your dreams reach back and rearrange all the fragments of what your mind has forgotten into new patterns. Long after you forget the names and faces, the other times and places, they're still part of you. Sometimes —sometimes it's frightening to think of it, that every person you've ever hated, or feared, or run away from is part of you . . ."

"But other times . . . ?" she said, as he paused to breathe, and he knew she was following.

"Other times, I think, it means you carry inside you every person you've ever learned from, every friend you ever knew. We were in China. I think we're going soon because we can't help any more. But part of us is in you, and it will be there; not a molecule of metal, but a grain of seed maybe that will grow again. You'll be here, and you're Chinese. But part of you is America because you learned there. And because Americans have passed here; and even Kwan came up the road with us, he's been entered by America and he saw Collins . . ."

"Collins," she said as if she had forgotten, "of course, Collins. But he was just a boy . . ."

"But somebody must have seen Collins that day," said Baldwin. "Somebody must have eaten some of the food that Collins put in the snow. Somebody saw an American putting it there; and maybe one or two of them will survive, and remember. Just as the people in Yang-an-Sing, if they survive, will remember. I don't know whether it works with people the way it does with metals. But I think so . . . Every child you've ever touched is part of you. And every woman, too.

Every woman you've ever touched is part of you, as you are part of her."

He could not say it more than that, and was glad that at that moment the captain was coming back.

The captain was bustling with efficiency, snapping at the heels of Baldwin's slow speech.

"We have contact with Kweiyang. Colonel Masterson of the American Liaison with the New Sixth is waiting. He is surprised that we have Americans with us."

Baldwin rose to his feet; he did not want to keep Colonel Masterson waiting—as soon as he spoke to whoever was Colonel Masterson, it would be over, off his shoulders. Yet he still did not know whether she would be with him in the morning or not.

"You're turning in now, I suppose?" he said to Su-Piao.

"Yes," she said, turning to Kwan to repeat the question, and he nodded, too.

"Will I see you in the morning?" he asked. He did not want to press her. Looking at her now once again, he could see the tiredness in her face, and his own imagination saw her again crying, saw her smiling, saw her angry, saw her once close and in his arms. And the smooth lines of her face, moving, shaped her lips; she was about to say something. And she shook her head, then a smile, caressing him, curved her lips and she had made up her mind.

"I suppose we'll see each other when they load the trucks in the morning," she said, "but I'll go out with Kwan on the captain's truck."

It was strange that the hurt was so little. But he was glad he had said it all to her already, and that she understood.

"If we don't see each other in the morning," he said, "Good-bye—and good luck."

He shook hands with both of them, American-fashion. He

noticed that Kwan's grip was firm, strong and friendly, and he squeezed back.

Her touch was soft and it lingered.

"*I lu p'ing an,*" she said quietly, as if giving him a blessing. He was glad he had learned the phrase.

"Until the Road's End, Peace and Safety," he replied, repeating the phrase in English, and turned away to follow the captain to the radio.

The radio operator handed Baldwin the earphones and after a moment his ear had caught the hum of the carrier wave. He tensed, realizing he was holding his breath because at the other end an American waited to meet him on the invisible path of the frequency in the China night. Baldwin flicked the switch button to SEND and said:

"This is Baldwin. Major Baldwin of Air Force Base Engineers. Do you hear me? Who is this? Over to you."

He snapped the switch to RECEIVE. A loud crackle spat in his ear, and then, in a voice remarkably loud and clear, almost as if it were a local telephone call, came the unmistakable sound of authority in American.

"This is Masterson. Colonel Masterson of New Sixth Liaison Group. Masterson of New Sixth Liaison. What's your message? What's your message? Masterson of New Sixth Liaison to Baldwin of Base Engineers. Over to you."

There was no need now for secrecy; he could talk in the clear; everything he knew the Japs must know.

"I hear you. I hear you. Will you relay this message to Hutcheson of Kunming Base Engineers. Report two bridges blown on way out, main highway bridge at Liu river outskirts of Liuchow, smaller bridge twenty miles up the road. Major demolition on road thirty miles south of Hochih, repeat Hochih, a sidehill blow, estimate ten days or two weeks before wheeled vehicles can pass the blow, but Jap cavalry probably beyond that point. Liquidated ammunition dumps at Tushan repeat Tushan today. Will arrive Kweiyang tomorrow." He hesitated, then added, "Three men killed, bearing their bodies with me. Can Hutcheson arrange for C47 to get in to Kweiyang tomorrow to evacuate them? I guess that's it, will you give it back to me, please, over to you."

The message came back, precisely as he had given it and then:

"You say the dumps at Tushan are blown? Repeat that, Baldwin, over to you."

"Dumps at Tushan all blown at fifteen hundred hours, over."

"Damn good," there was excitement in the colonel's voice, "damn good work, who did it, Baldwin? We've had an order out for forty-eight hours to get those dumps blown but we didn't know whether they'd do it or not. Who did it, Baldwin?"

"We did it. We came up the road from Liuchow."

"Was there much there?"

"Estimate between thirty and forty thousand tons."

Baldwin could not be sure that the whistle was in the colonel's voice. It might have been static.

"Anything we can do for you? You're only fifty miles by the coordinates from us right now."

"Not now. The men are sleeping it off. We'll be in tomorrow before noon. If you can put pressure on Kunming to get us a plane out of Kweiyang, and have the trucking companies take our trucks out, I'd like to get my team to base before evening."

"We have planes going out of here empty after they bring the troops up from Burma. We can put you on one of those whenever you get in."

"Good," said Baldwin.

"Great job you've done, Baldwin, great job. Anything else I can do?"

"Not tonight, thanks. I guess it's over and out."

"Over and out, Major."

Baldwin lifted the phones from his ears. He knew tonight's report from Kweiyang would credit him with blowing the dumps; the three dead would not be mentioned; nor the fight at Yang-an-Sing.

And then the room danced about him, the walls swayed, the light blinded him, the Chinese captain looking at him, smiling, seemed to be swaying and the Chinese operator at the radio was shimmering. Baldwin felt light, as if he had no weight, as if in a moment he would rise, gravity releasing him, and float up in the air. It had been lifted from him, there was nothing on his back, no burden, no responsibility. He had flicked the road and the responsibility and the burden over to Masterson, just like that, by flicking the switch from RECEIVE to SEND.

"I'd like to go out for some air," Baldwin said to the young Chinese captain.

"Air?" said the captain, puzzled.

"Outside. Air. I need a breath of fresh air."

"Oh, yes," said the captain, his English finally comprehending. "Oh, yes. Outside. But cold outside."

"Yes," said Baldwin flatly, he needed to drag some cold air into his lungs. "Outside. Now."

The captain led the way down a corridor, and opened a door, and Baldwin followed, and they were out, suddenly, in the clear, icy, knifing cold. He felt better.

Both of them shivered and the captain teetered on his toes, torn between the courtesy that required him to be with Baldwin, and the cold that urged him back indoors.

"Very pretty," said the captain, sweeping his arm across the sky with its stars. "All old temples are pretty."

Baldwin's pupils were opening to the dark. The temple like so many Chinese temples in the wild was set high on the edge of a hill, a box on a balcony, and the starlight faintly illuminated the various shades of deep blue, deep purple, luminous black, showing the folds and contours of the hills up which they must have come to this barrier.

"This temple built with good *feng-shui*," said the captain, shivering violently, "old-fashioned Chinese magic. Temples always sit north and south to catch the wind and luck. See, there is Tou Mu," and the captain pointed to the North Star hung like a lantern directly over the stone terrace on which they stood. Baldwin could see the wings of the temple about him, and the axis on which it was built, rigidly north-south. His eyes slowly oriented and he said:

"Yes, there's the Milky Way, too," pointing to the faint, silver milky way across the sky.

"In China," said the captain through his chattering teeth, "old-fashioned people say this is River of Heaven. Full of tears. When too many tears, too many cry, then are clouds, then river spills over and there is rain. One drop too much and big rain. Tonight very clear. No rain tomorrow. No tears."

While Baldwin pondered the thought the captain deferentially added:

"Very cold, Major. You stay here? I wait for you inside? All right, sir?"

"Yes," said Baldwin. "I'll be back in a minute."

He stood there when the captain had left, letting the cold punish him, and he enjoyed the cold all the way down into his lungs where it hurt when he breathed. The cold lay over the plateau, he knew, far, far away up into the roof of Tibet and far, far down the road to the burning shanties and gutted way-stations of the wanderers, and the cold wind from the high mountain had no mercy on anyone. It was freezing as far as he could imagine. And no tears. There could be no tears for all that had happened. He could see exactly where he had been wrong. But he could not see even now how it could have happened otherwise. The road was cut now. But not even the faintest stirring of exultation came with the thought. There was only what he had learned to comfort him. If he could add that to what he was, or had been, this was all he could take away from the mountain road.

Acknowledgements

The friends who helped me with their devoted advice and criticism throughout the work on this book are too numerous to mention; my gratitude to all of them has long been expressed directly.

I should like to record by name, however, two whose help has been outstanding:

Captain Ralph T. Hauert of the United States Army Corps of Engineers, not only for the research and experience he made available to me but for his continuous technical advice on the entire manuscript.

And Dr. Chiang Yi, of Columbia University, for his gracious kindness in helping me translate Tu Fu's "Jade Flower Palace" on page 276.

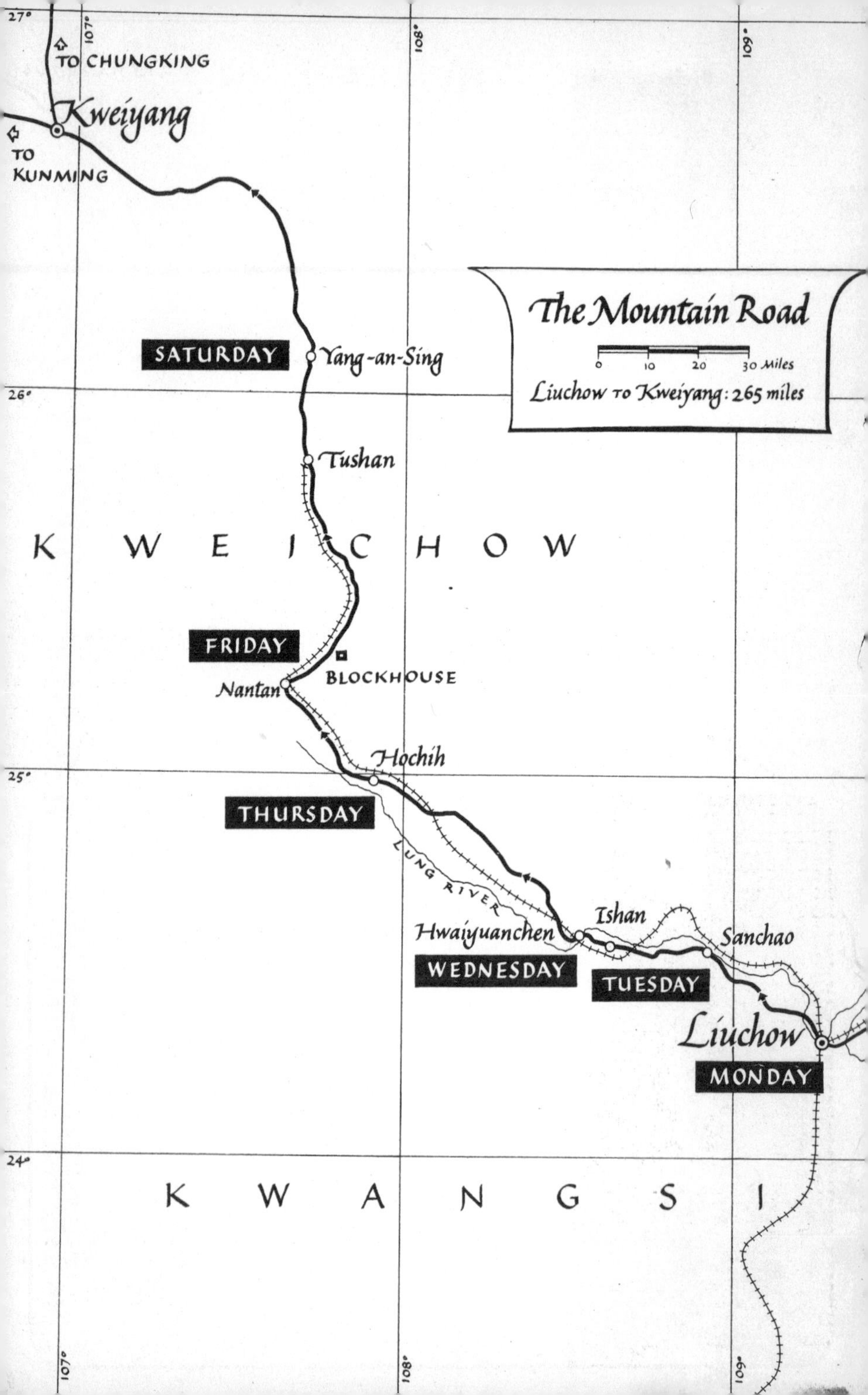

27°
107°
108°
109°
TO CHUNGKING
Kweiyang
TO KUNMING
The Mountain Road
0 10 20 30 Miles
Liuchow to Kweiyang: 265 miles
SATURDAY
Yang-an-Sing
26°
Tushan
KWEICHOW
FRIDAY
BLOCKHOUSE
Nantan
Hochih
25°
THURSDAY
LUNG RIVER
Ishan
Hwaiyuanchen
Sanchao
WEDNESDAY
TUESDAY
Liuchow
MONDAY
24°
KWANGSI
107°
108°
109°